HOMECOMING

RICKY BLACK

PROLOGUE
FRIDAY 16 NOVEMBER 2007

He hated drugs.

Justin Holmes, twenty-five-year-old high school dropout, walked the narrow path to *Hell*, carrying nothing but a container of tepid coffee. It wasn't Starbucks — he'd bought it from the local paper shop, but it would suffice. The wind howled around him as the frosty ground crunched beneath his boots. He pulled his jacket closer, but the gesture was meaningless. The cold penetrated the folds of his fleece jacket with ease.

Not far to go, he told himself, keeping his head down and clutching the coffee tighter.

As he approached his destination, the nearby streetlight highlighted another person. He was short and cocoa coloured, wrapped in a thick duffle coat and puffing on a cigarette. As he saw Justin, he straightened up. He reached for a pack of Silk Cut and handed him one. As Justin put it to his mouth, the man fumbled with a gaudy cannabis lighter and lit it. Justin inhaled, the release of nicotine causing him to gasp. He downed the coffee, then smoked the cigarette.

'One of the kids has asthma.'

'You're a considerate one, aren't you, Chip?'

'Must have learned from you.'

Justin grinned, savouring the cancer stick.

'How did you get stuck pulling babysitter duty?' Chip asked.

'King's sick. I offered to cover for him.'

Chip laughed, 'he's been working hard. He needs to chill.'

'King will be all right.' Justin stubbed the cigarette and signalled for Chip to follow him up the rickety steps to the crack spot, *Hell*. As Chip unlocked the door, they heard loud music mingled with video game explosions and cursing. It sounded like a party. Justin cut his eyes to Chip, but his partner only shrugged. Step quickening, they entered the living room, surprising the youths. Takeaway containers, cola cans, weed bags and powdery residue dominated the room.

When the kids saw Justin glaring, they froze. He was slender, with soft facial features, but his eyes betrayed him. They were caramel pools when he was in a loving mood, flint when he wasn't. Without a word, they scrambled to tidy the room. Behind him, Chip smirked.

'Get to work,' said Justin. 'People are waiting, and they don't care who gets the most kills on *Halo*.'

The kids did as ordered. Three of them stayed in the living room, the rest leaving.

'Is the work bagged?' Justin spoke to Chip.

'Almost.'

'Yo,' Justin called to one youth. 'Leave what you're doing and bag the rest of the work. It's almost time to reload. Do it now.'

The kid grumbled, but did as instructed.

'King's building a nice little squad here.'

Justin frowned at Chip's remark.

'They need proper supervision. They're too sloppy. Marlon would help. He's solid.'

Chip nodded. Marlon was a youngster who was shooting up the ranks. Justin had taken a liking to him.

'Marlon could work.'

The two friends headed to the kitchen. A youth scrubbed cocaine residue from the scales and other equipment, focused on his task. They cleared the faded brown table of a few plates and cups and sat down.

'Were you planning to go out tonight?' Chip asked. Justin nodded.

'I was taking Charlie for a meal. Haven't seen much of her lately.'

'Want me to cover? I'd have said if you'd rang me before you came.'

'I didn't know you'd be here.'

'My side-chick let me down.' Chip grinned. 'Her man came back on army leave early. Had to jet out of there.'

Justin laughed. It was typical Chip. 'You'll never learn.'

'You're right. I'm getting food for these little rugrats. You want anything?'

Before he could reply, they heard a sound that meant trouble in their world; sirens.

'Fuck!' Justin leapt to his feet, Chip mirroring his action. The kids shouted in the background. By the time the *'Enforcer'* battering ram smashed the front door, Chip had already unlocked the side entrance. He and Justin hurried through, startling the waiting officer.

'Oi,' he shouted, but Justin shoved him to the ground,

allowing Chip time to vault over the sturdy fence into the neighbouring garden. Justin followed, slipping over as the officer missed grabbing his leg. The pair surged forward, the shouts, sirens and blue flashing lights more pronounced. They were already panting, a bad sign. Justin stopped Chip.

'Keep going that way. I'll go out the front.'

'Nah, man! Let's stick together.'

'Don't argue. Hurry before that old man catches us.'

Chip frowned but nodded, vanishing out of sight. Justin hurried onto the main road in time to see police herding his young squad into a waiting police van. One kid spotted him and shouted. The police turned in his direction, but he was halfway down the road. Heavy boots thudded against the pavement behind him, but he kept going. He had a lead on the officers, but they were fitter, and he was lagging. Adrenaline kicked in, spurring him to go even faster. He hurtled around the corner and ran full-pelt into an older woman, sending her crashing to the floor. The officers were gaining, but when Justin saw the woman's eyes, he helped her up.

'Are you okay?'

Before she could answer, three officers rounded the corner and tackled Justin to the ground. He hit the pavement, a cut opening on his forehead as the officers wrestled with him, forcing him onto his stomach.

'Thought you could run, did ya?' One of them booted him in the ribs. Justin wasn't struggling, but it didn't stop the overzealous officer.

'Leave him alone! He's not resisting,' the woman shouted, sickened by the aggression.

'Stay out of it, or we'll arrest you,' one of the officers

said, not relinquishing the half-choke hold he had Justin in.

'He's not resisting. Let him breathe.'

'This man you're trying to protect is a scumbag drug dealer,' the same officer snarled. 'Go on about your business, before we arrest you as an accessory.'

The woman flounced away, glancing over her shoulder at Justin. Despite the aggression of the police, he met her eyes, unruffled.

'Where's your mate? Tell us where he's gone.'

'No idea what you're talking about,' said Justin. The officer who had choked him shook his head as they dragged him towards the crack spot. A crowd had gathered.

'Oi, let Justin go.'

'Fucking Pigs.'

'You should all die!'

The crowd hurled insults at the officers. The other kids from the crack spot had already been loaded into the police van. Justin didn't resist as he was pulled towards a nearby police car. Someone in the crowd threw a bottle, narrowly missing an officer and hitting the ground. The police warned the crowd to stop, but they only gained momentum. A brick smashed against the bonnet of the police car.

'We need to get him out of here now,' One of the officers called out, his colleague calling for backup. The officer that had choked Justin hurried to the car with him, people in the crowd hailing him by name as others surged forward. A few fearless young men were nose-to-nose with an officer, shouting in his face and calling him names.

'Justin Holmes, I'm arresting you on suspicion of

conspiracy to distribute a Class A substance. You do not have to say anything . . .'

The rest of the words faded away as he was led to a separate police car and tossed in the back. Doors closing, the police car drove away at speed, the police van following as more police cars wailed to the scene.

CHAPTER ONE
THURSDAY 4 OCTOBER, 2012

'It's good to see you, man.'

Justin nodded to Chip as they sped up the motorway, leaving the looming, Gothic prison in the dust. Chip's BMW purred, handling the roads with ease. He seemed slimmer, more confident, groomed, and better dressed. He nodded his head to the thumping rap song, eyes focused on the road. Justin glanced from the window, the scenery a mesh of blurred green fields and grey clouds. He wondered how new the car was. It reeked of leather and cheap freshener, mingled with aftershave and a lingering weed stink.

'Yes, it is,' he said. Chip opened his mouth, closed it, then pointed at the CD player.

'Is the music okay?'

He nodded. Chip glanced over. Justin had grown whilst in prison, which was normal. Everyone seemed to these days. Chip knew guys who went inside *just* to get bigger. He couldn't put his finger on it, but something seemed different with Justin. It wasn't the size. It was something in his demeanour.

'What was it like?' He blurted. Justin assessed him.

'Restrictive.'

'Look, J, I'm grateful for you keeping my name away from the Feds.'

'I'm just glad you got away. No sense both of us getting caught.'

'I suppose. Look at you, though. You've stacked on bloody size!' He cracked, trying to add levity. Justin laughed.

'You're still a fat bastard.'

'Fuck off.'

Justin was still chuckling. 'Seriously, you look good, Chip. Who's the unlucky girl?'

'Do you remember Marie?'

'Course I do. Surprised she hasn't killed you yet, the shit you put her through.'

'She's pregnant. We're engaged, man.'

'Congratulations.' Justin beamed. 'Are you ready?'

'I'm glad I've still got a few months to get my head around it.'

They sat in comfortable silence, the ice broken. Soon, they stopped for food at a local restaurant. The crisp air hit Justin as he climbed from the ride. In the sky, grey and white clouds tussled for supremacy. Rain the night before had extinguished the snow that fell a week earlier. The restaurant had condensation-riddled windows and tables littered with lint. An aroma of stale fat and body odour lingered in the air. They waited in the booth as a waitress with a rugby player's build stomped toward them.

'What can I get you?'

Justin reached for a menu. It had a discernible, syrupy substance on the end, causing it to stick to the table. He yanked at the menu and studied it, settling on a burger and a cup of coffee. Chip ordered the same, but with lemonade. Still not knowing what to talk about, they waited for the food to arrive.

'It's great to see you,' repeated Chip. He cleared his throat, rubbing the back of his neck. Their food arrived, and they took cautious bites. Satisfied they wouldn't die of immediate poisoning, they tucked in.

'Chip?'

'Yeah?'

Justin wiped his mouth. 'Whatever the bad news is, tell me.'

Chip hesitated and took a liberal sip of his lemonade, residue resting on his thick lips.

'Have you heard about Charlie?'

Justin's insides shifted as he fought to keep the neutral expression on his face. Prison was a cruel place; word had reached him of the relationship between Charlotte and his partner, King, long before the words left Chip's lips. Charlotte had been a good girl studying Business Management at university. They'd spoken of getting engaged, but fate had intervened. Justin broke up with her after his sentencing, insisting she and everyone else left him to do his time in peace.

'I overheard something. About her and King.'

Chip shot him a glance.

'They're engaged.'

Justin nodded, ignoring the lump in his throat.

'How's King doing?'

'He's on top of the world. Came out swinging after Karma's death.' Chip broke off, his expression contrite. Karma had remained one of the main men in Chapeltown for years and was always fair in dealing with people.

Justin, King, and Chip had all worked for him. 'Sorry, I know how close you two were.'

Justin nodded. 'He was a good man.'

'King didn't miss a step when he died; a few key people disappeared, and next thing, he's running the crew.' Chip rubbed his sleek leather jacket. 'Life is okay now.'

Justin took in everything he'd said whilst wrestling with his burger.

'He treats you right then?'

'I can't complain, bruv. I'm trying to maintain and put money away.'

'Have you ever thought about leaving?'

'Leaving what?' said Chip.

'The game. Have you ever considered leaving it behind?'

'To do what?'

'Anything is better than this.'

'I wouldn't know. Never done anything else. Neither have you.'

Justin nodded again. 'Doesn't mean I don't want to.'

CHAPTER TWO
THURSDAY 4 OCTOBER, 2012

JUSTIN'S MIND whirred as Chip drove onto a street in Harehills. He'd kept to himself when he was inside, but people often discussed street rumours. King's name came up occasionally, and people left him alone after learning of their connection. It still startled him. He recalled his old partner having a wicked temper. He wondered who was keeping King calm. As Chip cruised down the street, he checked the surroundings, unimpressed.

Boxy little cars, rusting bikes and mopeds littered the street. An old woman wrapped in a thick coat three times her size limped down the road. She stopped, spat on the floor, then resumed her slow walk. Further down the street, a man and woman stood nose to nose, screaming at one another.

'Shane's got it good round here,' Chip said, smirking at the entertainment. Other neighbours on the street watched, grinning.

'If you say so.' Justin's eyes zeroed in on the oil stains splotched on the rough tarmac. A solitary fried chicken box fluttered in the wind.

'Thanks for getting me.' He moved to climb from the car. Chip grabbed his arm.

'I'll pick you up at eight. For the party.'

'What party?'

'Your coming home party. People know you're touching down.'

Justin closed his eyes. 'I need sleep. It's been a long day.'

'Couple drinks, J. Just show your face.'

'Fine. Eight o'clock. I'll come for a little while.'

'That's my boy. I'll scoop you up.' Chip beamed. Justin grabbed his bag and knocked on the plastic door.

'Jus!' Shane Holmes wrenched the door open and grabbed him into a tight bear hug before he could say anything.

'I missed you, bro.' He grinned. Shane still towered over him but seemed less solid, bigger around the middle. His big eyes brimmed with genuine merriment.

'You were caged too long. The streets missed you. Come in. Put the bag down. You hungry?'

'Nah, I'm alright. I ate with Chip.'

'Fat bastard. Couldn't even say hi.' Shane frowned.

'He's gone to get ready for this party they sorted for me. Did he say anything about it?'

Shane shook his head, looking like an overgrown child.

'Let me show you around the house,' he said, taking Justin on a tour. They ended up in the living room.

'Check out these beauties.' He picked up a photo from a chipped cabinet and thrust it towards Justin. It was a picture of two smiling little girls dressed in matching outfits, both missing teeth.

'Jesus, Shane. Nobody told me you had kids.'

'They're not mine. My girl came into the relationship

with them. Their dads left them in the lurch. Pair of plonkers. No one told you anything because you said not to contact.'

Unable to argue, he inclined his head, 'Is this your woman?' he looked at another photo.

'Yeah. The bloody love of my life.'

'I'm sure I've seen her before,' said Justin.

'She grew up in Chapeltown. Met her a few years back. Been with her ever since.'

'I'm glad you're doing well.' Justin smiled again.

'I love them.' Shane's random response took him by surprise.

'Who?'

'My kids. They might not be mine by blood, but I'd do anything for them.' Shane's eyes were hard, his mouth tight.

'Neither of the fathers still around?'

'They both bailed.'

'Well, at least the girls have you.' Justin wasn't sure what to say.

'Yeah. What's your plan? Now you're out.'

'I hoped I could stay awhile. Until I get my shit together.'

Shane scratched his face. 'I'll check with Keeley. Can't see her having a problem, though.'

Shane's response surprised him, but he said nothing.

'Okay. You coming to this party, anyway? Chip's swinging by around eight.'

'I dunno, bro. Keeley will be home with the kids. She's had them all day. She'll be knackered.'

'Just one drink, bro. I won't be there all night.'

'One drink then. After that, I'm off.'

Justin's stomach lurched the moment he stepped from Chip's BMW. Chapeltown had been home all his life, and he still recalled the aura that seemed to surround it. The area always had a community vibe. It was a place where everyone knew everyone, and underneath the violence, drugs and war stories, there was a beauty. It was a concrete jungle but seemed tamer. On the ride down, he'd noticed several new buildings. Chapeltown Road looked neater. He wondered what it meant for the future.

'Whose house is this?' Shane asked, standing with his brother. He wore a t-shirt and jeans, his gut straining against the cotton lining.

'Some Hood chick's.' Chip locked up and slapped Justin on the back. 'C'mon, let's go get hammered.'

He led the way into a garden overrun with weeds, cigarette butts and Supermalt bottles. People mingled in the doorway, talking over one another. There was no gate to the garden, loud music drowning everything else out. Justin composed himself, following Chip, watching his friend greet people.

'Yes, Wally. What's happening? Stevie, you good? How's your mum? Do you guys remember Justin?'

'Yeah, course,' the guy called Wally said, his puzzled expression making it clear he didn't. Justin shook his hand, then they were inside. The flickering lighting immediately caught his. It was like an interview room from a mediocre cop show. The living room and hallway teemed with bodies, the stench of weed, aftershave, and body odour overwhelming. He stood in the corner next to a peeling wall, noticing a baby's bouncer and several stuffed toys. Scanning the room, he didn't recognise anyone. The CD kept skipping. No one else noticed.

'Here,' Chip pushed his way through the crowd and handed him a beer, 'get that down you. It's live in here.'

'I don't know anyone,' said Justin. Shane loomed in the middle of the room, drinking a beer and looking at his watch.

'Things change. People move on. This is the game.'

Justin turned back to Chip, 'Is this my party?'

'Course it is. Why?'

Justin shrugged.

'Seems like a random Hood party.'

Chip shook his head. 'Negative prick. Go shake a few hands. Make the party come to you. Either way, you've got a couple of surprises coming your way later. I'll be back.'

He strolled away. Justin saw a face he recognised and headed over.

'Joe?' He said.

'Justin? I haven't seen you in years. When did you get out?' Joe asked. He was a short, thin man who always dressed in black and kept his grey hair well-trimmed.

'Today. How's business? Still running that gambling spot?'

'Not anymore.' Joe shook his head. 'Business dried up, so I got out. What's your move now you're free?'

Before he could answer, the music paused. He turned. A man loomed over him, wearing a long-sleeved black top, jeans and black boots with loose laces. No one spoke. Justin noticed Chip and Shane watching.

'So, they let you out then?' The man said. His voice was low, almost a growl. Justin nodded.

'Seems they did.'

The pair sized up one another. King removed his

glasses, allowing his dark eyes to meet Justin's. A long moment passed before they embraced.

'It's good to see you, J.'

'You too, King.'

If he wasn't forewarned of King's rise, he would have known it now. Power resonated from his old partner, evidenced by his firm stance. He wore heavy jewellery; a long gold chain resting next to his heart, and a Rolex laden with diamonds. His crew posted nearby; young and hard-faced, brimming with an insatiable need to prove themselves. Justin knew King's agenda well. He'd always loved training the younger ones.

'You enjoying the party?' King scanned the room as he spoke.

'It's okay.'

'Yeah. Good turnout. You deserve it. These people know they're around a Hood legend.' King tried pumping up Justin, who rolled his eyes.

'I don't know about that.'

'Well, I do.' King glanced at his watch. 'Listen, I've got business. I've left something for you outside Shane's place. Are you free tomorrow? We need to talk.'

Justin nodded. 'I'm free.'

'Good man. Enjoy your party, bro.'

People flocked to Justin after King left. Soon, he made his way outside and sat on the step. He shivered, finding it chillier now. A few stragglers were in a corner of the garden, but he ignored them, preferring the isolation. He clambered to his feet to leave as Chip lumbered outside.

'There you are. Been looking for you,' he drawled, eyes red and drooping. He clutched the hand of a brown-skinned girl with watery hazel eyes. 'This is Cassie. It's her house.'

'How you doing, Cassie?' said Justin.

'Fine. You?' She wrung her hands, eyes shifting around the garden.

'I'm good. You have a lovely house.' Justin glanced at Chip, who smirked.

'Look, let's get to the point. Cassie is taking you upstairs for your *surprise*. Thank me later. Come get me when you're done, and we'll kick out.' Chip slapped him on the back and staggered inside.

When he left, Justin and Cassie didn't move, unable to make eye contact. She coughed, clearing her throat.

'Let's go inside then.'

Not knowing what to say, he followed her upstairs, the wooden floorboards creaking underneath them. They entered her bedroom, Cassie closing the door on the raucous party sounds. The room was dominated by a large metal bed, a wardrobe and a cot. Cassie looked at him.

'Let's do it then.'

Not immediately responding, he stared. She squirmed under the intensity of his gaze.

'Is that what you want?'

She nodded.

'It doesn't seem like it's what you want.'

'I do. It's your treat.' Her words were listless.

'Do you have a man?'

The question seemed to startle Cassie.

'Why does that matter?' She folded her arms.

'It doesn't.'

'My baby father's in prison. He did a robbery and got caught.' Cassie's voice was tight.

'Are you still together?'

'No. I can't wait for him. I have to focus on my son.'

'And sleeping with strange men is focusing on him?'

Cassie scowled. 'Don't judge me. You're fresh out. You can't question anything I'm doing. As long as my son has food and clothes, I don't care. In fact, get out of my room.'

Justin wiped his face and left. Shane had vanished by the time he reappeared in the main room. The music was louder, people were dancing, a few couples full-on grinding to the jams. In the corner, Chip whispered into the ear of a giggling girl. Watching this scene play out in front of him, Justin left, wondering if this world had been worth sacrificing his freedom for.

A new Honda CRV sat outside Shane's house when he arrived. A man climbed out. He was ratty looking and dressed in an expensive warm-up suit.

'King told me to give you these,' he said, tossing Justin the car keys. 'There's goodies in the glove compartment, plus numbers in case you need anything.'

'Cool,' said Justin. 'What's your name?'

'Pincer.'

'Good to meet you, Pincer.' Justin held out his hand. Pincer's lip curled. Another car parked behind the Honda beeped. Pincer climbed in the passenger seat, then glowered at Justin.

'I don't get what he sees.'

Without another word, the driver drove away. Justin scowled at the disrespect, watching the car disappear down the road. He used his key and headed to the kitchen, where another surprise awaited him.

CHAPTER THREE
THURSDAY 4 OCTOBER, 2012

Justin opened the door, tiptoeing inside. He switched on the living room light. A quilt and pillow had been tossed onto the sofa for him. He studied the room. The TV and sound system were top of the range, but everything else seemed dusty and peeling. On the coffee table were dirty cups and even a fork on top of a massive plate stained with gravy. Justin headed to the kitchen, planning to have one more drink.

'You can switch the light on.' A soft voice caused him to jump.

'Shit, sorry,' he said, turning on the light. Keeley sat at the kitchen table, looking up at him. She looked the same as her picture—light-skinned, straight brown hair and bright hazel eyes. A bottle of brandy rested in front of her, alongside a half-filled glass.

'Didn't think anyone else would be up.' Justin finished.

Keeley nodded. 'How was it?'

'How was what?'

'The party. Shane said everyone was having one for you.'

'That wasn't my party,' admitted Justin.

'How do you mean?' Keeley crossed her legs. She wore a camisole top and a pair of black shorts. He gazed at her legs, then glanced away.

'People said it was for me, but it wasn't.'

'You didn't enjoy it then?' Keeley ran a hand through her hair. He shook his head.

'I wanted a nightcap before bed.' Keeley motioned to the bottle. 'Do you want one?'

'You must have read my mind.' Justin grinned and sat opposite Keeley on a stiff metal chair, watching her pour the drink. They toasted one another and drank. The fiery brandy burned his throat, but he relished it.

'It must have been a rough night,' Keeley said, laughing. She poured him another, which he sipped.

'It feels like the world has moved on without me.' Justin voiced what was on his mind. He'd watched people around him talking, living, smiling, free. He thought of King, remembering the reaction when he'd arrived.

'You've been out a day. Give it time. You've got good people around you. Shane loves you. He'd do anything for you.'

'I'm glad he's doing so well.'

'Me too. He looks after the girls and me. He's a prince.' Keeley's words were positive, but her voice seemed hollow.

'You never said what you were doing up so late.'

'Your brother. He did his best to sneak into bed but still woke me up. That bloody snoring stopped me from getting back to sleep.'

'Sorry about that, going out was my idea.'

Keeley shook her magnificent head. 'He deserves a treat now and then.'

Justin glanced around the kitchen as they spoke. Nothing seemed clean. He wasn't sure if it was because of the young children, but it seemed grubby. In the sudden silence after Keeley's words, he listened to the soothing purr of the fridge fan. On the kitchen counter, he spotted a shaker filled with residue.

'I've told him about that.'

'Pardon?' He turned back to Keeley.

'Shane. He never out his containers. If it's not protein powder, there's tuna in the Tupperware.' She minutely shook her head. Justin smirked.

'He's trying to get back into shape,' Keeley continued. 'Dunno if you've noticed, but he's got a belly.'

'Good living.' Justin laughed. 'He's comfy. Nothing wrong with that.'

'I guess,' Keeley said. 'I keep this tight for him, though.' She gestured down her body. Against his better judgement, Justin followed. Keeley's supple brown legs glistened under the cheap light bulb. He swallowed and took another sip of brandy. She assessed him. Her eyes gleamed, but she looked calm. It was too much. The relaxed vibe had left the room, replaced by a weird one he didn't want to give voice to. He stood.

'I'm off to bed,' he said. Keeley's mouth fell open.

'You don't need to rush off.'

'It's been a long day. I'm tired.' Justin rubbed his forehead.

'Finish your drink at least.'

'I don't want it. Goodnight.'

Justin headed upstairs, washing his face and brushing his teeth. He changed into a vest top and flannel bottoms, and then returned to the living room. The lights were off in the kitchen. He lay down and stared at the dark ceiling, sighing as his eyes closed, wondering what the next day would bring.

CHAPTER FOUR
FRIDAY 5 OCTOBER, 2012

Chip bopped his head to booming rap music as Justin traipsed from Shane's house the following day. Despite the early chill, he wore sunglasses and a t-shirt, singing along with the vicious song. Justin climbed into the passenger seat with a yawn.

'Yes, J. You good? What happened to you last night?'

'I got tired, so I left early.' Justin spoke over the music. Chip turned it down.

'You missed out, man. I got in after six. Pincer rang me, reminding me about this meeting.' Chip stifled a yawn as they motored down the road.

'Where's King at these days?'

'All over. Moves around a lot during the day. He's got some little offices. We're going to one now.'

'Cool.'

Chip shot him a glance. 'You nervous?'

'No.'

'Are you sure?'

'Why would I lie?'

Chip cut in front of a speeding Volvo, ignoring the angry horn of the driver.

'Shit changes, man. I'd be a little nervous.'

'I'm not nervous.'

Chip turned the music up again. 'Tough bastard, aren't you, J?'

King's office was near Roundhay Road. It was a dull locale with a rusting gate and weathered redbrick wall. Two large men loomed nearby. As Justin approached the office, both men sized him up but didn't make a move. Despite its outer appearance, the inside sparkled. Mud-brown flooring, pale walls, and leather sofas dominated the room.

King stood as they entered, the sickly scent of incense following him as he trailed towards them, shaking Justin's hand.

'Take a seat,' he said, sinking onto the leather sofa again. Justin sat nearby. Chip slouched against the wall.

'Justin Holmes; Five damn years, man. Long time.'

'It was long for me too.'

King's eyes bored into his. 'No doubt. I know the police offered you everything to give Karma and me up, but you never did.'

'I'd never have done that.'

'People change in them interview rooms. I'm glad you didn't.'

King quietened, Justin wondering if he was threatening him. Chip fidgeted in the corner, but didn't speak.

'I want to show my appreciation, J. We're doing big things, and I want you front and centre, leading the way you should have been.'

'I'm out of the game, King.'

'I don't know everything about your situation, and I understand how you feel about handouts, but let me help you, man. If you hadn't got locked up, we'd have been right here together.'

'I've got things I'm working towards. I gave too much to this life.'

'What kinda things?'

'I'm a writer now.'

The reaction to this statement was immediate. King and Chip fell about, roaring with laughter. Justin resisted the urge to retort.

'What are you playing at? What did they do to you inside?'

'I finished a book,' said Justin. King's smile vanished. Behind them, Chip giggled harder.

'Go outside, Chip.'

Chip wiped his eyes as he left.

'J, I need you. Things are going on out there. Fuckers are coming for the throne. I need someone I can trust to watch the shop while I handle them.'

'Who?'

'Two little bitches. Hood dudes. Tunde and Bloon.'

Justin considered the names for a moment. 'I don't recall them.'

'They were the lowest of the low before you got locked down. They're nobodies.'

'What's changed then?'

'They've got their money up, and now they're cocky. If I don't have to worry about the business, I can handle them. That's where you come in.'

'What about Chip?'

'Chip's a joker. He's a soldier. You're a leader. Stand

with me.'

Justin shook his head.

'What about Karma? What if I told you those pricks killed him?'

He straightened, his nostrils flaring.

'Karma died in a car accident.'

'I had it investigated. Someone fucked with the brakes.'

'Why didn't you tell me earlier?'

King frowned. 'I'm telling you now. Those little fuckers benefited from Karma's death. They grew after it.'

'Was it an inside job?'

King nodded. 'Karma was getting old, and the world saw it. You can't show no weakness in front of the vultures. There's always someone waiting to take advantage.'

'But you ended up in charge,' said Justin, letting his words linger. King didn't blink.

'They tried to hit me, and I hit back harder. I hurt the traitors I could see. The rest hid in the shadows. It's only now they're getting brave.'

'Why not go after those two earlier? *Tunde and Bloon* or whatever they're called.'

'I didn't know they were involved then.' King shook his head, his face still serious. 'I need you, J.'

Justin wanted to say no. He owed Karma, though. He had put him on and allowed him to make money.

'I need to think.'

King nodded, his expression unchanging.

'I heard you're staying with family,' he replied after a moment. Justin nodded.

'Shane's putting me up.'

'I've got a place you can use. In St. Martin's. A nice little three-bedroom. I'll have the keys by this evening.'

'I don't know.' Justin hesitated.

'No strings. You held it down, and you need your own place. There's even a desk you can write at.'

That broke the tension, and they laughed like old friends. It felt good.

'Okay. I'll take it.'

King smiled again. 'Good man. I'll send someone round to Shane's later. It's furnished. Change what you need to change. We planned to use it as another spot for the guys to rest, but we've got other places for that.'

'Thanks, King. Means a lot.'

'Anytime, J.' King was about to rise.

'How is Charlotte doing?'

King froze. He straightened and glanced at him, his brow furrowed.

'Why?'

'Did I say something wrong?'

'Nah, it's just,' King paused, 'I meant to talk to you about this earlier. Me and Charlotte, it wasn't no snake shit. You dashed her, and we became friends. It developed from there.'

A painful tightness engulfed Justin's chest and throat. He marshalled his emotions. The last thing he needed was to become caught up.

'I understand. I just wondered how she was.'

'She works a lot. Stays busy.' King rubbed his face, clearly uncomfortable. Justin stood.

'I'll go see where Chip's got to.' He slapped hands with King. He'd reached the door when King spoke.

'J?'

He turned. King stared, his gaze inscrutable.

'I owe you,' he said.

Nodding, Justin left.

CHAPTER FIVE
FRIDAY 5 OCTOBER, 2012

It was early in the afternoon when Chip dropped Justin back at Shane's. After meeting King, he'd renewed his driver's licence, then asked Chip to drive to the new house. It was a simple, dirty white-bricked spot, but he liked it.

Keeley's girls sat on the sofa where he'd slept, a laptop squashed between them. They didn't even notice him, engrossed by a flashing cartoon. He shook his head. On the coffee table, a bag of Haribo's nestled alongside chocolate wrappers, juice cartons and the plate from the night before.

'Shane? You around?' Justin called, hurrying to the kitchen. Shane and Keeley were there, both looking in his direction as he entered. Shane sat at the table, his jaw set. Keeley was by the sink smoking a cigarette, ash spilling around her.

'Are you two okay?'

Neither spoke. Keeley met his eyes for a moment as she left the kitchen.

'Shane, what's up?'

Shane took a moment to peek up, not quite meeting his eyes.

'Bro, me and Keeley have talked, and there's just no room for you here. I'm sorry.'

Justin thought about her behaviour the night before. He'd rejected her, and this was her response.

'That's cool, man. Don't worry about it.' He recalled how tough his big brother used to be. Now, he seemed miserable and bloated.

'Where are you going to go, Jus?'

'I'll visit Janet. King found me a place, so I'll move in soon.'

'He needs to sort me too. We're brothers.'

'Sort you out to do what?' Justin rubbed his chin.

Shane shrugged. 'Anything. I'm struggling on the doors, arguing with students, getting nowhere. He could change that in an instant.'

Justin wondered who was talking here: Shane or Keeley.

'You don't even know what you'd want. Him helping makes no sense.'

'Whose side are you on? King throws money at you, and you're turning against your family?'

He frowned, unprepared for Shane's hostility.

'What are you talking about?'

'Nothing. Forget it,' snapped Shane. Justin stared at him for a moment, then left to get his things together. After grabbing his toothbrush from the bathroom, he saw Keeley waiting.

'You'll have to come around for dinner when you're settled,' she started. 'Where are you going to go?'

'I'll stop in on my sister.'

'*Crazy Janet* needs the company,' Keeley's words were cold. Justin's eyes narrowed.

'Don't insult my family,' he warned. Her eyes widened for a moment, then hardened.

'You know what, don't come for dinner. Stay away from my family.'

'Shane is my family too.'

'I can change that, though.' She looked around, lowering her voice. 'Your brother will do anything I say.'

'Don't test me.'

'No, you don't test *me*. I don't need you messing with Shane,' Keeley hissed.

'You're the one messing with him, not me. I think it's time for me to go.' He needed to get away from Keeley before he did something stupid.

'Remember why you're going too. Because it's what I wanted. Remember that.'

Justin pushed past her and went downstairs. She followed. Shane slouched in the living room, shoulders slumped. The brothers stared at one another before he looked away.

'Say bye to my girls. Kaci, Skye, Uncle Justin is going now.'

The girls didn't even look up from their device. Shane's nostrils flared as he glanced at Justin, then back to the girls.

'Girls, put the tablet down and say bye to your uncle, or I'm taking it.'

This got their attention. They shuffled to their feet and glared at Justin, standing in front of him. He glanced at Shane.

'Give them a hug then.'

Justin looked to Keeley, whose jaw was tight. When she

didn't speak, he hugged both girls for a few seconds. When he let them go, they went straight back to their game. Justin glared at his brother now. The whole thing had been a complete charade that he didn't quite understand. He needed to leave.

'I've called a taxi. I'll be back for the car.'

CHAPTER SIX
FRIDAY 5 OCTOBER, 2012

'Is this the street?'

'Yes.' Justin's head almost hung out of the window as the creaky taxi turned onto Sholebroke Place. The driver's grubby, navy polo shirt stuck to him, and the resulting smell of stale sweat had Justin savouring fresh air. On the street, young kids played under the baleful eyes of harassed parents. They stared as the taxi car pulled up, seizing the momentary break from routine. When he paid the driver and climbed out, he received a moment's interest. Climbing the cracked steps, he knocked on the door and then walked in.

Entering the living room and ignoring the generic morning show on the television, Justin scanned the room. It was the opposite of Shane's place. Everything, from the furniture to the two milk-white figurines on the chipped mantelpiece, seemed dated. Old. Frowning, he heard a noise and followed the sound, *Febreze* replaced with the smell of fried food, cinnamon, and nutmeg. A heavyset woman hunched over a boiling pot, mumbling to herself. She looked up when she saw him.

'Jus?' she moved from the hob and gave him a bone-breaking hug. He closed his eyes, savouring the moment. When they released one another, he wiped his eyes.

'It's good to see you, sis.'

'You can't stay too long. What happened at Shane's?'

'A night or two is fine.' Justin pulled out a battered, bone-coloured chair, perching on it. 'Nothing happened. There wasn't room with the kids.'

'*Her* kids, you mean.'

'Pardon?'

'The kids are hers. Not Shane's. She came into the relationship with them. Two different dads,' Janet Holmes said, pouring coffee into a large mug.

'So?'

'Shane's got no sense. That girl is nothing but trouble. She swans around, telling him what to do and flirting with everyone in sight.'

'Shane can handle himself.' He recalled Keeley's flirty manner the night before.

'No. *You* can handle yourself. Shane is a wimp. He thinks she'll leave him if he stands up to her.' Janet placed the cup in front of her brother. 'Have you eaten?'

'I had a sandwich. Maybe she would leave. She's feisty. Might be what Shane needs.'

'He needs to stop being whipped and stand up for himself. It's embarrassing how she talks to him.'

Justin shrugged, burning his lips on the black coffee. Janet still remembered how he liked it. He leaned back in his chair as much as he dared. Even her clothing seemed mismatched and old. A few minutes later, she slipped a massive plate in front of him, keeping up a steady amount of terse chatter.

'Your mate Chip, he's lost a lot of weight, hasn't he? He hasn't changed, though. Still cheating.'

'Chip is Chip,' said Justin, engrossed in the food. The turkey sausage, fried eggs and breadfruit were fantastic. 'This is brilliant.'

'There's more if you're still hungry after. People always seem to leave prison with a bigger appetite.'

'This is fine, thanks. Have you seen anything of King?'

'King!' Janet made a scoffing noise, lifting her cup to her full lips. Justin got an even stronger whiff of cinnamon, along with the sweet scent of honey. 'He's too good to speak to the likes of me. Too busy copying the old man.'

'Who? Karma?'

'Karma always had time for the people. He and Eddie, they always asked after you. All King cares about is himself,' said Janet. He didn't know what to say.

'Has King spoken to you yet?' She continued.

'Yeah,' Justin said, not adding anything further. She seemed to understand and finished her drink. He had questions, things he wanted to know about her situation. They would keep for now.

'Do you need money?'

Janet gnawed her lip. Justin thought he detected a gleam in her eye, but a moment later, it vanished.

'No, I'm all right, Jus. I have a job, remember.'

'You still with the council?'

'I'll be there until I die,' Janet said, laughing. 'What are you going to do now?'

'Get a job.'

'A legal, legit job?' Janet asked. He nodded.

'I wrote a lot when I was inside too. Finished a book. That's what I want to do, and it'll cost money to do it.'

'Mum used to write.' Janet tilted her head.

'Did she?'

'Poetry. She was great too.'

They looked away. Their mother had suffered for years, succumbing to cancer when Justin was fifteen.

'Do you still have them?'

'The poems?'

'Yeah.'

'I wouldn't throw them away. I'll find them for you later.'

CHAPTER SEVEN
FRIDAY 5 OCTOBER, 2012

Later, a taxi pulled up outside Shane's place, driving off with Justin's money and a tip. He looked at the CRV King had given him. He unlocked it, climbed in and started the engine, getting used to the controls. Putting his foot down, he felt the power as he motored off.

Justin pulled onto a quiet street in Moortown and parked. He grinned when he saw the man he'd come to see slouched in a garden chair, drinking a beer and watching a younger woman chase after a child. He hung back a moment. When Eddie noticed him, his face brightened, and he rose to his feet. Both smiled.

'Look at you,' whispered Eddie.

'I've never seen you looking so good,' replied Justin. 'This is a beautiful house.'

He wasn't lying. The house was semi-detached, with an old-fashioned jet-black roof and brownish-red bricks. It looked domestic, and anti-Eddie.

'Karma left me enough money to wise up and leave the streets behind.'

'I'm glad.' Justin's tone softened. 'I tried getting permission to go to the funeral, but—'

'You don't need to explain. Karma loved you like a son. You would have been there if able.'

Noticing Justin, the woman, and the young kid, walked towards them.

'Justin, I don't think you ever met my youngest daughter Stephanie. This little man is my grandson, Evan. You two, this is an old friend of mine, Justin.'

'Nice to meet you.' He shook hands with Stephanie. She was moon-faced and chubby, with a warm smile. He nodded at the kid, who returned the gesture.

'You too. Would you like a drink?'

Justin shook his head. 'No, thank you.'

'We'll be inside,' Stephanie said to her father. She left with Evan.

'It's their visiting time. She stops by a few days a week,' Eddie explained.

'I can come back another time. I just wanted to check you were okay.'

'Nonsense. You're here now. Are you adjusting to life outside those prison walls?'

'I'm trying to keep up with all the changes.'

'Five years is a long time.' Eddie had aged well compared to other men his age. Despite his lined face, his eyes shone with vitality, his movements still sharp.

'No arguments here,' said Justin.

'You shouldn't have gone.'

'How so?'

'You were the heart of the team. King should have gone to prison, not you.'

'It wasn't King's fault I was there. He's been good to me since I got out. He's looked out for me.'

Eddie waved this away. 'He has to. He's following the code. The streets are watching, and he can't let them see him not taking care of you. It's bad enough they don't believe in him.'

'I heard differently,' said Justin.

'From who? Chip?' Eddie coughed, doubling over in his chair.

'Are you okay?'

'Fine, just a tickle.' Eddie composed himself. 'Fact is. King is greedy. Everyone sees that. Treats the inner circle well and neglects the rest. You were never like that.'

Justin digested his words. As long as he had known him, he'd spoken little and had remained a source of good counsel. The pair grew close working under Karma, the head of the organisation. Karma and Eddie had come over from the West Indies in the seventies. Justin wondered if he was out of touch, or if there was truth to his words.

'He wants me back alongside him,' Justin admitted.

'Under him, you mean.'

'I don't want to be part of the life anymore.' Justin paused. 'Things change. I want to write.'

'Books?'

'Yes.' Justin braced himself for the mocking. He relaxed when Eddie smiled.

'That's a perfect goal for you, Justin. Keep at it, and don't let anyone tell you you can't do it. Follow your dream. There's no future in the streets. Stay away.'

CHAPTER EIGHT
MONDAY 8 OCTOBER, 2012

JUSTIN SAT at Janet's kitchen table, searching for jobs. She didn't have a computer, so he pored through the vacancies section of the Evening Post. Nothing called out to him. Even if it did, he was a high school dropout with a criminal record.

Justin thought of King as he fixed a drink. He still needed to give him a response. Eddie had given him money — forcing him to take it. It wouldn't last long. He needed something, and he needed it now. He placed the paper to the side and reached for a dog-eared notepad, most of the pages full of black ink. Justin picked up a Biro and was about to write when his phone rang.

'Yeah?'

'J, I'm outside, man. Hurry too. It's cold.'

Chip leant against his BMW when he opened the door. He wore a chunky cardigan and black combat trousers, designed to protect him from the biting cold. His eyes were fathomless.

'Have you driven it yet?' Chip motioned to the CRV.

'I visited Eddie.'

'Karma's Eddie?' said Chip. He nodded.

'What's that old man saying?'

'Enjoying retirement,' Justin rubbed his arm, the wind causing his t-shirt to ripple. 'What are you doing round here?'

'Came to give you this,' Chip handed him a set of keys. 'You wanna revisit the spot?'

'Gimme two minutes.' He picked up on the vibe. 'Has something happened?'

'This street shit, it's madness. King fill you in?' Chip spat on the floor. He looked up and down the empty street.

'He said two guys are stepping up.'

'Yeah. Tunde and Bloon. They're running their mouths in the streets. There's talk about a snitch in our camp too.'

'Do you agree with the talk?'

Chip shrugged.

'Where did the beef start from?' Justin continued. Chip rubbed his hands together, looking left and right again.

'A business deal flopped. They got the short end. King mugged them off, thinking they wouldn't do anything.'

'And?'

'And, they got their people together and made waves.'

'Are they going to be a problem? King seemed relaxed,' said Justin.

'It's not gonna be as easy as he thinks. King got respect when he took over from Karma. There were all kinds of rumours back then, and he used them.'

Justin straightened. 'What rumours?'

'A few guys vanished. Shit got pinned on King, and people stayed outta his way. That shit doesn't last forever, though. Tunde and Bloon are hungry. They won't play second fiddle forever now they're making money. Everybody wants more.'

Justin weighed up what Chip was saying, trying to understand the situation. He hadn't thought about what King would have had to deal with after Karma's death. He wondered how it would have played out if he was on the streets alongside him, instead of locked up.

'Anyway, I didn't come here to talk politics,' Chip said, laughing, 'I wanted to drop them keys on you. I've gotta handle something soon, so let's check this house real quick.'

'Let's go then.'

CHAPTER NINE
THURSDAY 11 OCTOBER, 2012

In a warehouse in the town of Garforth, a naked man whimpered, tied to a wooden chair, rough rope cutting into his wrists and ankles. A stone-faced man sipped an energy drink as he glared at him.

'Please, let me go,' Roy gasped, his face throbbing. The man ignored him, the silence almost as bad as the beating he had endured. Three sharp taps punctuated the quiet. The old guard opened the door, standing aside to allow two more knuckleheads in, followed by King.

'King—' said Roy.

'Any trouble?' King addressed the guard. He shook his head.

'Nah, he's just crying like a little bitch.' The warehouse door opening caused the outside chill to spread around the room. Roy shivered, his nose dripping. He couldn't even lift his hand to wipe it.

'Typical,' said King. Sinister laughter ensued. Roy scanned the faces. He didn't recognise the other men. He wondered where Chip and Pincer were.

Was the fact King's higher-ups weren't present a sign he would be released?

He clung to the notion, trying not to breathe in the smells in the room, the sweat, the coppery stench of blood, the vomit from earlier.

'King, please—'

'Now you wanna talk?' King's face contorted into a vicious mask of anger. 'You're a snake. Why should I listen to anything you're saying?'

Roy said nothing, still quivering from fear and cold. Signalling to an underling, King watched the goon hit Roy twice in the stomach and once in the face. He sagged in the chair, blood dripping from a cut below his eye onto the warehouse floor.

'Ain't shit you can say is there, sellout.'

'Please—' Roy said, his words thick, struggling to talk through swollen, throbbing lips.

'Please, what? Am I wrong?'

'Bloon is my boy. I was just talking. I didn't tell him nowt about you, King. I swear.'

'Swear on what? *God*? I'm your damn God.'

'I was on that stuff. Hard. Bloon helped me. That's it.'

'What did you tell him? No one shits for free.'

'Nothing. I promise.'

'Guess I don't need to keep you around then.' King again motioned to his goons.

'Wait! Kill me, and you'll always wonder what I said; If I said anything. Can you take that chance?' Roy saw the hesitation on King's face and believed he had scored a telling point. King smirked. At that moment, Roy knew. He threw up again, trying to lurch forward to avoid being sick on himself.

'Bloon and Tunde are on borrowed time. Those ounces I gave you, Lizzie, will work them off.'

Roy gasped at the reference to his lover.

'Lizzie's a good girl. She doesn't sell drugs.'

'Not drugs. Her body. She's going out on the corner until your debt's paid — along with a special tax for working against me.'

'No, King. Please. Lizzie's innocent!' Roy cried. King's smirk widened.

'How can she be if she's with a punk like you? Fuck that, anyway. Time to send a message.' King turned to his people. 'Open his mouth.'

King pulled a knife. Roy thrashed around in the chair, urinating on himself.

'Fuck! He pissed on my trainers.'

'I said, open his fucking mouth.' King ignored the complaints. They pried Roy's mouth open, ignoring his yelling as they half-gagged him. King tugged on Roy's slimy tongue as he spluttered, saliva and blood splashing King's arm. Almost smiling, he forced the sharp knife down against Roy's tongue, cutting through it until it dropped to the floor with a wet slapping sound. Without missing a beat, he dragged the knife across Roy's throat. Roy struggled, choking, gurgling and spitting torrents of blood until he was still. King wiped the blade on his slumped back.

'Clean this up.'

CHAPTER TEN
THURSDAY 12 OCTOBER, 2012

A WEEK PASSED BY. Justin kept to himself, getting to grips with his new house. It didn't need much in the way of repairs, but he dipped into his dwindling stash of money to replace the furniture.

He hunched over his oak desk, trying to write. Since leaving prison, he hadn't jotted a single word. He couldn't figure out what blocked him, but needed to sort it. He put the pen to the page but hesitated, unable to concentrate. His face contorted as he flung the pen across the room in frustration. Picking up his keys, he hurried from the house.

The day was breaking outside, and a fine haze appeared to descend from the sky. Justin walked towards Scott Hall Road, watching the steady throng of cars driving towards work. He rubbed his hands together, cursing himself for forgetting his gloves. He craved nicotine, a habit he had given up during his incarceration. A strange, jittery adrenaline pulsed through his body. He needed something to happen. He watched an elderly man totter along, using his stick to navigate the frosty path. He tensed when he saw

Justin, who turned to go back home. As Justin turned onto his street, he spotted King sitting on his doorstep. He wore a grey crew-neck, sweats, and black boots with thermal gloves.

'Have you been waiting long?'

King shook his head.

'Figured you couldn't have gone far if the car was parked here.' He looked at the CRV to illustrate his point. 'How's it running?'

'It's good. Thanks.'

'And the spot? Everything working?'

'Yeah. It's all good.'

'Anything's ever up, Pincer gave you the numbers, right?'

'Yeah, King, he did.'

Satisfied, he looked to the floor. Justin waited. He spoke after a few seconds.

'Let's go for a drive.'

Not arguing, Justin followed him to a black 4x4. They climbed in the back, and the driver, who Justin didn't know, drove away. The traffic hadn't picked up yet, and the journey to Chapeltown was swift. After a few more minutes, the ride stopped outside a house on Grange View. They climbed out, the driver remaining in the car. King knocked at the front door. A sleepy-looking man gazed out at them, straightening up when he saw King.

'King? You cool?' he asked. His voice shook.

'Yeah, Smithy. I'm good. You're not busy, are you?'

'No, no, course not.' Smithy led them to an empty room with a few tables and a customised bar. The stench of aftershave lingered. King sat opposite Justin, watching for Smithy, who disappeared behind the bar. After he rustled a bottle of brandy and a glass, Smithy set them down, then left the room. He returned with a pitcher of clear water and filled King's glass. When he finished, he excused himself. King took a sip of the water.

'Still don't drink?' Justin asked.

'That stuff is poison. I like to stay in control. Help yourself, though. That's good brandy.'

'It's barely seven in the morning.'

'So what? You're not working.' King's words hung in the air.

'That why you wanted to see me?'

'It's been a week. Shit out here is bad. Maybe someone told you.'

Chip stopped by a few days ago to christen the new spot. He'd mentioned that King had struck a blow against Tunde and Bloon.

'No. Haven't heard anything,' he lied.

'Thought Chip might have said something. Either way, I need an answer, man.'

Justin fingered the cold glass. He could see particles of dust collecting on the outside. He traced random shapes, planning his words.

'I don't wanna get back into the life, King.'

'And Karma? You're not bothered about that?'

'Course I am.'

'You tell Eddie I wanted you back on the team? I know you visited that old fool.' King's voice was scathing. Justin filed this reaction away.

'What if I did?'

'He loved Karma more than both of us. You don't think Eddie would want you to help avenge him?'

'King—'

'I need you. You're my only shot at winning this. You

know the drill better than anyone. Gimme the time I need to wipe these fucks out.'

'I'm legit now.'

'How? You're not working.'

'I will be soon.'

King laughed. 'After five years for drugs? You must be talking about cleaning, or off-the-books, five pounds an hour shit? Those companies can trip up and find dickheads to work shitloads of hours for them. Dudes without records. What hope is there for you?'

'I'll still try,' said Justin, refusing to let him know how much his words had hit home. King frowned.

'You can earn real money, then run off to Hollywood and do that writing shit.'

'I can't do it, King. I'm out of the life.'

King slammed his glass down and slid to his feet. He glared for a long moment, the veins in his neck prominent, his eyes narrowed.

'Fine,' he snarled, heading for the exit. After a moment, Justin sighed and left.

CHAPTER ELEVEN
MONDAY 29 OCTOBER, 2012

Justin sat in his garden early one morning, looking at the sky. It had become a habit of his. Prison had forced him to embrace waking early, and he'd continued. Even in his current situation, he tried to be productive. His notepad rested on his lap. He'd written a few more unimpressive pages. He wouldn't give up, though. He had something to work towards, and he needed to focus.

Justin hadn't spoken to King since he'd all but stormed out of the gambling spot a few days ago. Chip stopped by, but even his visits were becoming scarcer. Everyone in the Hood was preparing for war. Justin wondered how it would pan out. As he sipped from a lukewarm cup of coffee, a taxi pulling to a stop in front of his house piqued his interest. Janet stumbled out, gasping for breath.

'Thank God you're up,' she panted.

'What's happened?'

'It's Shane. Someone beat him up!'

Justin was on his feet. 'What?'

'He got jumped. He's in hospital.'

Locking the door, he followed her into the taxi, which sped off.

Hospitals reminded Justin of his mum's declining health—the odour of death seemed to mix in with that unique chemical smell. The walls were bland, which didn't surprise him. Everything about hospitals was neutral. They were so deceptive.

Janet spoke with the receptionist, and they hurried onto the ward. Shane slept, his facial bruises evident from a distance. By his side, Keeley sat teary-eyed, along with the kids, both of whom stared at the wall with drooping eyes.

'Are you okay?' said Justin, all previous hostilities forgotten.

'Just in shock.' Keeley flung her arms around him. 'They broke his jaw and bruised a couple of ribs.'

'Who did?' Janet glared at Keeley.

'The guys that jumped him. I don't know anything about it.'

'Why don't I believe you?'

'Because you're a bitter, twisted, lonely old woman who can't accept that her brother loves someone else.'

'My brother loves a slapper, you mean.' Janet fired back. Everyone on the ward watched.

'Both of you need to calm down,' Justin spoke now. 'Think about the kids, for God's sake.'

Both women quietened as one of the staff nurses hurried over.

'If you can't keep your voices down, I must ask you to leave,' she warned.

Justin gazed at his older brother and pondered the situation. Things weren't adding up. Janet had implied one person attacked Shane, but Keeley stated there were multiple people. He looked to her as she gnawed at her nails, her eyes watering. There was more going on. He sensed it.

'Jan, I'm getting off.' He moved toward the exit.

'What? That's our brother lying there.' Janet's voice rose.

'I know.'

'Where are you going then?'

'To find out who put him there.'

As he walked out of the hospital car park, he rang Chip. The first time, there was no answer. He gave him a minute and then called again.

'Who the fuck is this?' Chip sounded tired.

'It's me.'

'Are you on crack ringing me now? I've barely slept.'

'Cut the shit. I need to see you.' Justin heard him yawning and climbing out of bed.

'What's up?'

'My brother got jumped. He's in hospital,' said Justin. There was silence on the other end. 'Did you hear what I said?'

'I already knew. Told you them dudes were stepping up.'

'Which dudes? Chip, fucking talk. This is my brother,' snapped Justin.

'I know. I'm trying to wake up. Gimme a minute.'

Justin overheard a female voice mumbling in the background. He sat on a nearby bench, waiting.

'Okay, I'm back. I dunno how accurate this shit is, but everyone is saying the same thing.'

'What are they saying? Stop stalling.'

'J, if you're out, you're out. Don't get mixed up.'

'Chip, tell me.' Justin's voice hardened.

'Fine. Shane got jumped by Tunde and Bloon. Two of their other guys too.'

'Why?'

'It involves that girl he's trying to wife, I know that.'

'Keeley?'

'Yeah. I banged her years back myself. She's loopy. She's been grinding Tunde. Your bro found out and tried stepping to them. They smacked him up.'

Justin didn't respond, his mouth tightening with anger.

'Is he okay?' Chip continued.

'Where can I find them?'

'Jus, I—'

'I said, where can I find them?'

Loud Grime music shook the ground as Justin approached the house. He parked behind a green bin and climbed out. Gathorne Street had looked the same ever since he was a child. It was a long street with weathered red brick houses. The *Hell* crack spot had been located on this street, and he closed his eyes for a second, remembering.

Justin looked at the address Chip had given him. Four black men sat on the stoop, shouting and passing a stick of weed between them. When he entered the garden, they paused, three of them rising.

'Who are you?' One snapped.

Justin ignored him and focused his attention on the man still sitting. He was slight and smooth-skinned, with a shaped-up fade, red designer sweater, and a large chain around his neck. His eyes drooped as he glanced at Justin.

'Are you Tunde?' Justin asked.

'Who's asking?'

'Justin Holmes.'

Tunde looked less bored now, 'I know you.'

'You know my brother too. You jumped him.'

'If your bro is who I think it is, then he started it,' said Tunde, laughing. 'He stepped up like Rambo. Threw the first punch too.' He smirked, eyes red and unfocused.

'You think this is a joke?' Justin stepped forward, his path blocked by the other men. They scowled at him, eyes narrowed and ready to cause damage.

'Dig up before you end up in the bed next to your brother. I don't care about your name. You were big like ten years ago. Your time's done,' said Tunde.

One goon grabbed Justin's shoulder. 'You heard what he said. Move.'

'Don't touch me.' He shoved the man away, glaring at Tunde's smirking face. Furious but outnumbered, he left, Tunde's laughter ringing in his ears.

CHAPTER TWELVE
MONDAY 29 OCTOBER, 2012

Justin shook with rage in his car. Before considering what to do next, he dialled a number on his phone.

'Who's this?'

'King, I need to speak to you. Now.'

'I'm at a dinner party. Come through, and we'll talk.'

He took the address and hung up. It was early evening, the grey clouds in the sky darkening. The sky had a blood-red tint, giving it a ghoulish, sinister appearance. He parked and knocked at the door.

'You must be Justin,' a short black woman said, opening the door with a smile. 'Come in.'

She led him into the room. He stopped short when he saw who sat there. Her dark, chestnut brown hair was coiffed, her lips still sensuous. Her cold, smoke-grey eyes widened, mouth parting for a moment. He couldn't tear his eyes away, transfixed. His palms were clammy as he struggled to hold Charlotte's gaze.

'Nice to see you, J,' King rose, grinning. Justin had forgotten that he or anyone else was in the room. 'You okay?'

'I need to have a quick word.' Justin forced his attention to King. His stomach churned as his friend leant over Charlotte, kissing her on the cheek. Justin looked away, thinking about Shane.

'Let's go outside.'

The pair traipsed outside to the back garden, the damp grass soft under their feet. Mildew clashed with whatever aftershave King had doused himself in. Justin kept his eyes ahead. He'd seen King's smile. The meeting point hadn't been an accident. It was designed to shock him and had worked. His thoughts flitted to Charlotte, her presence tearing through his mind like paper. He was never truly over her.

'What's up then?' King asked.

'Did you hear about my bro?'

King's face softened. 'Chip told me. Listen, if there's anything—'

'Tunde and Bloon were behind it.'

'Heard that too.'

'That offer you made,' Justin started. 'Does it still stand?'

King surveyed him, then nodded.

'I accept, but I have conditions.'

'Name them.'

'I walk away when I'm ready—no ifs or buts.'

'Done.'

'I touch nothing. No product, no money. I control the people around me.'

'Anything else?' King leant forward, his grin widening.

'No. Tell me what you need.'

'Tomorrow. I'll scoop you up and give you the play.'

'Okay.' Justin steeled himself to head back inside and moved toward the door.

'Jus?'

He faced King again.

'Was it the beating that made you change your mind?'

Justin loathed the cocky expression on his old partner's face. A deal was a deal, though.

'Something like that.'

Justin groaned the next morning as he forced his eyes open. After leaving King, he'd headed to the first shop he could find, buying several bottles of wine and drinking as much as possible before passing out. He staggered to the shower, standing under the piping hot water, trying to clear his head and avoid thoughts of Charlotte. When he was ready, he tried to eat, but his mouth wouldn't cooperate.

'Show no weakness,' he murmured, abandoning his breakfast.

Chip showed a while later. He glanced over at Justin as his friend climbed into the car.

'King told me to come and get you.'

'He said he'd be in touch today.' Justin fastened his seat belt.

'Are we gonna talk about what's going on?'

Justin rubbed his head. He regretted his weakness. It was stupid to get drunk, and worse to do so over Charlotte.

'What do we have to talk about?'

'You know what. Are you working for King now? What about the writing?'

'I have a plan, Chip. That's all you need to know.'

'J, I'm on your side. A couple of the others won't like this situation, though. King's crew, they're vicious, and everyone wants to climb. It's competitive.'

'Like I said, I have a plan.' Justin wiped his eyes, missing the speculative look Chip gave him.

The spot was an industrial warehouse near Guiseley. Justin recognised it as one he'd visited with Karma years ago. King grinned when he saw him, and motioned for them to approach. He counted at least twenty people dotted around. Some snacked on sandwiches and drink, others chatted amongst themselves.

'Everyone listen,' King started. 'We're here for one reason. Our brother has come back to us. Justin Holmes came up with me and a few others. He's an old-school-soldier who stood tall and did five years without opening his mouth.' King patted him on the back and wrapped an arm around him. 'Listen to his orders like they're mine, and make sure you all play nice.' With another wide grin, he pushed him towards the crowd.

Justin tensed, but didn't respond. He studied the reactions of the men. Most stifled yawns, messing on their phones. A few glared at him with venomous looks. He sighed, ready for the work he needed to do.

King dismissed the men a while later, telling Chip and Pincer to stay. Justin stood near the door as Pincer fixed him with a glare.

'Why are you still here? You're a soldier.'

Before he could reply, King invaded his space again, clapping a large hand on his shoulder.

'J is the heir to the throne. He'll be here, and at every other meeting I decide.'

Pincer didn't argue, but Justin noticed he shared a quick look with Chip.

'Anyway, I'll bring you up to speed, J. Organisation-wise, we're similar to what you know. I handle money. Chip and Pincer handle day-to-day on the streets. We move crack, heroin, and lately, a lot of coke and weed. You're gonna oversee the organisation and money, reporting to me when necessary. You have free rein. Cool?'

Justin nodded. He sensed Pincer and Chip's eyes on him, but he focused on King. The man paced the room.

'Good. Now then, to business. Tunde and Bloon have to go.'

'Do they work with anyone?' Justin asked. King shook his head.

'They're independent. They've got links, but none that'll fight for them. They're always surrounded by people. They're flashy, and they like women.'

'Why don't we use Shane's girl?' Chip spoke. 'Tunde's already had her, and she'd do it for the right price.'

Pincer and King grinned. Justin fought to get his anger under control.

'No.'

Everyone turned to him. He scowled at Chip.

'My family are off limits.'

'Wait a sec,' Pincer stepped forward. 'You don't get to decide shit.'

They locked eyes. Justin's fist clenched, ready to punch a hole in his ratty face.

'He's right. You lot, leave his family alone. We'll come at Tunde and Bloon another way.'

'King, put me on this. I'll take them out,' said Chip.

King assessed him for a moment, then glanced at Justin.

'Get it done, and there'll be a nice bonus in it for you. Let's get out of here and get to work.'

CHAPTER THIRTEEN
TUESDAY 13 NOVEMBER, 2012

Charlotte Winters kept her eyes on the road, letting out a yawn. Work had been arduous, and as she angled into her driveway, she noted King's car already parked. As she climbed out, she saw another car across the road, watching the house.

King sprawled on the sofa watching football on the 60-inch screen, grinning like an overgrown man-child. Charlotte gave him a chaste kiss, placing her handbag and jacket on an armchair. Besides the TV, she had control over the décor, and the chocolate-coloured sofas and plush brown carpets were all her doing.

'We're gonna be okay.'

Charlotte made a face, waiting for him to elaborate.

'Justin's in. It's gonna be like back in the day. We're gonna run this city.'

She headed to the kitchen. King had cooked, and she helped herself to some fish and rice. As she tucked in, she winced from the pepper. She could still see Justin's shocked face when he entered the room at the dinner party. Weeks had passed, but she recalled his face hardening. His eyes had showcased the pain. She'd noted he looked well. Haunted, but healthier than expected.

'Justin's got that thing about him. He's gonna have people eating out of the palm of his hands.'

Charlotte agreed. Justin could always talk; he had the ability to draw people into his vision and had charmed her with ease. As she put her fork to the side, she wondered if he still loved her.

'Is he staying with Shane or Janet?'

King's eyes narrowed.

'Why?'

She cleared her plate.

'He never had a house of his own. He used to rent places.'

King didn't reply straight away. Charlotte wondered if she'd gone too far. Justin was a subject that they never broached. After he started spending time around her, it became awkward to mention Justin, so they didn't.

King let out a deep breath.

'I set him up with a place on St Martin's Road; gave him a little Honda jeep to drive.'

'Does that make up for prison?' Charlotte made herself some green tea, rubbing the back of her neck. King shot her a vicious look.

'I didn't have to help him.'

'I thought Justin was an asset? Sounds like you'll be helping each other.'

King had a sour look on his face as he approached. His nostrils flared, but she calmly watched him, blowing on her tea as he seethed.

'Justin works for me. I'm the boss, and you need to watch your mouth because you don't know what you're talking about.'

Charlotte slid away and sat back at the table. King bristled, glaring down at her. When she didn't react, he stomped back to the living room, missing the smirk that appeared on her face.

Justin sat in a safe house. It was a chill spot with no drugs, guns or money. Carlton, a young soldier in King's crew, sat with him. He was light-skinned with short black hair and an easy smile. He was well-liked among the crew, and Justin enjoyed his company.

'How old are you?' Justin asked.

'Sixteen.'

'Do you go to school?'

'I got kicked out, so here I am,' Carlton replied with a grin. Justin resisted the urge to lecture him. He thought about all the younger kids that had worked under them back in the day. Some had been locked up around the same time as him, but he knew a few escaped. He wondered what they were doing, whether his own experience scared them from the life.

Sighing, he wondered what he was doing, and how he was changing anything.

Justin hung around Carlton a while longer and then drove home. He made a meal and picked at it as he drank freely from a bottle of Hennessy. Being back in the life jarred him. He wasn't used to the paranoia. People were counting on him to fail, and he needed to watch his moves and outsmart them. He stumbled up the stairs, leaving the half-drunk brandy bottle on the table. Washing his face and brushing his teeth, he collapsed on the bed and closed his eyes.

Justin's eyes opened at the sound of the first bang. He struggled to his feet, wearing only a pair of cotton pyjama bottoms. A nearby empty bottle toppled. He ignored it, switching on the hallway light and padding down the stairs to open the door. He didn't check who was knocking, and he should have.

Charlotte lingered in the doorway. Her intense eyes searched his own, but she took a moment to speak.

'Hi.'

Justin shook his head and stood aside.

'Take a seat,' he said, stomping upstairs and throwing on a t-shirt. He smoothed out the crinkles, looking in the mirror at the tired visage. Splashing cold water on his face, he glanced again at the bloodshot eyes.

When he walked back into the front room, Charlotte was thumbing through his writing pad.

'Don't touch that.' He snatched it from her.

'Okay, no need to be territorial. Just ask.'

'What are you doing here?'

Charlotte shifted in her seat, her movements fluid. Justin caught himself staring at her frame and stopped.

'Have you been drinking?'

'Why?'

Charlotte shrugged. 'I saw the bottle.' She pointed at the bottle of brandy.

'Must be from the other night.'

'Must be.'

'You still haven't answered my question.'

'I wanted to check you were okay.'

'Why wouldn't I be?'

'Look,' Charlotte started, 'I know seeing me wasn't easy—'

'That was over two weeks ago,' Justin interrupted.

'I didn't know you were coming. King didn't say.'

'Did you know I was out?' Looking at Charlotte hurt, so he focused on the label on the bottle. He hadn't even checked it before he bought it.

'I did. You seem well. I'm happy about that.'

He yearned for her, remembering lazy days spending time together, reading, making love until the early hours of the morning.

'So, you turned up with no warning — a fortnight later — to tell me you didn't know I would be at a dinner party?'

'Look, a lot has changed.'

'Yeah. You're fucking my friend.'

Charlotte's face flushed. 'And you're working with him. You must be so proud.'

'You don't have the right to pass judgement on me.'

'After five years, I don't have the right, but you can make remarks about my sexual proclivity? Between my fiancé and me?'

'That's right. You're engaged. I should offer my congratulations.'

'It doesn't concern you. There's no need to congratulate me.'

'You don't need to be here, so run back to your big house. I dumped you, remember? Don't take the moral high ground when you've hopped from one friend to another.'

Charlotte's composure slipped, and her voice was barely above a whisper when she spoke again.

'Is that why you hate me? Because of King?'

'I don't feel a thing for you. You're not worth hating.'

She struck him, the crack ricocheting around the room. Justin touched his face and smiled through his rage, his veins surging with fury.

'I hope you enjoyed that. Now get out.'

Charlotte's eyes were ablaze. She took another step toward him, then turned on her heel and stormed out. He closed the door and stood still for a minute. He dragged himself upstairs, flopping on the bed and closing his eyes, trying to block out a headache and his own feelings. Groping for the bottle, he threw it across the room, giving way to his emotions.

It was after midnight, and the Hood was silent. Steady rain had relaxed to a drizzle, the dreary fog giving the entire road a horror film vibe. A BMW X6 ambled to the curb, the heavy bass from the music announcing the driver and his passengers.

Bloon stepped out, his tracksuit and black trainers immaculate, the clothing still carrying the price tags. Life had grown harder for he and Tunde lately. King and his team seemed more co-ordinated and harder to pin down. His driver opened his own door, his face dour as Bloon chatted on the phone.

'I hate this weather,' he grumbled in a low voice, several drops of rain landing on his head and running down his face.

'One sec—' Bloon said to the caller. He snaked his head towards his driver, '—shut up and go open the door. I'm talking here.'

The driver opened his mouth to reply. Before he could

speak, a black motorbike whizzed around the corner. They gawped, just able to make out two figures. By the time they spotted the passenger's gun, it was already too late. Bullets sprayed everywhere. Several struck the X6, setting off the car alarm. Bloon dropped the phone and turned to run as a bullet clipped him. He screamed in pain, holding his wounded shoulder and staggering along. He stumbled on the wet road, searching for safety. He made it five yards down the road before another bullet crashed into his back. Toppling onto the murky pavement, he couldn't move, his whole body racked with pain. Heavy footsteps hurried towards him, the silence punctuated by the gunman's heavy breathing, and screams in the background. Chip kicked him onto his back and aimed the gun at his face, his jaw tight.

'King said goodbye.'

Gunfire followed. Then darkness.

CHAPTER FOURTEEN
THURSDAY 11 APRIL, 2013

SPRING ARRIVED in a flurry of warmer, fresher weather. Clouds seemed to glide across the sky, obscuring the faint sun, peeking in and out, giving those below a brief, fiery vision.

'It went well, J.'

Justin didn't reply to Chip straight away. They were driving down Roundhay Road, a long winding stretch of path. Chip shot him a glance, then turned the radio down. Justin had waited in the car while he met his links. They were steady buyers associated with a powerful crew, and he was trying to raise his profile with King by getting them to buy more drugs.

'J, they're ready to step up; they need reassurances, and to meet with you or King.'

Justin glanced in his wing mirror and moved into another lane.

'J, man—I'm talking to you.'

'I'm listening.'

'Are you gonna meet them then?'

Justin shook his head.

'J, it's big money. One meeting won't hurt.'

'Business either talks or it doesn't. No meetings.'

'You're the boss.'

Chip had meant it as a slight, but he'd grown used to being in charge. Other than a few bumps, his transition had been smooth. He'd earned the respect of most of King's crew by ironing out what wasn't working, leading to more money for the team. He also gave big bonuses for good work, which motivated the troops to work harder. There were grumblings from the King loyalists he was changing too much, but he ignored the negativity. The smoother everything worked, the easier his money would come, and the quicker he could leave. The silence didn't last long before Chip spoke again.

'I might talk to King. He'll wanna do this deal.'

'I'm in charge. Not King. I said no, Chip. I don't trust them.'

'They're my people. I've known them for time.'

'Then they shouldn't need to meet with anyone,' Justin pointed out. Chip folded his arms and stared out of the window.

'How's the supply?'

'Fine,' replied Chip, his tone dismissive. Justin frowned, but held his tongue for now.

After dropping Chip, he drove through the city centre to the college on its outskirts. He locked his phones in the car, grabbed his rucksack from the back and waited inside after flashing his ID at the security guard. Most students had left. The cleaners had already tidied up.

The stench of ammonia and bleach stung his nostrils as

he headed to a classroom on the first floor and walked in. He was early—only two other students sat in the room, talking in low whispers. They paused their conversation for a moment, then resumed as he headed for his usual seat at the back of the classroom. Justin opened his textbook to the last page he'd read the night before. He glanced around the room. During the day, the classroom belonged to another department. Based on the graphs, projections, and number-based pieces hanging on the walls, Justin assumed it was a business class. He began reading his textbook, engrossed in the next section. The classroom filled around him, but he didn't notice.

'Sorry, people—traffic was a nightmare.' Their teacher hurried into the classroom, red-faced and breathing hard. 'Turn to the section titled *Giving Life to Characters* while I catch my breath.'

An hour later, everyone packed away. Justin had just closed his bag when Tyler — one of his classmates — approached.

'Mate, we're gonna go to the pub and get a quick drink. Interested?'

Justin smiled. 'Sorry. I've got a meeting. Next time.'

Tyler nodded. 'Yeah. Next time. See you next week.'

It was turning to darkness when he reached his ride. He turned his phones back on and started the engine. On Spencer Place, he parked across the road from a row of houses, then called a number.

'Yo,' a voice said.

'It's me. I'm outside.'

Moments later, Carlton emerged. Even in the growing darkness, Justin noted the focus on the youth's face. As he approached and climbed into the ride, he checked his surroundings.

'Yes, J,' he said, slapping Justin's hand.

'Carlton. How are we looking?'

'We're almost out.'

Justin tensed.

'Have you spoken to Chip?'

'Tried. He ain't answering.'

'Okay. Go to Jack's. Tell him I sent you, and to ring me if he needs it verified. He'll sort you.'

'Want me to try Chip again?'

'No.' Justin's face darkened. 'I'll speak to him.'

The next day, Justin drove to Chip's. It had rained earlier, but the sky was clear, save for a few mounds of dreary grey cloud. He smiled when Marie answered the door. She had a pregnant glow, even with her hair scraped back in a ponytail, and a round belly.

'Hey, J. You okay?' She beamed as they hugged.

'I'm looking for your fella. Is he around?'

'He left early this morning. Is everything okay?'

'Everything's fine. I thought we were meeting here.'

Marie frowned. 'Don't lie, Justin. Chip looked stressed when he left. What's happening?'

His heart went out to Marie. She was pregnant and hormonal, but there was nothing to tell her.

'Trust me, nothing is going on. Rest up. You're ready to pop, right?'

'Couple weeks to go yet. Are you sure?'

Justin smiled again. 'Yes, I'm sure.'

He drove to King's spot in Chapeltown. As always, a few guys milled outside. They greeted him, but he didn't stop to talk. Chip, Pincer and two other men were talking in loud voices. When he entered, they stopped. Pincer's eyes narrowed. Chip glanced at the floor. An open bottle of liquor and several glasses rested on the otherwise bare coffee table.

'Give us the room,' Justin told the others. They left.

'What are you doing here?' Pincer asked.

'Do we have a problem?' Justin directed his question to Chip, who scowled. He waited.

'No.'

'What was yesterday about then? Why, when I asked if we were low, did you say we weren't?'

'It was an oversight.'

'Was it?'

Chip's eyes narrowed. 'What are you trying to say?'

'I'll ask you again; do we have a problem?'

'We're cool, J.'

'Justin, Chip told me about that meeting — why aren't we doing it?' Pincer interjected.

'We are. Just not on their terms.'

'These guys associate with Teflon. Chip's got a personal relationship which gives us an edge. We should take advantage.'

'We don't need a meeting if his relationship is that productive,' said Justin.

'King might see it differently.'

'He might. But, he left me in charge, and unless profits were down, I doubt he'd be concerned.' He faced Pincer, looking down his nose at the ratty man. 'Are profits down?'

Pincer shook his head.

'Are profits up?'

'You know they are,' Pincer mumbled.

'You're right. And no matter what the two of you think, I know what I'm doing.'

'If you say so,' Pincer grumbled.

'I do.' Justin locked eyes with him, irritated by his ratty face. 'And you need to consider if you can work under me, because I won't tolerate disrespect.'

The tension was palpable. Both men glared, neither giving an inch.

'Like you said, you're the boss. I'm out.' Pincer eyed him one last time and left.

'Jus—' Chip started.

'King came to me.'

'What?' Chip frowned.

'He asked me to do this. You were there. Work with me or don't. But, don't fuck up on purpose.'

'Listen, no one's trying to fuck up. I don't see why you can't slide on this. They're my people—'

'I won't have my decisions questioned, do you understand?'

Chip reared back, his mouth hanging open.

'I'm your boy,' he said. Justin glowered, maintaining the fierce stare.

'This is business. My arse is on the line, same as yours. Work with me, not against me.'

Chip shook his head and stormed out after Pincer. Justin took a seat and swigged from the bottle.

'Listen, I ain't got time for this.'

King hung up, tossing the phone onto the seat next to him.

'Fucks sake. Justin's supposed to make shit easier,' he

grumbled. Charlotte stared out of the window, taking in the night sky.

'Are you okay, babe?'

She nodded, her face pale.

'You're not pregnant, are you?'

Charlotte snorted.

'Where did that come from?'

'Are you?'

'No! Course not.'

'It's not the right time, Char. I ain't got the time for a kid.'

'King, I'm not pregnant.'

'You'd better not be.'

An awkward silence ensued. She continued watching King. They'd dressed up for dinner, but he'd been distracted. He wasn't around as much, and she couldn't seem to get hold of him. Her face etched into a frown. After what seemed like an age, the driver stopped at Charlotte's place in Chapel Allerton. King stepped from the car with her trailing. The street was deserted, save for a young-looking man walking towards them. King glanced at him. Something about him seemed out of place. He didn't know why, but his instincts screamed a warning. He moved as the man drew a gun.

'Char, get down!' He said without looking back, his words drowned out by the clap of gunfire, followed by Charlotte's shrieking. The man fired three wild shots, but the driver stumbled from King's ride and returned fire. The shooter retreated, dropping the gun and running in the direction he had come from.

'Char! Are you hit?' King scrambled towards his fiancée. She lay in a heap on the floor but appeared unhurt. When he reached for her, she reared back, terrified. He grabbed her hand. 'We need to go inside.' He turned to the driver. 'Get outta here now!'

By now, neighbours converged. Gun smoke and the smell of gunpowder filled the night air. A few of the shell-shocked neighbours had phones in their hands. The driver did as ordered, jumping into the ride and speeding off. With one last panicked glance, King bundled Charlotte into the house.

CHAPTER FIFTEEN
THURSDAY 11 APRIL, 2013

THE FIRST THING Justin heard when he approached the spot was shouting.

'I want them dead. No more pissing about.'

Pincer, Chip, and several other higher-ups were present. At every corner, skinny, hard-faced youths watched with hawk-like attentiveness. Justin didn't hold their angry-at-the-world stares. He knew killers when he saw them.

'It was a young guy—I wanna know everything about him. Get hunting so I can finish him myself.' King was shirtless, his chiselled physique on show as he stomped around the room.

'No one's saying anything—' Pincer started.

'Make them say something. I want no one flopping on this. We should have already dealt with the bitch behind it.'

'Was it Tunde then?' Asked Chip. King turned on him.

'Who else? Should I be looking elsewhere?'

Chip looked at the floor, unwilling to reply. King glared a moment longer, then continued pacing. Though larger than most front rooms, there was limited space with all the bodies. Not that this stopped him.

'I shouldn't be exposed like that. You need to step your games up, show people why I'm on top.'

As he spoke, Justin poured himself a drink of Disaronno from a nearby bottle. The war talk bored him. Charlotte had been in the car too. He wondered if she was okay.

'What about you?' King noticed his movement.

'What about me?' He sipped his drink.

'Why are you here?'

'I'm here because someone tried to kill you. Also, you asked me to come.'

'Well, why aren't you contributing?' demanded King.

'To what?'

King looked around the room again, his expression disbelieving.

'To the damn discussion.'

'Because I'm not your counsellor.'

A hushed silence filled the room.

'What are you then?'

'Why did you bring me back?' Justin took another liberal sip, wishing he had something to mix it down with.

'To cost me money, if the shit I've heard is correct.'

Justin realised the reason behind his summoning.

'I wasn't aware takings were down,' he said, gathering his words.

'So that means we can turn down money?'

Everyone waited for his reply. King had put him on the spot.

'Am I in charge?' he asked.

'What?'

'Am I in charge, King?'

'What I'm trying to say is—'

'It's a simple question. We made an arrangement. Am I in charge or not?'

Silence descended. Even the shooters looked startled. None of them had ever seen anyone talk to King in such a manner before. King's eyes narrowed, almost molten with anger. His jaw clenched. Still, Justin met his gaze.

'You're in charge. You know what you're doing.' King approached. He picked up the bottle of Disaronno, filled Justin's glass, then, in a move that surprised everyone, took the glass from him and downed it.

'Everyone leave.'

CHAPTER SIXTEEN
THURSDAY 25 APRIL, 2013

Justin raised the cheap beer to his lips and took a liberal swig. DVD cases, bottles of pop and West Indian food boxes littered Shane's living room. Shane glared at the football match on the television as Keeley flounced in, wearing her jacket and carrying her handbag. She gave Justin a glance as she headed for the door.

'Where are you going?' said Shane.

'To the shop. We're out of bread and milk.'

He eyed her. 'What are you all dressed up for?'

'I thought you liked it when I look nice?'

'When it's for me, I do.'

'You know what, just fuck off, Shane. Why don't you get off the sofa and lose weight?'

'Go away, you slag. I shouldn't have got involved with a slapper like you.'

'Go to hell.' She stomped from the house.

'I swear, I'd leave if it wasn't for the kids,' Shane said. Not knowing what to say, Justin nursed his beer.

'Are you back at work yet?'

Shane chugged his beer, then let out an enormous

belch, wiping his mouth. Justin wished he would open a window.

'Not yet, bruv. It's early days.'

'Your boss isn't happy. He thinks you're taking the piss.'

'How do you know?'

'People talk.'

'People need to mind their bloody business. As for Ronnie, I've stuck by him from a lot of aggro, and now he wants to cut me loose?'

'Go back to work, bro. Get your structure back and—'

'Door work is dead.' Shane's expression became crafty. 'Why don't I work for you?'

'Excuse me?'

'I know what you're doing, J. Everyone knows. You're the main man out there. Put me on.'

'There's no future on the roads, Shane. Go back to work. Fix your relationship. The longer you leave it, the harder it'll be.'

'Don't bloody preach. I need help, not pity. I need you to put me on and give me a job.'

Justin stood and checked the time on his phone.

'Concentrate on the kids. I'll come by and check on you soon.'

As King left the gym in the afternoon, his bodyguard trailed behind him. Pincer waited by the car.

'Boss, we think we found him.'

'What do you mean *think*?' King was in no mood for games.

'A bird watching one of our weed spots—she said she

saw Tunde and another guy pull up across the road about ten minutes ago,' relayed Pincer. He had King's full attention now.

'Is she sure it's him?'

Pincer shrugged. 'Her friend used to bang him back in the day. I came to get you as soon as I received word.'

King moved towards the car. 'We'll grab tools on the way.'

Violence and murder on their minds, they clambered into the 4x4. The driver had just started the engine when they were blocked in on all sides by flashing police cars, shrill sirens piercing the quiet.

'What the fuck is this?' King hurried from the ride, followed by his people.

'Nice to see you, King. How are you doing after that shooting?' A balding detective ambled from one car.

'What the hell do you want?' snarled King.

'I'd like to escort you to the station so we can have a chat.'

'I'm not going anywhere.'

'Is that how you want it?' The officer seemed unruffled. King gazed at the police surrounding them. They watched the exchange with determined faces.

'You ain't got a charge. You must wanna get sued for harassment.'

'The charge is murder,' said the officer, taking pleasure at the expression that flitted across King's face. 'Lose your boyfriends before they get arrested for obstruction of justice.' He pulled a pair of handcuffs. 'Hands behind your back.'

CHAPTER SEVENTEEN
MONDAY 29 APRIL, 2013

A FEW DAYS LATER, Justin dragged himself from bed at seven in the morning for a run.

As he stepped from the house, the sky switched from pitch black to light grey, birdsong and car engines providing a soundtrack. He needed to clear his mind to survive. His new running shoes pounded the pavement as he plodded along, determined. His breathing became ragged, and his knees ached. He tried running through the pain, but soon enough, he bent at the waist, sucking in air.

'Fuck!' he shouted to no one in particular, giving his frustration a voice. He couldn't help but recall the day when the police had caught him. Fitness hadn't saved him that day, either. It wouldn't happen again.

So what was he doing then?

His mood hadn't improved by the time he made it back to his house. He lit a cigarette and rooted around for the bottle of Courvoisier he'd bought the night before. His hands trembled as he held the bottle, wanting to drown his feelings in a torrent of liquor. He put the bottle back and sat at his makeshift desk. It had evolved into a more functional writing space, with notepads, pens, books on writing technique with the price stickers still on, and a MacBook Pro. Justin booted it up, loading the last piece of work he had started. He closed his eyes and let his hands find the keys. It was futile. He wrote two jumbled lines, out of sync with the mediocre words that had come before them.

The streets dominated his mind. King was out on bail. Justin wondered how things would pan out if he was imprisoned, and what it would mean for the business. He deleted the lines he'd written, then the entire text that had preceded it, saving this before he changed his mind. He hated feeling so torn. For a second, he longed for prison—not the bars, but to slip back into the prolific state of mind he'd channelled to finish his first draft. Even now, he struggled to be free.

The door knocked. Justin sighed, closed the laptop and answered, letting Chip in.

'You're up early.'

'I was at the hospital with Marie.'

'Everything okay?'

'False alarm. Thought the kid was coming. Doctors said it was *Branston Hicks* or something,' said Chip.

'Marie's cool, though?'

'Yeah, just fat and bad-tempered.'

'I'll tell her you said that.'

Both laughed before Chip spoke again.

'I'm here for a reason, J.'

Justin flopped down on the sofa. 'What's up?'

Chip's brow furrowed. 'Shit's different with us. It's like we're not vibing.' He rubbed his nose. 'That shit with King shouldn't have gone so far.'

Justin nodded. Chip continued.

'I dunno what it is. Maybe I'm still not used to you being here. I wanted you to know I'm with you.'

'Sentimental prick.' Justin patted his back, touched by the words. 'It's all love, Chip. Always will be. You're my boy until the end.'

'Now who's being sentimental.' Chip's eyes zeroed in on his writing desk. 'You're serious about this writing shit, aren't you?'

'It's the first thing I've done in a long time that feels right.'

Chip nodded now, a thoughtful expression on his face. 'I know I laughed before, but—'

'All love, Chip. Like I said. I know you meant nothing bad.'

'Nah, I didn't. Dreams, y'know. They're just dreams. That's how I've always seen it anyway.'

Justin understood where he was coming from. There were few people to push them towards what they wanted as they grew up. Dreams were dismissed. It was why they gravitated towards the streets.

'It's only too late when you stop trying, Chip. Don't die because you think you have to. Focus on your child, and how you want them to grow up.'

Chip said nothing, but he was sure that his friend was getting it.

King sat in the plush office of his solicitor, sipping tea from an antique cup and scowling. The office had a smell of rich leather and varnished wood, dominated by papers and expensive stationery. A host of bound textbooks filled a mahogany bookshelf in the corner of the room. The splendour was lost on the thug. He focused on the man opposite him.

Simon Masters was diminutive and world-weary. He wore a well-cut grey suit to go with his malicious grin.

'Let me earn my money and handle this situation for you. I assure you I'll find the spill,' he said, his words and manner filled with unshakeable confidence.

'You agree that someone is talking?'

'It seems someone is working with the authorities. Those detectives were too pleased with themselves in that meeting.'

'I'm fucked then.'

'You hired me for a reason, Mr King, and that reason is that I am the absolute best. If the police have a credible witness, they still have to make their case. I have powerful cards still to play.'

'For how long? Si, I'm on bail with these police sitting on my place. They're not even subtle about it.'

'That's a good thing. A man took a shot at you.'

'Don't you think I can take care of myself?' King's eyes narrowed, but Simon continued to smile.

'I know you can, Mr King. You shouldn't deny protection when it is there, though.' Simon walked around to him, shaking his hand. 'In the meantime, consider the people around you, and which are best placed to do you serious harm.'

CHAPTER EIGHTEEN
FRIDAY 3 MAY, 2013

Riding the wave of reinvigorated friendship, Justin, Chip, and a few others partied one night in a nightclub in the heart of Leeds city centre.

Justin cradled a bottle of Kopparberg — his only drink of the night — watching Chip and the others trying to entice passing women into staying with them. They had snorted cocaine in the taxi. After a few shots, they were on the path to revelry, spending tons of money and making a lot of noise.

Through the flickered atmosphere, he studied them, thinking about the pre-prison days when he'd enjoyed the club scene. Now, that passion had diminished. The curtain had lifted, and now he saw it for the facade it was.

His eyes roved around the room, trying to view it through a writer's eyes, as his tutor suggested in their latest class. He spotted a curly-haired woman who seemed familiar. Feeling his eyes on her, she glanced back, warily at first, then with sudden intrigue. He turned away, refocusing on Chip and the gang. Seconds later, a soft hand tapped him on the shoulder.

'Are you Justin Holmes?' Her skin was a luscious olive colour, her hazel eyes sizing him up.

'Yes, I am.' Justin frowned. He couldn't place her.

'You don't remember me, do you?' She picked up on his confusion, 'I'm—'

'Karen Spratt.' From high school. Mrs Bennett's English class,' he said, remembering a skinny girl with glasses. 'Wow, you've—'

'Filled out?' Karen smirked at his attempt to subtly ogle her. *Filled out* seemed to cut it. Her curves certainly hugged the dress she wore.

'I would say grown-up,' said Justin. They both laughed.

'What are you up to these days?' Karen asked.

'Still trying to figure out my life. I imagine you're masterminding hostile takeovers. That or running a city.'

Karen giggled, a sweet melodic sound even against the loud House music pulsating in the background. He liked the laugh as much as he liked the Colgate smile.

'I'm an Events Marketing Manager, and I'm studying for my masters in Communications.'

'That's impressive. I always knew you'd do well.'

'Whatever, you didn't even recognise me.' Karen faked a pout.

'Course I did. Why do you think I looked over?'

'Figured you'd seen an attractive woman and wanted to stare,' Karen teased. He felt himself loosening up.

'That was my other reason.'

'J, come meet this little slut.' Chip chose that moment to lurch over and drape himself on Justin. He clutched a glass of champagne in each hand, his designer t-shirt matted with cocaine sweat. 'Who's this?' he leered at Karen, whose lip curled.

'An old friend.' Justin extricated himself from Chip, who seemed to get the hint.

'Didn't mean to interrupt.' Chip guzzled from one glass, spilling most on the floor as he swayed. 'We're gonna kick out soon and go bottom end of town. You coming with?'

He shook his head. 'I'm gonna get off soon.'

'Cool. Look after yourself.' Chip staggered away.

'He hasn't changed much. Apart from the drastic weight loss, anyway.'

'Chip will always be Chip.' Justin wondered how many times he'd uttered those exact words to different people.

'He tried sleeping with Tina Healy on the school fields. She turned him down, so he spread rumours about her.'

'Sounds like something Chip would do.'

Karen glanced at him. 'Tell me something. Why aren't you over there, living the high life and indulging with your friends?'

He considered this. Chip seemed to have forgotten his plan to leave. He and his cronies were pouring champagne onto the chest of a busty blonde and taking turns licking it off. Justin rubbed his forearm.

'It doesn't interest me anymore,' he said. 'Guess I'm boring now.'

'Not boring. Mature.' Karen's eyes met his again for a long moment.

'I hope you're right. I'm gonna go. Nice seeing you, Karen. I'm glad you're doing well.' He rubbed his throbbing temples, ready to head for the exit.

'Wow, you're not going to give me the line about staying in touch?' Karen feigned shock.

'Didn't want you having to explain to your boyfriend

why an old ruffian from school was trying to call you at inappropriate hours.'

'Good thing there's no boyfriend then. Pass me your phone.'

Justin unlocked his phone and handed it to her with a smirk. Once she'd saved her number, she gave it back.

'Balls in your court, *old-school-friend*. We can go for a drink when you're over your headache.'

Justin laughed. 'Definitely.' His smile faded as he glanced over Karen's shoulder. His sister Janet was in the same club. She hadn't spotted him, her attention focused on the man with her. He wore a brown suit and had a lined-up flat top. He whispered in her ear, and she giggled. Justin's eyes narrowed as he saw her hand the man several notes from her bag. The man swaggered towards the bar with a smirk.

'Justin?'

He snapped his eyes back to Karen. Her eyebrows were raised, concern evident.

'Sorry about that,' he said.

'Are you okay? You seem dazed.'

'I was thinking hard of witty scenarios of how to contact you,' he joked. Karen laughed again, her concern dissipating.

'Don't overexert yourself. I'm a simple girl. I'll speak to you soon, Mr Holmes.'

She walked away then, Justin watching her, a smile tugging the corners of his mouth.

CHAPTER NINETEEN
FRIDAY 10 MAY, 2013

THEY WENT for dinner a week later.

Karen picked the restaurant. She wanted Italian, and Justin didn't argue. He picked out a nice charcoal shirt and black trousers, shined his shoes, and jammed all the negativity running around his mind to one side.

The restaurant was packed to capacity, doing nothing to settle his nerves. They were led to an onyx table with gold trim around the edges. He helped Karen into her seat and took his own. They ordered white wine and waited for the menus.

'I haven't eaten here in a while,' Karen remarked, taking a sip of wine when it came.

'I've never been. The setup seems nice, though.'

Karen smiled. He studied her. Her eyes sparkled, brought out by subtle smoky eyeshadow. Her dark-fitted dress accentuated every curve.

'I'm surprised you called me.'

That intrigued him.

'Why?'

'In the club that night. You seemed disconnected. From your friends, from everything around you.'

'I won't lie and say you're not right. You weren't included in that, though. You were a breath of fresh air on a dismal night.'

Karen couldn't hide her glee at his comment. Her eyes gleamed.

'You must be trying to win me over with lines like that.'

He grinned, but didn't reply. Karen put the drink down.

'I want you to know that I'm aware of your background.'

Justin still didn't reply, but his fingers tightened around his glass. Karen surveyed him.

'It doesn't have to define you. Plenty of people go to prison. Some of them still manage to make positive lives for themselves. Why are you letting it weigh you down?'

'It's not so simple to shake it. The life, Chapeltown, everything that goes with it. I'm trying my best to navigate it. I have dreams I'm working toward.'

Karen leant forward. 'What are these dreams?'

'I write, so I want to take that as far as I can,' replied Justin. Admitting he wrote still felt strange. Every time he said it, he expected more laughter. Karen's eyes widened.

'You write? That's amazing. What do you write?'

'Honestly, my first book was about nothing. This time around, I'm trying to write something Chapeltown-related. Show all the little knuckleheads that there's more out there. People in the Hood are going through so much, and no one is really trying to tell those stories, so I guess I can.'

Karen nodded. 'How do you do it?' She giggled and

took a sip of wine. 'I mean, I can read and write, but sitting and writing a book is a different story. I couldn't imagine sitting and coming up with ideas.'

Justin scratched his chin. 'It's hard to explain. When I was inside, I had so much going on in my head that I decided to get it all on the page. I threw away the first few pages because they were trash. Didn't know what I was doing, and I was ashamed at how bad it was.' Justin paused, recalling the prison cell. 'I carried on with it, and it became something more. When I put pen to paper, I was able to escape the reality of my situation, and that desire fuelled me to write more. The rush of writing, of filling pages with words I created, few things in life could compare. Whenever I wrote, I felt like a whole person again, instead of a hollow shell . . .' His voice trailed off as he saw the expression on Karen's face. She gazed at him, openmouthed, a bemused half-smile tugging her lips. His face burned.

'Sorry, I got a bit carried away,' he mumbled, reaching for his drink to alleviate his embarrassment. A moment later, Karen shook her head, her eyes brimming with something he hadn't expected: admiration.

'Like I said to you earlier, I saw you that night in the club, and you were closed-off from everyone around you. I could feel your anxiety even as you looked at me. When you were speaking just then, I felt your passion, the struggle, and the journey you must have gone through to survive in what I'm sure was a hellhole. That same passion wasn't there in the club. You're doing what you want to do in life, and I love that.'

Both looked away at that point, abashed at their mutual disclosures. Their food arrived, and they began eating. Justin glanced at Karen from time to time, comparing her to Charlotte. He wondered if that was the attraction; the fact they both spoke their mind.

'When do you think your next book will be finished?' Karen asked after a comfortable silence.

'I wish I had the answer. Writing about the streets should be easy, but it's not clicking in the way I want it to.' It was the most honest answer he had. In an ideal world, he would bunker down and focus on his writing, but the actual streets stole his attention.

Tunde hadn't resurfaced, and King wanted people searching for him night and day — no matter the cost or effect. Morale was low, which irritated Justin after all the effort he'd administered. The fact King had been arrested meant he looked at everyone around him as a potential snitch, and people down the ranks felt the tension. Everyone was on edge, and he found it impossible to slip into the writing zone after hours on end spent in safe houses, planning strategy as he attempted to keep everyone placated.

'Can I ask you something?' Karen said after their plates had been tidied away.

'Of course.' Justin gestured for her to speak.

'Did you have a girl before prison?'

Justin's stomach lurched, an image of holding hands with Charlotte as they sat in a cinema consuming him. The film's name evaded him, but the memory of her beaming face as she stared at the big screen wasn't easy to shake.

'It's not worth talking about.'

Before Karen could say anything, she glanced at something to his left. He turned to see a face he hadn't seen in a long time. The man was casually dressed; long-sleeved navy t-shirt, jeans and shoes. His hair was styled, his rosewood eyes stained with red, but twinkling. He resonated an effortless power that outshone anyone Justin had been around, excluding Karma. Both men grinned.

'I heard you were back around,' the man said as Justin rose to shake his hand. 'I see you're already picking up beautiful women.' The man focused his attention on Karen, whose cheeks coloured under his praise. She beamed.

'You have good taste in females.'

Justin interjected, 'this is Lamont Jones. Lamont, this is my date, Karen.'

'Nice to meet you, Karen. You're in fantastic company with Justin here.'

The group laughed. He looked past Lamont to his table. A pretty brown-skinned woman watched their exchange with narrowed eyes.

'Mind if I borrow your date for a minute, Karen?'

Karen signalled it was okay, and Justin followed him to a corner of the room. Both men sized one another up.

'I'll get to it. I know you're back in. I want you to come and work with me.'

It took Justin a moment to find his voice.

'Why?'

'You're sharp. Always have been, and people tell me you haven't missed a step since you got out. I want you in an upper management position, nothing directly street-related. You'd get a flat weekly fee, a percentage of the take, and you can make your own side moves. Everything clean, paid to an account for you to use. What do you say?'

Justin mulled it over. Lamont Jones, known as *Teflon* on the streets of Leeds, was an upper-echelon kingpin. He had grinded and fought to the top of the crime pile long before Justin had been locked up. The offer was fantastic, and he realised it would eclipse anything he would make working for King.

'I can't.'

Lamont's expression remained unchanged. Justin waited a beat.

'It's not that I don't want to. It's complicated.'

'Complicated how?'

'I made a commitment to King. He took care of me when I got out, and if I walk away from that, it'll cause headaches.'

Justin stared at the floor for a moment in contemplation. After a few seconds of silence, he glanced up at Lamont. His eyebrow rose slightly when he noticed Lamont had taken out his phone, and was typing away. More seconds passed, the nervousness replaced with frustration. He tried masking it, forcing himself to wait.

Finally, Lamont locked eyes with him. Slowly turning his phone, he motioned toward the call button, his mouth curling into a crooked smile. On the screen was a number he didn't recognise.

'Say the word, and he's dealt with,' Lamont said coldly.

There wasn't a single part of Justin that believed Lamont was lying. He was aware of some of the killers Lamont had at his beck and call, and they wouldn't think twice about eliminating King if he ordered it. Like Lamont's offer of employment, it was tempting, but he wanted to handle his own problems. The last thing he wanted was for Lamont to be fighting his battles.

'I can handle things, L. Thanks, though.'

Nodding, Lamont smiled warmly, then put his phone in his inside pocket. Straightening, he put his hand on his shoulder.

'Come and see me when you're ready.'

The pair shook hands, and he headed back to Karen.

'So, you're friends with big-time gangsters?'

Justin chuckled. 'You know who that was?'

'I think everyone knows who Lamont is — or whatever street name he goes by. I suppose you can't tell me what he wanted?'

'He just wanted to make sure I was doing okay.' It wasn't a lie, either. If Karen suspected there was more, she didn't press. Pouring more drinks, they enjoyed the rest of their time. They debated who would pay the bill at the end of the night. Justin won. They shared a taxi, heading to Karen's first. He walked her to the door.

'Thanks for an interesting night,' Karen said. She gazed into Justin's eyes, kissing him on the cheek.

'You're not ready yet.'

With that, she headed inside and closed the door.

Charlotte Winters gnawed at her nails as she sat on the sofa. Ever since a random thug had shot at her, she lived in a state of fear. A show she was struggling to follow played on the TV screen. She muted the TV as King stormed in.

'I don't want excuses. Find him. I don't care. Get him, or someone else will find you both. Got that?'

As King's heavy footsteps grew closer, Charlotte unmuted the television.

'You okay, babes?' He sauntered into the room, his face lined with stress, vivid bags under his eyes.

'Just watching this.' She motioned to the screen, accepting the perfunctory kiss King planted on her cheek.

'Why are you always watching this American crap?'

He took the remote from Charlotte and changed the channel.

'I was watching that!'

'It's shit,' said King, as if that was adequate justification.

'So what? You weren't watching it. I was.'

'Don't forget who bought the TV,' he told her. Picking up the bottle of red, he guzzled from it.

'Why are you drinking?' As long as Charlotte had known King, she had never seen him drink alcohol.

'Because I'm thirsty.' He set the bottle back down, wiping his mouth with the back of his hand.

'Can you put my show back on, please?'

'No. It's crap.' He collapsed onto the sofa, rubbing his stomach. 'Grab another bottle, babe.'

'That was the last one.'

'A cuppa will do then. Five sugars,' said King with a grunt. Charlotte gritted her teeth. She didn't know what was going on, but she didn't appreciate him projecting on her.

'Make your own tea,' she replied. King cut his eyes to her.

'You can be such a cunt sometimes.'

Charlotte's head snapped towards him. He sneered, knocking the bottle of Prosecco to one side with his feet.

'Get fucked.' She flounced upstairs and threw herself onto the bed, screaming into her pillow. It didn't take long before the stairs creaked. Charlotte's stomach lurched as she felt King's presence in the doorway. Something landed on the bed next to her. It was the television remote.

'What's your problem, Char?' King said when she knocked the remote onto the floor.

'You're my problem. Why can't you let me be? Why dominate everything?'

King was at a loss for words. Charlotte was feisty, but she had never challenged his authority.

'Take the remote, okay? I shouldn't have called you a cunt.'

'I want you to leave my house.'

King kissed his teeth and rubbed his eyes.

'You know what, I'll be downstairs. Come down when you're off your period.'

Charlotte stood, her anger lending her confidence as she faced King down.

'I said I want you to go. This. Us. I've had enough.'

King's mouth was agape. He coughed.

'Char, babe, I dunno where this crap is coming from, but I'm gonna go downstairs and give you space. Take a nap and sleep off the drink.' He nodded, reassuring himself. 'You're drunk, that's why you're saying all this.'

'I was drunk to think it would ever work with you, Charles, or do you prefer *King*? You're impossible.'

King's disbelief ebbed toward annoyance. He didn't like being defied.

'You think I'm just gonna let you go?'

'I'm a grown woman. I'm not living like this anymore. It's gone on for too long.'

King laughed.

'I looked after you when Justin got banged up. I bankrolled your shitty business. You owe me.'

'I don't owe you a thing. I paid you back a long time ago. Whatever insecurities you have over Justin are your problem. I'm leaving.'

That was it.

'Yeah?' King roared. Sensing danger, Charlotte tried to

run. 'Where are you going?' Gripping his fiancée by her hair, he delivered a pair of vicious slaps that span her around. She crumpled to the floor, too shocked to even cry. He loomed over her, a frothy-mouthed madman.

'You think I'm a loser you can talk to like a piece of shit?'

Charlotte looked up at King. He clenched his fist and drew back again to strike. She closed her eyes, but he punched a fist-sized hole into the wall behind her.

'I own you. Try leaving me, and I'll kill you. Are you listening? You only leave when you're dead.'

CHAPTER TWENTY
SATURDAY 18 MAY, 2013

Justin slumped over his desk, punching keys on the Mac as his phone vibrated. He tried ignoring it, but relented and answered the call.

'Did I catch you at a bad time?'

Justin smiled. After their date ended, he hadn't expected to hear from Karen. They'd begun texting, however, deciding to take things slow.

'I was just trying to write. No drama. How may I help you this evening?'

'I'd hate to feel I was disturbing you, Mr Holmes.'

'You could never disturb me. You know your company is always welcome.'

'Why are we talking over the phone then?'

Justin beamed. He loved when Karen showed her playful side.

'You tell me. Do you think I'm ready now?'

'Come see me, and we'll find out.'

Before he could reply, there was a steady knocking at the door. He told Karen he would call her back, and went to answer. He took a step back when he saw Charlotte.

'Sorry for turning up again,' she mumbled. He noticed the split lip and tear-streaked face.

'Charlie, what the hell happened?'

'I, it was—'

Justin's eyes widened. 'Did King do this to you?'

She hung her head. Justin tilted her chin, so she looked at him.

'Did he?' he repeated. Charlotte nodded. Justin's eyes flared, his expression matching the murderous one of King's earlier. She watched, transfixed by the bulging veins in his neck. A second later — it may have been longer — he was still.

'Stay here.' He headed for the door, but she grabbed him.

'I didn't come for that. Please, don't make it worse.'

Justin took a deep breath and regained his composure.

'Sit down,' he said. Charlotte sat in the living room. He followed. 'Drink?'

Charlotte shook her head. He handed her a tissue. She took it with quiet thanks. Justin headed to the kitchen, allowing her to check out the living room. The house seemed more lived in. There were pictures on the wall from old sporting events, assorted DVDs and books on the table, and an organised writing space in the corner.

Justin re-entered with a cup of coffee in one hand and a cheap energy drink in the other. He sat opposite Charlotte and took liberal sips from each. She made a face.

'How can you drink those together?'

'What happened?' Justin ignored her, his eyes scrutinising. Charlotte looked at the floor.

'We argued, and then King got drunk and passed out.'

'About what?'

'Something trivial.'

'So trivial that King struck you?'

Charlotte swallowed.

'I shouldn't have come.'

'You did, though, Charlie. Why?'

'What do you mean *why*?'

'You know what I mean. Why here, of all places?'

'I'm going.' She moved towards the door.

'Fine. You're nothing but a coward, anyway.'

Charlotte froze. Turning to face Justin, she glowered at him. He finished his coffee, not taking his eyes from her.

'What did you say?'

'You heard. You're a coward, and you're the last person I thought I'd ever say that to.'

'Where do you get off? You think you have all the answers? The criminal?' Charlotte gathered her words. 'What was your big plan? To march over to King and challenge him to a fight? How would that have ended?'

'I—' Justin faltered.

'Save it. Let me say what you're too weak to admit. King would have killed you. Or he would have had someone else do it. He's a killer,' she spoke those words for the first time. Justin didn't respond.

'What about you?'

'What about me?'

'Are you a killer too? Is that what you were doing, all those nights you weren't with me?'

Justin stood so fast he didn't realise he'd moved. The energy drink clattered to the floor, the lime-green substance billowing over the carpet.

'What do you think?' He demanded, invading her space.

'Pardon?' Charlotte instinctively stepped back.

'Do you think I was a killer?' Justin glared at Charlotte, who closed her eyes, taking shaky breaths.

'No. How do I know, though? This is all so fucked up.'

'That's why I ended things. Not because I didn't love you anymore. I tried to save you, and you got with King instead.'

'I needed someone!' Charlotte screamed. 'Don't you get it? I was up all night, crying, worried about you having to survive in there,' Her voice fell, tears pooling in those haunting grey eyes. 'I needed comfort.'

'I know, Charlie.' Justin held her close as she cried. The icy wall thawed as they shared their first embrace in over five years. He recalled how Charlotte's body used to mould to his own. When she reached up and met his lips, it felt perfect. When they kissed, all his senses seemed to come alive at once. It was a rush of adrenaline, everything he had been missing, brightening every crevice of his gloomy mindset. The kiss grew more insistent as they spilled to the sofa, Charlotte's bra askew as he mauled her neck, breasts, any part he could reach as she moaned and writhed beneath him. Justin opened his eyes and saw something in Charlotte's. Beyond the lust, there appeared to be uncertainty. The spell broke. It didn't feel right anymore. He pulled away.

'What are you doing?' She sat up.

'We can't do this.'

'Why not?'

'Because we're doing it for the wrong reasons.'

'Doesn't mean we can't do it anyway,' Charlotte said after a minute. Her voice lacked passion, though.

'As much as I wish things were different, we can't go backwards. Too much has changed.'

'I'm sorry,' said Charlotte, putting her clothes back on.

'No, I'm sorry. Things with us should have been better.'

Charlotte kissed him chastely on the lips. 'We both wish things were different. You're right, though, Justin. We can't change the past.'

Justin nodded, understanding.

'I don't want you going back home tonight.'

'I'll be okay. It wouldn't be smart to stay. Don't worry about me.'

He wanted to argue but held his tongue. When Charlotte had gathered her things, he walked her to her car. She was about to climb in when she paused.

'Can I read your book?'

Justin hesitated.

'Of course, you can.'

CHAPTER TWENTY-ONE
TUESDAY 21 MAY, 2013

King's nostrils flared.

He perched in his office, mobile phone in hand, resisting the urge to throw the thing across the room. His solicitor had advised caution, but he didn't know what he was talking about. The streets had their own laws. He needed to act.

'Boss,' Pincer knocked and walked in, his eyes wide, 'we need to—'

'Rudy is moving funny. I need a new supplier. I swear, they're—' King rambled on, ignoring Pincer's face.

'Boss, we got hit.'

King straightened in his leather chair.

'Tunde again? We need to finish that fucker. No more games.'

'It wasn't Tunde.' Pincer struggled to find the words. 'It's looking like an inside job. Our people were strapped like you wanted. We got one robber.'

'Dead?' King beamed. Pincer nodded.

'One of our youths got him. Hands shook so much he popped him in the head when he aimed for the body.'

'Make sure he gets a bonus. How do we know Tunde wasn't involved? That fucker ripped us for almost fifteen grand last week alone. Prick thinks he's smart targeting all our smaller spots,' said King.

'I hit the scene. We stripped the place. The dude we shot, I recognised him.'

'Stop double-talking me and tell me who it was,' King snapped. Pincer still looked strained.

'It was Justin's bro. Shane did it.'

Justin had the weight of the world on his shoulders as he knocked on Keeley's door. He tried the door handle, finding it unlocked. The two young girls played on the floor in the living room. A thick layer of dust seemed to cover the room. He searched the kitchen for Keeley, finding only dirty dishes and cups.

'Where's your mummy?' He asked the children. They pointed towards the ceiling. The soft sounds of *Mary. J. Blige* crooning about *Real Love* increased as he neared the top. The sobs became louder when the bedroom door opened. On a king-sized purple bedspread, Keeley slumped, her face blotchy from crying. The satin-red dressing gown she wore clashed with the bed cover. When she looked up, she hurried from the bed to give Justin a hug.

'I'm so sorry, Keeley,' he repeated over and over, stroking her hair.

'It doesn't seem real. I can't believe what he tried to do,' she said.

'His back was to the wall. He couldn't see a way out.'

'I thought *you* were his way out?' Keeley pulled away.

'Shane was doing fine without me.'

'Shane was struggling, and you know it. He knew what you had going on. You could have helped, but you didn't.'

'You could have not cheated on him, couldn't you?' Justin replied, watching as Keeley's face slackened.

'It's not about that.'

'You don't think throwing yourself at an up-and-coming ghetto superstar might make your man upset?' Justin took a deep breath. 'This isn't why I came, Keeley. You and I have plenty of time to blame one another. Take care of those little girls. They need their mum.'

'My girls are fine. I've raised them to be strong.'

Justin snorted.

'They're sat down there, covered in dust and dirt, staring at a screen like robots. What part of that is strong?'

'Just fuck off, Justin! Fuck off and leave us alone.'

He swallowed his anger and gazed at the pathetic woman who'd stolen Shane's heart.

'I've got money that you can use to tide yourself over. Clean yourself up. I'll be back in an hour.'

Justin drove to his sister Janet's house. He found her in the kitchen.

'Jesus, Justin, you scared me.' She clutched her chest. She wore an apron, her hands covered in flour. In front of her on the counter was a bowl full of chicken.

'Having a party?'

'A little gathering.'

'Jan, our brother is dead.' Justin's brows furrowed.

'He did a robbery. For whatever reason, the oaf thought he'd get away with it.'

'He's still family. Is food and drink the best way to deal with what happened?'

'I'm not dealing with anything. Shane was old enough to know better. He should have been thinking about that slut and those two babies he loved that weren't his.'

Justin shook his head.

'I'm here to raid the *Writing Fund*.'

Janet's eyes widened.

'Is that smart? You'll never get any money back that you give her.'

'A few thousand should tide her over until she's back on her feet.'

'I don't think it's a good idea, Justin.'

'I know what I'm doing. Where's it at?'

'Upstairs,' said Janet with a sigh.

Justin stood in the doorway as she rooted around in her cupboard. She handed a red shoe box to him. He opened it, thumbing through the arranged stacks. He frowned.

'This is light.'

'Is it?'

Justin glared at his sister, causing her to take a cautionary step back.

'You dipped into my money?'

Janet hesitated. 'J-Just a little. I-I was behind with rent, and—'

'You knew I'd give you the money. Why didn't you ask?'

'I'm supposed to look after you, not the other way around. I was gonna put it back again when I got paid.'

'Where's your money?'

'I have bills to pay. The cost of living. It's difficult.'

'What about *Blair Goodison*, the man you're seeing?'

Janet reared back, her mouth hanging open.

'Who?'

'Don't bullshit me. Is that where your money went? And mine too?'

Janet sobbed, 'bad people threatened him, and he begged me to help.'

'You can't be this fucking stupid, Jan. Do you know what he is?'

'People tell lies about him. He's a good man.'

'He's a ponce. He pimps women, so save any stories. How long has he been juicing you?'

'We love each other.'

'How long!' The force of Justin's tone scared Janet, but she held her ground.

'We've been together almost a year.'

'I thought you were smarter than this.' He rubbed his forehead, his veins surging with rage.

'You have no right to judge me, Justin. You're supposed to be super smart, and you ended up doing five years. Save your platitudes for someone else.'

'Throw it in my face all you want; I came out focused. Now, we will deal with this Blair Goodison problem when I get back. Tell him I want my money. Today, or—' His ringing phone cut him off mid-sentence. '—Chip, this isn't a good time.'

'I'm outside Jan's. You need to come out here.'

Chip hung up. Justin stowed his phone, dropping the box of money back on the bed. 'I want the cash back, Jan. Tell your fancy man I said that.'

Chip waited on the front step, dark circles flourishing under his eyes. He fumbled with the drawstrings of his grey hooded top as Justin approached.

'What's up, Chip? I'm dealing with stuff in there. About my bro.'

Before Chip could speak, two of King's henchmen climbed from Chip's BMW, entering Janet's garden.

'Chip, what's going on?' Justin cut his eyes to his friend.

'King wants to see us.'

'Tell him I'll get with him later after I've handled everything.'

One goon cleared his throat, glowering.

'It's about Shane. What he did.' Chip couldn't meet Justin's eyes.

'I'll make it right. King knows what Shane's like. He wasn't in his right mind—'

'J, Shane wasn't working alone. Bower was behind it.' Chip's voice shook.

'As in your cousin Bower?'

Chip tilted his head, grimacing as he massaged his temples.

'King wants to see us both. Now.'

CHAPTER TWENTY-TWO

TUESDAY 21 MAY, 2013

Four goons joined King, Pincer, Justin, and Chip in the office. No one spoke. All eyes rested on Justin and Chip. All except King's. He fingered an empty glass, staring at it.

'Sit down,' said Pincer. Two chairs faced King's seat. Chip slumped into one. Justin copied him.

'You two got anything you wanna tell me?' demanded King.

'About what?' Justin asked.

'About your brother.' King looked at Chip now. 'And your cousin.'

Chip was about to reply, but Justin spoke again.

'Why would we know anything about that?'

'Because your brother and his idiot cousin don't have a brain between them.'

'Shane wanted me to bring him in on what I'm doing for you. I said no. He did something stupid in return. The blame stops well short of us, King.'

'What about you?' King faced Chip. He was pale and nervous in his chair.

'Huh?'

'Don't fucking *huh* me. One of you two is lying. I know you were with your cousin earlier. What were you doing? Making sure he remembered the plan?'

'You calling me a snake?' Chip shot to his feet. Two of the killers lunged. They kicked his chair aside and laid into him with heavy punches. One held his arms while the other smashed his fist into Chip's nose. There was a sickening squelch, followed by a stream of blood. Justin rose as they stomped on his ribs, unwilling to watch his friend's beating.

'Don't do it, J. You're my brother, so sit and watch him take his medicine,' King warned.

'Chip didn't do it. How long have you known him?'

'Time doesn't matter one bit. This dumb bastard thought he should lead.' King clicked his fingers, and the beating stopped. 'He wanted my power.'

Justin knelt by Chip, listening to him moan in pain.

'He didn't do this.' He glanced at King, who glared back.

'Did you then? Because one of you motherfuckers did.' King rounded the desk and stood in front of him. 'I thought it was him. Maybe it's you.'

Justin stood, eyeing King. Pincer and the goons watched, wanting the green light to tear him apart. He was oblivious to this, exhibiting a cold force that everyone felt.

'If you're gonna accuse me, then be a man. Don't hide behind your people.'

The room waited. Only Chip's whimpering punctuated the silence. Just then, another of King's people burst in, startled when all eyes shot in his direction.

'What do you want?' snapped King.

'We got confirmation on Tunde at a house in Harehills. Lizzie's there with him. She's keeping him company.'

King turned from Justin. 'Pincer, take ten of our people, go down there and drag him from that spot. Take him alive. I wanna talk to him before he goes down.'

Pincer hurried from the room, glancing at Justin as he did so. Without a word, King turned to his remaining goons.

'Clean him up, then let them go. We'll finish this later.'

'Shit . . .'

Chip massaged his ribs as Justin drove the BMW, his mind analysing everything that had transpired.

'Can't believe King did this; after all these years.'

'You need a doctor.'

'Fuck that. We need to get outta town. King's gonna kill me. You too.'

'I can't leave. Not yet, anyway. I need to sort Janet and Keeley. King'll use them to get to me otherwise.'

Chip leant back in the seat, grimacing in pain as he drove them to Janet's. As he pulled up, he noticed the front gate and windows were wide open. He peered through the window, noting half the living room contents were gone.

'No.' He kicked open the door, rushing into Janet's room. He stopped short. Several drawers had been emptied, but there were still clothes hanging in the wardrobe. The shoe box remained. Justin's heart plummeted when he wrenched it open and found it empty.

'J, what's happened? Where's Jan?' Chip entered.

'Gone. Doesn't appear she's coming back.' He swallowed back tears.

'Crap. What was in the box? Money?'

He nodded. Chip kissed his teeth.

'Fuck. Snaked by family.'

'We're both in that boat. We need to make moves. No time to dwell. How much money you got?'

Chip rubbed his ribs again. The blood had dried on his face and stained his clothing.

'I can get to a few grand.'

'Go home. Send Marie somewhere safe. Tell her you'll join her soon. We'll form a plan.'

'Got it.' Chip limped to the door. Justin followed.

King paced around, waiting on confirmation. When Tunde was dead, King had to consider his old friend Justin Holmes. He had called King out in front of his people. It would need rectifying.

King's phone rang. *Pincer.*

'Boss, we got set up!'

'What?'

'It was a setup. They locked up everyone.'

'What are you on about?' King pressed the phone closer to his ear.

'Lizzie was working with the police. She's the one who put them onto you. She told them that you slashed Roy.'

'Little slut. Tunde was never there then?'

'He was there all right. Watched the squad get locked up.'

'You're the only one who got clear then?' King frowned.

'I was still in one car. We had eight or nine dudes, all strapped. They didn't need me.'

'Get your arse back here.'

'Boss, you need to leave that spot. Feds might be on their way—'

'On their way for what? I'm on bail. Lizzie's a crack-fiend who doesn't know what she's talking about.'

'But, the dudes who got locked up—'

'Are yours. You said they were loyal. You changing your mind now?' said King, his voice laced with danger.

'No, King. They're cool.'

'Good. Now, get back here after you've done one more thing.'

'What thing?'

'Call Shav. Tell him where to find Chip,' King paused. 'Justin too. No loose ends.'

CHAPTER TWENTY-THREE
TUESDAY 21 MAY, 2013

JUSTIN HURRIED AROUND THE HOUSE, getting things together. Clothes and other essentials were stuffed into a sports bag along with the laptop. He paused, holding one of his notebooks. Thumbing through a few pages, he stowed it away. He'd left Chip a few hours ago, and ever since, his mind had worked overtime trying to devise a plan. Depending on how much money Chip had, they would have to flip it and make more to sustain them.

He'd tried calling Janet, but the number was unavailable. He'd told Keeley to stay somewhere else. Chip would take care of Marie. As he dragged the heavy bag to the car, he wondered if he should contact Charlotte to get his book back. He put the bag in the boot, locked it, glanced into the darkness, and stepped back inside.

Shav stood in the garden across from Justin's place. As soon as Pincer contacted him, he had posted up here. The house owner was away, so he wasn't worried about his position. Justin had carried several bags to the car. It looked like he was making a run for it. Watching as a light turned on upstairs, he drew his silenced pistol. Holding it by his side, he hurried across the road as fast as his bulky build allowed. Pincer had given him a spare key to unlock the door, but he found he didn't need it. Justin had left the door open.

Shav advanced to the stairs. He heard Justin's clipped, authoritative tones as he spoke on the phone, but couldn't make out what was being said. It wasn't important. He paused outside the bedroom door, then raised the gun and burst in as the lights cut out, plummeting the room into darkness. Before Shav could get his bearings, a figure hurtled towards him. They struggled, grunts and pinging sounds breaking the silence as the gun sounded three times. Shav kneed Justin in the stomach, pushed him away, and tried to aim the weapon. Justin lunged back at him, his survival instincts on full alert. He needed to stay close. He grappled with Shav again and wrenched the gun from the shooter. It skidded across the floor. He pushed him against the wall, hitting him again and again. With his free hand, he turned the light back on. The assassin was hook-nosed, bristling, his sallow face twisted in a mingled combination of anger and pain. Justin ignored the stitch in his side and hit him again.

'King send you? Huh? Are you the one?'

Rather than respond, Shav kicked out, his foot catching Justin's pelvis and knocking him off balance. He flung him to the ground and reached for his gun. Before he could aim, a bang from downstairs distracted him. Justin stunned Shav with a blow to the head. He scrambled back to his feet and pointed the gun at Shav. There were footsteps now. Chip's voice shouted his name.

'J! Where you at?'

'Don't move,' Justin ordered Shav, as Chip entered the room. He too was armed. He pointed his gun at Shav, moving further into the bedroom. Shav faced them. Like Justin, his face bore the results of the struggle.

'Chip,' Justin started. 'This—'

Justin's words caught in his throat. Chip grabbed a pillow from a pile on the floor to muffle the sound. With no hesitation, he shot Shav twice. The assassin toppled to the floor, dead.

'You killed him,' said Justin, staring at the dead man.

'Shav was dangerous. King's used him before.' Chip surveyed the room, which looked like a bomb had hit it. 'Y'all did damage. We need to clear this mess up.' He kissed his teeth. 'My contacts are all King's. He'll know.'

Justin already had his phone out. 'I might know someone.'

CHAPTER TWENTY-FOUR
WEDNESDAY 22 MAY, 2013

EDDIE TOOK his time entering Justin's place. He wore an old tracksuit, his alert eyes widening at the state of Chip and Justin.

'King?' he asked. They nodded.

'This is serious. I knew he couldn't be trusted.'

'I couldn't think of anyone else to call.'

Eddie shook his head. 'I'll always help you, Justin. You know that. We'll get this tidied up.

'Thank you.'

'You need to leave Leeds. My eldest nephew is outside. He'll take care of that for you.'

'I'm not leaving, Eddie. Not yet, anyway. King needs stopping.'

Eddie removed his glasses.

'Are you planning on writing a book about it?'

Confused, Justin shook his head. 'Course not.'

'Then you need to leave. King's not your problem. He is under the scrutiny of the law now.' Eddie put his glasses back on. 'It's my understanding they have a witness. A young woman named Lizzie. King murdered her boyfriend.'

'How do you know?'

'Because I orchestrated her cooperation.'

'What?' Justin and Chip spluttered.

'King planned the murder of my oldest friend. Karma's death was all his doing. After this, he capitalised and took control.'

'But, he said—'

'That it was the clowns he had problems with? You're smarter than that, Justin. Those thugs couldn't have got close enough to Karma to shake his hand, never mind organise a professional car crash. King lied because he wanted you on his team.' Eddie removed a weathered brown envelope from his jacket pocket, which he passed to Justin.

'I toyed with whether or not to give you this.'

'What is it?'

'A letter Karma wanted you to have.'

Justin's hands shook as he opened it. It contained several pieces of paper. The first was a yellowing letter. He read, recognising the slanted handwriting of his mentor:

Justin,
If you're reading this, it means I'm gone, and that you survived that hellhole. I hope you've learnt a lesson in the powers of trust.
King is different now. He doesn't even try to hide the naked ambition burning within him. He wants it all, and he doesn't have you keeping him grounded anymore.
I'm telling you this not so you will take him on, but so that you heed the message and stay away from him and that life.

The other papers contain details relating to a property I own. The solicitor has arranged a sale, and the profits will be managed. Use this money to free yourself. The contact details are overleaf.
Stay safe.

Justin read the letter twice, his eyes tearing as he absorbed the words. Chip and Eddie watched, moved by the emotion.

'Karma loved you like a son. I don't know what the letter says, but we spoke often, and I'm aware he left you something. He didn't want you involved.'

'Why didn't you give me this earlier?'

'I wanted to see how you would carry your freedom first. When you ran back to King, I held off.'

'You should have told me.'

'You should have listened. I warned you about King.'

'Let's go, Chip.' Justin didn't want to argue anymore.

'Wait.'

They paused. Eddie stared them down.

'I don't know your intentions, but you need to leave those weapons. They're evidence. I'll destroy them.'

Justin had forgotten he still held Shav's gun. He handed it to one of Eddie's men, now in the room with them. Chip did the same. They headed for the door.

'Karma has given you a future,' Eddie's final words followed them.

They kept walking.

CHAPTER TWENTY-FIVE
WEDNESDAY 22 MAY, 2013

'He needs to go.'

Chip sighed, his face lined with tiredness, intensified by the marks from the beating. He looked around the murky street, searching for more killers.

'No going back then?'

'He beat the crap out of you and sent someone to kill me. It won't end there.'

Chip's eyes filled with resolve. He nodded once as if internally deciding.

'You're right.'

They drove to an old-lockup Chip owned. He rummaged until he found what he was looking for; a worn sawn-off shotgun.

'There should be more straps. Grab one,' he told Justin. After rooting in a drawer, he picked a silver Colt. It looked like a ponce's gun. For a second, he remembered Janet and her pimp boyfriend, nostrils flaring.

'King'll be waiting for the confirmation,' Chip said as they got back in the car and drove away. 'He's not the kinda guy to leave shit to chance.'

'He could send more people after us. Either that or they could be guarding his place.'

'King lost key dudes today — they got licked by police. At least eight of his upper guys. Maybe more. Takes time to restructure that.'

'You could get a promotion,' Justin said. Chip smiled.

'Eddie man, what a guy,' he shook his head. 'Did you know he was involved?'

'You heard what he said. He never trusted me.'

'Bollocks. They both did. Eddie wanted you to feel out the situation. He knew King would turn on you.'

Justin turned to him.

'Do you believe him about King? That he had a hand in Karma's death?'

Chip shrugged as he changed gears. 'Sounds far-fetched. Cutting brakes and sabotaging rides? That's government assassination shit.'

Justin again wiped his eyes, glancing out of the window. The heavy pistol rested on his lap.

'Have you heard from your cousin?'

Chip's face was set. 'He won't contact me. I dunno who put the idea in his head, but I'll find them after we settle up here.' He scratched the underside of his chin. 'What about your sis? You gonna go after her?'

'She can keep the money,' Justin said with a sigh. 'Jan raised me. Dunno how she got caught up, but she kinda earned that money. I hope she ditches the pimp.' He fingered the pistol.

'We're here now. We'll park and jump out.'

'Why here?' said Justin. They were several streets away from King's spot.

'It's easier if he's got lookouts. I know a way inside. We'll be alright.' Chip checked the shells in the shotgun.

'I need a minute. Gotta make a phone call.'

'Now? Can't it wait?'

He shook his head. Chip shrugged and headed out of sight, keeping the shotgun low. It rained now, a slow, steady drizzle coming down from the sky. Justin found the number he wanted and dialled.

Charlotte was drinking green tea in bed when her phone rang.

'Justin?'

'Hey, Charlie.'

'Are you okay? What's wrong?'

'Why does something have to be wrong?'

Charlotte closed her eyes.

'I don't know.'

Justin cleared his throat. 'I wanted to check on the book.'

'I've only read a little. Work has—'

'If anything happens, keep it and do what you want with it. Publish it, burn it. Whatever.'

'Justin, I couldn't. It's your work.'

'Charlie, you inspired all that.'

Charlotte didn't speak. He spoke again, words tumbling as quickly as the raindrops.

'I cut you off, but you were always on my mind. I needed to survive, and so I wrote. First, poems, and then I moved on and wrote everything in my head. It kept me sane and stopped me thinking about you twenty-four-seven. Do you understand?'

'I,' Charlotte struggled to find her words, 'why does this feel like goodbye?'

'If you read my book, you'll understand at the end. Remember what I said, and look after yourself.' Justin hung up. Charlotte stared at her phone. She hurried to find his manuscript and skimmed to the last page. After reading it, she broke down, crying harder than she had in her life.

'He should have checked in by now.'

King puffed on a cigarette. The hits needed to be quick, yet he was still waiting for word.

'He's not picking up. Might be doing it now,' said Pincer, phone pressed to his ear.

'He better be. I want it done. Justin's too sneaky for his own good.'

The door burst open as the words left King's mouth. The shotgun blast reverberated around the room. Pincer slammed into the wall and slid to the ground. Chip and Justin hurried into sight, Chip wielding the sawn-off as Justin clutched a pistol.

'What the hell is this?' spluttered King.

'Don't play dumb. You know what this is.' Chip glared, pointing the still-smoking shotgun barrels at him. King cut his eyes to Justin.

'J, what are you doing?'

'You sent a message. I'm returning it,' replied Justin. An older had once told him to aim for the chest in a shootout. He recalled the knowledge.

'J, man, I—'

'Shut up. You tried having me killed. You started this,' Justin cut across King.

'J, you proved your point. I'm done. Take it all. Just let me live. Charlotte . . .' King's lips trembled, '. . . Take her too. Just please let me go.'

'Why did you kill Karma?' Justin's hand shook.

'What?' King pretended he hadn't heard.

'You said it was Tunde and Bloon. But, it was you.'

'Nah, J. You're wrong. I wouldn't do that.'

The pop of the Colt drowned out King's frantic words. Justin's wrist jerked from the kickback, but he maintained his grip. King dropped to the floor, holding his left leg.

'I'm not playing, King. Why did you do it?' Justin repeated.

'Because I knew!' King burst out, gritting his teeth. 'I knew what he did.'

'What did he do?' Justin pressed.

'Don't act like you didn't know. That motherfucker tried setting me up. You were in on it with him.'

CHAPTER TWENTY-SIX
WEDNESDAY 22 MAY, 2013

Justin lowered the gun. King noticed, his expression giving him strength.

'Yeah, I knew! I knew what you two were concocting, trying to get me taken out,' King's voice rose, fear forgotten. 'I was loyal, J. Until y'all gave me a reason not to be.'

Justin froze again, as he realised.

'You set me up?' His voice choked.

King didn't reply.

'That night, that's why you wanted me to cover. It was you. You called the police.'

King's eyes watered with pain. His mouth remained closed.

'Admit it!'

King shot him a hateful glare.

'Fine. Yeah, I called the police. I did you like you and that old bastard were gonna do me.'

Justin's face hardened. The gun barked three more times, hitting King twice in the chest, the final shot embedding in the wall. He dropped the pistol, breathing hard, nauseous as he stared at the prone form of his former friend. He closed his eyes.

The shotgun clicked, and Justin hoped he was dreaming.

'Don't turn around,' Chip murmured. 'I don't wanna see your face.'

'Why?' Justin's eyes remained closed.

'It's the game, J. This is my time now. You should have walked away.'

The shotgun blast hit Justin in the spine. He crumpled face down, the rough wooden floor breaking his fall.

'I'm sorry, J.' Chip sounded like he was in tears. There were heavy footsteps and then silence. Overwhelming silence.

His thought process staggered. His eyes dimmed.

He thought about Charlotte, and how she would feel about him and King being shot.

He wondered if she had loved King more than him; if she would publish his book.

Justin's final thoughts as the darkness claimed him were of his and Charlotte's first date.

He remembered holding her hand, feeling like life was complete.

DID YOU ENJOY THE READ?

Thank you for reading Homecoming!

Compared to some of my other releases, it had a much shorter lifespan — I wrote the first draft in 2012, and kept working on it alongside my Target books. I love the end result and hope you do too.

Please take a minute or two to help me by leaving a review – even if it's just a few lines. Reviews help massively with getting my books in front of new readers. I personally read every review and take all feedback on board.

To support me, please click the relevant link below:
 UK: http://www.amazon.co.uk/review/create-review?&asin= B07H49HMV4

US: http://www.amazon.com/review/create-review?&asin= B07H49HMV4

Make sure you're following me on Amazon to keep up to date with my releases, or that you're signed up to my email list, and I'll see you at the next book!

If you're looking for your next read, check out my gritty Target series.

ORIGINS PREVIEW

Check out the FIRST CHAPTER of Origins, BOOK 1 in the Target series.

CHAPTER 1

MONDAY 10 MARCH, 1997

He just needed a few more seconds.

His arm stretched out, the stacks of twenty and fifty-pound notes within reach. He grinned as he grabbed the money.

'Lamont!'

Lamont Jones jerked awake, vaulting from the bed. Stretching and wiping his eyes, he quickly trundled downstairs. Carmen Jones sat at the table, a middle-aged black woman with long black hair and excellent bone structure, just barely hanging onto the looks that had once enticed many men.

'Good morning, Auntie.'

Carmen ignored her nephew, looking over him with a critical eye. Lamont was gangly, with similar cheekbones to his Aunt, and messily curly hair. A jagged scar at the bottom of his chin slightly marred his features. He was long-limbed with a quizzical nature and dark, rosewood eyes that showed a vulnerability that intrigued those around him. Auntie was immune to it.

'Get back upstairs and wash your face. You look disgusting,' she said.

Lamont hurried to obey, heading back downstairs afterwards. Auntie had lit a cigarette, the disgusting smoke wafting around the kitchen. He was getting over a chest infection, and the smoke tickled his lungs. If Auntie noticed, it didn't show.

'Get started on breakfast. Your sister will be up soon, and I don't want her to be late.'

Lamont busied himself turning on the hob, then went to the fridge for eggs and bacon. Auntie watched, eyes narrowing.

'Comb your hair too. You're a mess.'

The usual anger simmering within, Lamont ignored Auntie. She did this daily, and rising to it would only make things worse. Instead, he skilfully prepared and served breakfast, made her a cup of tea, and then went to wake his sister. Marika Jones snored softly, the quilt pulled over her head.

'Rika . . .' He gently rocked her. 'Rika, you need to wake up.'

'Mhmm.' Marika stirred, looked at Lamont and then closed her eyes again. Mumbling, Lamont yanked away the quilt.

'Oi, what are you doing?'

'You've got school today.'

'I'm tired. I wanna go back to sleep.'

'Don't make me get Auntie.' He would never act on this threat, but it often paid dividends.

'I don't care. I'll tell her I'm ill.' Marika pulled the quilt back over herself.

'Fine.' Lamont left to take a shower. Auntie normally timed him, so he made sure he was out within minutes to avoid her complaints about him using all the hot water. Like everything else in the house, the shower was top of the line, but Auntie still found fault. Dressing for school in a worn pair of jeans and a baggy shirt, he threw on a pair of cheap trainers with damaged soles. Marika was drinking a glass of milk in the kitchen, beaming, when he re-entered the room.

'Hurry, Rika. Are you going to school by yourself, or with Danielle?' Her friend's mum had a car and usually drove Marika to school. He had wanted Marika at his high school so he could keep an eye on her, but Auntie hadn't cared, choosing to send her somewhere else.

'Marika isn't going to school today. She doesn't feel well,' said Auntie.

'She's lying, Auntie.' Lamont glared at his sister, whose smile widened.

'You don't dictate to me. My niece said she is ill, so she isn't going to school.' Auntie lit another cigarette. This time, she unlocked the back door and stood outside.

'How often do you think you're gonna get away with this?' Lamont hissed. Giggling, Marika continued sipping her milk and dismissed him. She seemed to take several days off school a week. Whereas Lamont attended school every day, even when he was ill, she took liberties.

Lamont could do nothing about it. He had no say in the household. School was his way out, and because of that, he soaked up everything taught to him.

Grabbing a jacket and his school bag, Lamont left the house. He embraced the air of Chapeltown, or the *Hood* as it was affectionately known. A diverse, multicultural suburb in Leeds, Chapeltown had a reputation for violence. Lamont saw beyond that. There was beauty in the Hood, a certain energy that sometimes made the hairs on his arms stand on end. He couldn't explain it, but he felt it.

Lamont headed towards the main road, his steps halting when he saw the group of boys skulking on the corner. They smirked when they saw him.

'Look who it is; *Trampy Lamont*,' one of them, a lanky kid named Tower, called out. He came from a big family and had several brothers. He was always throwing his weight about and targeting Lamont. They'd fought before, but his friends always jumped in when it looked like he would lose.

Lamont sighed, knowing he couldn't avoid them. If he tried to run, they would either chase him or spread the word that he was a coward. He froze as the group approached.

'Where'd you get them trainers from? Africa?' Tower stood in front of Lamont. His friends guffawed as if he had told the funniest joke in the world.

'Nah, even the Africans wouldn't wear them,' Another boy piped up.

'Look how his toes are nearly poking through! And look at them trousers,' Tower continued. Lamont stood, hands in his pockets, taking the insults. Tower was trying to bait him, and he would not rise. Seeing that his strategy wasn't working, Tower tried another tactic.

'Gimme all the money you've got. Now.'

'I don't have anything, Tower.'

'Why do you talk like that?'

'I don't talk like anything.'

'Yeah, you do. You talk like a white man, all prim and proper. You're from the Hood. Act like it,' Tower snarled. 'Gimme your money. If I don't get a pound in sixty seconds, we're gonna rush you.'

Sighing, Lamont removed his school bag and jacket. Putting them on the floor, he faced the boys.

'Why are you taking your coat off? You wanna go?' Tower taunted. Lamont tensed, waiting for them to make the first move. Before Tower could do anything, another voice spoke up.

'I'll go with you.'

Tower and his cronies froze, recognising the harsh voice. Tower swore quietly as Marcus strolled towards them. Marcus Daniels was sixteen years old, but he was over six feet tall, with the build and the attitude to prove it. He glared at Tower and his gang, eyeing each of them. None met his gaze.

'Yo, safe, Marcus.' Tower's tone softened.

'Don't *safe* me. Why are you lot surrounding my brother?' Marcus asked in his slow voice. He was soft-spoken, his eyes constantly showing his true intent. They were full of malice and rage against the world. Anyone who knew him, knew Marcus was the real deal.

'Nah, we were just playing with him. Lamont's cool,' Tower back-pedalled. His boys slowly backed away.

'L, are they troubling you?'

Lamont needed only a second to reply.

'Nah. Like Tower said, we were just messing.'

Tower shot him a look, pursing his lips and tilting his head to one side.

'Are you sure?'

'Yeah, man. I'm sure.'

'You lot, go away. Trouble my bro, you'll have me to deal with,' Marcus promised. The boys hurried up the road.

'You should have let me stomp them out.'

'There's no point. It'll just make it worse next time,' replied Lamont.

'Doesn't matter. Sometimes you need to take the licks.

People will never respect you if you don't stand up for yourself.'

Lamont knew Marcus meant well, but resented being spoken down to by anyone. It was easy for Marcus to preach about standing up for himself. Everyone feared him. Lamont was on his own most of the time and had no one to back him up.

'Whatever, man. Have you been out all night?' He changed the subject.

Marcus grinned. 'Had some business, then I stayed with Mia.'

Lamont laughed. Mia was Marcus's girlfriend, for lack of a better term. She lived with her older sister. Marcus was always around, and if the rumours were true, had also slept with Mia's sister.

'What kind of business?'

'Don't worry your head about it, *schoolboy*.' Marcus reached into his jeans pocket and peeled off five, ten-pound notes. 'Keep hold of that. Don't let the witch see it.'

'I won't.' The first time Marcus had given him money, Lamont foolishly left it on his bedside table. The next day he awoke to the lash of the belt striking his legs and Auntie screaming that he was a thief.

'I'm gonna head home. Why don't you skip school and come with me?'

Lamont shook his head. 'I'm not missing school. I'll get with you later if you're about.'

'Let me know if Tower and his people trouble you again.'

'I will,' Lamont lied. Tower was an annoyance, but the last thing he needed was people thinking he needed Marcus to fight his battles.

Marcus had lived with Lamont, his Auntie, and Marika

for the past few years. The son of a pair of hardcore drug abusers, his father was murdered trying to rob a drug crew, and his mother died of an overdose when he was six. Marcus had been in his fair share of foster homes. Moving in with Lamont had calmed him down, but the demon still lived below the surface.

Once he turned to walk home, Lamont quickened his pace. If he didn't hurry, he would have to get the bus. Folding the money Marcus had given him, he put it in his sock and was on his way.

Lamont was hurrying out of the school gates that afternoon when he heard someone call his name. Tower strode toward him with his gang following.

'Oi, don't think you're rough because you've got *Psycho Marcus* backing you. My brother will end him if he steps out of line, understood?' Tower pushed out his chest.

'I do,' Lamont said listlessly.

'You better. I want some money tomorrow. Don't try avoiding me either, because I'll come to your yard and smack up you and your sister, you get me?'

'Don't talk about my sister,' Lamont's tone became cold. Tower and his people picked up on it.

'Or what? What are you gonna do?' Tower said. Lamont glared, his eyes blazing. The sight of his stare made Tower feel uneasy. He glanced at his crew.

'Don't forget what I said. Come, you guys. Let's go.' They hurried away. Lamont took a deep breath, not realising he'd clenched his fists.

'Are you walking home, L?'

Lamont hid the smile that appeared on his face as Erica

Anderson sashayed into view, two of her friends flanking her. Erica was tall, with skin the colour of dark honey. Lamont had liked her for the longest time, but painfully knew he was in the friend zone. She had an older boyfriend, but often talked with Lamont, and would walk home with him.

'Hey, Erica. Yeah, I am. Are you?' he said, resisting the urge to fidget.

'Yeah. These two are getting the bus, but I'm meeting Leon at the park. Do you mind if I walk with you?'

'No, course not.' Lamont's smile widened. Erica's friends giggled, shaking their heads.

'Let's go then. See you two later,' Erica said to her friends. Walking with Lamont, the two of them crossed the road, walking down the long path that led to the park.

'Did you do Mr Silver's homework?' Erica asked as they walked.

'Did it on Sunday. Did you?'

'Yeah, I did it at Leon's house. When he let me anyway. I swear, all he does is try to feel me up!'

'Bet that's annoying,' Lamont said, feeling a flash of anger as his stomach hardened.

'It's sweet. He's not a talker, so I guess it's his way of telling me what I mean to him.' Erica giggled, running a hand through her hair.

'Yeah, there's always that.'

'What were Tower and his boys saying? You looked mad.'

'Nothing. Just Tower being Tower.' Lamont didn't want to think about him.

'Okay. Just be careful. You know what he's like.'

'I'm always careful,' replied Lamont, smiling. Erica grinned back.

'What are you doing this evening?'

Lamont shrugged. 'Should be good. All the washing, or if I'm lucky, Auntie will let me do the ironing or cooking.'

'She treats you worse than a slave.'

Lamont had confided in Erica about Auntie's treatment. Once, he'd even shown her the welts on his back from the belt. Marcus was his best friend, but he wasn't the easiest to converse with. Erica showed him the affection and sympathy that he needed.

'I'll be out of there soon,' Lamont said, his voice firm.

'How? How will you live?' Erica looked thoughtful.

'I'll get a part-time job and start college. I can't stay under that roof forever.'

Erica nodded. Lamont had mentioned his desire to leave home before. They walked along, talking about school life and playground dramas.

'Lavinia likes you. Do you like her?' Erica was referring to a girl in their year at school.

'She's all right. Not my type, though.'

'Really? So what's your type then?' Erica pressed.

You, Lamont wanted to say.

'I don't have a proper type. I just know that Lavinia's not for me. She's cool to talk to, but I don't have feelings for her.'

Erica smiled. 'Give her a chance. I bet she'd let you sleep with her.'

'I'm not interested in that,' Lamont lied. He was sixteen. It was all he thought about.

'You're not? Have you done it before?' Erica asked.

'Yeah. Loads of times,' Lamont's voice took on a boastful tone, the lie growing. He had virtually no experience with the opposite sex, other than a few kisses and fumbles. Between his mismatched clothing and being prey for every bully going, Lamont wasn't top of the social spectrum. Life had dealt him nothing. He was smart, but it was getting him nowhere. Lamont hoped adult life would change things for him, but struggled to see how it could.

'Really? Who with?' Erica leaned into him, her eyebrows raised.

'No one you know,' Lamont furtively replied.

'You're no fun. Did you enjoy it? I always do.'

Lamont's stomach lurched at Erica's words. He knew she had slept with Leon, but didn't want to hear about it.

'It was okay. Nothing special.' Lamont hated himself for lying, wishing he could tell Erica the truth; that she was the only girl he wanted to sleep with, mainly because of the kindness she had shown him. He couldn't. He had committed himself to the lie, and now he would have to see it through.

'You must not be doing it right. Talk to Leon. He's great at it. Suppose it's because he's older.'

'Yeah, must be,' Lamont grumbled. The park was coming into sight now.

'Gosh, you're so moody sometimes, L.' Erica linked arms with him and kissed him on the cheek. Lamont's face burned, his jeans tightening. She smelled amazing. Like apricots.

'Shut up,' He said good-naturedly, enjoying the contact. They crossed the road and trudged up the steps to the park. Lamont spotted Leon and his friends sitting on the swings. They were all hard-faced, towering over Lamont. Leon, a bullet-headed eighteen-year-old with facial hair and a sneer, looked him up and down. He disentangled himself from Erica.

'I guess I'll see you tomorrow at school then,' he said, not liking the way Leon and his friends were staring.

'Why don't you stay and hang out? Leon won't mind. His friends are cool.'

Lamont shook his head.

'Nah. Auntie will flip. I'll see you later.'

Lamont hurried away. Washing his hands and face as soon as he got in, he headed to the kitchen. Raucous laughter greeted him. Auntie and two of her friends sat around the table, smoking, drinking and laughing almost manically at some joke. They all looked up as Lamont entered.

'Good afternoon, Auntie,' The practised words rolled from Lamont's tongue with passable conviction. She stopped laughing.

'Don't stand around talking. Grab the dustpan and brush and sweep the stairs. Come back when you're done. I've got more for you to do.'

Lamont did as instructed. It was tedious work, bending over to sweep the stairs causing him backache. He didn't know why he couldn't use the big brush, but the last time he had asked, Auntie had hit him in the head with it.

When he finished, he looked into Marika's room, where she was draped on her bed, reading a magazine. She looked at Lamont haughtily when she saw him.

'What do you want?'

'Where did you get that magazine?'

'Auntie bought it for me. For being so good today.' Marika grinned. Lamont clenched his fists.

'You little faker. You could've at least swept the stairs for me.'

Marika made a face.

'Whatever. Is Marcus in?' He continued.

'He's in his room. Think he's sleeping,' Marika replied, turning back to her magazine.

Lamont left, picking up the dustpan and brush. Emptying the dirt into the bin downstairs, he rewashed his hands, put the dustpan away, and returned to Auntie for further instructions.

When all his chores were finished, Lamont flopped onto his bed, spent. He was sure that Auntie made up jobs for him to do. She seemed to get a kick out of watching him sweat. He had homework, but before he started, he needed to relax. Yawning, he stared up at the ceiling, gathering his thoughts.

Lamont dreamed of a time when he would be on his own. He would be a working man, free to live his life any way he wanted. The thought was daunting, yet something he did for himself now. Other than the roof over his head, Auntie provided nothing for him. He did everything. He had tried making money getting part-time jobs in the past, but Auntie always seemed to scupper his hustle.

School was nearly finished now. If all went well, he would not have to suffer much longer.

'L?' There was a heavy knocking at the door.

'Come in, Marcus,' he called out. Marcus sauntered into the room, smirking when he saw Lamont lying down.

'The fuck are you doing, thinking and strategising and shit!' he laughed.

'Just trying to get my mind right.'

'Get money, you get your mind right. Money opens doors,' Marcus said matter-of-factly. To him, it was that simple.

'When I finish school, I'll get money,' Lamont assured his friend. Marcus made a face.

'When? Any job you get, it's gonna take time to make real cash,' Marcus pointed out. Lamont didn't respond. Marcus had touched upon the flaw in his life plan. Whatever job he ended up in, it would take time to build up. He would need to be patient.

'Forget that, anyway.' Marcus scratched his head. 'We're going out.'

'Nah, I'm tired,' Lamont replied, stifling another yawn.

'I'm not asking. I'm tired of seeing you sitting up here, night in, night out. Throw on some aftershave too; we're gonna be around women.'

READ BLOOD AND BUSINESS

Tyrone Dunn wants to take over Leeds, and he is willing to battle anyone who gets in his way.

Even family.

Will it be settled by blood . . . or business?

Order now, and find out.

ALSO BY RICKY BLACK

The Target Series:

Origins: The Road to Power

Target

Target Part 2: The Takedown

Target Part 3: Absolute Power

The Complete Target Collection

The Deeds Family Series:

Blood & Business

Good Deed, Bad Deeds

Deeds to the City

ABOUT RICKY BLACK

Ricky Black was born and raised in Chapeltown, Leeds. He began writing seriously in 2004, working on mainly crime pieces.

In 2016, he published the first of his crime series, Target, and has published seven more books since.

Visit https://rickyblackbooks.com for information regarding new releases and special offers and promotions.

For Maya. Always.

Copyright © 2018 by Ricky Black

All rights reserved worldwide. Except as provided by the Copyright Act. No part of this publication may be reproduced, stored in a retrieval system or transmitted in any means without the prior written permission of the publisher.

This book is a work of fiction. Characters and events in this novel are the product of the Author's imagination. Any similarity to persons living or dead is purely coincidental.

Printed in Great Britain
by Amazon

TALES YOU WIN

CONTENTS

Foreword	xiii
Book Playlist	xv
Prologue	1
Chapter 1	3
Chapter 2	12
Chapter 3	29
Chapter 4	43
Chapter 5	52
Chapter 6	65
Chapter 7	77
Chapter 8	92
Chapter 9	103
Chapter 10	115
Chapter 11	128
Chapter 12	142
Chapter 13	157
Chapter 14	174
Chapter 15	189
Chapter 16	199
Chapter 17	206
Chapter 18	216
Chapter 19	229
Chapter 20	239
Chapter 21	258
Chapter 22	271
Chapter 23	280
Chapter 24	294

Author Note	309
About the Author	313
Also by Bea Paige	315

Kelly Stock writing as Bea Paige to be identified as author of this work has been asserted by her in accordance with sections 77 and 78 of the Copyright, Designs and Patents Act 1988.

All rights reserved. No part of this publication may be reproduced, stored in retrieval system, copied in any form or by any means, electronic, mechanical, photocopying, recording or otherwise transmitted without written permission from the publisher. You must not circulate this book in any format.

This book is licensed for your personal enjoyment only. This e-book may not be resold or given away to other people. If you would like to share this book with another person, please purchase an additional copy for each recipient. Thank you for respecting the hard work of this author.

Copyright © Kelly Stock writing as Bea Paige

First published: 30th April 2022

Cover Design by Everly Yours Cover Designs

Photograph by Michelle Lancaster

Cover Model: Chase Cassels

Title Page Artwork: STOCKE @stockysartworks on IG

❧ Created with Vellum

Dear Reader,

*Beast wants you to know that he's a ride or die kinda man.
If you don't enjoy riding his dick (even if it is in your imagination) then he'll die of fucking shame.
Grim wants you to know that if you ever try riding his dick (even if it is in your imagination), she'll cut it off and bury him and his womanising dick six feet underground.
They love each other really...
Happy Reading!*
Love Bea xoxo

"You are mine, and I am yours, and no one in the world can alter that."

—*Jacob Grimm, quote from Grimms' Fairy Tales*

FOREWORD

Dear Reader

For those of you who fell in love with Beast and Grim in the Academy of Stardom series, this one's for you! I've been wanting to write about their love story for some time now. In fact, when Grim first appeared in the Academy of Misfits trilogy, I knew then she was a character who deserved her own story, but it wasn't until her voice, and that of Beast's, grew so loud in Academy of Stardom that I had the real need to write their story.

Initially I wanted this to be a standalone, but it soon became apparent that one book would not suffice, so now they're getting a duet. **Heads You Lose**, book two of the duet will be out early summer. This will conclude their story and introduce some old friends.

If you're a regular reader of mine, you know that I LOVE a book playlist. This time I've decided to do something a little differently and give each chapter a specific song. Each song is listed at the top of the chapter with a link to the playlist. I hope you enjoy them!

In addition, this story opens with a prologue which is a letter written by Grim (aka Kate) to her daughter, Iris, and refers to something that happens at the end of the Academy of Stardom series and plays out in Their Obsession duet. If you haven't read either of these two series, it may be a little confusing. However, it was imperative to pull these three separate series together, and will make perfect sense to those of you who've read both Academy of Stardom series and Their Obsession Duet.

If you've not read either, then you may scratch your head and wonder about the contents of the prologue. Firstly, I hope it intrigues you enough to read Academy of Stardom and Their Obsession Duet (in that order), but if it doesn't, then the rest of the story won't be spoiled by it. You can absolutely read this book without reading the other series.

Like I've said, Grim & Beast have been around in this world I've created for some time, so there are lots of crossovers in this duet with characters that already have their own story.

My recommended reading order is:

Brothers Freed trilogy
Academy of Misfits
Beyond the Horizon
Finding Their Muse
Academy of Stardom
Their Obsession Duet
Beast and Grim Duet

BOOK PLAYLIST

If you're familiar with my books you'll know that I love a book playlist. Each chapter of **Tales You Win** has a song that I've selected which is specific to that chapter, but if you want the playlist in full, then you can find it on Spotify here: **Tales You Win**.

PROLOGUE

Dear Iris,

I'M NOT great with words. I act. That's what I'm doing now.

You see, my sweet baby girl, I have a sister. Her name's Christy and she's in trouble.

Real bad trouble.

Some men have taken her, stolen her away and locked her up in their castle.

They're bad, bad men and they'll hurt her.

I have to rescue her. I have to bring her home.

That's what I do. I protect my own. Family means everything to me. Everything.

Which means I have to do the one thing I hoped never to do and that's leave you behind. I can't put you in danger.

I won't.

Instead, I'm trusting my friend Pen and her men, Xeno, Dax, Zayn and York to take care of you whilst I'm gone. They're good people, the best. They will love you and care for you whilst your dad and I go slay the monsters.

You're too young to understand how dangerous this is. We might never come back. It *hurts my heart to admit that I may be making a choice where you are left an orphan with no parents.*

It hurts me beyond repair, and I will live with the wound forever, whether I live or die.

But I have to go. We have to go, your dad and me.

I have entrusted you to my friends who will love you until we return, and if we don't... will love you always.

If this is the end of your dad's and my story, then so be it.

Either way, I've left you a gift.

It's my story.

Actually, it's our love story.

Your dad's and mine.

His words, and mine. His memories and my memories, all scrawled down on the pages of these notebooks.

You see, Iris, a long time ago a coin was thrown.

A coin that would decide my fate.

Tales you win.

Heads you lose.

I won, and my dad, your grandfather, lost.

Though admittedly it didn't feel that way at the time.

What I do know is that everything happens for a reason. Your dad and I were always supposed to be together, it just took a while to get there.

This might not be the perfect fairy tale, but it is our fairy tale, and now it's yours.

Ma x

CHAPTER ONE

It started with a... kiss fight.

"Fists up, protect your face, keep light on your toes," the growly bastard yells at me.

"I'm trying!" I snap, stomping my foot against the canvas in frustration as I drop my guard and glare at Beast, my dad's enforcer and my fucking bodyguard. Sweat trickles down my spine and between my tits, causing my t-shirt to stick to my chest and back.

"Has *Princess* had enough for one day?" he asks, snorting with laughter as he pulls off the boxing pad and tussles my hair with his huge hands. We've been training regularly for the last six months and I'm getting stronger and fitter with every session, but Beast still runs me ragged.

"It's *Grim*," I protest, slapping his hands away.

Beast cocks his head. "Nope, still *Princess* to me."

"I'm not a princess, you arsehole!"

He chuckles. "Yeah, yeah. Now are we done?"

"Not nearly, *Roger*," I retort, shoving him off me and using his given name because I know it pisses him off. Ever since my dad aka *The Boss*, aka Carter Davidson, aka the ruler of Tales— an underground fight club—started calling me Grim after my love of reading Grimms' Fairy Tales, Beast and the other men who work for my father started calling me Princess.

It's fucking annoying.

His smile drops. "You ain't too old to be put over my knee and given a spanking. Don't push your luck, kid."

Kid? Okay, that's worse than being called Princess, the fucking twat. In a month I'll be eighteen. Besides, I haven't been a kid for a very long time. Comes with the territory of being a gangster's daughter.

"Ha! As if you would. I think my dad would have a few things to say about an *old* wanker like you getting his rocks off over spanking a *kid*!" I sass back, knowing I'm pushing all his buttons and loving every minute of it. Firstly, he's not all that older than me, maybe around twenty-three. Secondly, he'd never raise a hand to me, unless it's in the ring and he's teaching me how to defend myself. Thirdly, he might be a fucking maniac and kill people for a living, but he isn't a predator. The guy's a straight up saint when it comes to women. In fact, I've heard he's a gentleman, except in bed when, apparently, he's an animal or rather a *beast*, but only to women who are well over the age of consent. Not that I've asked around or anything. My cheeks flush at the thought, and I preoccupy myself with trying to pull off my gloves, which is no easy feat when you don't have the use of your fingers.

"You know that mouth of yours is gonna get you in a shitload of trouble one of these days," Beast remarks, chucking the boxing pads he was holding at Dom—my dad's third in command—who catches them easily.

The reflexes on that man are insane. I witnessed him catching a knife by the blade once. Straight up thought it was going to bury itself in his forehead. It didn't, though. Dom's got a four inch scar on his palm for the trouble. In fact, he's covered in them. He's been involved in more fights than the local tomcat and that tomcat takes on *dogs*. Both of them are certifiably insane, like all my dad's men, or 'soldiers' as he calls them. Funnily enough he looks like more of a beast than Beast does with a shorn head, squashed nose from it being broken so many times, and missing half an ear from when it was ripped off by an opposing fighter in the cage.

Yeah, the fights get bloody at Tales.

"What do you mean *going* to get her in a shitload of trouble?" Dom asks, winking at me whilst I glare back at him. "She's already causing a fucking problem with the local hoodrats. That fucker Hudson came over today sniffing around for Princess."

"Hud is my friend, not a *hoodrat,* and I am NOT a princess!"

"Touchy subject, Princess?" Dom teases.

"Fuck you, *Dom-I've-got-a-limp-dick,*" I retort with a wan smile.

"Oh Princess, my dick most definitely limps. Have you seen the way it drags across the floor when I walk?"

Beast roars with laughter as my eyes stupidly drop to Dom's crotch and the very sizeable bulge he has there. What is it with these men and their dick appreciation? If I had a sack of skin swinging between my legs like some elephant trunk, I wouldn't be bragging about it. Fucking ugly if you ask me. I much prefer tits. Not that I have any... Maybe I'm a lesbian? I mull that thought over as I glance back at Beast who is watching me with a sudden intensity that makes my skin cover in goosebumps, my stomach lurch and my traitorous pussy tingle. Okay, so definitely into men then.

"Fuck sake," I mutter under my breath.

"What's the matter, Princess, cat got your tongue?" Beast asks, his voice low and lethal sounding.

I gulp. "Nope. Perfectly fucking fine, thank you very much," I reply, arching a brow.

"I'll leave you to lock up and get Princess home, yeah?" Dom asks, completely ignoring me and smirking at Beast.

"Yep. I got this," Beast replies, turning his attention back to me as the door to the gym slams shut and Dom leaves us alone together. He stares at me, his leaf-green eyes bright in the fluorescent lights as I continue to struggle to remove my boxing gloves. "So you were saying something about me getting off on spanking kids?"

"It was a *joke*," I say, rolling my eyes and turning my back on him as I stride over to the other side of the ring. Only I don't make it that far as Beast lifts me up and chucks me over his shoulder. "WHAT ARE YOU DOING!" I scream from my upside-down position, my face practically pressed against his ridiculously firm arse.

"I thought that was obvious," he retorts with a low, rumbly chuckle that has my insides fucking squirming.

Jesus, I need to get a grip. I do not like *Roger Smith*, a bland name for a man who's far from it. "My dad will kill you if you even think about raising a hand to me." I punch him on his arse and the back of his tree-trunk thighs. The fucker doesn't even flinch.

"Your father has given me free rein to do whatever the fuck I want..." he warns, his voice dropping an octave or two and sounding far more sexy than it has any right to. "...*Inside the ring.*"

"Fuck that, you moron! Put me down!"

He chuckles, clearing his throat, then drops me unceremoniously onto the stool situated in the corner of the ring. I let out a whoosh of air from the impact and immediately stand, not liking, or perhaps liking too much, the fact that he's towering over me all sweaty and big and fucking sexy as sin. He's tall. Six foot five to my five foot seven. A fucking giant, no... *Beast.*

"Urgh, you're an arsehole!" I say, punching him as hard as I can on the nearest bodily part which happens to be his very wide, abnormally firm, stomach. I mean there's six packs and then there's *six packs*, and his happens to be accompanied with a V muscle that turns all women's insides liquid. Except mine, because once you've seen one, you've seen them all, and every fighter at Tales has one.

So I'm immune.

Except his muscles are covered in tattoos, and my immunity stops there. Tattoos are my weak spot and I happen to find them insanely attractive. My eyes rove over his bare chest, all slick with sweat as I drink in the familiar geometric patterns that criss-cross his chest and stomach, and the single eye staring at me from his right pec. Not to mention the beautifully detailed side profile of a lion, its gaze focusing on his navel. God, his tattoos are fucking epic...

"Are you gaping at my dick?" Beast asks, chuckling.

"What? No!" I reply, quickly lifting my gaze and rubbing at my sweaty, *flushed* cheeks.

"Then don't be staring like that, Princess. You might give a man the wrong impression," he says, placing his large, bear-sized hands on my shoulders. "Sit!"

I sit.

Dropping to his knees before me, he reaches for my gloved hands and starts untying them. His thick fingers are nimble and mesmerising despite their size, and don't even get me started on his hands with his wide palms, the thick wrists, the veins and the tattoos. You know what they say about a man and his hands... Wait, perhaps it's the feet? Fuck, whatever. Either way, big hands, big dick.

"I don't fancy you, Roger, if that's what you're getting at," I say, lying through my teeth. "Your physique might turn the average bimbo with fewer brain cells than a gnat on, but not me. I prefer my men with more upstairs. Know what I mean?"

Beast scoffs and I can't help but smile at the way he yanks at the string of my gloves. "Are we back to that Hudson prick again? Jumped-up shit who thinks he's gonna run the world, that one. More balls than a rugby team playing at Twickenham stadium, but a lot less sense."

"Hud is *smart*," I counter. "Don't underestimate him."

"Princess, I make a habit of never underestimating anyone because I *am* smart."

"Says the man who has ride or die tattooed on his lower

stomach. Yeah, smart. More like fucking *obvious*," I scoff. "Is that the male equivalent of a tramp stamp?"

Beast's fingers still. "No, just the fucking truth. I'm a ride or die kinda man, both in life and in the bedroom. Any woman I invite into my bed can vouch for that," he says, and I have to grit my teeth and lock down the urge to squirm. I do not want to give him the satisfaction.

"Well, whatever. I prefer the smarts. Besides, Hudson's about a thousand times more attractive than you..." And whilst that's not strictly true as they're both equally attractive, just in different ways, he doesn't need to know that.

Beast snorts, back to concentrating on what he's doing. "If you're trying to offend me, don't bother, Princess. I'm not interested in the slightest. You're my boss's daughter, *underage* and entirely off fucking limits. So let's just get back to being cool, okay?"

"What, as opposed to hot? Are you saying I'm *hot*, Roger? Do you want a nice tight piece of underage arse?" I don't know why I push him like this, but I can't seem to help myself. Not to mention the fact I'll be eighteen in a couple of months and officially classified as an adult, so there's that. This time he does look up, and I swallow hard at the look of anger in his eyes.

"Even if you were of fucking age, I still wouldn't touch you."

"You do realise that the age of consent in the UK is sixteen, right?" I say, taunting him.

"I don't give a fuck what the law says. My age of consent is firmly fixed at twenty, got it?"

"Why twenty? You're also considered an adult at eighteen in this country."

"Just because..." he replies, refusing to explain. "Besides, you're not my type."

Removing my gloves, his fingers curling around my wrists, all warm and firm and, surprisingly, soft. For a couple of seconds he just stares at the spot where our skin touches and I wonder if he feels it too, that electric current humming between us.

"No?" I question softly, my heart racing in my chest as he leans in close. I'm pretty sure he can feel my pulse racing under his fingers.

"No," he repeats, whispering in my ear. "I like my women with a bit of meat on their bones. Come back to me when you've turned into one, yeah?" I suck in an offended breath and he laughs, letting me go. "I'll call you a cab," he says, standing abruptly.

"I thought *you* were taking me home?"

"Nope." He strides over to the other side of the ring and ducks between the ropes, dropping to the floor.

"Where are you going?" I shout after him, hating the way my voice catches and my skin burns from his touch.

"I've got work to do."

"What work?" I ask, frowning.

"Carter has got wind of some news he ain't happy with. Nothing to concern yourself with."

"News?"

Beast ignores me "Babysitting duties are up. Catch you later, *Princess*."

And with that he's gone.

"It's Grim!" I yell after him.

Staring at the door that Beast just left through, I grind my teeth. He's the only one of my dad's men who knows how to really push my buttons, the arrogant, cocky bastard. Then again he's the only one of my dad's men that really knows me at all. As I try to calm my thrashing heart, I reassure myself with the fact that there will come a time when I'll be queen of this fight club and Beast will be answering to me. Though whether that's as my lover or as my soldier isn't clear just yet.

CHAPTER TWO

Jungle

"Start talking or I'll cut off another damn toe!" I growl, swiping the back of my hand against my sweaty forehead. Cutting bone is fucking hard work, plus there's no air-con down here in the basement of Tales and it's as hot as a hooker's coochie in summer.

The cocky prick who's strapped naked to the metal gurney spits, a glob of saliva and blood hitting the concrete floor by my feet. "Fuck you!"

I lift a brow, impressed. This is one tough motherfucker. Normally just being strapped to this table and showing them the blunt edge of a well-used knife is enough to get the fuckers talking. Not this man. He's kept his mouth shut, and he's now minus both big toes for the trouble. "I ain't saying shit!"

"Yeah, I'm getting that impression," I muse, a note of respect in my voice.

Either he's got a very high pain threshold or he's high as a fucking kite on some kind of opioid. I'm guessing the latter given the size of his pupils.

"Listen, mate. You could walk... *hobble*," I correct myself, glancing at his ruined feet as Carter snorts with derision from the other side of the room. Obviously, this guy walking out of here ain't gonna happen, but usually the possibility of it gets them singing like a canary. "Carter is happy to let you *hobble* on your way," I continue, cracking my neck. "So long as you give us the name of the prick who's been organising sly bets on our fights right under our fucking noses."

"You'll let me go?" The guy scoffs. "I'm not an idiot, but I am pissed off that it's your face I have to see before I die."

"Then you're a fucking martyr covering for a man who doesn't deserve it!" I retort, losing my patience. "I mean Saxon, for fuck's sake, would sell out his own mother just to save his arse!"

The guy laughs hysterically, flicking his gaze to Carter. "And you think *he's* any better? And people say you're smart..."

"What's that supposed to mean, you little prick?"

Before I even know what's happening, Carter strides over to the trolley loaded with torture implements, picks up a screwdriver and slams it into the guy's shoulder. "Tell me what I want to fucking know, you piece of shit!"

"I ain't no grass!" the little twat roars back, adrenaline and the drug he's taken keeping him from passing the fuck out.

I ease Carter away from him, shaking my head. "Boss, I *got* this."

"Fucking cunt!" Carter snarls before pulling a cigarette from his packet and lighting it up. He drags in a deep breath and blows out a stream of smoke. "The next time you disrespect me, I will drive that screwdriver through your fucking eyeball!" He looks down at his Armani suit, which is no longer pristine given droplets of blood have splashed over the lapel, and frowns. "Fuck sake! If you weren't already going to die, I would've killed you my fucking self for getting blood all over my suit!"

I'm about to say it's not really the guy's fault that he stabbed him with a screwdriver but I hold my tongue. I need this over and fucking done with, and getting into a spat with the boss ain't gonna make that happen. Besides, I've got a major case of *blueballitis* that has been plaguing me ever since Princess provoked me during training a couple of days ago. She's been playing on my damn mind ever since, and I cannot and will not travel down that road. Hence needing to get out of here quickly so I can relieve some of the pressure in my pants with *anyone* other than her.

"Listen, mate, on any other day I'd be impressed with your loyalty, but I've got plans tonight that include sinking balls deep into some top class stripper pussy, so do us a solid and tell us what we want to know!"

"And I told you, I ain't no grass!"

Shaking my head, I glare at the prick. "Look, you hairy scrotum, I'm normally a patient fucking man, but I got pussy waiting on me and I'm fucking starving, so start fessing up!"

The dickhead has the gall to laugh. Fuck me, he really does have a death wish.

"Fuck this, Beast! Cut him up into little pieces and deliver them to Saxon. We all know that cunt is behind this," Carter snaps, his dark brown eyes flashing.

"Boss, you hired me for my ability to break the toughest

motherfuckers. I'd appreciate it if you'd let me do my job. We need to hear it from the horse's mouth or we can't make a move. You know that."

Carter narrows his eyes at me through a plume of blue-grey smoke, but he knows I'm right. I'm really fucking good at my job. "Fine. I've got business to attend to anyway. I'm heading home for a bit before the next fight tonight. Swing by my place once you've confirmed a name, and pick up Grim on your way over. She's with Hudson."

I give Carter a surprised look. "You approve?"

He shrugs. "He's a smart guy, it's the only reason he's still alive. That and the fact I know he ain't interested in Grim."

"He's gay?"

"Nope, he's *focused*. He's only got one thing on his mind and it certainly ain't pussy. He hasn't got time for a relationship, not whilst he's trying to claw his way out of the gutter."

"You sure? I could rough him up a bit, warn him off?"

"Positive. I'm keeping a close eye on Hudson Freed and his brothers, they might come in useful at a later date. Know what I'm saying?"

"Yep."

"Anyway, enough of the chit-chat. Get me proof."

"Got it," I reply, waiting for the heavy iron door to click shut before I turn my attention back to this stupid fucking cunt who is rapidly ruining my night.

Rolling my head, I drop the serrated knife onto the metal table, droplets of blood splattering across the surface as I pick up a pair of gardening shears. Rusty and covered in dried blood, they're about as sharp as a butter knife, making them perfect for what I'm about to do next. I don't profess to like chopping off a man's dick, not because I feel bad about it or anything, but because it makes my own dick metaphorically shrivel up, and that ain't good for my mental or physical health, particularly not the way my balls are feeling tonight.

"Just fucking kill me and be done with it, coz I ain't talking," the guy mumbles, bashing the back of his head against the metal table like he's trying to do the job for me.

I lean over him and press my palm against his forehead to hold him still and get real close. "Okay, I'll level with you. You were right, you ain't walking, or hobbling, or fucking crawling out of here for that matter. These will be your last few minutes on Earth, so I'm gonna give you a choice. You tell me what Carter wants to know, and I can make this quick. Or you can choose to hold out on me, and I'll make sure you bleed out slow. But I can assure you, you'll tell me what I want to know regardless. So what's it to be?" I ask.

"Go fuck yourself!" he shouts, the veins in his neck straining as he bares his teeth at me.

"Yeah, I figured that's what you might say," I reply, lowering the shears towards his dick. "But that's alright, I can get some pussy later. I'm more than happy to wait until the drug you've taken has worn off and all your nerve endings are back to firing properly."

There's a flicker of fear in his eyes, and whilst that isn't unusual given the circumstances, I recognise that fear for what it is. This man ain't afraid to die, but he is afraid of what will happen if he talks and we all know that grassing usually ends with not only your death but the death of your loved ones too. If that cunt Saxon is behind this, then he'll already have a marker on this man's family. No question.

"Fuck, man! I never wanted to bring them into this."

"Okay, spit it out," I demand, tapping his limp dick with the shears. "Whose life has Saxon threatened if you talk?"

He meets my gaze, his fear barrelling out of control now. *Bingo.*

"My kid sister. She's only fucking ten."

"Ah fuck." I let out a heavy sigh. Dealing with toerags like this man ain't usually an issue for me, especially when they work for a prick like Saxon, but when you start bringing innocents into the mix... "You know what, sometimes I hate my fucking job."

"What?" he asks, blinking up at me.

"Does she have anyone else?"

"Anyone else?" he asks, a flash of confusion crossing his features.

"To look after her?"

"She lives with my aunt."

"Not with you?"

He shakes his head, his teeth rattling now with adrenaline. Looks like talk of his sister has sent his system into a downward spiral. Believe it or not, physical pain can often be controlled by people in situations like this. I've witnessed a lot of men take their fair share of torture before cracking, but as soon as you bring up something that will fuck with their head and their heart... Yeah, most don't last five minutes.

"Where?"

"Essex."

"Address?"

"Why?" he asks, suddenly testing the restraints. I know he's wondering if he can somehow escape and get back to his little sister. We both know that ain't happening.

"Because, *Einstein*, I'm gonna send some men to go collect her and your aunt. We can protect them."

"Why would Carter do that?" he asks, surprised.

"Carter wouldn't. I would."

"*Why?*"

"Because they're innocent and don't deserve to die because you're affiliated with the wrong fucking man. Do you want their deaths on your conscience?"

"No! Fuck! I'm all they've got!"

"Well not anymore," I say, dropping the garden shears onto the table. "Just confirm that it's Saxon who's pissing in the wrong territory, and give me the address of your family and I'll make sure they're taken care of."

He meets my gaze. "You promise?"

"Yes."

He nods. "15 Southside Road, Chelmsford."

"Good man," I mutter, pulling out my phone and sending a quick text message to Connall, my go-to in situations like this. He's not Carter's man, he's my oldest friend and one of the O'Briens, a well-known, not to be fucked with, Irish mafia family who own all of the Irish pubs in London and a few dodgy side businesses involving bootlegged liquor and firearms. Not that I give a shit. We go way back and it's not as if I'm clean. You could lock me away for three life sentences given the amount of shit I've done in the name of my boss. It's why I'm head of security and his most trusted soldier, hence the babysitting duties with Princess. He trusts very few people with his baby girl. I don't fucking blame him. Princess has a way of burying her sharp little claws into your skin.

And your dick...

"Fuck!"

"What?! What did they say?"

"Don't worry, your sister and aunt will be taken care of," I reply, tucking my mobile phone back into my pocket.

"What's gonna happen to them?" he asks, his teeth chattering so loud I can barely make out the words.

"I'll get them to a safe house"

"But they don't have much money..."

"Is that why you started to work for Saxon... Money?"

He nods. "Yeah."

"And you think selling drugs to minors is the right way of going about that? I heard that a kid not much older than your baby sister took one of his dodgy pills and died. What do you think about that, huh?" I ask, gearing myself up to the fact that I'm gonna end this prick's life any second now. I ain't sad for him, he's just another cunt who'll do anything for money, but I do feel bad for his kid sister and aunt. No doubt they love him and he keeps his nefarious shit away from them. Until now.

"It wasn't me that sold the drugs to that kid."

"But I bet you have, right?"

He doesn't answer and I nod, grabbing the Glock 21 semi-automatic pistol and pressing the muzzle against his temple. "Name."

"I have money stashed in the floorboards of my aunt's spare bedroom. She doesn't know it's there. Make sure my aunt takes it. It'll be enough to get her and my sister set up again."

"I'll make sure she gets the message. *Name*," I repeat.

"It was Saxon. He's been doing it for months now."

"Thank you," I reply, then pull the trigger, not flinching as brain and skull matter explode out of the side of his head, painting the floor and wall scarlet. "What a fucking waste."

Holstering my pistol, and giving him no more than a cursory glance before I stride from the room, I send a quick message to Dom so he can get the cleaners in to clear up the mess and dispose of the body.

My phone rings. It's Connall. "Sorted?" I ask.

"Yeah, we're on our way over to pick them up now. How long will they need the safe house?" he asks me.

"Until Saxon's dealt with and we can organise somewhere more permanent for them both."

"My guys will take good care of them."

"I know it. Thanks, Connall."

He chuckles down the phone. "You know you're a bit of a bleeding heart these days."

"Tell that to the fucker missing two toes and half his head blown off. Pretty sure he'd disagree with you."

Connall scoffs. "You can act like a beast all you like, but I know there's a heart of gold inside that hairy as fuck chest of yours."

"Shut the fuck up. I ain't hairy," I grind out, his laughter echoing through the loudspeaker as I punch the off button and climb the stairs.

Flicking a slither of flesh off my bare arm, I head towards the changing room, understanding that taking a shower isn't going to wash away my sins, but knowing that a ten year old girl and her aunt are going to be safe sure as fuck helps ease my conscience a little. Besides, I can't be covered in blood and gore when I go pick Princess up, I've got some standards.

"I'M outside Hudson's place. Where are you?" I growl into my phone an hour later, rattling the door even though I know they're not inside.

"Obviously not at Hud's flat," she replies, laughter in her voice. I can hear chatter in the background and music, and groan internally. I'm not in the mood to go and drag her arse from a club.

"Princess!" I warn, pushing off from the door and striding back to my car. "You've got two seconds to tell me where the fuck you are, or so help me I'll—"

"Jesus, calm down, Roger. Bad day at the office?"

"You could say that," I grind out, yanking the door to my car open and climbing inside. Not even the heated seats and sleek lines of my Mercedes G Wagon can cheer me up tonight. I'm in a bad fucking mood and Princess is making it worse. "Look, Carter sent me to pick you up. He was expecting you to be at Hudson's place. You're not. Do I need to give him a call and tell him his daughter's out past her bedtime?"

"Oh, screw you! I'm a fucking adult. I can do what I want."

"We both know that isn't true. Carter says—"

"I don't care what Carter says!"

I blow out a breath, trying to maintain my cool. "Why the fuck do you call your dad Carter anyway?"

"Why the fuck do you care?"

"Okay, fine, you're not in the mood to talk. Guess what, neither am I. So here's the thing. I was planning on getting thoroughly screwed by a beautiful woman tonight, but you've managed to fuck that up being where you shouldn't be. You *owe* me," I say, pressing the console on my dash and connecting to bluetooth so I can have this stupid conversation handsfree whilst I drive the damn car.

"I don't owe you anything. I didn't ask you to babysit me."

"Princess, just tell me where you are." She goes quiet and I can hear the muffled sound of a male voice. I know it's Hudson, and fuck if it doesn't piss me off. "Princess!"

"Macey's Bar. We're just having a drink. It's not a big deal."

"I'll be there in ten," I reply, disconnecting the call before putting the car in drive and hitting the gas. Fuck this bullshit. I did not sign up to look after a tempestuous smartarse who happens to look good in gym gear and gives me fucking ball ache. Fuck, no I did not.

Exactly eight minutes later the bouncer at Macey's Bar greets me with a welcoming slap on the back. "Good to see you, mate. It's been a while."

"Yeah, I've been busy with work these past few weeks," I say vaguely.

"I know exactly what you mean," he replies with a grin, waving me through ahead of the waiting patrons.

"Sure," I mutter, highly doubtful. He's a bouncer, I'm an enforcer. There's a big difference in our line of work. Namely a shit load of dead bodies.

"Have a good night!" he calls after me as I take the stairs down into the club and head towards the bar. I need a drink, then I'll go get Princess.

Ordering a Jack and Coke from Suzy, the hot blonde behind

the bar, I rest against the counter and sweep my gaze over the room. It's busy, but I sensed Princess's whereabouts the second I stepped onto the floor. She's sitting with Hudson and another bloke I don't recognise in a booth on the other side of the room, laughing and chatting like she hasn't got a care in the world. I'm pretty sure she clocked me as I walked in too. The way we know where each other is in a room without really trying fucks with my head, in all honesty. I don't need or want that kind of connection. If she were anyone else and past the age of twenty, I would've fucked her and got her out of my system, but as it is she's not in the cards, or on the table, or against the motherfucking wall for that matter. Besides, I don't do relationships. Never have.

Taking a sip of my drink, I watch her from behind the rim of my glass as she throws her head back and laughs raucously at something Hudson's just said. He grins, wrapping an arm around her shoulder and pulling her into his side in a hug. Jealousy spikes in my chest, and it takes a great deal of control not to storm over there and punch his fucking lights out. Not because I don't *want* to punch the turd, but because no matter what I feel about Hudson Freed, Grim cares about him and she isn't the type of girl to let many people in. That says a lot.

Truthfully, when she's not verbally sparring with me, she's guarded and cautious. It's no surprise given who her dad is and the environment she's grown up in, so I can't begrudge her their friendship, not to mention I've no right to. But one thing I do know for certain is that if he ever fucks her over, he's a dead man walking.

"Penny for your thoughts," a posh, but very sexy, female voice says from my left.

I give whoever's trying to chat me up a cursory look, clocking a leggy brunette with big blue eyes, lips pumped full of filler, and breasts just as fake. She's attractive, and I have nothing against a woman changing their appearance to make them feel better about themselves, but I'm suddenly not in the mood to hook up with a stranger, despite my severe case of *blue-ballitis*. Keeping my gaze firmly fixed on Kate, I knock back the remains of my Jack and Coke and say, "Love, you'd need to pay me a lot more than a penny to get inside my head right now."

She reaches for my arm as I place the empty glass on the bar. "Is that so? Well, I happen to be loaded."

I meet her gaze and grin. "I bet, beautiful. Thing is, I ain't no one's bit of rough. Paid or otherwise. Though it's been nice to meet you..." I say, bringing her delicate hand up to my lips and kissing her knuckles as I wait for a name.

"Lucy." She blushes, and any other night I'd be kicking myself in the bollocks for not tapping that, but I'm too distracted by Princess's laughter that seems suddenly too loud for her to still be over on the other side of the room.

"And there's me thinking you were here to take *me* home..."

Sighing, I drop Lucy's hand, ignoring her look of confusion, and turn my attention to Kate who's looking pretty damn cute in a faded Guns and Roses t-shirt and cut-off denim shorts paired with fishnet tights and biker boots. "Princess. Grab your shit and let's go."

"You're here now. Why not have a drink first," she replies, nudging her way between me and the posh bird, Lucy, who looks up at me with a question in her eyes.

"She's my job," I say by way of explanation, which only seems to confuse her more.

"And he's a *daily* pain in my arse," Kate adds with a sultry voice, false smile and a wiggle of her butt in my direction.

"Got it," Lucy replies, backing away from Kate and disappearing into the crowd of people dancing.

"Was that really necessary?" I ask, turning sideways to face the little vixen. As I move, her upper arm brushes against my chest, and that minor contact sets off my dick in a way I wish it fucking wouldn't.

"Was what necessary?" she replies innocently as she waves over the barmaid and orders her drinks.

"Being such a bitch."

Kate snaps her head around and narrows her eyes at me. "I just did you a favour, you ungrateful arsehole."

"Yeah, and how did you work that out?" I ask, loving the way her anger flares to the surface. There's something about pissing Kate off that amuses me, and I can't help but stoke the fire.

"She's an upmarket escort and has had more dicks inside of her than you've dipped your wick in other women, and that's saying something."

"And there's me thinking she wanted to buy *me* for the night."

"What?!" Princess snaps, murmuring her thanks to the barmaid who's loaded her order of drinks onto a tray.

I chuckle. "Like I said, I'm pretty sure she was willing to buy me for the night and, honestly, I would've banged her for free."

"Urgh, you're incorrigible," Kate scoffs, grabbing the tray and somehow expertly weaving her way around the crowded dance floor without spilling a drop. I follow her, ready to grab her and go the second she's settled the tray on the table.

"Big words tonight, Princess. I like it when you talk dirty to me," I say before I can rein my fucking neck in. Really though, what the fuck is wrong with me?

She makes a kind of strangled noise that's a cross between a laugh, a snort and a groan. I'd find it cute if I didn't want to throat punch myself for overstepping the mark. She's my boss's daughter and I'm her fucking bodyguard. I *need* to remember that.

Reaching the booth, Kate slides the tray into the centre of the table. I don't bother to acknowledge Hudson or his mate, my focus is completely consumed by Princess and the heated way she glares at me.

"You alright, Grim?" Hudson questions, earning him a death glare, which he doesn't cower from like others would.

He's got balls, I'll give him that.

Not sure I like the look I'm getting from the guy sitting next to him either. Haven't seen him around before, but I'd remember a man with eyes so blue they cut through the dim light of the club. He's a good-looking fucker, with a mixed background given his skin tone, and has the same kind of aura about him that Hudson has. Smart, streetwise, and confident. I'd appreciate that if I didn't want to drop kick them both for just breathing in the same air space as Princess.

Fuck, man. I've got to get a grip.

"Grim?" Hudson persists, pissing me off even more. I'm no threat to her.

"Of course she's—"

"I'm going to dance," Kate says, cutting me off before

pushing through the crowd and into the centre of the dance floor.

"For fuck's sake!" I mutter.

"Look, Beast. Don't be pissed at Grim. I suggested we come here tonight. This is on me."

I snap my head back around and glare at Hudson. "Is that right? Well, you can explain to Carter why the fuck she ain't at your place like she was supposed to be. I mean the sheer fact he *lets* her hang out with you is beyond me, but that's neither here nor there."

"Carter's alright with me," Hudson replies with a shrug. "He knows I'm not like that with Grim."

The guy next to him grins, winking at me. It doesn't look like he's all that convinced either, the shithead.

"You got something you want to say, pretty boy?"

"The name's Cal, and nope, nothing to add."

"Good, because I wouldn't want to mess up that pretty face of yours," I reply, briefly considering doing just that. "Lucky for you I've had a pissy day and I need to go home and get some sleep. So we'll bench this..." I wave my hand between us, scowling, "For now."

"Fair enough," Hudson says with laughter in his eyes—the little prick—before jerking his chin towards the dance floor. "Looks like some dude's getting handsy with your Princess though."

"The fuck?!"

I spin on my feet, my gaze honing in on the tosser who looks like a secondhand version of that bloke from the Lord of the Rings movies minus the fae get up. Like Hudson said, he's got his hands all over Kate and what's more, she seems to fucking like it.

Striding through the crowd, I tap the bastard on his shoulder as Kate peers up at me, a smirk on her face. "Take your fucking hands off her, *Orlando!*"

CHAPTER THREE

Ain't No Other Man

"Orlando?" the guy scoffs, turning around to face Beast and almost choking on his tongue when he gets a good look at the man who drives me insane.

"Yeah, you heard me. Take your motherfucking hands off of her. NOW!" Beast bellows, making the poor guy practically jump out of his skin and the people dancing nearby give us some space. I have to hold in a laugh, because despite how irritating Beast is, the look on Orlando's— I mean, *John*'s face is priceless. Well, I think he's called John, I couldn't quite catch his name over the music.

"Woah!" John replies, letting me go and holding his hands up. "She didn't say she had a boyfriend."

"*She*? Who's she, the cat's fucking mother?" Beast grinds out, grabbing his scruff and getting in his face. The guy practically pisses himself.

"I meant Alice. Fuck, man. Sorry!"

"*Alice*?! Who the fuck is Alice?"

John peers over at me, and this time I can't help but laugh. It breaks out of me like a bubble bursting. "Sorry, I wasn't about to give you my real name," I say, biting down on another laugh as I point towards Beast. "You can see why, right?"

Beast narrows his eyes, then lets John go with a shove. "Get the fuck out of here. I catch you coming onto *Alice* again I'm gonna fuck you up so bad you're gonna look more like one of those ugly fucking orcs than that pretty, long-haired fae boy."

John shakes his head looking thoroughly confused and it's only then I realise the connection—Beast thinks he looks like the actor Orlando Bloom—which causes another bout of laughter to burst out of me. I practically bend over in half, I'm laughing so hard. By the time I've calmed down enough to straighten up, Beast is staring at me, his thick arms crossed over his chest. A furious expression on his face.

"What the fuck is so funny?" he exclaims.

"You. You're hysterical, do you know that?"

"Yeah I'm full of laughs. Now get your shit and let's go!"

I cock my head and pretend to think about it, then smile. "No, I don't think I will."

Beast's top lip curls up in a snarl that is way too sexy to be intimidating. "You don't have a choice. Do as you're told."

I roll my eyes ready to cuss him out some more when the DJ starts playing *Ain't No Other Man* by Christina Aguilera. The girl knows how to write a mean arse song, and her voice? Pure fucking sex.

"I came here to dance. So I'm dancing," I retort, then turn my back to Beast, bend my knees and drop it like it's hot.

"Princess!" I hear him warn, but it only spurns me on as I push back upwards, raise my hands in the air and dance, shaking my arse right in his crotch.

This song is about a woman claiming her power, *and* her man, and that's exactly how I feel in the moment, even though I have no right to. Beast isn't mine, but I can't deny that I want him to be. I have for a while now. Maybe it's the several shots of vodka I've knocked back, or maybe I'm digging the way he handled that guy just now. Either way, I'm feeling suddenly confident in my ability to pull Beast despite what he said to me in the gym the other day.

"If you don't stop wiggling your arse like that, I'm gonna have to take drastic action, Princess," he says, his rumbling voice vibrating up my spine as my arse presses back against his crotch harder.

"Do you mean like this?" I ask sweetly, looking back up at him whilst doing my best impression of the strippers at Nine Lives, the club my dad owns. Those women know how to move their bodies to make men weak. There's a power in that, and I respect them immensely for it even if it does piss me off that most of them have rubbed up against Beast in the same way, *naked* and in his bedroom.

"Princess, I'm in no mood for your shit," he grumbles, attempting to put space between us, but I just step back against him once more.

"Oh come on, dance with me. Why not let your hair down for once and loosen up a bit?"

"Loosening up *isn't* the fucking problem, Princess," he growls, grabbing my arm and spinning me around to face him. I throw my hands up automatically to stop myself from colliding with his body. My fingers curl into his shirt as I glare up at him.

"Then what *is* your problem?" I snap, all the fun of the moment leaving me with a rush of anger.

"You," he mutters, squeezing my arm a little too tightly.

Not that I care, because despite my anger, I want his hands on me. So I take a step closer towards him, not away. "This dickish behaviour is beginning to piss me the fuck off. You're not like this with any other woman. What gives?"

"You ain't special, Princess. If that's what you're getting at," he argues.

"No? So leave then. Hud and Cal will drop me off at home."

"Not happening!" he snaps. "Now move your feet before I move them for you."

"Seriously, Beast, what gives?" I ask in frustration.

Yes, I know he works for my dad and there's certain expectations, but would it really kill him to hang out with me for a bit? I might not be his type, but I'm pretty fun to be around when given the chance. We could at least be friends. I don't have many of them and could use some more.

"*Princess.*"

Another growl, another warning.

Everything about this whole situation is screaming for me to take a step back. He's angry, that much is obvious, and I should be wary.

But I'm not.

I know he's not going to hurt me and that makes me bold.

We glare at each other, and with every intake of breath I seem to edge closer to him until Christina Aguilera's voice is drowned out by the rushing and thumping of my pulse beating loudly in my ear.

"Well?" I prompt, my heart galloping as he releases his grip on my arm and his palms find their way to my hips. His hands are so huge that they practically meet over the bottom of my spine. For long, agonising moments he just stares down at me, an unreadable expression on his face, and whilst I stopped gyrating like a stripper the second he flipped me around to face him, I'm still swaying from side to side *wanting* to dance with him, daring him to dance with me too.

"We should go," he says, but to my surprise he mirrors my movements and the steady thump of my heart misses a beat as he pulls me even closer. It's all I can do not to press my lips against his throat and slide my tongue across his tattooed skin, but I do take the opportunity to breathe him in, his masculine scent of whisky, sweat and leather stirring a longing deep within me.

"Dance with me," I whisper against the column of his neck, and this time he doesn't deny me.

Heat builds beneath my skin where our bodies touch, and in the places I *wish* he would touch, and for a few blissful moments we leave behind our personas and just move fluidly together. Right here in the middle of a packed dance floor, in this grimy basement club, he's no longer Beast, the man who kills for Carter, and I'm no longer Grim, the woman who is destined to take her father's place. In this moment we're just us. Just two people attracted to one another. Two people who might belong to each other if the world we live in didn't get in the way.

And it feels *good*.

My cheek presses against his chest, my fingers curling into his shirt tightly as he wraps his arms around me in an embrace that simultaneously gives me strength and protects me from all the things that could hurt me, of which there are many.

I'm not used to feeling safe, but in his arms I do.

"Princess..." he murmurs, cupping the back of my head, his fingers curling into my hair and tugging gently. He looks down at me, a fierce kind of agony in his eyes as he lowers his head and presses his lips against my ear. "It's time to go."

"I just want..." I reply, a little breathlessly if I'm honest. I've never been a woman to pant after a man, but Beast is the *only* man who's ever made me lightheaded and a little crazy. There's no way I'd let anyone else get to me the way he does.

"You just want, what...?" he asks, his voice low, gruff, as his hands slide down my back and his fingers curl around the waistband of my jean shorts, pulling the material so tight that I can feel the seam between my legs rubbing against my clit.

"I just want..." I gasp, unable to finish the sentence.

You.

My voice trails off as he pulls me closer, his whole body a wall of muscle and masculinity that scrambles my head and makes my knees weak. The pull he has over me is like nothing I've felt before. It's an attraction, yes, but it's also so much more than that, and it's terrifying because for all my flirtation, I'm not exactly experienced. Not that he needs to know. I would rather cut out my own tongue than admit that.

"I know, Princess. I *know*," he murmurs, his lips brushing over the top of my head as he speaks.

"Just a little longer..." I say, but it comes out like a plea, and I hate myself for it.

Knowing that I want him is one thing, but being vulnerable like this is quite another. Maybe it's the tone of my voice, or maybe it's the sudden realisation that he's gotten way too close to his boss's daughter, but either way he stiffens and takes a step back.

"Carter wants you home, so home it is," he says, then picks me up and chucks me over his shoulder, breaking the spell and reminding me that I don't live in a fairy tale, but in the real world with men who wear tattoos like armour and have no problem throwing a woman over their shoulder when the mood takes them.

"YOU'RE A DICK, YOU KNOW THAT?" I say, still fuming as he parks the car outside my house half an hour later. "Putting me over your shoulder like some caveman. It was embarrassing!"

"I'm just doing my job, Princess," he replies, but I can't help but notice the heaviness of the sigh that follows. He makes no move to get out of the car, so neither do I.

"What is it?" I ask him.

Unclicking his seatbelt, he twists in his seat to face me. "So now you want to talk? You've been giving me the silent treatment all the way back from the club."

"You pissed me off." *You made a fool out of me.*

"I do that a lot, it would seem."

I frown. "Don't pretend you're upset about it. You love winding me up, makes your day go quicker, right?"

He gives me a half smile, swiping his hand through his cropped brown hair. "You got me there."

"Yeah, I get it," I say, smarting a little, but covering up my hurt by rolling my eyes. "I'm just a source of amusement for you. That was well played."

"Princess..."

I wave my hand in the air pretending I don't give a shit. "Whatever. I'm already over it."

He chews on his lip, glancing at his phone charging on the dash. This G Wagon has all the latest electrical gadgets and I briefly wonder how much my dad is paying him. Must be a shit load to be able to afford this beauty and to put up with my antics, I guess.

"This is bullshit," he mutters after a while.

"Do you want to tell me what's up? Something's clearly bothering you."

"Nothing's bothering me."

"Tell that to your bottom lip," I scoff, glancing at the tiny bead of blood where he's gnawed at it.

"What?"

"You have a tell. You chew on your bottom lip when you've got something on your mind."

"I do-fucking-not."

"You're bleeding." I point out.

He reaches up and swipes at his lip with his thumb, widening his eyes when he sees the blood. "Interesting."

"What is?" I ask. "The fact that you didn't realise you had a tell, or the fact I noticed?"

He doesn't respond, just stares at his thumb like he's never seen his own blood before, and I have this sudden, inexplicable urge to climb onto his lap and take his mind off whatever's bothering him. I don't. Instead, I reach forward and gently press my fingers against his knee. "Beast?"

"I killed a man today," he says, scrubbing a hand over his face as he looks back at me. There's a haunted look about his eyes that I haven't seen before now.

"Ah fuck," I whisper, drawing my hand back, not because I'm disgusted with him, but because I'm finding it increasingly hard not to smooth my palm up his thigh. Now is not the time to seduce him, or make a fool out of myself for that matter.

"Yeah."

For a moment he doesn't say a word but tells me everything with his silence. Beast has a reputation for being a cold-blooded killer, and that's true, he is. But there's more to him than that. Over the last year I've been watching him closely. He's loyal, protective, funny when he allows himself to be, and a good leader even if he acts like a caveman sometimes. I know that I've only just scratched the surface of who he really is and I want to know more.

"What did he do to warrant his death?" I ask instead.

"Carter needed information," Beast replies. "The guy I killed had it."

"Right." I nod, picking at a piece of non-existent lint on my jean shorts.

It's not like I don't know my dad's a bad man. I do. But he's still my dad. He's still the man who took me from a deadbeat mother when I was a baby and brought me up the best way he knew how. He's still the man who wants to teach me how to be a savvy businesswoman who can survive in a world full of cutthroat criminals.

"He was selling drugs to minors..." Beast says, as though he's trying to convince himself that killing that man today was a good thing, and given what he just said, it is. Adults can make their own decisions, but it takes an extra special kind of arsehole to deal drugs to kids like they're fucking sweeties.

"He sounds like a piece of work. What a dick."

"Would it have made me a better man for killing him because of that reason?" he asks me.

"You feel bad about killing him?" I throw back.

He lifts his gaze to meet mine, his green eyes glinting in the light coming from the porch. "I should, but I don't, and I ain't sure if that's because I've lost the ability to give a shit about the value of human life after years of fucking taking it at the whim of other men, or if it's because I really don't give a shit that he's dead."

"He sold drugs to children. You've probably saved a few lives by taking him out even if that wasn't why you killed him."

"Yeah, until the next man steps in to take his place."

"I didn't know you—"

"What, care?" he snorts. "I don't, not for dirtbags like him. Except..."

"Except?" I prompt, cocking my head to the side as I study his face.

"He had a kid sister, and an aunt."

"Every bad man has a family," I say with a shrug even though there's this tightness in my chest that makes me feel like a victim somehow. Especially when Beast looks at me like that's exactly what I am. I frown, not liking the feeling.

"I'm well aware of that fact, but his choices aren't their fault. They loved him regardless, and that's what I have trouble with. I've taken someone they love even if he was a bad man."

"Then they're better off without him, right? He'd only bring trouble to their door eventually."

"Which is why we've got them somewhere safe."

My eyes widen with surprise. "You have?"

"He was working for Saxon, and that guttersnake will have a target on their heads just because they were related to the prick who grassed on him. I won't have their deaths on my conscience too."

"Wow. How did you even pull that off?"

"I have my ways. For now, they're out of Saxon's reach. Once we take him out, they'll be safe."

"I didn't realise Carter did stuff like that," I say, completely shocked that my dad would even care about some small-time drug dealer's family.

"Yeah, your dad's a good man," Beast says, giving me a smile that doesn't reach his eyes.

"Beast?" I question, seeing the lie written boldly across his face, but his phone beeps with a new message and he grabs it from the dash, swiping his finger across the screen, ignoring me.

"Fuck!"

"What?"

"I gotta go. Out you get," he bites out.

"Is it the little girl?" I ask.

He shakes his head. "No. Something's going down at Tales. Your dad's already there."

"Then I'll come."

Beast shakes his head. "No."

"Beast, it's my club too."

"Not yet it ain't. Get out of the car, Princess."

"You can't protect me from this life. This is my future, Beast. I'm coming."

"THE. FUCK. YOU. ARE!" he snarls, shoving open his door and striding around the car to the passenger side. He yanks my door open, ducking inside to unclip my seatbelt and haul me out of the vehicle, slamming the door closed behind me.

"Get your hands off me!" I yell, and without thinking it through, I throw a punch that hits him square in the jaw.

A snarl rips out of his mouth as he backs me up against the side of the car, his hands gripping the roof either side of my head as he crouches slightly so that his eyes are at the same level as mine. They flash with anger, but also the kind of pain you never want to see in the eyes of someone you care about.

"Don't you *ever* raise your fist to me outside of the ring again, you hear me?"

"Then don't manhandle me like I'm a piece of damn meat. It goes both ways!" I snap back, refusing to back down.

His nostrils flare, but after a moment he nods. "You're right. I'm sorry."

"You are?" I reply, shocked at his apology frankly, but given he's big enough to do so, I decide to do the same. "Fine, I'm sorry too. I know you're only doing your job."

He shakes his head. "No, if I were doing my job I'd be bringing you along right now just like Carter wants me to do."

"What?" I question as he reaches up and trails his fingers over my cheek, heat tracing over my skin from his touch as he stares at me intently.

"Carter's got Saxon and he's about to execute the fucker. *I don't want you there.*"

"*You* don't want me there?" I shake my head incredulously as his hand drops away.

"Yeah, me."

"I don't need protecting, Beast. Don't you understand that? This is my life and I'm not some feeble woman who'll cry at the first sight of blood. I know what will happen tonight. I've been preparing for it my whole life."

"I know you're not feeble," he retorts, biting down on whatever else he wants to say but is stopping himself from doing so. I wish he'd just come out with it.

"Look, this is going to be my business one day and I won't be seen as some weak fucking crybaby. I'm coming!" I argue, pressing my hands against his chest as I try to shove him away.

He shakes his head, pushing back against me, his hips pressing against mine, keeping me in place. "I *know* you're not weak. I *know* this is your life. I *know* you don't cry, that you're strong, capable. I know you can handle a gun, that you would go up in the cage against the best of us. I *know* you're gonna be Queen of Tales one day. I know all of that, Kate."

Kate.

His use of my real name makes my stomach flip over. I both hate my name and love hearing it on his lips. Kate was the name my mother gave me and the girl I've been trying to separate myself from for a long time now, but hearing Beast use it makes me feel differently somehow.

"Then what are you trying to prove?"

"I'm not trying to prove anything. I'm trying to—"

"To *what*?"

"To give you more time."

"Time?"

"To be *Kate*."

"I don't understand."

He draws in a deep breath, stepping back away from me. "Yes, you do."

"I don't. Explain."

"*Princess* is the girl I've been hired to protect. *Grim* is the woman your father wants you to be, but Kate... She's the person who has a chance to choose."

"Choose what?"

"Fuck! A different life! A better one without men like your father, like *me* within it. Make the right choice before it's too late," he says, before striding around the car and climbing in the driver's seat. His words sink beneath my skin and burn into my bones as he hits the gas and speeds out of the drive.

As I watch him drive away, one thought pops into my head...

It's already too late. I've made my choice.

I *want* to be Queen of Tales, and I *want* Beast too.

CHAPTER FOUR

Lean on

"Where the fuck is she?" Carter asks the second I step into Tales without Kate. He's in the cage, Saxon kneeling before him, his face a bloody, pulpy mess. Rodriguez is with them, a new guy who Carter brought in a couple of months back. He's a little bit older than me, has connections to the Perez crime family that settled in North London, and not someone I've had much chance to spend time with. As far as I'm concerned he's Carter's bitch and not one of *my* men.

"I left her back at your place," I reply, shrugging out of my jacket and tossing it over one of the chairs nearby. I roll up the sleeves of my shirt as I stride towards the cage.

"What do you mean you left her back at my place? I specifically told you to bring her here!"

"She ain't ready," I say, eyeing Saxon as he groans, blood

oozing from a split lip and eyebrow, as well as a nasty gash to his cheek. Given the way his nose has collapsed against his face, I'd say that it was broken too. Rodriguez has certainly made a good start in my absence.

"What do *you* mean she isn't ready?" he snarls.

"What I said. She ain't ready to see this shit yet."

"She's a motherfucking Davidson. She was born ready," Carter explodes, and if the human body were capable of making steam come out of its ears in anger, I'm pretty fucking positive he'd be a human choo-choo train right now.

"I made a call. I don't regret it."

"You think you know my daughter better than I do?" he questions.

I know I do, I think.

"No," I reply instead. "I think you hired me to protect what matters to you the most. She ain't ready."

Carter scowls, taking his measure of me. I wait for whatever it is he's going to say, rolling my shoulders and loosening up my muscles from clenching them so tightly. Dancing with Kate has got me in fucking knots. Today I let her in more than I should've, and now I've got to deal with the consequences of that.

"You've been training her," he says finally, and it's more of an accusation than a statement.

"To protect herself. Not to kill."

"Same difference," he snaps, eyeing me. "You know as well as I do that in this life you're fighting to survive. She needs to be prepared."

"And she *will* be, just not yet," I insist.

"I hired you as my *enforcer* and as her trainer," Carter replies sharply. "Not someone to psychoanalyse my own fucking daughter."

"And you've also hired me to look out for her," I remind him. "I'm doing that now. Kate *isn't* ready."

Carter's nostrils flare, but he doesn't pursue it. Instead he motions for me to step inside the cage. "Get in here."

I'm not fool enough to believe that this conversation is over, Carter isn't the type of man to let disobedience go, but for now his mind is back on Saxon.

"You got it," I reply, flicking my gaze to Rodriguez who's watching the exchange with interest. Too much interest. I don't know the fucker, and right now I don't want to know him given the way he's smirking. "Got something to say, *el cabrón*?"

The smile slips from Rodriguez's face, but he jerks his chin. "Not a thing, *Beast*."

"Good because I have no issues wiping that smirk off your face... permanently."

Climbing inside the cage, my gaze drops to the growing pool of blood spreading out over the canvas floor beneath Saxon. He mutters something as I approach but it comes out garbled as cherry-red blood drips down his chin. That's way too much blood loss for a few missing teeth.

"I cut out his tongue," Rodriquez says, answering my internal question as he points at a slab of bloody muscle beside Saxon's leg.

"*You* cut out his tongue?" I ask, not surprised per se, just taken aback that Rodriguez was the one who did it.

"He was spouting bullshit lies. I was tired of listening,"

Carter interjects, pressing the muzzle of the gun against Saxon's forehead. "Rodriguez got the job done."

"What kind of lies?" I ask, ignoring his veiled dig.

"The kind that gets a man's tongue cut out," Carter snaps back, unwilling to share, or at least unwilling to share right now.

I flick my gaze to Rodriguez, who's removing his knuckle dusters and avoiding eye contact with me. Not sure I like the fact he's stepped into my shoes so fucking easily. *I'm* Carter's enforcer after all, the punk can fuck right off if he thinks he can wiggle his way into my fucking role. He's not the first to try and I doubt he'll be the last, but he'll learn pretty fucking quickly where his bread's buttered and that ain't at Carter's side.

"Got it." I nod, knowing that now is clearly not the time to push the subject given everyone's being so fucking cagey. "So what did you need me for then?"

Carter makes a snorting sound. "I needed you to bring me Grim."

"Next time?" I offer, maintaining eye contact with him because if there's one thing I know for sure about Carter Davidson is that he doesn't like a pussy, and whilst I might enjoy eating pussy a great deal, I ain't one.

"There's no need for a next time..."

The. Fuck. She. Didn't.

My head snaps around as Kate enters the gym. I open my mouth to tell her to get the fuck out, but slam it shut just as quickly. What the hell does she think she's doing here?

"Grim!" Carter says, surprise in his voice.

"Carter," she responds, a tight smile plastered to her face as she nods in greeting to her father and Rodriguez, completely avoiding eye contact with me.

"How did you get here?" I grind out as Saxon gurgles and splutters, trying to speak. An uneasy feeling settles in my stomach as he motions to Kate, as though whatever the fuck he's trying to say is aimed at her.

Carter flicks his gaze to me, jerking his chin at the fucker. I know what that look means. Without missing a beat, I raise my fist and punch Saxon as hard as I can. He falls to the side, shaking his head as droplets of blood splatter the canvas and our clothes. Kate takes it all in, her eyes dropping to Saxon, then slowly rising upwards to meet my gaze.

"I called a cab," she replies as calm as fuck.

"You called a fucking *cab*?" I reply.

Carter chuckles, a smirk pulling up his lips as he motions for her to join us. "Grim ain't ready, my arse," he says, flicking his gaze to me before motioning for her to join us in the cage.

It's all I can do not to level the cunt.

I *know* she isn't ready. Kate is here to prove a point, but it's the wrong fucking one. This is bravado and bluster. He doesn't see how her fingers are curled into fists to stop her hands from shaking, or the way she keeps licking her lips and flicking her gaze to the man who's about to die. She's fucking terrified. Kate might've noticed my tell earlier, but she's got a few of her own. Glaring at her, I hold back the words I want to say and reach over, grabbing Saxon by the hair pulling him upright.

"What now, boss?"

"Now Grim is going to shoot the bastard thief," Carter replies, as Kate steps into the cage.

Her step falters, but only briefly. If Carter were paying any kind of attention he would see that she didn't expect to be the one to kill Saxon. Witness his death, yes. Kill him? No.

Fuck no, according to the glimmer of fear stuttering across her features that she shuts down in the four steps it takes to reach her father's side.

"Did you get what you needed from him?" she asks, the slightest tremor in her voice only noticeable to those who know her well enough. Either Carter notices and doesn't give a shit, or he really doesn't know his own flesh and blood. Right now I'm having a hard time figuring out which is true.

"To a degree," he answers, holding out the gun to her. "But what I really want is this prick to pay. That will only happen when his brains are splattered across this canvas."

Grim looks at the proffered gun then back up to Carter who's watching her closely. This is a test, that much is obvious. Taking someone's life ain't easy, no matter how much you psych yourself up to do it. I remember my first kill and despite the dicksplash being a murdering cunt, I will never forget how it felt to see the life leave his eyes. Never.

It changes you, permanently, and there's no turning back.

"Grim?" Carter questions.

She swallows hard. "I—"

"I'll do it," I say quickly. Too quickly, given the way Carter snaps his head around to look at me.

"I said, *Grim* is going to do it. After all, she's the one he's stealing from."

"I am?" she replies.

"Tales is going to be your club one day, Grim. So you need to send a message out to anyone who thinks they can fuck over the Davidsons. Understand?"

"Yes," she nods tightly, taking the gun from him. Her tongue peeks out of her mouth, wetting her parched lips. I bet her mouth is just as fucking dry. "Where?"

"Where what?" Carter replies, kicking Saxon in the stomach as he tries to grasp his suit jacket. Saxon doubles over, his chest heaving.

"Where do you want me to shoot him?" Kate asks as Carter moves out of her way so she can step in front of Saxon. He slowly pushes up from the floor, his hands reaching for her now. I step in and slap his hands away.

"Hands off!" I growl.

Rodriguez snorts, earning him a narrowed look from Kate. "What's *your* problem?" she asks.

"You asked where you need to shoot him. It's obvious, no? In the *head*," he replies with a wink.

"Don't you want to... Fuck him up some more?" She turns to look at her dad, a question in her eyes, and maybe a plea of sorts. Despite her now steady voice, she can't hide her true feelings. At least not from me. I was right. She ain't ready to kill a man.

"No, we're done here. Shoot him in the head," Carter says offhandedly.

Kate nods, then presses the muzzle against Saxon's forehead. Her hand is shaking and she tenses every muscle in her body in an attempt to get a hold of herself.

"Carter..." I begin, but he holds his hand up, cutting me off.

"She's *ready*," he insists.

Kate swallows hard, gritting her teeth as her focus is pinned on the bloody and beaten man kneeling before her. Saxon stares back, his bloodshot eyes begging her not to kill him. In one last ditch attempt to save his pitiful life, he puts his palms together and attempts to form a sentence, his tears mingling with the blood that pumps from his severed tongue.

"Carter..." Kate says, uncertainty creeping into her voice.

"Pull the damn trigger, Grim," he grinds out, patience waning.

Her nostrils flare, and I want to ask her why she came, why she didn't listen to a damn word I said, but I don't. I can't. Not here. Not now. Later maybe when this is fucking over, I'll get the chance.

"Do it!" Carter orders.

She wavers on her feet and her indecision fucking kills me. She's in way over her head right now. "Let me," I interject.

"The fuck you will," Carter snaps, stepping up beside her. "Kill the motherfucker, Grim. Show me you got what it takes to run this place alongside me. Do it. Now!"

"Dad," she whispers.

It's a plea, one he chooses to ignore. She's shaking so much that she has to cup her hand holding the gun to steady her aim.

"I said *do it!*" he shouts.

Kate jumps, and without giving it a second thought, I press my chest against her back and slide my hands down her arms. Grasping her hands in mine, I reposition the gun, helping her to hold it steady against Saxon's head.

"The fuck, Beast?" Carter spits, but I ignore him.

I don't give a fuck what this looks like. Right now the only person I give a shit about is Kate. If her dad's not willing to do what's right, then I will. I fucking will. I'll steady her hand whilst she takes a life.

She releases a breath from her mouth, her muscles relaxing the tiniest amount, telling me that for whatever reason she feels safe in my arms. For the briefest of moments I allow myself to bask in that knowledge, then I lower my mouth to her ear, and not giving two fucks who's watching, whisper, "*Choose.*"

She knows what I mean even if no one else does.

Kill Saxon and become Grim. Step away and remain Kate.

She chooses.

CHAPTER FIVE

Princesses Don't Cry

Peeling off my clothes, I climb into the shower and let the scalding water saturate my hair and run over my body before picking up the shower gel and squeezing a generous amount into my hand. I wash myself harshly, scrubbing at my skin with a loofah until it's dusted pink all over. Then repeat the process again before washing my hair.

By the time I turn off the shower an hour has passed and there isn't one inch of me left unclean.

Not that it matters.

I'll never feel clean again.

Ever.

And that isn't because I put a bullet in Saxon's brain, it's because I *didn't*.

I feel dirty.

Tarnished.

Ashamed.

When I'd withdrawn my hands from Beast's and handed him the gun, my father gave me a look of pure disgust. I've never felt less of a Davidson in my life than I did when Carter looked at me like I was nothing, like I was a disappointment. I chose to be Kate in that moment and look how that turned out for me. Swiping at the mist covering the mirror, I look at my reflection remembering the harsh words my father had uttered when I'd allowed Beast to do what I should've.

"This is a prime fucking example why women are the inferior species. Bleeding from their cunts as well as their hearts."

My anger flares, hot and fiery as I stare at my reflection. I'd never felt smaller in my life but I've only got myself to blame. I should never have listened to Beast. Shaking hands and dry mouth aside, I made the wrong choice. I should've put a bullet in Saxon's head and sucked it the fuck up. Whilst I don't appreciate the shitty derogatory remark—because fuck you *Dad* for bringing my sex into this—I get where he's coming from. Weakness is not tolerated in our line of business, and mercy is out of the fucking question when you've been wronged.

"Fuck!" I grind out, so angry at myself that I could fucking cry.

Which I won't do. Ever.

Grabbing a towel, I dry myself quickly then pull on my leggings, vest, grey hoodie, and a pair of warm socks before running a comb through my hair. I yank at the strands until I'm satisfied I've got all the tangles out, then head into my bedroom and pick up my copy of Grimms' fairy tales, opening it up on the story, *The Juniper Tree*, a gruesome fairy tale about a young man murdered by his evil stepmother who cooks the boy and feeds him to his father.

Nothing like a dark story to take my mind off everything.

Getting under the covers, I turn on my side and read, too engrossed in the twisted minds of the Grimm brothers to notice someone entering my room.

"Are you asleep?" Beast asks, making me jump.

"Jesus Christ, ever heard of knocking?!" I snap, sitting up in bed to face him.

"I did. You were too busy reading..." he replies, eyeing the book left discarded next to me. "Which story are you reading tonight?"

"What do you want?" I retort, not wanting to talk.

Beast steps towards the bed, and I narrow my eyes at him. Things could've gone so differently tonight if he hadn't put thoughts in my head. I need to prove to Carter that I'm *not* a bleeding heart. That I can, and will, be able to run Tales by his side, and Beast clearly isn't the man who's going to help me to do that. I'm not sure why that makes me feel both unutterably safe in his presence and simultaneously furious. It's confusing as fuck.

"Carter wanted me to pass on a message."

"And why can't he do that himself?" I ask, shifting in bed as I draw my knees up and clutch them to my chest, only to promptly let them go when I realise how fucking pathetic it is to self-comfort myself in this moment.

Beast frowns watching me as I shift about. "Because he's gone to Nine Lives."

"Of course he has."

"Yeah. Said he needed to forget about what went down tonight and... *unwind*."

"What, inside one of the strippers?" I snort, ignoring the way my stomach turns over. "Yeah, sounds about right." Carter isn't an apologetic man so his actions shouldn't surprise me in the least, but it still stings that he can't even bear to be under the same roof as me.

"He also wanted me to go over the rebuild plans for Tales with you."

I blink in surprise. "After everything that happened tonight he still trusts me to handle it?"

Beast nods. "You're smart, Princess. Capable. He'd be a fool not to notice that. The plans are on the kitchen table. I've made coffee."

"But I'm also the inferior species, right?" I scoff, shoving back the covers, climbing out of bed and moving past him into the hallway.

"That was a low fucking blow," Beast admits as we stride down the stairs.

"True though, at least part of it," I say as I reach the kitchen table and glance at the plans laid out there.

"*None* of it's true," Beast argues, pulling out a chair and sitting down next to me. He hands me a mug of coffee with cream. I take a sip, tasting the sweetness of honey.

"You know how I take my coffee?" I ask.

He cocks his head to the side. "I pay attention."

"Hmm," I mutter, glancing at him behind the rim of my mug as I drink the perfectly made coffee and try to unravel everything that's gone down tonight. If he knows that I'm staring he doesn't make a point of it. Instead he takes a sip of his own coffee and looks at the plans, a little crease forming between his eyes.

"Can I ask you something?" I ask eventually.

"Sure," he replies, focusing back on me as he places his mug on the table.

"Why?"

"Why what?"

"Why do you want me to be Kate and not Grim?"

Beast chews on his bottom lip, then remembering that I know it's his tell, frees it from between his teeth. "Because you've got a good heart."

"So *you* think I'm a bleeding heart as well? Figures," I snort, shaking my head and focusing back on the plans, not really taking any of it in. Carter has been wanting to fix up Tales for a while now, and a couple of months back he gave me the responsibility to oversee the build starting in a few weeks. Of course I jumped at the chance. Now my *heart* isn't really in it. The fucking irony.

"No, I don't. But I do think you have the potential to be so much more than—"

"What? A criminal?" I roll my eyes.

"Well, I was gonna say a murderer, but yeah, that too," he says with a straight face.

"Pot, Kettle... Are you suddenly getting a conscience or something?" He doesn't break out into a smile at my response, or have that usual twinkle in his eyes. Tonight he's serious as fuck, and it's more unnerving than when he's pissed off or angry. "What?" I press.

"Do you think I wanted this life?" he asks me, adjusting his chair so that he's facing me. His knees brush against my thighs, and my stomach does a little flip at the slight contact.

Frowning, I adjust my position too, so that I'm facing him more. "You didn't?"

"No one chooses this life, Princess."

"They don't? Could've fooled me. Have you met the patrons of Tales?"

"Okay, so maybe some people walk into this life with their eyes wide open," he concedes. "But a lot of them ended up here because there was no other way. They were either brought up in it and they really didn't have a fucking choice, or they fell into it because they couldn't see any other way."

"And here's Carter calling *me* a bleeding heart," I sass, trying to make light of a serious discussion.

Beast sighs. "I don't enjoy killing people for a living, Princess."

"No?" My brows shoot up at that because a part of me always wondered.

"No." His finger taps at the table as he considers what to say next. "I'm numb to it now, and it's true that taking someone's life doesn't affect me, but I've never gotten any kicks out of it. I do what I need to do for myself or for the people I'm loyal to. That's it. That's all."

"So you're a lover not a fighter?" I joke, trying my damndest to make him smile, because serious Beast makes me way more nervous than any other version of him that I've met already.

"I'm both," he smiles then. It's a small, sexy smile, and I try my hardest not to stare at his handsome face for too long. "But I'm also a cold-blooded killer."

I grin, nudging his knee with mine. "You don't scare me, Beast."

The look he gives me next has my smile slipping from my face. "I know and that's a huge fucking problem."

"Why?"

"Because you *should* be scared. I'm not a good fucking man, Princess. None of us are. There's a darkness in me that I've come to accept. That will never go away. Not ever. I can't be saved, and I've long since lost the ability to fucking choose the man I want to be. *This life*, my life, is nothing to aspire to."

"You're well respected. Dom and the guys look up to you," I argue.

"Maybe so, that doesn't mean I'm not a bad man."

"They *like* you."

"Perhaps that's true, and maybe that's only because they're just the same as me. But how much can you truly like a man who could end your life just like that?" he says, snapping his fingers. "I'm respected, yes. Liked…? That's a matter of opinion."

"Connall would say otherwise."

"Connall is like a brother to me. We knew each other before."

"Before?" I ask him, keen to find out about his past and where he came from. All I know is that he was a fighter at Ransom's club and he grew up in Birmingham before moving here to work for my dad a year ago.

"Connall was a childhood friend. He lived in Shirley too. Moved to London a couple of years before me to work for his family. One of the reasons I took the job was so I could hang out with him again."

"You went to school together?" I ask.

Beast laughs, and this time his eyes twinkle. "We skipped school together. Got up to the usual shit."

"Like what?"

"Like pulling girls older than ourselves, smoking weed, getting into fights. You know, that kind of thing. Wherever trouble was, so were we. Best fucking years of my life."

"I can imagine." I grin, but when his smile drops, mine does too. "What is it?"

"I didn't make things easy for my mum. She was a good woman, and for a while I caused her a lot of grief. I regret it."

"Was it just you and her?" I ask tentatively.

His expression darkens. "I had a dad too. He was a dick."

I nod. "That bad, huh?"

Beast scrapes a hand over his face. "A womaniser and a fucking drunk. Mum got sick with cancer, and he left us to look after each other. She died when I was seventeen."

"I'm sorry," I say, reaching for him. My fingers wrap around his arm, squeezing gently. "That must've been hard."

"It was. Watching her waste away before my eyes with stomach cancer was the single fucking hardest thing I ever had to endure."

"Your dad didn't help at all?"

"No." Beast's jaw tightens at the memory. "But he did have the gall to turn up at the funeral half cut, saying how much he fucking loved her when he hadn't seen either of us in two fucking years. I lost my head and almost beat him to death. If Connall wasn't there to pull me off of him, I would've."

"Fuck," I whisper, meeting his gaze and feeling his rage like it's my own. To have to take care of your mum whilst she's dying of cancer is bad enough, but to do it alone? Fucking unforgivable.

"That day I went to the funeral as Roger, and left as Beast. I made *my* choice, and here I am."

"And your dad, is he still alive?"

"Barely. Last I heard he was living in an abandoned warehouse wasting away from liver disease and addiction. I don't give a fuck, honestly. He deserves whatever shitty life he's barely living."

"Yeah," I agree.

"You know, I often wonder if things would've turned out differently had my mum still been alive."

"Would they have?"

"Maybe. She was a straight talking woman. A *good* woman." He sighs, scraping a hand over his head. "And I might've been a good man for her. Or at least tried harder to be."

"You *are* a good man, Beast."

"I think you've got me all wrong, Princess," he scoffs, shaking his head.

"I don't think I do. You have a moral compass. Look what you did for that little girl and her aunt..." I say, knowing deep down that was all on him and had nothing to do with Carter.

That thought stings, because for a long time Carter had been my idol of sorts. Of late my rose tinted glasses have been removed, and I'm beginning to see him as others do.

"That was guilt," he mutters, taking another sip of his coffee.

"No," I disagree. "Maybe there's more of your mum inside of you than you think."

"It's a nice thought, but I know who and what I am, Princess, as should you."

"But I do."

"You don't. But that's irrelevant." He gives me a guarded look then asks, "Why did you come tonight when I told you not to?"

"Because no one tells me what I can and can't do," I reply, twisting my body away from him, and blindly staring at the plans.

"Maybe that's part of it, because we all know you're stubborn, but there's more to it than that."

"Carter wanted me there," I shrug. "I figured it would be for a good reason."

"Yeah, to put a bullet in Saxon's brain. He was testing you."

"And I failed."

"That all depends."

"On what?"

"On whose point of view."

"Carter's point of view is the only one that matters." Even as I say the words I hate the way it sounds.

"Really, the *only* one?" he questions, stealing another glance at me.

"Yours then?"

"Fuck no." He shakes his head, chuckling. "What I think is irrelevant when all is said and done."

"Yet you didn't want me to go to the club tonight. You didn't want me to shoot Saxon."

"Of course I fucking didn't."

"Why? Why does it matter to you so much?" I ask.

"I just wanted to give you time to make the right choice for you," he says with a wry smile. "I thought that was obvious."

"I get that, but *why* does it matter so much to you whether I make the right choice, *for me?*" I press, needing him to give me something, anything. There's an attraction between us. I felt it. I *feel* it. He cares for me beyond his role as my bodyguard. I know he does.

"Because sometimes all we need is someone to guide us in the right direction in order to save us from ourselves."

"And you're that person for me?"

"In this case, I guess I am." He side-eyes me, adding, "Don't think too much into it. I don't want you to get the wrong impression."

"And what impression would that be?"

"Tonight I overstepped."

"What, so now you're saying you shouldn't have said anything?"

"No, I'm not talking about that. I'm talking about the fact we danced at Macey's Bar."

"It was just a dance," I reply, knowing full well it was way more than that. I felt the way his heart hammered beneath my cheek, how warm his hands felt on my skin, how hard he was.

He frowns, shaking his head. "Whatever it was, it ain't happening again."

"Sure thing," I take a sip of my coffee pretending I don't give a shit.

For a moment we fall silent, but then I ask, "If you could go back and change the fact you beat up your dad, becoming Beast, would you?"

"Fuck no. I'd make sure I finished the job."

"Same applies to me," I reply. "If I could do tonight over again, I would. I should've shot Saxon. I should've shown Carter what I'm capable of. Now I just look like a fool. A woman who can't handle her emotions, who listened to her bleeding fucking heart instead of her head."

"You made the *right* choice," Beast insists, as I huff out a frustrated breath.

"No. I didn't. Whether you like it or not, I'm a Davidson. This life, this is who I am." Standing, I push back the chair. "Thanks for the coffee, but I'm suddenly not in the mood to go over the plans tonight."

"Princess..." Beast begins but I shake my head, cutting him off.

"It's *Grim*, okay?"

"But I kind of like the way Princess rolls off my tongue," he says, back to the flirty banter. It's like a security blanket for him, and it successfully puts an invisible barrier between us. I roll my eyes, but when I move to walk away, Beast grabs my wrist, his fingers wrapping around me tightly.

"There's one more thing I wanted to say."

My gaze flicks from his face to his hand squeezing my wrist. I swallow hard ignoring the way my skin heats from his touch. "Go on then."

"I appreciate the chat tonight. It's been a long time since I've talked with anyone about my mum. Thank you," he says earnestly.

"No problem," I reply, my stomach flipping over as his thumb glides over the sensitive skin of my wrist. I can feel my cheeks heating, but I ignore it. "Thank *you* for the coffee."

He looks from the heat creeping up my neck and cheeks

down to his hand holding my wrist and blanches like he's only just realised he's touching me. Dropping my wrist, he clears his throat and says, "If you're intent on being Grim, then I won't stop you. If that's the choice you make, then I'll watch your back. *Always*."

"I appreciate that." My expression softens, my heart thumping at his promise. He notices.

"But I'll do it in the same capacity as I do for Carter, as an *employee*. I'm not and never will be anything more than that to you. Are we clear?"

"Perfectly," I reply, moving to walk away. Only after a few paces, I stop and twist on my heel to face him. "But are you?"

"Am I what?"

"Clear?"

"I just said—"

"Oh, I heard the words that came out of your mouth, Beast, but perhaps you need to have a chat with your body, because that's telling a whole other story," I reply, before striding out of the kitchen and back to my room.

CHAPTER SIX

Medicine

"I don't fucking care, Grim!" Carter shouts from inside his office, a week after I shot Saxon in the head not more than a few metres from this spot. "You need to learn to toe the damn line!"

"Toe the line?" she scoffs, a bitter laugh escaping her lips as I push open the door without bothering to knock. Thank fuck the gym cleared out half hour ago, otherwise the patrons would be having a field day listening to this shit.

"What the fuck do you want?" Carter shouts as I step into the room. The vein in his forehead bulging with anger.

"Just a reminder that you've got a meeting scheduled in an hour."

Meeting, my arse. Carter's got an appointment with his regular fuck at The Crib Club, and an evening of gambling with his friends. Of course, that's a truth he'd rather keep to himself.

"And you couldn't fucking knock first?" he retorts, scowling.

"I did, you didn't hear," I lie.

The fact of the matter is, they've been arguing for the past ten minutes about Kate's *extracurricular* activities after Carter sent her to his strip club a few days ago to go over the books and learn a few things about running a successful business with Matilda, the manager. Only she ended up learning more than he'd bargained for. According to Matty, as we all call Matilda, she's really good at pole dancing. All that upper body strength she's gained from sparring in the ring with me, and yoga shit she likes to do, has given her the perfect tools to spin around a pole. She's flexible *and* strong.

Clearly, Carter's just found out and is pissing fire about it.

Can't say I blame him. The thought of Kate spinning around a pole in heeled platform shoes has got me feeling all kinds of ways too. Mostly dick-as-hard-as-rock ways, combined with whose-eyes-do-I-need-to-gouge-out ways. Seriously, *the fuck?*

Carter scrapes a hand through his hair and eyes Grim. "We'll talk about this later. I've got work to do."

"There's nothing left to talk about. I was having *fun*. The club was empty apart from the girls. It was no big deal. It wasn't as if I flashed my tits at a bunch of desperate men like *him*," she argues, folding her arms across her chest in anger as she jerks her chin at me.

Desperate? *Rude*. But also, thank fuck. My inner possessive arsehole takes a calming breath now that he knows the club was closed.

"Excuse me?" I raise a brow at her sass, which of course she fucking ignores. "I've never been desperate in my life. Women flock to me, not the other way around."

She smirks. "Whatever you tell yourself to make you feel better."

Carter's fist lands on the table with a loud thump, making Kate jump. "I don't give a fuck if you were having fun. You're a Davidson," Carter seethes, thumping his fist against the table to drive the point home. "You act accordingly. Do I make myself clear?"

"Crystal," she bites out.

"Good because I'm done with your shit tonight." Carter stands, pulling on his suit jacket and grabbing his phone and wallet from the desk, dismissing her with a wave of his hand. I can see the rage bubbling beneath her skin and she opens her mouth to argue, but I cut in.

"I've got the car pulled up out front."

"Good, I'll get Dom to drive me. You can take Grim home and make sure she fucking stays there."

"I don't need a babysitter!" Kate argues, taking the words right out of my mouth because I sure as fuck don't want to babysit her either. Every time we're alone together something stupid fucking happens and I need to keep my distance.

"What you need is a lesson in respect!" Carter roars, his face turning red as he stalks around his desk and strides over to Kate. She stands her ground, too stubborn to back down.

"Carter—" I begin.

"Stay the *fuck* out of this!" he shouts, turning his rage back on Kate. "Who the fuck do you think you're talking to?"

She glares back at him, her fire meeting his. "You once told me that I need to stand up for myself. That I should never let *anyone*, no matter who they are, walk all over me. I'm doing that now, *Dad*," she adds with as much venom as she can muster.

Fuck me, she's fierce tonight.

I wait for Carter to explode because the only thing he hates more than being disrespected is being called out. I ready myself to grab him, because whilst he's my boss and I respect him, I don't respect any man that hits a woman. They face off, nose to nose, and then Carter does something that surprises me, he laughs. Tipping his head back, he roars with fucking laughter. Kate's as shocked as I am by his sudden change of attitude.

"Carter?" she questions, looking far more bothered by his laughter than she was by his anger.

"You're right, I did," he eventually says, chuckling now.

Kate frowns. "Did what?"

"Tell you not to let anyone walk all over you, and whilst I'd like to point out that I'm not walking all over you, merely protecting our motherfucking *name*," he scowls, giving her a warning glare that quietens the words forming on her tongue, "I'm your dad and I know this world better than anyone. Don't act like a slut, or you'll be treated like one."

A slut? The fucking prick. "Carter," I warn, unable to help myself. Kate's no more of a slut than I am a fucking virgin.

"And you," he says, turning on me. "Do your fucking job."

"My job? And at what point haven't I done my job?" I ask, as calmly as humanly possible because what the actual fuck is this bullshit?

"Grim has a name to uphold. You know that. Making friends with the strippers at Nine Lives and spending her time there spinning around a motherfucking pole isn't what gets the job done, and neither is backing off from shooting the cunt who dared steal from us. Do. Your. Job!"

"*His* job?" Kate blurts out, as shocked as I am.

One, I'm not her dad, *he is*. Two, fuck him if he thinks I'm the kind of man who will mold a woman to suit my needs. Admittedly, I didn't like the thought of her dancing for another man, and am relieved to find out she was just having some fun with the girls, but who the fuck am I to tell her what she can and can't do? Ultimately that ain't my fucking business.

"You're my eyes and ears when I'm not around to watch over her," Carter continues. "Where the fuck were you when Grim was spinning around a pole, huh?"

Dragging your sorry arse out of The Crib Club, half-cut and ten grand down after losing a game of cards and shagging some top class pussy, I almost say, but hold my tongue. That answer will likely get me shot, and I'd rather not die tonight if I can help it.

"Noted. I'll do my *job* better," I say, even though it grinds my gears to do so.

Kate shakes her head, barking out a laugh and earning a glare from me. I don't need her going off about the fact I wasn't really doing my fucking job when I danced with her at Macey's the other night. I do actually want to keep my bollocks.

"Good!" He starts to move towards the door, then stops, spinning on his heels. "Actually scrap taking Grim home, you can start doing a proper job with her right the fuck now."

"What are you thinking?" I ask, because let's face it, I'm on unsteady ground here. Who the fuck knows what he's getting at. Carter has always had a short fuse, but I've never seen him go off on Kate like this before and I ain't about to get myself fired for not reading his fucking mind correctly.

"Take her to the shooting range. Don't leave until she can handle a gun."

"I know how to handle a gun, Carter," Kate protests, and she does. Carter's been teaching her how to shoot since she was a kid. What happened the other night had nothing to do with her form and everything to do with the thoughts *I'd* put in her head. "Carter, I know how to handle a gun," she repeats.

"That's what I'd thought. Only looks like you need a fucking reminder. Maybe you'll pay more attention if Beast is teaching you instead of me?" he asks, looking between us.

Neither of us respond. Not sure what point he's trying to make here, but I ain't about to second guess that either. Pretty sure if he thought I was fucking Grim I'd be dead already.

"Don't wait up. I expect it to be a long meeting," he adds, before striding from the room.

The second the front door to the club slams shut, Kate lets out a frustrated scream and storms into the gym taking her anger out on the punch bag hanging in the corner of the room. Her fists aren't wrapped and it isn't long before she's cursing the air blue from the splits to her knuckles.

"Not the wisest decision you made," I remark, leaning against the wall as I watch her pace up and down in fury, her knuckles dripping blood.

"Don't you fucking start! I was just having fun!"

"I wasn't talking about you pole dancing, though I'd like to have seen that." I smirk, and she picks up a discarded boxing glove and chucks it at my head. I catch it easily and drop it on the mat at my feet.

"Shut the fuck up!"

Biting back the laugh that threatens to spill from my lips, I approach her. "Let me see."

"I'm fine," she says, turning her back to me.

"You're bleeding," I point out, stepping around her. "Let me see."

She huffs out a breath, and realising I'm not going to give up, holds out her hands. "What have I taught you?" I ask, gently inspecting her wounds.

"Clearly, I'm shit at being a student as well as a daughter," she sasses back, hissing when I press on her middle knuckle that's not split but clearly tender, and will no doubt bruise.

"That hurt?"

"Not in the slightest," she lies.

"I don't think they're broken, but I will clean and wrap them up, that should help when we go to the shooting range."

"I'm not going," she says stubbornly.

"You're going," I reply just as stubbornly.

"What's the matter, scared you're going to get fired if I refuse to go with you?" she asks, as I grasp her elbow and walk her over to the small medical room just off the gym.

"Sit down."

"Oh my God, you are, aren't you?" she laughs. "The great Beast is really a fucking pussy."

"Sit the fuck down, Princess!" I growl, losing my fucking patience as I gather up some cotton wool pads, iodine solution and a bandage to wrap her knuckles once I've cleaned them up.

She's on a downward spiral tonight, and whilst I get where she's coming from, understanding she feels trapped by her father and resenting the fact that she can't let loose like any other person her age can, there's a line she's crossing with me right now and I'm not fucking cool with it.

"Or *what*?" she counters, picking a fight, clearly needing to take her frustrations out on someone, and that someone happens to be me.

"Or nothing. I'll leave you to fix yourself up and wait outside. Then I'll drive you to the shooting range just like Carter asked me to do."

"You didn't do what Carter wanted you to do the other night though, did you? Pretty sure he'd have something to say about you slow dancing with me."

"Listen, Princess," I snap, striding towards her so quickly that she stumbles back, her arse dropping to the gurney. "If you think for one second I'm going to stand here and listen to this bullshit, you can think again. You're angry at Carter, I get it, but don't take your shit with him out on me. I'm just doing my fucking job!"

She snorts with derision. "Like you were doing your job the other night?"

"We've gone over this already. It won't happen again."

We stare at each other, a series of mingled breaths and heavy breathing as I stand between her parted legs, my hands flat on the gurney beside her hips as she leans away from me. I hadn't even realised I'd gotten so close, and right now I can't seem to back the fuck up either.

"Why not?" she asks eventually, and her voice is so quiet, so tinged with disappointment that I can't help being affected by it.

Fuck, I want to pull her in my arms and reassure her that one day *I'll* be the man who will treat her the way she deserves to be treated and not talked down to or ridiculed like her dad has been doing lately, but I don't, because what's worse than hope... False hope. So, instead I give her the truth.

"I can't get involved with my boss's daughter."

"Can't or won't?"

"Both."

"So you've thought about it?"

"What gave you that impression? I overstepped once," I counter evenly. If she thinks she can get me to admit I'm attracted to her, she can think again. "Now give me your damn hands."

"I'm pretty sure this is overstepping," she murmurs, shifting forward an inch as I move closer.

"Nope, this is me taking care of you," I reply, pressing my hips against the edge of the gurney so that I can keep my bastard dick in check.

"Exactly. This isn't part of your job description."

"I'm your bodyguard—"

"Babysitter," she interrupts.

"Bodyguard," I insist, trying not to pay attention to the way her inner thighs rub against my legs as she shifts on the gurney, but failing spectacularly. "And it's my job to keep you safe, to take care of you."

Her eyes twinkle at that and I ready myself for her smart-arsed reply. There's a lot that I like about Kate, and that starts with her fiery nature and continues with her smart mouth, everything else is just gravy. She makes me smile like no one else. She's like a medicine to my grumpy arse, moody-as-fuck nature. I shouldn't like that but fuck, I do.

"Tomayto, Tomahto," she replies with a huge grin.

"Pretty sure you're getting on my last fucking nerve," I grumble, unscrewing the cap of the iodine solution and soaking the cotton wool, refusing to acknowledge how she's affecting me, but secretly loving it.

"Ditto," she replies, eyes dropping to my crotch and rising back upwards. She's smirking now, and if she were anyone else, I'd lay her over my lap and smack her arse for being so damned infuriating.

"Hand," I demand.

Rolling her eyes, she rests her palm in mine. "Fine."

I do my damndest not to react to the way her touch makes my dick jerk and my balls tingle. Instead, I concentrate on blotting her skin and clearing up the blood. When I'm happy she's cleaned up, I gently press against each knuckle, and the bones in her hand and fingers to make sure she's not got a fracture.

"I think you're good," I say, and grabbing the bandages, wrap her knuckles, tying them off. My fingers linger on her skin longer than they should and, of course, she takes this as a perfect opportunity to push the boundaries between us some more.

"Don't I get a kiss better too?" she asks, a small smile tugging up her perfect cupid's bow lips.

Damn her.

If she were mine for the night, the things I'd do to her. I imagine sliding my hands into her hair, fucking her mouth with my tongue and dry-humping her on this gurney until she comes, just to show her that she shouldn't ask for something she can't fucking handle. Then I'd give her all those things, until she was so turned on that she'd be begging me to make her come again and again and again.

"*Beast?*"

"We should head over to the shooting range now," I reply, blinking away those dangerous thoughts. I chuck the bloody cotton pads in the bin and put the iodine solution and cotton wool back in the medicine cabinet.

She sighs, standing. "Yeah, I guess we should."

With my back still turned to her, I take a moment to clear my head and will my dick to deflate. Every time I'm alone with her things get intense, and it's a sucker punch to the gut every damn time. I don't like the feeling of wanting something I can't have. It's fucking with my head.

"Look, I'm sorry if I was out of order tonight," she says, sensing my change of mood. It's a genuine apology and I take it as one.

"No need to apologise to me, Princess," I reply, giving her a tight smile as I turn around to face her.

Her returning look is one that I can't interpret, and one that makes me a little uncomfortable if truth be told. I take pride in being able to read people well, or at least get a handle on their motivations for doing something, but with Kate it's not so easy. Sometimes she's an open book, other times she's so closed off it's hard to know what she's feeling, let alone take a punt at what she might be thinking. Either way, right now she's shutting down in a way that I don't particularly like but have no business trying to prevent her from doing.

"Shall we go?" I ask her as she chews on the inside of her lip.

"I don't suppose I have a choice."

"No," I agree.

"And yet the other night you tried to convince me that I did, that I could walk away from this life. Only we both know that's impossible. *You* think it's because of Carter and his hold over me, but I know the truth."

"And what's that?"

"Despite my frustration today, despite the fact I hate Carter curbing my fun and controlling my actions, I *want* to be Queen of Tales, and I will do whatever it takes to get there."

I frown. "Even killing someone?"

"Yeah, even that."

CHAPTER SEVEN

Secrets and Lies

"Well that was fun," I remark dryly as Beast and I step out of the shooting range and head towards his car. We've spent the last hour shooting the shit out of the bullseye paper target. Pretty sure we're evenly matched in terms of accuracy and I'm more than positive I can handle a fucking gun.

"Your form is good, Princess. I'm impressed," Beast replies, reaching for the passenger door before I can open it myself.

His fingers brush against mine and I remove them quickly, shifting slightly out of the way so that I don't do something crazy like step into him and drag my nose against the open collar of his shirt just so that I can breathe him in. He smells good enough to eat and I find my gaze dropping to his crotch and lingering there. I've never given a man a blowjob, but I'm pretty sure I'd enjoy giving him one.

"Princess?" Eyes snapping up, I give him a bland smile that

he returns with a broad one of his own. "In you get," he says, pulling the door open.

Since when does he open car doors for me? I wrinkle my nose, not sure how to take this gentlemanly behaviour. Is this how he treats all his women? No wonder he's so popular with the ladies. "Thanks?"

"Don't look so surprised," he says, chuckling as I climb into my seat and pull the door shut.

"What was that?" I ask him the minute he climbs into the car.

"What was what?"

"The whole opening the door for me thing."

Beast snorts. "Why does it bother you so much? I was being a gent."

"You've never done that before," I reply.

"Then I apologise for being a shitty human. I will endeavour to open more doors for you in the future."

"Have you taken something?" I ask, side-eyeing him as he puts the car in drive and we head out onto the street. "You're acting weird. First the compliment, then opening the door for me. It's not like you."

"Not taken a damn thing," he shrugs.

I study his side profile, waiting for him to burst out laughing. He doesn't.

"That's good then," I reply lamely as I look out of the window and blink away the image of his straight nose, cut cheekbones and sharp jaw covered in a two day old stubble. His kind of attractiveness should be outlawed. I'm pretty sure he's a danger to my health.

Turning my attention to the passing scenery, I try to push

all thoughts of Beast's attractiveness out of my head and focus on my rumbling stomach that's decided to make itself known. I haven't eaten since breakfast and my stomach feels like my throat has been cut given it's now dark and pushing eight o'clock in the evening.

"Hungry?" Beast asks.

"Starving," I admit, glancing over at him.

"I know a place. Want to join me for dinner?" he asks all casually like it's no big deal, and it didn't just sound like he'd asked me on a date. Probably because he hadn't.

It's not like we haven't eaten together before. Beast spends an awful lot of time over at my house purely because he's always needed by Carter for one thing or another. He's even got a room at the house in case work meetings go late and he needs a place to crash. That and the fact that Carter insists I'm not left alone whilst he does fuck knows what, with fuck knows who. When I said Beast is a glorified babysitter, I meant it.

"Sure, why not?"

"Great."

Half an hour later we're parked down a quiet side street in Soho. I jump out of the car before Beast can open the door for me. It feels weird waiting for a man to do something that I can do for myself just as easily. Besides, I'm getting hangry and need to eat something before I set on someone.

"This place serves food?" I ask, looking up at the nondescript building in front of me. It has blacked-out windows and a boarded-up door.

"It's a speakeasy," he explains.

"You're shitting me?!"

"Nope. It's owned by the Ricci family."

"*The* Ricci family? Aren't they Italian mobsters?"

"Ain't we gangsters?"

I laugh. "Point taken. How do you know about this place?"

"I know a lot of people, Princess."

"And this speakeasy doubles up as a restaurant."

"Best Italian food in London, for those with the password, that is," he replies with a smirk as he strides over to the boarded-up door and raps his knuckles against the wood. A wooden slot slides open at about eye level and dark brown eyes with thick black eyebrows peer out at us. They crinkle at the edges when they notice who's standing at the door.

"Password?" a thick, heavily accented male voice commands.

"Amore," Beast replies.

Love.

Having an Italian housekeeper has come in handy it would seem. The question is why is Beast taking me to a speakeasy where the password is *love*. Am I reading too much into this?

"Welcome Beast, I see you've brought a friend," the voice replies as the sound of several locks unclick and the door swings open revealing a handsome, smartly dressed man of about thirty years old with neatly groomed black hair and perfect white teeth.

"Good to see you, Romeo," Beast replies as the two men shake hands. "This is Miss Davidson. Carter's daughter."

"Ah! Yes, I've heard much about you."

"You have?"

"Beast speaks very highly of you," he replies with a wide grin as he opens the door and steps aside to let us in. "Welcome to Sapori."

I glance up at Beast, a frown pulling my brows together. "You do?" I whisper.

He just shrugs, a smile in his eyes as he rests his hand on the small of my back. "Ladies first."

My skin tingles beneath his touch and I'm hyper aware of his nearness as we follow Romeo down a darkened hallway and a set of stairs. The walls and floors are painted black, and a strip of red LEDs running either side of the hallway gives us just enough light to see where we're going.

Stopping in front of a door at the bottom of the stairs, Romeo turns to me with a warm smile that really doesn't befit his reputation, then says, "I think you'll enjoy what Sapori has to offer, Beast certainly has in the past."

"Thank you," I reply, not quite sure how to interpret that comment, then suddenly not caring as Romeo opens the door and we look down into wonderland. "Wow!" I exclaim, totally taken aback by what I see before me.

"You like?" Romeo asks, moving to one side to allow us to step onto the balcony overlooking the room below.

"It's incredible," I say, my gaze taking in every detail with more than a little bit of awe and wonder.

The whole room is wrapped in floor to ceiling stained glass windows that are backlit by spotlights instead of daylight given this is a basement. Splatters of prismatic light filter through the different coloured panes of glass and it's as though an artist has painted the room in a flurry of colour that is both sensual and rich all at the same time.

Couples sit at every table, candles flickering between them as they eat, enjoying the sultry sound of a woman singing. Her voice is pure, undiluted sex, and I search the room, finding the owner of such an incredible voice perched on a stool next to a baby grand piano in the corner of the room. She sings whilst an older gentleman with slicked back grey hair and a handlebar moustache plays.

"Who's that?" I can't help but ask as Romeo guides us down the ornate gold staircase to a small table tucked into the corner of the room that's slightly set back from the main dining area affording more privacy than the other tables.

"That's my brother's wife, Nina Ricci. She's outstanding, don't you agree?"

"I've never heard anyone sing so beautifully," I reply in awe, staring at her like the rest of the captive audience is.

Not only does her voice sound like pure sex, her figure is to die for. She has the kind of dips and curves and softness that most, if not all, men find attractive. My figure is far more lean from spending the past year training with the fighters of Tales and sparring in the ring with Beast. I'm envious of her milky white breasts confined in a corset top that jiggle when she sings and can't help but appreciate her auburn hair that falls in waves around her face. She's wearing a fascinator with thick black lace attached, covering her face. There's something about the way she holds herself that's melancholy, and I have the urge to get a closer look at her, to set eyes on the face of the woman who sings like temptation personified.

"Take a seat. I will bring you our finest red wine produced in my family's vineyard back home in Oltrepò Pavese," Romeo says, his gaze flicking to his sister-in-law on the other side of the room. I want to ask why a woman who sings like she does isn't in the spotlight, but hold my tongue. It's not my business to know.

"Sounds good, Romeo," Beast says, pulling out my chair so that I can sit down.

I blink up at him, completely thrown off guard by his continued gentlemanly behaviour and the wonder of such a place. It's a far cry from what I've grown up used to. Tales is a fight club filled with sweaty, testosterone fuelled men, and on most weekends, blood and spilt booze. This place oozes sophistication. It's classy, reeks of money and refinery. I love everything about it.

"This place is amazing," I exclaim, my head filling with so many ideas for the future of Tales, and the Davidsons' family business. Imagine a fight club that's just as sophisticated as this place? We could have the rawness and grit of a bloody fight between two worthy opponents set against a backdrop that reeks of elegance and finesse. Perhaps we could even provide similar entertainment like this between fights?

"It is, isn't it? The Ricci family know their shit. Good food, fine wines, great entertainment and a club to be envious of."

"Do you know her well?" I ask, wondering how friendly he is with Nina Ricci. She's married, and if I know Beast as well as I think I do, he doesn't go after married women, especially women married to acquaintances of his. That's a whole mess I think he's got the smarts not to get embroiled in.

"I've never met her formally, though we've been in the same room on occasion over the years. Her husband Alfonso keeps her to himself mostly. She only sings here when he's in London on business, and never mingles with the guests. I didn't know she'd be singing here tonight. We got lucky, I guess."

I nod, smiling up at Romeo who's returned with a bottle of wine.

"Would you like to taste it first?" he asks, uncorking the bottle and pouring a drop into my glass, not Beast's. That small token of respect makes me like him even more than I already do from first impressions. I'm so used to everyone speaking over me to Carter, or any other man that I might be accompanying, including Beast, that him not offering the first taste to Beast is a good sign. This man is respectful of women. I like that.

"No, I'm sure it's delicious," I reply, feeling my cheeks heat from his attention. He's a good looking man, but far too clean-cut for my tastes. I like my men a little rough around the edges.

"Very well," he replies, pouring us both a glass then sets the bottle on the table between us. "Tonight we are serving a selection of antipasti to start, including tender grilled octopus with zesty salmoriglio sauce. For primi we have a creamy mushroom risotto with truffle and for secondi, a beef brisket with red wine sauce on a layer of fluffy potato."

I flick my gaze at Beast whose expression remains deadpan. When he asked if I wanted dinner, I thought we'd swing by the local chip shop. I wasn't expecting a fine dining experience.

"Wow, that's a lot of food."

"I've not finished yet, bella," he continues with a wink.

"There's more?"

"Sì, we have formaggi e frutta and dolce."

"Whatever you serve, I'm sure it'll be banging," Beast says.

"Perfecto," Romeo responds, taking that as his cue to leave. "I shall return with the antipasti shortly."

"Thank you," I reply, watching him as he strides across the room, stopping to talk briefly to other couples as he makes his way to the kitchen to place our order. "He's very attentive."

"He's a very astute businessman," Beast says, picking up his glass of wine and taking a sip. "A Good looking fucker too."

I tip my head to the side. Is that a thread of jealousy I detect in his voice? Deciding that I need to have some fun with Beast, I bite my bottom lip, sucking it into my mouth before letting it go with a slight smile. "You're right, he is. I didn't see a wedding ring..." I muse, allowing my gaze to find Romeo in the room.

"Absolutely fucking not," Beast replies, taking the bait just like I knew he would. "He's old enough to be your dad!"

"What can I say, I'm partial to an older man... Besides I'd say he's more in the age bracket of an older brother, rather than a dad, wouldn't you say?"

"I don't much give a fuck either way. He's not for you."

"What's the matter, Beast? Jealous?" I ask, returning my attention to him. "I'm betting with a name like that he's outstanding in bed too."

Beast clamps his mouth shut as Romeo returns with the antipasti, laying the dishes out on the table. My stomach rumbles, and I give him a sheepish smile. "It smells so good, thank you, Romeo," I say, giving him my most flirtatious smile.

Out of the corner of my eye Beast's fingers curl into fists and I suppress my glee. You can't tell me that there's nothing between us when he gives me cues like that. Either he's playing games with me or he's fooling himself. Maybe it's a bit of both?

"You're welcome. Matteo, my head waiter, will serve the rest of your dinner. I need to speak with Nina for a moment. If you'll excuse me?"

"Of course, thank you for your hospitality," I say, smiling up at him as he rests his hand briefly on my shoulder in a very platonic way before striding over to Nina who's currently lingering by the bar nestled in the corner of the room. Piano music still plays, but without her voice harmonising it's just not the same.

"Romeo is a fair man, but he can be ruthless. You might want to remember that when you give him fuck-me eyes," Beast says evenly, and even though his voice is level, calm, his shoulders are stiff as he leans forward and helps himself to a forkful of octopus.

I wait for him to put the food in his mouth and chew before commenting. "And you might want to remember that you're *not* my dad. You're just my bodyguard, right?"

He chews slowly, his jaw working as he stares at me. Watching him eat shouldn't be a turn on, but it is. God help me, it is. My eyes track to his tattooed throat, watching as his Adam's apple bobs up and down as he swallows. Why am I so obsessed with his throat and the intricate tattoos that darken his skin there? Why am I so obsessed with him full-stop?

"Eat," he demands.

I smirk then allow my gaze to fall to the dishes laid out between us, not sure where to start first. Picking up my fork, I decide to try the octopus too. Spearing the meat, I lift it to my mouth instantly tasting the garlic followed by this tangy hit of lemon. It's delicious and I can't help but hum in appreciation as I chew.

"You like that?" Beast asks, shifting forward in his seat and resting his elbows on the table as he watches me, his gaze flicking from my eyes to my mouth and back again. The way he asks the question seems filled with so much more than a general interest in whether I like what I'm eating.

"So much," I reply, needing more. I go to spear another

piece of octopus, but instead he pinches a large green olive stuffed with capers between his forefinger and thumb and holds it to my lips.

"Try this."

"I can feed myself, you know," I say, locking eyes with him. His returning look is one that makes my skin heat and sends tingles of awareness scattering down my spine.

"Yeah, I know," he replies softly, the candlelight flickering in his eyes as he regards me. "I just thought maybe your knuckles might still be sore."

"They're not."

"Still..."

The tension between us grows as he swipes the olive against my bottom lip. Without thinking too much about it, I allow the tip of my tongue to taste what he's offering before pulling back slightly and saying, "I think this goes way beyond your duty as babysitter."

He smiles with something more than friendly banter glistening in his eyes. "Oh, I don't know. Don't babysitters usually have to feed the kids they look after?"

And there he goes again, pushing my buttons.

"I'm not a kid—!"

But my sentence is cut short when he places the olive in my mouth and I find myself too distracted by the taste of the olive exploding on my tongue to hold onto my anger.

"Chew," he instructs with a smirk.

I chew, and his eyes don't leave my lips the whole time that I do.

"More?"

"You want to continue to feed me?" I ask.

"Only if you want me to."

"If this isn't overstepping, I don't know what is," I say, spearing a prawn soaked in oil.

His smile falters, as if he suddenly realises what he's doing and reality sinks back in. I see him hesitate, his hand lowering and an apology hovering on his lips.

"This is just a bit of fun, right? It doesn't mean anything?" I ask, lifting the prawn to his lips. "What's the matter, Beast, afraid you might like it?"

"Nah, but I am worried *you* might like it a little too much," he retorts in an even tone that belies the flicker of apprehension in his gaze.

"We've established that you're a tease and that I'm game. Why don't we just bench the complexities of our relationship and just go with the flow?" I suggest as calmly as possible.

He narrows his eyes at me, studying my face as though he's waiting for me to crack and show how I'm truly feeling beneath the calm facade.

I don't.

There's something to be said about playing it cool, and whilst on the surface I might appear to be at home in my skin, confident in my actions, I'm really a fireball of lust and want.

My knickers are soaked. *Drenched*, in fact.

As soon as I get home I'm going to relieve the tension that's been building between us all bloody afternoon. For now, squeezing my thighs together will have to do.

"I'm not a tease," he says and this time it's my turn to laugh.

"Yeah, and I don't have a piercing in my clitoral hood."

When his mouth drops open in shock I take the opportunity to fill it with the prawn. "Chew."

He chews, chasing the prawn down with a glug of wine, swallowing hard.

"Tell me you're joking," he says.

"Tell me you're not a tease."

"I'm not a fucking tease."

I grin, a smile pulling up my lips. "Yeah, and I don't have a piercing in my clitoral hood."

He narrows his eyes at me then stabs a prawn with his fork none too gently. "I think you need to try one," he says, lifting a prawn to my parted lips.

I take it between my teeth, a droplet of oil sliding down my chin as he slowly removes the fork from my mouth. Reaching up, I try to swipe the oil away, but he gets there first, the pad of his thumb gliding up my chin and capturing the droplet. He brings his hand to his lips, and sucks the oil free from his thumb. His plump lips taking it all the way into his mouth, his cheeks hollowing out as he sucks, before he pulls his thumb free. It takes every single last drop of restraint not to melt in a puddle right here on the chair. Fortunately for us both, I'm better at keeping myself in check.

I *think*.

"Delicious," he mutters, and I can't help it, I let out a nervous laugh that sounds far too mocking than I'd intended. "What's so funny?"

"Seriously, you don't know?"

"Know what?" he asks as he grabs his glass of wine and knocks it back in one long gulp. I'm pretty sure his cheeks are flushing, though I can't be one hundred percent certain, given all of the dappled light from the stained glass windows. I don't think I've ever seen Beast blush, it's endearing.

"This," I say, waving a hand between us. "You're flirting with me."

"I'm not," he retorts, grabbing a slice of bread and slathering it in aioli before taking a huge bite, the sauce dripping out of the corner of his mouth. All the refinement of a moment ago of gently spearing the food and tenderly feeding it to me is now gone. He's acting more beast than gentleman and I can't help but find that amusing. I've unsettled him. Good, now he knows what it feels like.

"Oh come on, admit it. We're on a date. You've taken me on a date," I tease.

"No, I haven't," he argues. "You were hungry and so was I, figured we could eat together."

"So bringing me to an intimate speakeasy and feeding me all whilst staring into my eyes like it's *me* you want to feast on wasn't what you were doing just now?" I ask with a sweet smile, internally giggling at how flummoxed he is.

"I—" he splutters, dropping the slathered bread onto his side plate and swiping at his mouth with the back of his hand.

"Because as much as I've enjoyed this meal so far," I interrupt, "Maybe it's me who should put some boundaries between us, given everything you've already said tonight? You *can't and won't* make a move on your boss's daughter, right?"

"Princess," he says, and it comes out like an apology that makes me feel far more awkward about what's happening between us than his flirty behaviour ever has. I don't like the sound of regret in his voice. It pisses me off.

"Look, I'm not someone you can come onto one minute, then disregard the next. I'm not your plaything, Beast," I say, and despite the relaxed smile I give him, I mean every word.

"You're right." He nods, swiping a hand over his face. "Looks like I need a lesson in chivalry. I wasn't thinking. I meant no harm. I apologise."

"You're only human," I reply with an easy shrug. "Can't say I blame you for wanting what I've got to offer."

Beast shakes his head, and I see him shutting down, all the flirtatiousness making way for seriousness once more. "And now that I've been effortlessly put into my place, shall we just eat using our own forks this time?"

"Sure," I reply, digging into the food, the rest of our conversation drowned out by Nina's seductive voice singing as we eat.

I feel Beast's eyes on me throughout the whole meal and there's no denying that Beast wants me as much as I want him. He can lie to himself all he wants, but I know his secret.

I also know what it means for us.

Nothing good, at least not where Carter's concerned.

CHAPTER EIGHT

She Drives Me Crazy

"Beast, eyes on the prize man," Dom says, shoving his fist into my bicep a few days later. "Look at that piece of ass, fucking delicious."

Lifting my hazy-as-fuck gaze from the bottom of my triple shot glass of bourbon, I look up at Nancy shaking her arse before me, the strobe lights of the strip club fucking with my ability to see straight. Well, that and the half bottle of bourbon I've sunk in the last hour. Yeah, she's fit. Sexy as fuck, in fact, but these past couple weeks my dick has decided to go on a leave of fucking absence and nothing and no one is turning me on. Which is a fucking shame because I really could use a good fuck to clear my head.

"Pretty," I mumble, knocking back the burning liquid and jerking my chin towards Natalie, tapping my glass. She gives me a warm smile that's filled with the promise of a really good fuck.

Dom chuckles as she walks over. "Ah, I get it. You're after the brunette tonight, not the blonde. Fancy a change of scenery?" he asks.

"Something like that," I agree, holding out my glass as Natalie fills it up.

We've slept together before, several times actually. She's a good lay and whilst I appreciate her come-hither eyes, my cock is in a coma, and I'm starting to worry it might never fucking wake up again.

"Are you free later?" Natalie asks me, earning her a glare from Nancy who doubles-down with her provocative dancing and starts shaking her beautiful pendulous tits in a way that has Dom shifting uncomfortably in his seat. Fuck it, he can have her. She knows the score, they all do. I'm very good to the women I choose to take into my bedroom, but I'm not the type of man you tie down.

"Sorry, sweetcheeks, I'm busy."

Natalie nods, her fingers curling around my forearm briefly. "Shame, I've missed you."

Dom snorts out a laugh, and without taking his eyes off of Nancy—who's doing her best to make me jealous—says, "Babe, get in line. Beast's cock is legendary."

"Oh, don't I know it," she laughs, pressing a cheeky kiss against my cheek before sashaying off towards the table where Carter is entertaining the *King*, aka no-one-knows-his-real-name-because-he's-a-secretive-certifiable-wankstain of epic proportions. I don't like him.

His *name* precedes him, and nothing about him is good. I mean, nothing about any of us is good, but at least I don't beat on women. That dick has a cock so small he feels the need to take out his underwhelming manhood on every woman he abuses. The prick. But Carter does what Carter wants, and despite my advice not to get mixed up with the King, he fucking ignored me.

So, here we are.

I take another swig of my drink, relishing the burn. I really shouldn't be drinking this much, but Dom and the rest of the guys have got this. Besides, it's my day off. Kind of. Getting pissed isn't usually my bag, but I'm in need of forgetting a certain someone who is so beyond off limits, it's not even funny.

"Hey, Beast." Sammy, another stripper and regular fuck, waves from the other side of the club. She gives me a smile, coyly biting her lip like she's an innocent virgin. I can confirm she is neither innocent nor virginal.

"Hey!" I grunt, tipping my head in acknowledgment.

"Fuck, I don't know how you do it, man," Dom says, side-eying me. "They're *all* hot for you. Every single dancer in the club, *and* all the staff. Even the fucking men."

"What can I say," I shrug, "Everyone wants a ride on my dick."

"Seriously though, how the fuck do you do it?"

"That's easy, mate. I put their needs first and no woman leaves my bed unless they've had multiple orgasms. It's a pride thing. I ain't about wham, bam, thank you ma'am. You should try it sometime."

"Dom pleasing a woman? He's got a better chance pleasing his mum," Mark comments as he steps up beside us.

"Fuck you, prick," Dom retorts with a smirk as he looks up at his best mate who was also supposed to be off tonight, but clearly Carter had other ideas.

"You know it's true. Or maybe that's me who's got a better chance at pleasing your mum. How is Dolly anyway?" Mark asks, winking at me.

Dom snorts with laughter. "Funny ha ha! You're just jealous because your scrawny arse can't get the girls."

We all laugh then, because there isn't one soldier of Carter's who could be classed as scrawny. Mark is a big guy too, and with his Mediterranean heritage, his dark hair and deep blue eyes are a firm favourite with the ladies. He's a good man. Solid. Fucking hilarious too, especially when he starts winding up the fighters of Tales. He never means any disrespect and it's all harmless banter.

"Everything alright, Mark? Didn't think you were on duty tonight," I say, fist bumping him.

"Wasn't supposed to be, but Carter called me in given we've got an extra special guest to look after tonight."

"Yeah, he's certainly fucking special," I mutter, eyeing the King as I knock back another mouthful.

"Well, I'd better get over there. Catch you at the club for training soon, yeah?"

"Yeah," we both reply in chorus as he heads over to the table.

"So," Dom begins as soon as Mark's out of earshot, "You're a selfless lover then. Fuck, I'd never have thought it."

"Back to that again? Anyone would think that you're obsessed with my cock," I say smirking, my attention drawn back to Nancy as she drops to her hands and knees on the small stage in front of us and wobbles her assets. Dom's tongue practically rolls out of his mouth at the display.

"We're all obsessed with your cock," Nancy says, licking her lips before giving Dom a face massage with her tits. "Beast is a man of his word. The last time we fucked I squirted all over his dick. Didn't I, babe?"

"You sure did, Nancy, you sure did." I chuckle, remembering only too well. That was one hell of a night. She's a good lay, and intelligent too. A perfect woman for whoever's lucky enough to nab her. That person just ain't me.

"Fucking hell, Beast. Talk about a lot to live up to!" Dom groans as Nancy pulls back and shimmies upwards onto her high heels. He looks fucking bereft that her tits are no longer smothering him. Ordinarily there's a no touching rule in the club, but that doesn't apply to us. We've got certain perks as Carter's soldiers, and so long as the ladies are willing, we get more than a lap dance.

"I suggest you take a leaf out of my book and you might even get a rep like me. Treat a woman right and she'll tell all her friends. Treat 'em wrong and you got yourself a problem. Women can be vindictive and I quite like keeping my balls."

The truth is, if a woman were to spend a night with me, I would make her the single focus of my universe, but it's never a permanent thing. For one night I love them hard, and fuck them even harder, but as soon as the sun rises on a new day, I'm off. It's better for everyone that way.

The only woman... *girl*, that has had more attention from me than any other is Kate and that's only because I'm her fucking glorified babysitter. I *have* to spend more time with her. Well, that's what I tell my bastard dick when it gets other ideas about how much time I should be spending with her. Speaking of which, my phone vibrates. I already know it's Kate. She's the only one who has the balls to call me on my day off.

"What?!" I snap, covering the mouthpiece and indicating to Dom that I need to take the call.

"Princess?" he asks.

I nod, flicking my eyes to Carter who's still deep in conversation with the King. "Looks like he's in for the long haul."

"Me and the guys have got this," Dom says, waving me away. "Besides, it's strictly your day off. Shouldn't you be buried deep in some hot chick and not chasing around after Princess?"

"Yeah, I fucking should," I reply bitterly, wishing it was that simple. If only I could lose myself in some sweet pussy without feeling like I'm cheating on someone who doesn't even fucking belong to me and never will.

"Good luck with that, man," Dom says, chuckling. The fucking bastard.

"ROGER!" Kate shouts down the line in frustration, loud enough for Dom to hear.

He barks out a laugh and I groan, striding away from him and towards the exit. "Who the fuck do you think you're screaming at?" I demand, pissed off that I don't even get the chance to wallow in alcohol all fucking afternoon, or better yet, some guilt-free sex.

"You answered the phone and then ignored me. What do you expect?" she answers back.

Fuck, this girl pushes all my buttons.

"I expect you not to call me on my day off, especially since I was enjoying watching a real woman shake her assets for me. What do you want?" I grind out.

She falls silent on the end of the line, and I feel like a first class dick. I made a promise to my mum that I'd never treat women the way my father treated her, and look at me being that exact same dick. Fuck. But I can't seem to get my head on straight around her, and my feelings have become even more fucking complicated ever since our meal at Sapori.

She was right, of course, to put me in my place, what cunt says one thing and then does another? I've been giving her mixed signals and it's gotta stop, but I shouldn't be an arsehole about it. This isn't her fault, it's mine. I'm the one with a fucking problematic dick that has a mind of it's own when it comes to Kate.

"Listen... Shit, you just caught me off guard. What can I do for you?" I ask, striding over to my car that I shouldn't even contemplate driving because I'm drunk as fuck.

"Can you come pick me up...?" she asks.

There's a vulnerability in her voice which immediately puts me on high alert. In many ways Kate is very different from her father, but when it comes to being tough she's a chip off the old block. So whatever's upsetting her, it's gotta be big for her to sound so upset.

"Where are you?" I bark out, pressing my thumb and finger against my eyelids. I really, really shouldn't have drunk this much.

"Eastside estate."

"You're at the children's home?"

"In the abandoned car park just along the street."

"I know the one. Why're you there?"

"Hud got into some shit, so I went to help. He's kinda fucked up right now."

"You want me to come get you *both*?"

"He needs some stitches, and I think he has a concussion."

"If it's that bad call him a fucking ambulance," I grunt, my head spinning from the booze. I need this shit like a hole in the head.

"He's got Bryce and Max to think of. They've only got a few weeks before they can leave the children's home and live with him, he doesn't need that kind of attention."

"Perhaps he should've thought of that before he got himself into whatever shit he's dragged you into. That prick should know better."

"He didn't drag me into anything, *I* chose to help him because that's what friends do."

"Yeah, yeah," I mutter, rubbing at my temple.

"Look, Beast, he's trying to do right by his brothers, and I'm trying to do right by him."

For some reason that just pisses me off more. She's so fucking loyal and the fact she's giving her loyalty to Hudson, a man not all that much younger than me, makes my blood boil. I don't even want to think about why that is.

"What's up with that relationship anyway? They aren't even his real family," I ask, forcing my thoughts to a less dangerous place.

Kate lets out a frustrated breath. "And Connall isn't your brother? Just because they're not blood, doesn't mean they aren't family. You know that better than anyone."

She's got a point, which I refuse to acknowledge because I've got a splitting fucking headache and a cock that keeps fucking twitching at the sound of her voice. "Are you hurt?" I growl instead, pressing the palm of my hand against my dick and mentally telling it to calm the fuck down. This is not fucking happening right now.

"Just a couple of bruises. Might have a broken rib..."

"The FUCK, Princess!" I yell, my concern for her making me lose my calm. "You're one royal pain in my arse!"

"Yeah, so you've told me repeatedly."

"Ah shit, I didn't mean that," I grumble under my breath, yanking open the door to my car, but the buzz in my head and the way the floor tips under my feet tell me I can't hold my drink as well as I thought.

"Can you come or not?" Kate asks, the crack in her voice causing a chasm to open up in my gut. How the fuck have I let her get under my damn skin like this? I should tell her to deal with her own shit. I don't.

"I'm a little drunk, Princess."

"Of course, you are," she retorts, getting my back up.

"It's my day off!" I remind her.

"Look, don't worry about it. I'll get him sorted myself."

"Just stay fucking put—"

She hangs up without bothering to acknowledge me.

"Fuck!" For half a minute I consider letting her get on with it. Then I remember that it's my job to take care of her, that I *can't* see her in trouble. "She needs a good fucking spanking," I mutter, then groan as my dick twitches, agreeing with me. Gritting my teeth, I fish my phone out of my jacket pocket and swipe the screen. With one eye squinted, I pull up the number I'm looking for and hit dial.

"Beast, what can I do for you?" Connall answers half a beat later.

"Fuck!" I exclaim. "Fuck! Fuck! Fuck!"

"Beast? Are you gonna tell me what's up?"

"Yeah, shit," I reply, forcing myself to concentrate on our

conversation and not thoughts of Princess over my knee. "Can I ask you a favour?"

"You don't need to ask me that. Of course. What is it?" he asks.

"I need picking up from Nine Lives. *Princess* has got herself in a jam and needs some help, and I'm too cut to drive."

"Have you been getting high on stripper pussy?"

"No, just half a bottle of bourbon."

"You're drunk? That's new."

"Don't lecture me, I needed to let loose a bit. Besides, it's my day off."

"It's your day off and you're not six feet deep into some prime pussy? Hmm, are you sick?"

"I ain't feeling it."

"My point exactly..." His voice trails off and I can hear the smirk in his voice. "You sure the problem ain't the fact that you're desperate for some *Princess* pussy?" Connall asks, bursting out laughing. If I didn't really need his help, I'd tell him to fuck right off. The fact that he's picked up on something I'm trying very hard to deny ain't good.

"Funny! Can I get a lift or what?" I ask dryly.

"Mate, you can't kid a kidder..."

"Why the fuck does everyone think I'm interested in her? For fuck's sake. Princess is not, and never will be, anything more than a job to me," I say firmly.

Ever since my chat with Princess I've tried putting space between us. For one stupid fucking moment, I let my emotions get a hold of me and let her in, telling her about my mum and my cunt of a dad. Not to mention fucking dancing with her, then taking her out to dinner a few days later. I can't afford to blur the lines again.

"Yeah, and I'm not Irish," Connall snorts.

"Fuck off. She's my boss's kid, not my type whatso-fucking-ever."

"What's that saying…" Connall muses, then puts on a fake posh British accent. "Ah, yeah, *he doth protest too much.*"

"FUCK OFF!"

Connall barks out a laugh. "Fine, I'll be there in five."

"Oh, and Connall?" I say quickly, rubbing at the headache that's beginning to pound into my skull like an inexperienced virgin fucking a woman for the first time.

"Yeah?"

"Bring me a coffee. I need to sober up and fast."

Connall laughs. "To be sure," he says before hanging up, his laughter ringing in my ears.

I glance back at my phone, swiping the screen until I find the tracker app that I also sneakily added to her phone after she fucked off to Macey's without Carter's permission. Clicking on it, I frown as I watch the little dot that represents Kate blinking up at me. She's no longer at the carpark but is moving towards the recreation ground behind it.

"Where the fuck do you think you're going?" I mutter, knowing that as soon as I've dealt with her shit I'm gonna need another bottle of bourbon and a willing pussy to sink my tongue into.

Fucking Kate. *She drives me crazy.*

CHAPTER NINE

Trouble

"Where the fuck do you think you're going?" Dougie Slimon, aka *Slimy Dickless Prick*, drawls.

"Ah shit," Hudson mutters, bending over and throwing up. His puke splatters against the asphalt, covering my brand new DM's. This day is just getting better and better.

"Oh no, you got a headache, *Huddy*? Need a pill to ease the pain? Better yet, why don't I just finish the job, huh?"

"Come back for seconds?" I goad, propping Hudson against the wooden base of the slide so that I can deal with these arseholes once and for all. My side is killing me, but I don't let the pain show, I can handle a broken rib.

"You didn't think we'd let you off that easily? Hudson owes us five grand, and we're here to collect."

"I don't owe you shit," Hudson slurs, trying to push up to his feet, and failing.

"Stay put!" I hiss, then turn back around to face the prick, loving the fact that he hasn't gotten off lightly either. His right eye is swelling and his lip is split from where I managed to throw a pretty hard left hook. Just a shame I didn't manage to knock some of his veneers out. I'd love to fuck up that smarmy thousand pound smile he's so well known for.

"Leave it, Grim," Hudson warns, his gaze swimming as he slides down the wooden frame, in no shape to stand, let alone fight.

"If you'd let me finish it, we wouldn't have this problem right now, Hud," I reply, pissed at him for stepping in when he did and getting his head smashed in for the trouble. I was handling my opponents just fine before he went all knight in shining armour on my arse and tried to take them all on himself. I'm not scared of Dougie and his gang of cronies. They're just another bunch of rich pricks trying to play gangster. In reality, they're as far from *gangster* as they come. Brought up with a silver spoon stuck up their arse and daddy clearing up their messes, they wouldn't know how to survive on the street if the concrete beneath their feet rose up and gave them a helping hand.

"Yeah, what's up with that? Getting a girl to fight your battles," Dougie taunts.

"I wasn't fighting his battles, *dickhead*. We were fighting them together, you misogynistic prick," I counter, eyeing up his crew. There might be four of them and only one of me, but I've trained with some of the toughest men in London, and I know how to handle myself, mainly thanks to Beast. These arseholes would've found that out if they hadn't run the second a police car went hurtling past the car park. It scared them off enough for us to make our escape, not because I was afraid, but because I knew Hudson needed a doctor and quick.

"He was hiding behind you. Just like he is now."

"He's got a fucking concussion, *shit for brains*. He can't fight, but if you really want to end this, let's go," I say, cracking my neck and rolling my shoulders.

He tips his head back and laughs, then lunges for me with his arms wide.

The fool.

I spin on the ball of my foot and kick him square in the stomach, my steel toe-cap boot burying itself in his non-existent abs. The surprise on his face is a picture as he falls to the floor, winded. Not that I get very long before his cronies pile in.

All of my training with Beast comes to the surface, and I duck punches and defend myself with relative ease until one fucker—who's a bit more streetwise than I first gave him credit for—lands a blow to my broken rib. It knocks me off-kilter, and I stumble a little, giving one of the others enough time to land a punch to my jaw.

"YOU FUCKER!" I roar, losing all sense of control as I launch myself at him.

Beast has always taught me to keep my anger under control when in a fight. He constantly reminds me that the best fighters, and the ones who consistently win in the cage, are the ones who fight *smart*. He'd be pissed off if he saw me now. Still, it doesn't stop me from following through. I land a punch to the guy's gut, winding him, only to receive a blow to the side of my head from one of the other arseholes.

Stumbling sideways, I fall over Hudson's legs. Hitting the

asphalt, I glance at him and try not to panic at the paleness of his skin and the fact he's now unconscious.

Fuck!

"What's the matter," Dougie drawls, standing over me, "Met your match?"

"You fucking wish," I retort, pushing up onto my feet and ignoring the ache in my rib and jaw. "I've eaten better fighters for breakfast."

He grins, his cronies flanking him. "I bet you have. Rumour has it you regularly *eat* them for breakfast. In fact, word on the street is that your dad likes to loan you out to deal with his debts. Quite the little whore, aren't you?"

"Yeah, I enjoy a good nosh on a cock in the morning," I retort with a roll of my eyes, dismissing his remark.

"Fucking *slut*. I bet you like it hard, don't you?"

My fist meets his cheek before he can even blink, and this time I don't stop throwing punches until I'm pulled roughly off of him. Satisfaction fills my veins as he spits out a tooth, his perfect smile ruined by my fist. Behind me one of his men has my arms twisted up my back. I'm not worried, I can get him off me when the timing is right.

"You fucking bitch!" Dougie snarls, swiping the back of his hand over his face and smearing blood all over his cheek. "Do you know how much these cost?"

"I couldn't give a flying fuck," I retort, smirking to hide the stab of pain I feel in my side when the arsehole holding me jabs his fist into my ribs.

Dougie spits out a glob of blood. "You're going to pay for this!"

"Yeah, yeah, like you keep saying."

"What do you want to do with her?" the arsehole behind me asks, his lips closer to my cheek than I'd like, the fucking creep.

"Hmm," Dougie replies, cocking his head as his salacious gaze roves over my body. "What should we do with the bitch?"

I bark out a laugh. "If you're thinking what I think you're thinking I suggest you stop right the fuck now, unless you want to be sent back to daddy dearest in a black fucking bag!"

"Now, now, we both know that I've got the upper hand here..." Dougie taunts.

"You really are thick as shit, aren't you?" I retort, then snap my head back as hard as I can. I hear the crack of a nose breaking right before a cry of pain pierces the air. Dougie's crony lets me go so he can stem the flow of blood, and I use the opportunity to twist around and land two more punches, the one to his temple knocking him out cold.

Then I attack.

With single-minded focus and a real desperate need to get Hud to a doctor, I lay out the two other men in quick succession.

I don't hesitate. I don't wait. I go for the kill.

Bones snap as I break one of the guy's legs, slamming my foot into his knee cap. It bends backwards, and his scream of pain reverberates around the playground. I dropkick the other guy and then, when he's sprawled out onto the floor, slam my foot against his right arm, breaking it.

Then I turn on Dougie and grin at the look of horror on his face.

"Now there's just us," I goad, licking my lips and cracking my knuckles. A strange kind of energy is firing through my blood, and I'm humming with the need for violence.

Fuck, it feels good. If only Carter could see me now. Maybe when word gets back to him about this fight he'll reconsider his recent appraisal of me.

I'm not a bleeding heart. I'm a Davidson.

No, I'm Grim.

"Looks that way, *Princess*," Dougie retorts with a smirk, hiding his fear with bravado.

I'm about to respond with a cutting remark when a familiar figure striding towards us freezes the words on my tongue.

"I suggest you take her name out of your motherfucking mouth, wankstain!"

Beast.

For a moment, my heart stops beating. It literally stops as I take in the man who both annoys the shit out of me and turns me into a puddle of hormonal desire every time he's close by. I hate that that's how I react to him. It pisses me off, but my pussy, she doesn't give a fuck. She flutters and gets all tingly like she's just about to have a session with my favourite vibrator, the greedy bitch.

"What the fuck—" Dougie spins on his feet only to meet a fist three times the size of mine. He goes down like a sack of potatoes and when Dougie turns his head to the side, he spits out three more teeth and a crap load of blood.

"You piece of shit," Beast snarls, kicking him in the stomach. Dougie groans, curling in on himself, but Beast doesn't stop there, he reaches for him, fisting his collar and dragging Dougie to his feet. There's a rage in his eyes that speaks of only one outcome... *Murder.*

"He's mine!" I snap, swiping at the blood dripping from my

lip, I hadn't even registered that I was bleeding. "If anyone gets to kill him, it's me!"

Beast's gaze meets mine and I suck in a sharp breath at the anger I see bubbling in his eyes, anger that is aimed squarely at *me*. "No!"

"What the fuck is your problem?"

Beast's nostrils flare and he jerks his head to a familiar face standing behind him. "Connall, grab Hudson and get him to the car. I'll deal with this fucking mess."

"Why is Connall here?" I ask ungratefully, glancing at Beast's best friend.

"The fucker was too intoxicated on booze and stripper pussy to drive," Connall retorts with a wink as he passes me by. "So I'm your chauffeur. Good to see you again, *gorgeous*—"

Beast snarls at him like some feral dog and Connall holds his hands up and laughs. "I mean, *Grim*."

"Connall," I mutter back, hating the fact my cheeks are heating at the way Beast is reacting right now, but more so from a sudden burst of jealousy that I've no right to feel. He has every right to fuck whoever he wants. He's not mine, and I'm certainly not his. After our meal at Sapori he kept things strictly professional, as though that night never even happened.

It stings.

"You did good," Connall adds with a smile that is way more flirty than it should be.

"Don't fucking encourage her!" Beast snaps, shaking Dougie like a rag doll. I can tell that he really wants to do that to me, and probably Connall too.

"I did what I had to do," I shrug, flicking my gaze to Connall who picks up Hudson and carries him off to the other side of the park where their car is situated. The guy is just as built as Beast, but a lot more friendly, which is just as well because I don't think I could handle two moody fuckers right now. I'm already at the end of my rope.

"You disobeyed me! I told you to stay put!" he says as soon as Connall is out of earshot.

"And I told you I could deal with this myself!" I shout back.

"You called me first, remember?!" he argues.

Dougie groans again, and with an annoyed sigh, Beast pulls back his fist and punches him in the face. The sound of more bones breaking is loud in my ear, and even I wince. That's got to fucking hurt. Dropping Dougie, who's now passed out cold, he stalks towards me, all pent up anger and tense shoulders. I can see the muscle in his jaw flickering with how tightly he grits his teeth.

Despite the fact I know he won't hurt me, I find myself backing up away from him. When my back hits the wooden base of the slide, and Beast boxes me in with his body, air rushes from my lungs as heat pools low in my belly.

"You're pushing your fucking luck with me, *Princess*," he growls, gripping my jaw in his huge hand, his face so close I can smell alcohol, coffee and peppermint on his breath.

"Get your hands off me!" I grind out through gritted teeth, angry that we're back to this again. This push and pull that drives me insane.

He smiles, or rather bares his teeth at me. "Make me."

Reaching up between us, I shove him in his chest. Even I know that's a stupid fucking move, the guy's made of stone and steel and of course, he doesn't budge an inch.

"Really?" he says, cocking a brow. "Is that all you got? I thought I taught you better than that."

Instead of taking that opportunity to knee him in the balls, I end up curling my fingers into his t-shirt and saying something really fucking stupid instead. "Believe me, I've got all the skills and more, I just don't think you'd be able to handle them."

"Handle them?" he scoffs, shoving his thigh between my legs before grabbing my wrists and pinning them to my side. For a moment my brain short-circuits at the feel of his thigh pressing against my pussy. "You might be able to handle a few *boys*, but you can't handle a man like me, Princess," he says, his voice low, filled with a mixture of rage and something that seems suspiciously like lust.

I have to tense every single muscle in my body so he doesn't feel me trembling from his touch. I'm not scared of him, the exact opposite in fact. It's all I can do not to rub myself against him like the fucking horny bitch I am.

"Are you sure about that?" I reply, my voice unrecognisable even to my own ears.

I sound like a woman well versed in seducing men, not an inexperienced virgin. A sore point of mine, but the truth nevertheless. Despite being surrounded by very fuckable men, I've got as much of a chance of losing my virginity as Mother Theresa. My dad would kill any man who dared try to kiss me, let alone fuck me. The only reason he's allowed my friendship with Hudson is because of how smart he is and the fact Hudson treats me like his sister and nothing more. Though that might change after what happened today.

"Well?" I taunt, pissed off and hurt and *achy*, and by achy I mean turned on.

Beast's nostrils flare and for one clit-pulsating second I think he's going to kiss me. Instead he steps back, slides one arm around my back, and the other arm behind my knees, then lifts me up into his arms bridal style.

"Put me down! I can walk, you know!" I screech, fucking sick of him chucking me around like a rag doll.

His grip tightens. "I. Don't. Give. A. Fuck. Next time you go rogue I'm going to put you on a damn leash! Count your blessings that I don't make you crawl across this field for disobeying me."

"Fuck you," I mutter, wincing as the pain in my side grows from a dull throb to a stabbing pain now that the adrenaline from the fight is beginning to wear off. "I thought we were past this caveman bullshit."

"That was before you ignored me. AGAIN! Next time I tell you to do something, you motherfucking do it!" he booms, stepping over Dougie, before pressing the heel of his boot against the neck of the guy whose arm I broke. He thrashes around, gurgling, his face going redder and redder by the second. "I want you to pass on a message to that prick when he wakes up. Come for Hudson or my girl again and not only will his guts end up as a necklace hanging around his throat, I will cut his motherfucking heart out and serve it up to Princess on a platter. Got it?"

The guy nods, or at least I think he does, because I'm hyper focused on the fact that Beast just called me *his* girl.

"Did you just—?"

"Good!" Beast retorts, lifting his heel off the guy's throat and completely ignoring me as he strides towards the car.

'Did you just say I was *your* girl?" I ask again.

"Stop talking, Princess."

"But you said—"

He huffs, completely fucking ignoring me.

"Beast!"

"Shut the hell up!" he snaps, that muscle in his jaw jumping like an addict waiting for his next fix.

"You really are a fucking arsehole," I mutter, even though I know he isn't. He's doing all of this not just because he's paid to, but because he cares. I *know* he does.

"Yeah, I am, and don't you fucking forget it," he replies.

When we reach the car he slides me onto the back seat and straps me in like I'm a fucking toddler. "I can do it myself!" I say, slapping his hand away.

"Connall, drive us to Joey's," Beast orders. "Let's get Hudson fixed up, so I can beat the shit out of him for ruining my fucking day off."

Up front Hudson groans in his semi-conscious state. Connall flicks his gaze to my best friend before looking back at Beast. "I've already called ahead. He's waiting for us."

"Great, let's fucking go," Beast says, slamming the door and rounding the car.

Connall grins, his hazel eyes sparkling with mirth as he looks over his shoulder at me. "You really know how to wind the big guy up, don't ya?"

"If he wasn't such a wanker, I wouldn't have to," I retort.

Connall laughs. "You two really should just fuck and get it over with."

"What?!" I exclaim, my cheeks flushing as Beast opens the door and climbs in the car next to me.

"What's so fucking funny?" Beast asks, glancing between us both as Connall cracks up.

"Nothing!" I say quickly. "Absolutely *nothing*."

"Connall?"

"I was just saying how much trouble Grim is..."

"Fucking tell me about it," Beast grumbles, his huge size taking up most of the backseat and leaving me very little wiggle room. He's nothing but a hunk of well-defined muscles that has no business being so attractive.

"I'm not the one who's *trouble*..." I whisper under my breath, my pulse racing for an entirely different reason as Connall puts the car in drive and Beast's thigh presses against my own.

CHAPTER TEN

Creep

"How's the little shit?" I ask Joey as he strides out of his makeshift operating room, which is basically the back room of his garage. He fixes cars as a front for his illegal activity of fixing criminals when they've got themselves in a spot of bother.

"Concussed. Some bruises and scrapes, but otherwise he'll live. I've checked him over and given him some painkillers. I suggest he goes home to rest," Joey says, pulling off his plastic gloves and chucking them in the trash can.

"And Princess?"

"Bruised rib. Busted lip. Black eye. Split skin across her knuckles. She'll live too—"

"Not if I don't fucking kill her first!" I grumble.

Joey swipes a hand through his long grey hair. He's basically a Father Christmas look alike but a lot slimmer and way edgier. "She's a bundle of trouble, that one. I like her. She's got to be tough, given the world she lives in," he remarks, giving me a look.

I know what's coming, Joey might've been struck off from practising but he hasn't lost the need to dole out advice like prescription drugs.

"What?" I ask, flicking my gaze to the door that he's left slightly ajar. Beyond I can see Kate talking to Hudson, she's got her hand on his forearm. My teeth grind together in annoyance.

"She said you're training her?" he asks.

"Yep, orders from the boss. She knows how to look after herself. I made sure of it."

"Right," he nods, squinting his eyes at me.

"What? Spit it out, old man."

"I'm gonna give you a piece of advice."

"Yeah?" I fold my arms across my chest as I glare at Hudson and Kate chatting and laughing. I'm not in the fucking mood for advice of any kind. Pretty sure I just want to throttle Hudson and be done with it.

"Don't fuck with the princess because one day she's gonna be queen, and at that point she'll fuck *you* up good and proper."

My head snaps around to look at Joey. "I don't intend on fucking with her."

"Did I say fuck *with* her? I meant fuck her. Don't. She's way out of your league, Beast," Joey says with a chuckle, gripping my shoulder in that fatherly way of his.

"Why does every dirty bastard think I want to fuck her?" I seethe, getting more and more pissed off. "I'm not a fucking *creep*."

Joey rolls his eyes. "We know you're not, but she won't be a princess forever, and when she turns into a queen, you better believe you'll be on your knees for her."

I scoff, scraping a hand over my face. "Whatever you say, old man."

Pushing off from the wall, I take a step towards the room so I can break up the fucking party then break Hudson's nose, but Joey grips my arm.

"I've only met one woman in my life capable of bringing a man to their knees, and I recognise that ability in Grim. Be careful with her, she trusts you. Don't break her heart because she'll eat yours for breakfast. Catch my drift?"

"Yeah, loud and clear. Can I fucking go now? I need a goddamn drink."

Joey snorts with laughter. "I suggest you find some pussy and try and fuck Grim out of your system, and if that don't work then try a few rounds in the gym with your best fighter."

"Got it. Thanks, Doc," I grunt, striding across the room and shoving the door open. It slams against the wall. Kate snaps her head around but I don't look at her, my attention is solely focused on Hudson. "Tell me why I shouldn't wring your fucking neck?"

"Beast!" Kate exclaims, shifting herself in front of Hudson, one arm on his knee as though to warn him not to react. She's protecting him, and it's all I can do not to fucking snatch her against my chest and claim her with a kiss to show him and every other fucker that's she's *mine*.

Fuck. Fuck. Fuck!

Joey was right, same as Connall. I need to deal with this problem now. She ain't mine. She's Carter's daughter and off the motherfucking menu. *Permanently*.

"It's alright, Grim, he has a right to be angry, I shouldn't have involved you in my shit," the little dickhead responds. Getting to his feet, he sidesteps her. "Do what you need to do."

"What? No fucking way!" Kate exclaims, getting between us.

"Get out of the way, Princess," I say, my eyes fixed on Hudson as I take another step forward.

Her hands fly upwards, pressing against my pecs. I can feel her nails digging in my skin, and fuck me if my cock doesn't spring to life. "The hell I will, Beast. He's my best friend, and I won't let you hurt him."

"Get out of the motherfucking way, or I'll make you."

"Grim, just let him do what he needs to do. I can take it."

"Shut up, Hud! You haven't been punched by Beast before, you'll be knocked out and this time you might not wake up!" she argues. Stepping into my space, she pushes against my chest, her whole body pressing against me now. "He's a good guy, one of the best. Don't do this. *Please*. For me?"

Her voice is quiet, or maybe it's the rush of blood in my ears from the fact that my whole body is so acutely aware of hers. My fingers flex and curl as I try my damndest not to grab her face and kiss her stupid. "He put you in danger," I say, my voice gruff.

"I put *myself* in danger. He had nothing to do with it," she replies, her cheeks flushing red, her fingers curling into my shirt. My cock grows and I know she can feel it pressing against her stomach, I can tell by the way her pupils widen and her mouth parts on a breath.

It's that reaction that saves the little prick from a coma.

Gripping Kate's shoulders, I push her away from me, my

eyes fixed on Hudson who's looking more uncomfortable by my interaction with Kate than the fact I could kill him with one punch. "Next time you get into any shit, you come to me. I will not have her put in harm's way again, got it?"

Hudson nods. "Got it."

Kate blows out a breath. "Thank you, Beast—"

I glance down at her, ignoring the way she's looking at me. "Get in the motherfucking car. I'm taking you home."

"And Hudson?"

"Connall's dropping him off."

"Aren't you still drunk?" she asks.

"Believe me, Princess, I've sobered the fuck up. Now say your goodbyes, I'll be waiting."

With that I stride out of the room, passing Joey who gives me a knowing look. I give him the middle finger and he just laughs.

"Hey, Beast, you alright, mate?" Connall calls from the other side of the garage, laughter in his voice.

"Drop that little prick off for me. I'm taking Princess home," I say, ignoring his question because no, I'm not fucking alright. I've got a boner the size of a baseball bat in my pants and I need to get the fuck out of here, stat.

"OW, SHIT!" Kate curses from inside her bedroom an hour later.

"What's up?"

"Are you *still* here?" she asks, yanking open her bedroom door and glaring at me.

"Looks that way, doesn't it?"

Frankly, I should be four hours deep inside Natalie's pussy according to the doctor's orders, but instead I'm *still* babysitting Kate, hovering in the hallway outside her bedroom like some fucking stalker. Carter took off with the King on business pretty soon after I left the strip club and that meant me spending more time with fucking temptation. The man lost his shit when he found out Kate had been involved in a fight, and the text he sent me after their conversation ended had very strict instructions.

Kill Dougie Slimon and the cunts who thought they could disrespect me.

Could disrespect *him*. Not the cunts who hurt Kate.

He didn't even ask her if she was okay. Not fucking once.

"Beast, I'm talking to you!" she says, drawing my attention back to her.

"Yeah, what?" I ask, leaning against her door frame, my arms folded across my chest as I take in my fill of her and push thoughts of Carter out of my head. I don't know what's up with him lately but his attitude towards Kate fucking stinks, so maybe I don't feel so bad sticking around to watch over her when that arsehole can't even bring himself to ask her if she's alright.

"You should go home," she says, frowning as I step into her bedroom.

Her long dark hair is dishevelled and the bruise around her eye is deepening to a nasty purple. Her lips are swollen from the her split lip, but it's the pain in her eyes that fucks me up more than I care to admit. She's good at covering up the things that hurt her. I'd seen the look on her face when her dad hadn't once asked her if she was okay during their conversation or applauded her for dealing with four grown arse men pretty much on her own. If that had pissed me off, then Christ knows how it made her feel.

"Nah, I'm good." Without thinking, I take a step closer to her and gently press my fingers against her cheek. "It hurt?"

"I'm fine," she replies, swallowing hard, her gaze flicking from my eyes to my lips and back again. She steps backward, my hand falling away.

"Didn't Joey give you any painkillers?" I ask, tucking my hands into my pockets to prevent me from touching her again, because fuck if she wasn't right about me saying one thing and my body doing another. I've got to reel my fucking urges in around her, or rather my hands.

"He did, they just haven't kicked in yet..."

"What's up then?"

"I want to take a shower."

"Okay?" I frown. "So what's stopping you?"

Kate's cheeks flush a deep red. "I can't take off my clothes, it hurts like a bitch every time I move," she whispers and her vulnerability kills me. She's not someone who easily shows her emotions; in fact, she does everything in her power to never show weakness. It's been drilled into her to never let anyone see what hurts you the most. Just like the rest of us. We're a bunch of tough motherfuckers.

"Where's Nadia? Can't she help?" Nadia is their housemaid, a little Italian woman with more fire and spunk than all the entire fighters of Tales. Plus she cooks a mean carbonara. I like her.

"It's her night off."

"So call her and tell her to get back here."

Kate shakes her head. "Her son is visiting, she's got her family around tonight for dinner. Besides, I've already ruined your day off, I don't want to ruin hers too."

I let out a breath and scrape my hand over my face. "You didn't ruin my day off. I'm glad you called me."

Kate pulls a face. "Is that because my dad has given you a bonus for stepping in today?"

"No, it's got nothing to do with that," I reply tightly, even though it's true and Carter's done exactly that. Doesn't sit right with me that he's rewarded me for my involvement, but ignored the fact his own daughter handled the situation like the badass she is.

"Yeah," she scoffs, shaking her head.

"I've always said that if you need me, then you call me. You did that at least, even if you didn't stay fucking put like I told you to."

"Like I've said before, I don't much like being told what to do," she retorts, dragging the sleeve of her hoody over her hand and letting out a hiss of pain as she pulls her right arm out of the sleeve.

"Well, it's about fucking time you started!" I snipe, and without really thinking it through, I grab the hem of her jumper and step closer.

"What are you doing?" she asks, her voice hitching.

What the fuck am I doing?

"Helping you undress, that's why you brought the subject up, right?"

"This is *exactly* what I was talking about," she mutters, her lips smooshing to the side as she chews on the inside of her cheek. "You can't stay away."

"Don't get carried away. There's nothing in it," I say, not certain who I'm trying to convince more.

"But—"

"Just keep still. Let me help."

She nods tightly. "Fine."

God, I fucking love the way she reacts every time I'm close to her. Kate's normally so full of spunk and fire, and here she is all pretty and blush for me. That thought has my dick leaping like a jack rabbit. I love her strength and her smart mouth, but right now it's her coyness, her shyness, that has me all up in my head for her.

"Fuck," I hiss. This is a bad idea.

"What?"

"Nothing."

I ignore my bastard cock as I grip the hem of her hoodie and t-shirt beneath it, then drag the material up and over her head, careful not to touch any part of her. Gently, I tug the gathered material down her arm and pull it free leaving her in a sports bra and jeans. Her tits are encased in black lycra, and a little zip down the front has me begging to pull on it. I imagine them spilling out and my hands cupping them. I bet they're a perfect fucking handful, and given her skin tone, I imagine she has perfect blush nipples too.

Jesus, Mary and Joseph.

If I wasn't going to Hell before, then I sure as fuck am now.

"What the hell is that?" I blurt out, staring at her sports bra that, despite its plainness, is a thousand times sexier than any lacy underwear I've ever seen on another woman.

"What, these?" she points to her tits and smirks. "I'm pretty sure you've seen a pair of tits before, several pairs of tits given how much time you spend at Nine Lives."

"Yeah, but I ain't seen yours," I mutter back, biting down on my motherfucking tongue so hard the metallic taste of blood fills my mouth. Fuck man, I need to be better at covering up my thoughts when I'm around her. Whatever this is between us, it's dangerous.

"Right," she replies, chewing on her lip.

I swallow hard, hyper focused on the way her perfect white teeth gnaw on something I'd really like to fucking nibble. Trailing my gaze down over her flat stomach, I stare at the waistband of her jeans, my fingers twitching, *itching* to touch her. "Your jeans?"

"It's fine, I can manage," she replies, waving me off and unzipping the zipper. She wiggles her hips, trying to shuck them off but drags in another sharp breath. "Ow, shit!"

Her face pales with the pain and yet again my hands fly out before I can stop them as I grab the waistband of her jeans. The moment my fingers curl over the material and my knuckles graze her smooth skin, she freezes, a funny little squeak releasing from between her lips. I look down at her, at the blush rising up her chest and my own fucking breath stills.

"Keep still," I order, cursing myself internally.

"I am!" she retorts.

"Just do as you're told."

"You're so fucking bossy," she grumbles under her breath as I crouch down before her and drag her jeans over her hips, which are far more womanly than they have any right to be.

"Quiet!" I snap.

When I catch a glimpse of her cherry red knickers, I have to turn my head to the side so I'm not tempted to do something really fucking stupid like press my nose against her slit and breathe in her scent. She's only a few weeks away from her eighteenth birthday, but I meant what I said, I don't fuck women younger than twenty. I'm not a fucking creep. Not that it makes a fucking difference because I ain't touching Kate. *Ever.*

In pure frustration, I yank a little too hard, sliding her jeans past her knees. She wobbles on her feet, squeaking in pain, and a growly noise rumbles up my chest. "Grab hold of my shoulders, Princess. I ain't gonna bite!"

"Shame," Kate murmurs, her fingers pressing against my shoulder blade, her voice filled with fuck me vibes that has me wishing I'd never stepped foot in this damn room.

"*Princess...*" I warn. She's playing with fucking fire and I'm usually not the type of man to put it out. In fact, call me a fucking pyromaniac and hand me a can of petrol so I can watch that shit burn. With her I can't. I just fucking can't.

"Alright, calm down. I'm just playing with you," she sasses.

"That wouldn't be wise."

"No?" She laughs, and that just annoys me more. "You seem to have a lot of fun playing games with me. Don't like it when the shoe's on the other foot?"

"For the record," I grind out, refusing to answer her question because she's fucking right. "I won't be biting any part of you, *Princess*. Not now, not tomorrow, not next year, not when you reach fucking twenty... *Never*. Understand?"

"Perfectly," she retorts, her nails digging into my skin as she lifts one foot out of the pooled material at her feet. Fuck, even her feet turn me on. I ain't averse to giving a woman's toes a suck and I bet hers are fucking delectable.

"Good." I reach for her other ankle still encased in denim, feeling the electricity sparking between us as I guide her foot out of the material. Heat licks at my insides, and the tension intensifies a thousand fold. I should remove my goddamn hands from her right now. Except my fucking fingers are stuck to her skin as though glued there.

"You can let go now," she says, after a beat too long. There's a breathiness to her voice that has my balls aching.

I pull back my hands and stand abruptly, taking a step back. Tearing my gaze away from her semi-naked form, I look behind her only to find myself staring at her bare arse on display in the reflection of the mirror, her rounded cheeks perfectly fucking formed.

She's wearing a motherfucking thong!

I rip my gaze away, frantically looking about the room for something other than her to focus on and not that peachy fucking arse I'd sure like to bury my teeth into. That song, Creep by Radiohead starts playing in my head, adding insult to injury. I'm so fucking screwed.

"Motherfucker," I whisper under my breath.

"I think I can manage now," she says, and there's a look of triumph in her eyes as she walks into the bathroom, her hips swaying as she moves.

"Fuck!" I exclaim, clenching my fists.

"What was that?" she calls through the partly open doorway, her voice light with mirth.

"I said I've got to go and fuck some shit up. Be back soon."

"Wait! I thought you were on *babysitting* duties this weekend, given Carter is away again?"

She catches me staring at her reflection in the mirror, her

fingers hovering over the zipper of her sports bra. A large, very dangerous, very fucking stupid part of me wants her to lower the zipper and show me what she's got. The other part knows I should get the hell out of her bedroom.

"There's a takeaway menu on the counter. Don't wait up," I reply.

She meets my gaze, a smirk pulling up her lip. "Will you be home to tuck me into bed... *Daddy?*"

Daddy?!

I don't respond, I get the fuck out of there, her laughter following me out.

CHAPTER ELEVEN

Bad Liar

I hear the sound of the front door opening several hours later, the familiar thump of Beast's footsteps loud over the wooden flooring in the hallway. He couldn't be a silent assassin even if he tried. I smile inwardly at that. Beast isn't someone who hides in the shadows, he's an *in-your-face-and-fuck-you-up* kind of guy. I like that about him. Though I'd never tell him that, I wouldn't want to stroke his ego, it's already the size of a small country.

"Beast?" I call out, turning on the coffee percolator and leaning against the counter as I wait for him to enter the kitchen. It's past two in the morning and I've not been able to sleep. Partly because of the pain in my side from my bruised rib and partly because my skin still burns from his touch. Despite what he said to me, I'd felt the connection between us, even though he'd denied it.

Fuck, I called him Daddy.

My cheeks heat at the thought, and my clit... Well, she throbs.

The expression on his face just before he twisted on his feet and strode from my room was one of shock, yes, but for a fleeting moment there'd been desire. He'd *liked* it. My toes curl at the thought, my freshly painted red toenails scraping against the tiled floor.

"What're you still doing up?"

I lift my gaze from my bare feet, wishing I'd worn something sexier than a pair of baggy joggers and an old t-shirt, then suck in a sharp breath at the blood pouring from a gash in Beast's cheek and covering his clothes.

"What the hell happened?" I ask as he places a metal box on the counter and helps himself to a bottle of whisky from the liquor cupboard. Scarlet droplets slide down his face and fall from his chin onto the white tiled floor. I grimace. Nadia, our housemaid, will be cursing him tomorrow. The last time she lost her shit with Beast was when he trampled mud all the way through the house after burying an enemy of my father's in Bracknell Forest. He was grovelling for weeks for her forgiveness. Nadia doesn't like a mess and Beast hates pissing her off. It's kind of cute really, a big guy like him afraid of a little Italian woman.

Unscrewing the cap, Beast takes a long swig. "What do you think happened, Princess?" he growls, swiping the back of his hand across his lips, smearing blood across his face.

"Dougie...?"

"Dead, of course," he replies, meeting my gaze.

"You took care of the body?" I ask as though we're talking

about the weather and not the fact he's killed a man. I'm turning into my father. Hard, cold, and completely detached.

"*Bodies*," he corrects, chugging some more whisky. "Those fucking pricks who attacked you never stood a chance."

"You make it sound like I was a victim. They didn't exactly attack me, we *fought*. I was winning before you butted in."

My voice trails off as he glares at me. "You think that matters, Princess? The second they laid a finger on you, their death sentence was set in stone."

"Where?" I ask flatly.

"The new flyover being built in West London. A friend of mine was pouring concrete in one of the archways."

"I see, so that's what you meant by their deaths being set in stone?" It's not the first time my dad had Beast dump bodies in the concrete foundations of various buildings around London. I'm pretty sure most of the new builds across East London have a body or two buried beneath them.

He chuckles, but it's a tired kind of sound. "Yeah. Exactly."

"So what's in that?" I ask, pointing at the metal box on the counter.

"Hearts."

"*Hearts?* What do you mean, hearts?" I ask, looking between him and the metal box. "You're not suggesting..." My voice trails off when he nods.

"They're for you."

"*Me?!* Why the hell would I want their hearts, Beast?" I screech, my own heart thumping so hard against my rib cage that I swear he can hear it.

"They wronged you so I took their hearts. Just like I promised I would. Though I'm sorry I turned up looking like this," he apologises, grimacing at the mess he's making. "Should've changed first."

"Wait, just back up a minute," I say, holding my hands up as he watches me, a smirk pulling up his lip.

Part of me feels sick at the thought of their hearts sitting in a metal box on the goddamn kitchen counter, but another part of me, a much bigger part, is turned on by it. He brought me their hearts. If that's not something straight out of a Grimms' fairy tale, I don't know what is.

Beast is the hunter of my story, except instead of cutting out the heart of a virgin, he's cutting out the hearts of her enemies instead.

"Are you honestly more concerned about not changing rather than the fact you actually brought me their hearts?"

He shrugs. "I've got standards."

"But you brought me their hearts, Beast!" I practically shout. "That's not normal behaviour."

"You were right there when I warned them, Princess. Why is this such a surprise? I told you. I'm a killer," he says calmly, and in such a way it sounds like he's trying to discourage me from liking him. The opposite couldn't be more true. This is probably the most fucked-up, most romantic thing anyone has ever done for me.

"You said you would cut out their hearts if they came near Hud or me again which, unless I'm missing something, they haven't."

"Did I?" he shrugs. "Well, whatever. Carter wanted them dead. They're dead."

"Did he ask you to cut out their hearts?"

He chuckles, taking another deep pull on the drink. "Nope.

That was all on me. When I say I'm gonna do something, I do it."

"Fuck, okay!" I shake my head. "But why bring them here?" I ask, pointing at the metal box. I should be freaking the fuck out some more, but all I can think of right now is that we need to get rid of the evidence.

"I just wanted you to know they were dead, and you didn't have to worry about them anymore. I'll get rid of the hearts, don't worry."

"That's, erm..." My voice trails off as I try to find the right words. But there are none. "You could've just told me they were dead."

"Now where's the fun in that?"

"You're a little unhinged, you know that, right?"

"They don't call me Beast for nothing, Princess."

"I honestly thought that was because..."

"Because what?"

"Because you were... *Big*."

"Big? He lifts a brow smoothing his palm over his abs. "I ain't fat."

"No, I meant—"

"Ah! So you've been talking to the strippers at Nine Lives, right? My cock *is* fucking legendary."

"What?! No, I haven't. I just meant you're tall, built, that kind of thing," I say waving my hand in his general direction. How has this conversation gone from carving out human hearts to the size of his dick? Jesus, if I didn't already feel wide awake I'd have to pinch myself just to be certain I wasn't dreaming.

"Well, now you know. I'm called Beast because I'm an *animal* in all the best *and* all the worst fucking ways. Know what I mean?" he says darkly and just like that, all of the amusement leaves his voice.

We fall silent and I watch him down almost half the bottle before I speak again. "You know Nadia is gonna be pissed with you. Look at the mess you're making," I say, pointing at the blood dripping from his cheek and onto the spotless floor.

"I'll clean it up later." I glance at his hands and the fact there's not a speck of blood on them. He notices me staring. "Gloves, Princess."

"Of course," I reply.

Pushing off from the counter, I grab some kitchen roll, wet it under the tap, fully aware that I should probably be a little more freaked out than I am right now. Growing up the daughter of a criminal hardens you to certain things, murder being one of them. I don't care that the bastards are dead, but I am concerned there will be backlash for the people I do care about.

"What about Dougie's father, isn't he some rich banker or something? Won't he be worrying about his son's whereabouts."

"He won't be an issue," Beast replies, eying me as I approach him with the kitchen roll. Instead of taking it from me, he places the bottle of whisky on the island and grips the counter top. I guess that's my cue to clean him up.

"No?" I ask, concentrating on cleaning up the blood on his face and not the fact his intense gaze is boring holes into my skin.

"Your dad's got some shit on him that will put him away for a long time. He won't be contacting the police," Beast says, watching me carefully as I dab the wet tissue against his cheek.

"But that's his son."

"You think that matters when it comes to selfish men?"

"It should."

"It doesn't," Beast points out.

"Okay, so he won't talk, what about the others?"

"Unimportant in the grand scheme of things."

"But—" Frowning, I fold the tissue in half and dab at his cheek some more.

"Are you worried this will somehow fall back on Hudson?" he asks, his thick fingers curling around my wrist, warm and strong. I stare at him, suddenly aware that I've stepped between his parted legs and my stomach is pressed up against his crotch. The last time we got this close he had a semi in his pants. If Hudson hadn't been in the room, I'd like to think I would've acted upon that, but now I have the chance to be brave and kiss him, a sudden nervousness fills my chest.

"No," I reply, allowing him to take the tissue from me as I ease backwards. "I'm worried it will fall back on you."

He cocks his head to the side and grins, his green eyes flashing with mirth. "Anyone would think you actually gave a shit about me?"

"You know I do."

He meets my gaze and nods. "Yeah."

"You shouldn't take the fall for something you didn't do," I say truthfully.

"Pretty sure it was me who shot Dougie and those little crybaby pricks in the head then carved out their hearts." Beast shrugs, dropping the bloody tissue into the bin.

"You know what I mean." I sigh, feeling the guilt churn my stomach. "If I hadn't gone to help Hudson, none of this would've happened."

"What's done is done. Besides, even if your dad hadn't

ordered me to off the fuckers, I would've done it anyway." He shrugs off his jacket and strides over to the dining table, chucking it over the back of a chair.

"Why?"

"Because I meant what I said. No one touches our girl and gets away with it."

"*Our* girl? Didn't you say I was *your* girl?" I can't help but ask, chewing on the inside of my cheek to stop myself from smiling.

"Same difference."

I pull a face. "Nope, it's completely different."

Scraping a hand through his cropped hair, Beast rolls his eyes. "I just meant you belong to the fighters of Tales. You know, like one of those mascots that run around at basketball games."

"A *mascot*?" I raise my brows and place a hand on my hip, indignation spiking my anger. "Do I look like a fucking beaver?"

"I dunno, does it?" Beast replies, his gaze fixing on my crotch, before he flicks his eyes back up again, amusement in his gaze.

"Ha ha! I'll have you know that I have a very neatly trimmed bush that is very un-beaver like, thank you very much."

"Always wise to keep the beaver tidy, you never know when it might be time to let it out to play."

"Funny." My cheeks heat and Beast laughs at my expense, the tosser.

"I'm gonna go take a shower. I'd kill for a cup of that coffee you've got percolating. Smells good, is that Arabica beans?" he asks.

"I have literally no idea..." I reply, shaking my head in

wonder that he even knows what type of bean I'm using and completely ignoring the fact he was talking about my *beaver* coming out to play.

"Smells rich, almost woodsy," he replies without a smirk in sight.

"I didn't know you were a coffee connoisseur."

"There are plenty of things that you don't know about me, Princess," he says, pulling off his hoodie and t-shirt and dropping them onto the floor at his feet, his broad shoulders and chest rippling with muscles. I swallow hard, trying and failing not to stare. I've seen him bare chested a million times before in the ring at Tales, but never here, at home, with just the two of us. It seems far too intimate somehow.

"Yeah, like what?" I ask, tucking my hands in my joggers and acting way more unbothered than I actually feel.

"Now that would be telling." Beast points to the pile of clothes. "Wouldn't mind sticking them in the washing machine, would you, seeing as we're family now, *baby*..." he asks, before striding off towards the stairs, leaving me fuming at his audacity and quaking at the implication.

I really, really shouldn't have called him Daddy.

"WANT TO WATCH A MOVIE?" I ask as Beast steps into the lounge half an hour later, dressed in a pair of joggers and a t-shirt. He doesn't live with us at the house, but my dad gave him a key and one of the spare rooms so he can stay over whenever he needs which, as of late, is more often than not, given Carter is away so much on business.

"I need to get rid of the hearts," he replies.

"No need. Dom came and collected them. He's on it."

"Well, shit, thanks," he says, dropping onto the sofa next to me. "I could do with unwinding a bit. A movie would be good."

"You should've got Joey to look at that," I say, pointing at the gash on his cheek held together with some medical tape. It's clean, but weeping a little still.

"I went to his place before I came here but he was busy fucking one of his dolly birds."

"Really?" I pull a face.

Beast shrugs. "He may be in his sixties but that man has got a queue of women waiting to bed him." Pointing to the mug of coffee and the bacon sandwich on the coffee table, he asks, "Is that mine?"

"I thought you might be hungry."

"You thought right." He grins at me. "Cheers, Princess, I could get used to this."

"Don't get any funny ideas, I'm not your skivvy."

He smiles around a mouthful of sandwich. "I don't suppose you put my clothes in the wash?"

I raise a brow. "Didn't anyone tell you it's rude to speak with your mouth full?"

"I take it that's a no?"

"It's a *hell no*. Just because I'm a girl it doesn't mean I'm automatically hardwired to serve an ignorant fuckwit who thinks it's okay to dump his dirty clothes on the floor and expect me to clean up after him. It was more than enough to clean up your blood from the kitchen floor and scrub the counter."

Beast chuckles. "Yet you did that *and* made me a sandwich and a cup of coffee…"

"Because *I* wanted to," I grind out. "I don't, however, want to deal with your dirty washing, so I suggest you pick it up off the floor before Nadia arrives on her shift in a few hours because you know she hates a mess."

"As soon as we've watched this movie and I've tucked you in bed, I *promise* I'll do that."

Snatching up the remote, I flick through the selection of movies on screen, ignoring his comment about tucking me into bed and the smirk on his face as he eats. Eventually I find what I'm looking for and press play.

"*Lock, Stock and Two Smoking Barrels?* Are you shitting me?" Beast asks, setting his empty plate back on the table and slurping on his coffee.

"I happen to like Jason Statham. Have you got a problem with that?"

Beast tips his head back and laughs, not caring that he could aggravate his gash. "Jason-fucking-Statham, *really?*"

"What can I say? I like my men older and a little rough around the edges."

Beast snaps his head around, eyes narrowing. "What, and fucking *bald?*"

"It's not about how much hair he has on his head," I counter. "It's his sex appeal."

"He's got about as much sex appeal as a rat on steroids."

"Says the meathead—"

"Meathead? I'm fucking insulted."

"That was the general idea," I snip back, grinning internally at the way he slams his empty mug of coffee onto the table and folds his arms across his chest.

"Banter is one thing, but a straight up insult is something

altogether different. A meathead would imply I'm as thick as shit. I'm not fucking stupid, Princess."

I burst out laughing, only vaguely aware of the opening title sequence playing on the TV screen. "Sensitive much? It was a joke."

"What, like calling me *Daddy* was, huh?"

My laughter dies on my lips as he shifts in his seat and turns to face me. His expression is serious as his knee brushes against my thigh and his arm rests on the back of the sofa. "Beast..."

"Listen, Princess, I'm a straight talking kind of guy and I do my best not to play games," he says, absentmindedly fiddling with the ends of my hair.

I scoff, rolling my eyes. "Says the man playing with my hair," I retort, then instantly regret it when he drops his hand. "Besides, *I'm* not the one playing games."

"You think I don't notice how you look at me all the time, huh? You've got some kind of crush and it stops now."

"One, I do not look at you all the time and two, this is *not* a crush—" It's so, so much more than that.

"I mean, I totally fucking get it. I'm a catch."

"You've got such a big fucking head!" I snap, meeting his gaze. I hate that he's trying to turn this all around on me as though he hasn't had a part in this growing attraction between us. I thought better of him.

He arches a brow, lifting his knuckles to my cheek. "You forget I know you."

"You don't. Nobody does," I counter.

"Not even Hudson?"

"Not even him," I admit.

Beast nods, something close to relief flashing across his face. "Tell me, Princess, have you ever fucked a man before?"

"*What?!*" I exclaim, my whole body stiffening.

Beast shifts closer and as he moves I get a hit of his freshly-showered scent of soap and deodorant. I try hard not to take a deep breath.

"I asked whether you've fucked a man, because whilst you've got the chat, I'm a thousand percent certain you haven't got the game," he says, his t-shirt pulling across his broad shoulders, hugging the muscles. I'm momentarily jealous of that piece of material for being so close to his skin.

"That's none of your business."

He cocks his head, narrowing his eyes at me. "Do you know what I think?" he asks, licking his lips in a way that makes my insides squirm.

"No, what?"

"Not only do I know that you've never been fucked, I also know that you've never been touched, licked, stroked or even *kissed*."

"You forget I have a piercing in my clitoral hood. I don't know many virgins who've got that area of their body pierced, do you?"

He smirks. "I don't believe you. You're lying."

"You don't know shit." I snap my head to the side, this time failing to hide the rapid rise and fall of my chest. I'm angry for being called out, turned on, and fucking terrified of admitting the truth. He's wrong about the piercing, but he's right about everything else.

Beast grips my chin with his fingers, forcing me to look at him. "*I know...*" he counters, staring at me intently as he leans in close, his mouth inches from mine, "That these lips are as virginal as your pussy. I can tell."

"How?"

"Just call it instinct."

"I'm not pure, Beast," I reply, because I'm not. Not in my thoughts anyway.

For long moments we just stare at each other, that same pull crackling and snapping in the air between us just like it did at Macey's Bar, and just like it did at Sapori. I'm pretty sure if someone were to light a match right underneath us, we'd go up in flames.

"Don't lie, Princess. You're as virginal as they come."

"If that's the case, then what're you gonna do about it?" I eventually whisper, the question spilling from my lips before I can stop it. Did I just offer myself up on a platter?

Beast's eyes flash with something close to possession, but he shuts it down quickly with a smirk. "Absolutely *nothing*," he replies, dropping my chin and settling back onto the sofa. I watch him as he lifts his bare feet up onto the coffee table and grabs a cushion, hugging it against his chest. "Are we gonna watch this movie or what?"

My stomach flips with nausea, and the sting of his rebuff has me feeling all kinds of ways, but I refuse to let my feelings show.

Fuck him. Two can play at that game.

Reaching forward I grab the remote control and chuck it in his lap, getting up. "Nah, I think I'll go to bed and play with my pussy whilst thinking about all the men I've fucked," I reply, then twist on my feet and stride towards the stairs, leaving him open-mouthed and staring after me.

CHAPTER TWELVE

Temptation

"Carter called, he wants us to meet him at Chez Etienne for dinner. He'll be there within the hour," I say, entering the kitchen a full forty-eight hours after I killed Dougie and his cronies.

"Surely he's tired after his trip? Why doesn't he just come home?" Kate asks, glancing up from the plans for the refit at Tales spread out in front of her on the kitchen table. Her brows lift at my outfit. It's not often you see me in a tailored suit. "Why're you so dressed up?"

"Boss's orders. I've laid a dress out on your bed for you to wear tonight."

Kate scowls as she gathers up the plans. "Presumptuous much? You know I *am* capable of picking out my own clothes to wear."

"Carter requested you wear something suitable for dinner," I reply evenly.

"Suitable? I don't see why I need to dress up, it's just dinner," she says, eying me with suspicion.

"Apparently not. Carter wants you to meet someone," I reply, fiddling with my cufflinks.

"Who?"

"He didn't say," I reply, turning my attention to Nadia who's quietly watching our exchange with humour in her eyes. "Good evening, Nadia."

Nadia dips her head respectfully. "Good evening, Mr Beast."

"You know it's just Beast," I say, striding over to her and pressing a kiss against her cheek. Her face flushes and she mutters something in Italian under her breath. My Italian is rusty, but I'm pretty sure she just said I look deliciously devilish. She ain't wrong. "I aim to please."

"Indeed." She grins, glancing at Kate who's still staring at me like she hasn't seen a man in a suit before. "Perhaps you should go and get ready, Miss Kate?" Nadia urges.

"I really don't want to go out," Kate says, wincing.

She's still in pain from her bruised rib and whilst the swelling around her eye has gone down, the bruise hasn't. She's got a proper shiner. I don't blame her for not wanting to go out. I had explained this to her dad but he didn't much care which, I must admit, pissed me off. That and the fact he asked me to pick out a dress for Kate. He'd been very specific about what he wanted her to wear. Something that was knee-length, covered her up. Made her look demure, respectable. His fucking words, not mine.

Something about that got my back up.

"I can cook us all a meal, I'm not completely useless," Kate continues. "He can ask his friend here."

"No! You cannot cook *ragazza dolce*, you will all die," Nadia says in that dramatic way of hers.

I can't help but laugh which only earns me another death stare from Kate.

"Our Princess might be a shit cook but she's most definitely not a *sweet girl*," I remark with a knowing smile as I check my gun then slide it into the holster strapped to my chest, before pulling on my dinner jacket. "Besides, this is business, not pleasure. Go and get changed."

"Don't order me about!" Kate retorts, folding her arms across her chest. "You've been nothing but a pain in my arse all weekend."

I meet her gaze. "You *wish* I was a pain in your arse."

Her eyes narrow at me, and I chuckle. Truthfully, I've been avoiding her as best I can all weekend and she fucking knows it. After whatever-the-fuck that conversation was on Friday night, I've made sure I've stayed out of her way, especially since my dick got rock hard at the thought of her pleasuring herself. Fuck, she knew exactly which buttons to push and it took every last shred of control not to chase her up the stairs and take all of her firsts in one moment of madness. If she's not a virgin them I'm the fucking Pope.

"Whatever you say," Kate replies, giving me a look that I'd love to fucking kiss off her face.

We stare at one another way past what is comfortable or socially acceptable only looking away when Nadia clears her throat.

"*Bella*, go shower and change. If your father wishes for you to dress up then it must be for a good reason, hmm?" Nadia says, ushering her out of her seat.

Kate rolls her eyes. "Fine. I'll go get ready," she agrees, traversing the table, her gaze meeting mine. "But you better believe I'm wearing what *I* want to wear. The day I let a man dress me is the day I lose my lady balls."

Nadia smiles, her pretty brown eyes flashing with amusement and pride. "That's my girl."

"Lady balls?" I scoff, shaking my head.

"There's a reason why God is a woman, Beast."

"Yeah, and how do you figure that?" I ask, not that I believe in God or anything, but wanting to hear her reasoning, if only because I can't resist the opportunity to tease her.

"Because she made sure women can bring a man to their knees just by grabbing their balls. Not so easy to do in reverse, eh, given ours are tucked safely inside of us?"

Nadia bursts out laughing as Kate climbs the stairs leaving me mentally adjusting my bollocks at the thought. Fuck, this girl is gonna be the death of me.

Forty minutes later and still no sign of Kate, I trudge up the steps ready to drag her arse out of her bedroom even if she isn't ready. Carter is not a patient man at the best of times and I'm going to need to break a few speed limits to get us to the restaurant on time if she doesn't hurry the fuck up.

"Princess, we gotta get moving," I say, rapping my knuckles against her bedroom door.

"Just a second, I'm just putting on my shoes."

I look at my wrist watch, a beautiful gold Rolex that I bought just under a year ago after winning a fight in a club up north run by Carter's uncle Ransom. That was the night Carter offered me the job as head of his security after I snapped the neck of some punk who was sent to kill him. He'd told me about his new business venture in London, backed by his uncle, and his need for a security team and experienced fighters. I took the job having no idea that part of my responsibilities would be to guard his feisty daughter. By the time I'd arrived in London, set up in a flat that I barely live in now, it was too late to back out. Kate's been nothing but trouble ever since, in more ways than one.

"You've got ten seconds before I sling you over my shoulder and carry you out to the car. Don't piss me off!" I warn, opening the top button of my shirt and rolling my shoulders. I rarely do smart, it always feels like I'm being strangled. I'd rather suffocate from a face full of pussy than suffer the tightness of a stiff collar like this. "Kate!"

"For Christ's sake, I'm ready," she retorts, pulling the door open angrily.

My snarky response is ripped from my lips when I'm confronted with the absolutely stunning vision before me. Pretty sure my motherfucking tongue is hanging out of my mouth right about now. A slow smile pulls up Kate's ruby red lips as she cocks her head to the side, her long dark hair falling over her bare shoulder in loose curls. She's wearing a low cut, figure skimming red silk dress that drops to the floor and has a slit to the top of her thigh, showing off her shapely legs. Given how the material skirts her skin and there are no visible lines beneath it, I know she's not wearing any underwear.

FUCK ME.

I'm in deep shit. Deep, *deep* shit.

"What's the matter, Beast, cat got your tongue?" she asks, brushing past me in a pair of Louboutin black heels with stilettos so sharp she could use them to kill a man. I watch agog as she walks along the hall, her hips swaying, her bare back on show from the low cut of the dress. I can practically see the top of her arse and honestly I've no idea how the dress stays on her body given it's held together with shoestring straps.

"Wait!" I call, coughing to remove the fucking tightness in my throat.

She stills, looking over her shoulder at me, her thick black eyeliner making her brown eyes look even more feline, the bruise hidden beneath carefully applied makeup. "What?"

"That is *not* the dress I put out for you," I say, and it's all I can do not to grab my dick and give it a squeeze to stop it from punching a fucking hole through my trousers.

"And I told you that I wear what I want. Besides, the last time I wore that dress I was fifteen. Do you *want* me to look like a child?" she asks, looking me up and down in a sinfully sexy way.

"Yes. *No*! Fuck. Just put on something else," I grind out, hoping to fuck she doesn't notice my semi.

"Nope," she replies, popping the p in a way that both grates my nerves and makes me want to throw her over my lap and spank her arse.

"Princess!"

But she ignores me, gliding down the stairs just like Vivien Leigh in that old black and white movie *Gone With the Wind* my mum used to love to watch.

"Fuck!" I exclaim, not in the slightest bit ready to face another night with a girl trying her damndest to get my dick chopped off. Because that's exactly what'll happen if her dad gets wind of whatever the fuck is going on between us.

Which is absolutely fucking *nothing*.

"GRIM, I'd like you to meet the King," Carter says thirty minutes later as he pushes back his chair and introduces the shady cunt to Kate. This is who Carter wanted her to meet? So far he's kept Kate out of one on one meetings with whoever he's doing shady shit with, and I know that she'd have to meet these men eventually, but why the King first? He's a fucking tool.

"Grim?" the self-titled King questions, his eyes flashing with interest.

I scowl. Carter notices and he gives me a look that I've only seen him use a handful of times before. It's his *don't overstep look* and it pisses me the fuck off, but it's the way he glares at Kate that grinds my gears more. I know she ain't wearing what he wanted, but there's no denying how fucking incredible she looks. *Powerful*, actually. He should be fucking proud, not giving her the motherfucking stink-eye.

"It's a nickname," Carter explains, plastering on a smile. "My daughter is an avid reader of Grimms' fairy tales."

The King nods. "That's quite a morbid interest you've got there."

"Not to me," Kate replies, taking his proffered hand and giving him a polite smile. "It's a pleasure to meet you."

She might be used to speaking on a level with me and the other guys who work for Carter, and has the ability to put us all to shame with her cursing, but she sure as fuck can switch on the role of obedient, respectful daughter when she needs to. I think I prefer her sass, frankly.

"Oh believe me, the pleasure is *all* mine," the King replies, lifting her knuckles to his mouth and running his lips over them as he drinks her in.

Kate stiffens, her gaze shifting between the King and her father who just gives her a bland, approving smile. What in the actual fuck is going on here? If any other man, potential business partner or not, tried to do the same they'd have a fucking bullet in the brain before they could even blink.

"This is Beast, my second in command and head of security," Carter says, introducing me officially to the fuckwit even though we met before at Nine Lives. I didn't like him then, and I sure as fuck don't like him now.

"Beast," the King replies, side-eyeing me because he's busy mentally undressing Kate with his hand still wrapped around hers.

I grit my jaw, my fingers curling into my palms as a rush of fucking anger bolts up my spine. It's just as well the dicksplash drops Kate's hand and sits down right at that moment, otherwise I would've taken great pleasure in knocking the cunt out.

"Princess," I growl under my breath, uncertain why I'm taking my anger out on her but unable to help myself. It's not her fault that the King's a fucking predatory bastard with a penchant for beating women, and he's looking at Kate like she's his next fucking meal. I pull out a chair for her, and to her credit she doesn't react to my shitty attitude. She just gives me a guarded smile instead.

"How was your business trip?" she asks Carter evenly, though the look she gives me as I sit beside her is unmistakably one of confusion as much as it is suspicion. Kate senses something shady going on as much as I do, she's just better at controlling her emotions and hiding her reactions than I am.

"It was very successful," the King answers. The fact Carter doesn't punch the dick for speaking on his behalf is telling. My fucking spine goes rigid. "Your father and I have come to a very agreeable business deal that I'm looking forward to completing very soon."

Kate looks at her dad, who's grinning like a fucking moron. Is he on drugs? The guy looks wired. A quick glance around the restaurant tells me we're alone and this isn't some elaborate ruse to jump us all. Still, I've not got to where I am today by resting on my laurels. This King fucker is up to some shit, and Carter is neck deep in it.

"I see, and what might that be?" she asks, picking up the menu and glancing at it.

"Well, here's the thing—" the King begins, but Carter raises his hand and cuts him off. Thank fuck, there's the Carter I know and respect. My shoulders relax a smidge.

"Not tonight. Tonight we'll enjoy a meal together. There's been enough business for one weekend," Carter says, motioning over the waiter.

The King nods. "You're absolutely right, of course. There's time to go over our deal at a later date once everything is fixed in place and contracts are signed, yes?"

"Indeed," Carter replies, before instructing the waiter to serve the wine.

My fucking *bullshitometor* starts ringing in my ears like a fucking foghorn. What the horseshit is going on? What contract? I'm Carter's second in command for a reason and usually I know everything that's happening when it comes to his business. So why the fuck am I suddenly in the dark?

"Boss, is there anything I need to be aware of?" I ask, as the waiter moves around the table and takes everyone's orders. When he reaches my side I point to some random shit on the menu having no idea what I've just ordered, given it's all written in French. I'm not fucking hungry anyway.

"We'll have a discussion later, for now let's enjoy this meal," Carter replies, taking a sip of his red wine. I'm pretty sure the bottle costs more than your average weekly wage. He's really pushing the boat out for this prick.

"So, Grim, tell me about the subjects you're studying at school?" the King asks, focusing his slimy, good-for-nothing bastard attention back on her. "I must say, I'd have placed you a little older than school age…"

He allows that comment to hang in the air and I can't help but notice how Carter shifts in his seat, avoiding eye contact with Kate, let alone me. The fuck kind of comment is that anyway?

Kate folds her hands in her lap and looks the King directly in his eyes, taking her measure of him. "I'm no longer at *school*, Mr…" she allows her voice to trail off.

"Just call me King," he replies, licking his lips as he watches her.

She nods. "As I was saying, *Mr King*, I'm not at school. I left college this summer and I'm learning the ins and outs of the business. In fact, right now I'm going over the plans for the Tales rebuild, ensuring the architect has everything in place ready for when the builders come in. Isn't that right, *Father*?"

Carter nods, seemingly oblivious to that little tell. Kate's pissed. She never refers to Carter as Father, it's either Carter or Dad. To look at her now you wouldn't know it though. She's poised and cool as a fucking cucumber, not to mention smoking fucking hot. Which is a big fucking problem, given the King is staring at her in a way that makes me want to pick up the steak knife resting beside my hand and stab it into his motherfucking eye.

King shifts in his seat. "Is that so? Carter tells me you've quite the business brain, that you're smart."

"Smart enough," she agrees coolly.

Smart enough to suss this guy out in less than ten seconds, that's for damn sure. Kate might think no one knows her, but I do. I know that right now her inner warning bells are going off just like mine are. You don't grow up surrounded by criminals without knowing very quickly who you can trust and who you need to shoot in the motherfucking head when the time is right. This guy has a bullet with his name etched on the surface just waiting to blow his brains out. Not that I'd share my thoughts with her, after all, her dad's my boss and whether I like it or not I have to respect his decisions, even if I don't fucking like them.

"You want to run Tales when you're older?" he asks, cocking his head at her.

"I'm learning the business so I can run Tales alongside my father *now*," she retorts, jerking her chin at the waiter and tapping the wine glass. "You seem to have forgotten to pour me some."

The waiter's cheeks flush a deep red and he mumbles his apologies whilst trying not to spill the wine all over the damn table cloth. Picking up the glass, she takes a sip, watching the King over the rim of her glass.

"Aren't you a little young to be taking on such responsibility? Surely there are far more interesting things that you should be concerning yourself with. A beauty like yourself would make the perfect queen for the right man."

Without even thinking about what I'm doing, my fingers wrap around the handle of the knife resting on the table. No one but Kate appears to notice, and beneath the table she rests her hand on my thigh, squeezing it gently. It does the fucking trick and stills my hand.

"Mr King, not only am I old enough to run *any* business I set my sights on, but I'm also fully capable of becoming queen without the need of a man. In fact, I'm certain I could take on the title of king too," she replies sweetly, but there's no mistaking the fire or the warning in her eyes.

Her dad snaps his gaze to her. It's a not so sly dig to him as well, and I can't help but feel a well of pride bloom in my chest. She might not have shot Saxon in the head, but she sure as fuck is showing that she means business.

That's my girl.

My girl? I shove that thought to the back of my head. I can't afford any more distractions tonight. Carter clears his throat, casting his gaze from Kate to the King, a nerve ticking in his eyelid. I've rarely seen him get nervous, but right now he's shitting a brick and I want to know why.

"Yes, Kate has her uses."

Uses?

My teeth grind together so hard that the sound is unmistakable. Next to me Kate flinches as though slapped, but to her credit that's the only physical reaction to her dad's disparaging remark that she reveals.

"That's good to know," the King replies with a smirk that I want to wipe off his face. "But women have no place in business, especially not the kind of business we deal in."

"Says the fuck who... *You?*" I ask, unable to stop myself.

The King turns his attention to me as Carter squirms in his seat. I can't help but imagine grabbing both their heads and slamming them together for being such fucking pricks. The King because he's clearly a hater of women, particularly those who're smarter than him, and Carter for not stepping in and putting a stop to this bullshit or reeling his own neck in.

"Do you disagree?" the King asks me.

"You bet your fucking—"

"Beast, could you pour me a glass of water?" Kate interjects, giving my leg another squeeze. I barely register her touch over the fucking rage fizzing through my blood right now. "Beast?" she prompts, firmer this time.

My fingers release from around the knife handle because as much as I want to slit this motherfucker's throat, I'm also all too aware that there's some deeper shit at play here and I need to keep my head to find out exactly what that is. Kate's picked up on it too, and she's playing the long game. I need to take a leaf out of her book.

"Apologies, no offence meant. I'm what you call *old school*. I appreciate the value of a good woman running a household and bearing my children. That is far more impressive than running a business in my humble opinion," the King says, smiling in what I assume he believes is a charming way, but only makes him look more like the slimy snake he is.

"It *is* impressive, you're right," Kate replies, her finger tapping against the table top, the only tell that she's losing her patience too. "Bringing up children and running a household is underestimated by most men, but I disagree that women have no place in business. It's an archaic and, frankly, misogynistic view of the world. Tell me, Mr King, how does your wife feel about such matters?"

Kate's gaze rests on the wedding ring the King wears before raising her brows. Carter looks as though he's either about to lose his shit or hide under the table, neither of which are appropriate responses for how well Kate is handling herself right now. He should be stepping in and backing her instead of allowing this horseshit to continue.

"Soon to be ex-wife," the King replies, twisting the band on his finger.

"And yet you're still wearing your wedding ring."

"Force of habit," the King shrugs, removing the ring and pocketing it. "That better?"

Kate keeps her expression blank. "For her, I imagine it is."

I snort, biting down the laugh that threatens to erupt. The King's eyes narrow and Carter's face pales but we're all saved by the waiter who delivers our food. I look down at my plate, eyes wide.

"What the fuck is this?" I bark out, causing the waiter to jump and almost drop the tray he's holding.

Kate laughs, the sound is light and carefree despite the evening's events and the smouldering look the King is giving her for insulting him so eloquently. "You ordered escargot... *Snails*," she adds when I snatch my head around to look at her.

"And you didn't think to tell me I was going to get a plate full of garden munchers?"

"Garden munchers?" Kate snorts with laughter then quickly straightens her expression.

"Would you rather I call them snot balls?"

"*Escargot* is a delicacy in France. Try something new, you might like it," she replies, the innuendo not lost on me as she flashes a smile that has my cock jumping.

"I would advise against that," the King says, watching our exchange as he carves into the barely dead slab of meat in front of him. "In my experience it's better to stick with what you know rather than indulge in something that could disagree with you, don't you think?"

I narrow my eyes at him, pick up the weird-shaped fork the waiter set down for me and pull out the snail from its shell, popping it in my mouth. Chewing, I swallow, surprised by how tasty it is. "You know what, Princess, you're right, I do like it. Trying new things ain't so bad after all. I could go as far as saying that it's pretty fucking tempting."

She grins. "Told you."

The King chews on his steak, focusing his gaze on Kate as he swallows. "Isn't temptation man's greatest downfall?"

Kate dabs her mouth with her napkin before responding. "I think that depends on the man, don't you?"

CHAPTER THIRTEEN

Let Me Down Slowly

"Do you want to tell me what's going on?" I ask, twisting in my seat to face Carter as Beast drives us home. I catch his gaze in the rear view mirror, unable to discern the look in his eyes.

My dad swipes a hand over his face, before pinching the bridge of his nose. "We've gone into business together."

"The club?" I ask, hating the way he won't look at me. Everything feels off.

"Yes and no."

"What's that supposed to mean?" I push, flinching at the sharp look he gives me.

"It means what it means. Stop asking questions, Grim."

"Dad—"

"I said enough! When the time is right you'll know. Right now I need to take a couple of sleeping pills and pass the fuck out. I've got a splitting fucking headache. It's been a long weekend." He rubs at his temples, groaning.

"Then why invite me to dinner tonight if you're not going to let me in on what deal you've got going with the King, who's a chauvinistic pig by the way. I have a right to know what's going on."

Dropping his hands, Carter twists his body to face me. "Firstly, whilst I might have given you more insight into the business and some responsibility with the refit, Tales is *my* club. Who I choose to do business with has fuck all to do with you. Know your place."

I suck in a sharp breath. "My *place?*"

"That's right. I'm the boss. I decide who I do business with, not you. Do you understand me?"

"But—" My voice comes out in a croak, and I hate it. I hate that my own dad has been able to cut me so deep, so easily.

"No buts. This is *my* business."

"I thought you said that you wanted me to be your partner? Why have you given me the responsibility of the refit if you didn't think I was capable of overseeing it?"

He looks me up and down, and I feel his disgust sink into my skin. What the hell is wrong with him? "Is dressing like an attention-seeking whore befitting of someone I want running the club beside me, huh? I think fucking not."

Beast slams on the brakes, my gasp lost beneath the sounds of the tires squealing as we're all thrown forward in our seats. My father throws his hands out, slamming them onto the back of Beast's seat.

"What the fuck, Beast?!" he shouts, oblivious to the tear that fucking escapes my eye. I swipe at it, refusing to let my dad see how hurt I am by his words. It's surprisingly painful.

"Apologies, a cat just ran into the road," Beast replies, twisting in his seat. He looks at me, an unreadable expression on his face. "You alright?"

"I'm fine," I reply tightly.

"Just take us fucking home," Carter snaps.

"Yes, *boss*." Beast puts the car into drive, his fingers gripping the wheel so tightly his knuckles are white.

The rest of the journey is spent in awkward silence. By the time we've pulled up outside the house it's nearing midnight, but the last thing I want to do is go inside. Carter's words are like a fucking dagger to my heart and there's no way I'm ready to sleep under the same roof as him. Beast cuts the engine and Carter reaches for the handle like he can't wait to get away from me.

"Carter. *Dad*..."

"We'll talk tomorrow," he grinds out, opening the door and striding towards the house without a backwards glance.

I stare after him, stunned by his attitude towards me. "What the fuck did I do wrong?" I mumble, more to myself than to Beast who is staring at me in the rear view mirror.

"Princess..."

"Don't. Whatever it is you're about to say, I don't want to fucking hear it."

"*Kate*, listen to me," he begins.

"Just get me out of here."

"What?"

"I said get me out of here. I don't want to go inside. Just take me somewhere, anywhere away from here," I reply, unclipping my seatbelt and leaning over to pull the door shut. I fall back in my seat, feeling the heat of Beast's gaze on me. Out of the corner of my eye I can see he's twisted in his seat and is staring heatedly at me. "What?"

"Your dress," he replies, his gaze snapping up when I look at him.

"What about it?" I let out a heavy sigh. "What's so fucking wrong with what I'm wearing?"

"That's not what I meant. It's just—"

"What?!" I snap, glaring at him.

"I can see your…" He gulps, twisting in his seat and facing forward, stepping on the gas as he drives us back down the driveway and onto the main road. "Fuck."

A slow heat creeps over my skin as my gaze slowly drops to my lap. My dress has ridden up and the thigh slit has shifted to reveal my neatly trimmed pussy. "Shit!" I exclaim, pulling the material down, my whole body aflame as I rest my head back against the headrest and press my palms over my face. I hadn't worn any underwear to provoke Beast. I'd done it on purpose, to get his attention, but now that I have it, it doesn't feel half as good as I hoped it would. I'm exactly what my dad accused me of being.

"He was right. How can anyone take me seriously when I'm dressed like a whore?"

"The fuck you say?" Beast growls, stepping on the brake for the second time tonight.

"You heard me," I reply, pulling my seatbelt around me and clicking it into place. Despite my humiliation, I don't want to die because I wasn't smart enough to put a seatbelt on.

"That's bullshit! Don't ever let me hear you speak about yourself like that again. Got me?"

"Why? It's true."

"The fuck it is," he snaps, hitting the gas again and speeding off down the road. I've no idea where he's taking me, but I don't question it. Instead, I stare out of the window as silence descends between us. This is the most vulnerable I've ever been and I hate it. I'm not this girl who lets shit get to her, who feels sorry for herself. Yet, here I am doing exactly that.

"Firstly, you ain't dressed like a whore, you're a perfect fucking vision of beauty *and* badassery," Beast suddenly says a few minutes of awkward silence later. My gaze snaps to him as he concentrates on the road ahead. I can't help but notice how that muscle in his jaw jumps as he grits his teeth. "Secondly, and for the motherfucking record, what you wear should never have any bearing on your value or your worth. None. Thirdly, and most importantly, the way you handled yourself tonight was nothing less than regal. You're a fucking *Queen*."

I scoff. "If that were true then why did you ask me to wear something else, Beast? Admit it, you thought the exact same thing."

"You've no idea what I was thinking."

"Whatever you say," I retort bitterly.

"I mean it, Princess. You don't know shit."

"I know enough."

Beast doesn't reply. He doesn't say another word until we pull up outside a large white house on a tree-lined suburban street twenty minutes later. It has four floors, and a big green door with several doorbells indicating the house is split into flats. I can see a woman talking on a telephone through one of the windows on the fourth floor, and a soft pink glow from a window on the first. Putting the car in park, Beast kills the engine, turning around to face me.

"Well, here we are."

"Where's here exactly?"

"My place."

"*Your* place?"

"Don't sound so surprised, where did you think I'd take you?"

"To a bar or a club. I was hoping to get drunk."

"Exactly."

I roll my eyes. "What are you going to do, make me a cup of cocoa and put me to bed like a good little girl?"

"Pretty much, yeah," he replies, climbing out of the car and slamming the door behind him. When I don't follow him he strides around to my side of the car and yanks open the door.

"Out."

"Just call me a cab. I'll head over to Macey's Bar. You don't need to babysit me anymore. I'll give Hudson a call when I get there. He'll keep me company."

He scowls. "Yeah, not happening."

"Look, I got this. I've had my mini meltdown. I'm *fine* now. I just want to blow off some steam," I say, letting out a light laugh in an attempt to convince both Beast and myself that my dad's insults and the weirdness this evening hasn't thrown me through a loop.

"Not tonight you won't, because you'll be spending some quality time with me," Beast says as he leans over and unclips my seatbelt before grasping my elbow and guiding me out of the car.

"Don't you have better things to do? You really are taking your job responsibilities one step too far," I say, pulling out of his hold and wrapping my arms around myself.

"Just get inside."

"No."

"Do you really want me to sling you over my shoulder? Because I will. You know I will," he warns, raising his eyebrows. I almost, *almost* test his threat, then I remember I'm not wearing any underwear and I really don't need the added humiliation of anyone else seeing my lady garden tonight. What the fuck was I thinking?

"Fine," I retort, striding towards the front door so he can't see how red my cheeks flame.

Beast locks the car then jogs to catch up with me, opening the front door and leading me inside. The communal hallway is blandly decorated with a black and white tiled floor and white walls, he stops briefly to pick up a pile of post resting on the hall table before striding towards the end of the corridor.

"Mine's the garden flat. You'll have to excuse the mess. I'm not exactly used to visitors."

"Really? I thought you were like the Don Giovanni of East London."

"Don Giovanni, who's that?" Beast frowns as he opens the door to his place, and ushers me inside.

"You mean you don't know the story about the world's greatest lover?" I ask, with a smirk.

"Funny. Just make yourself at home," he replies, turning on the light switch and illuminating his small but surprisingly tidy flat.

"I thought you said it was a mess," I say, kicking off my

stilettos and groaning as my feet sink into the carpet. It's a very minimalist space, with a big brown leather couch in the centre of the room and a large wall-mounted TV, a coffee table and a bookshelf filled with books. I wander over to it, passing french doors on the right and a small, but perfectly adequate kitchen on the left.

"Looks like my cleaner came today," Beast replies from what must be his bedroom. He's left the door ajar and I can see him shucking off his jacket and shirt, pulling on a t-shirt and hoodie. He's got his back to me, and I've got the perfect view of his broad shoulders and tattooed back. When he reaches down to undo his trousers I drag my gaze away from him and to the bookshelf in front of me, running my fingers over the spines to distract me from the fact that my nipples have hardened and my pussy is doing her best impression of a butterfly's wings quivering in the sun. Jesus, even my skin feels hot.

"I didn't know you were a big reader," I say, pulling out a copy of Lady Chatterley's Lover and flipping it open.

"They're not my books," Beast says from behind me.

I turn to face him, my mouth drying at the way he studies me. "Who do they belong to then?" I ask as he approaches me with a pair of boxer shorts and t-shirt. He takes the book from me and hands me the clothes. I clutch them to my chest, almost lowering my head to the material so I can breathe in his familiar scent, but manage to stop myself.

"My mum was an avid reader. She loved all of that romantic shit, not like those weird as fuck fairy tales you read," he replies, running his fingers over the cover before leaning over me and sliding the book back into its spot on the shelf.

"They're not weird. Well, maybe a bit…" My voice trails off

as he looks down at me, his gaze meeting mine. There's a whole host of pain in his eyes and I want so fucking badly for him to open up to me again.

"Well, it ain't no Disney shit, that's for sure."

"That's why I like it. Life isn't like a fairy tale and neither are the books I read."

"You're not wrong there, Princess." He nods, a faraway look in his eyes.

"Do you want to tell me some more about her...?" I ask, my voice trailing off when he lifts his other hand and grips the shelf behind me, trapping me between his body and the bookcase.

"No point in talking about ghosts. It doesn't do anyone any good."

"Okay," I reply and he nods, holding my gaze for so long that for a second I think he's going to kiss me. I freeze, my stomach flipping. "Beast?"

"Go change. You can take my bed. I'll sleep on the couch," he says, stepping back abruptly.

"You don't have to do that."

"I do," he insists.

"I can take the couch. Seriously, it's fine."

"Princess, for once in your life just do as you're told," he says with exasperation.

"Sure, okay," I concede. "I'll just be a minute."

"I'll put the kettle on, unless you want that cup of cocoa?" He grins, some of the tension between us releasing with his smile.

"I could do with something stronger. Got any bourbon?"

"Sure do," he replies as I head into his bedroom, which is as sparse as the front room, and he strides into the kitchen.

I quickly change, removing my dress and chucking it on the bed before pulling on his boxer shorts that slip low on my hips given he's that much bigger than me. His t-shirt is like a nightie but I don't care though, wearing his clothes makes me feel safe somehow.

By the time I've changed, he's sitting on the couch with a glass of bourbon in his hand, staring at the liquid like it holds answers to all the questions that are clearly troubling him. I wonder if he's as thrown by tonight's events as I am. Given how he reacted to the King, I'm sure he is.

There's no denying that Carter was acting weird, the sheer fact he's going into business with that creepy arsehole is testament to that. I don't like the King, and neither does Beast, which has me questioning why Carter trusts him. I thought he was smarter than that.

"Thanks for the clothes," I say, stepping into Beast's line of sight.

He slowly lifts his gaze, his eyes dragging up my bare legs, over my t-shirt covered chest until they finally rest on my face. Heat rises beneath my skin from his slow perusal and there's nothing I can do to hide the fact that my nipples stand to attention beneath his heated gaze.

"You're welcome," he murmurs, lifting the glass to his lips and taking a sip as he passes me a glass already filled.

I take a seat, pulling my legs up and under me as I twist to face him. "What do you think Carter's up to?"

Beast sighs, knocking back the rest of his drink. He places the glass on the table and folds his hands into his lap. "I'm sure he knows what he's doing."

I take a sip of the bourbon, relishing the burn. "You really think that?"

"He's an astute businessman, Princess."

"And an arsehole."

"I reckon he's just having an off day," Beast says, playing it down. "Don't take too much notice."

"An off day? He's been shitty towards me ever since I handed you the gun to shoot Saxon."

He doesn't agree but he doesn't say anything to the contrary either.

"And the King, what do you think about him?" I ask, knowing full well he dislikes the man as much as I do, that much was obvious from the way he reacted to him this evening.

"I'm not a fan."

"He's a dick..." My voice trails off as I nurse my shot of bourbon and we fall into an awkward silence that I just don't seem to have the energy to fill. I'm exhausted all of a sudden and honestly, all I want is some human comfort. A hug. Apart from the occasional brotherly hug from Hudson, I'm sorely lacking in that department.

"Princess, about what Carter said earlier," Beast says after a while, drawing my attention back to him.

"What, about dressing like an *attention-seeking whore*?" I laugh bitterly, still feeling the sting.

"Yeah." He nods. "Your dad was wrong."

"So you said."

Beast shifts forward in his seat, and I catch a whiff of his scent as he moves. Fuck, he really smells good. "I mean it. That was a shitty fucking thing to say."

"True though."

"Not in the fucking slightest!"

Knocking back the bourbon for dutch courage, I settle the glass on the coffee table and meet Beast's angry glare. "But it was. You were right about everything, Beast."

"Right about what?"

"Before when you said that I was flirting with you, I *was*. I dressed like I did tonight to get you to notice me," I admit.

"Princess, don't do this," he warns.

"I wanted to tempt you. I wanted you to want me. Fucking stupid because to you I'm just a kid, *right?*" I press, knowing in my heart that he's been lying to himself as much as he's been lying to me.

"Princess, I've told you—"

"To the King, I'm a mindless bimbo whose only purpose is to be someone's trophy wife, and to my dad, I'm no better than a fucking whore, a *disappointment*," I interrupt. When he doesn't argue, I heave out a sigh. "I've grown up around bad men my whole life, Beast. I've seen and heard shit that would screw with most people's heads. The irony is I stopped being a kid a long time ago, yet the moment I dress like a woman I'm made to feel worthless. It fucking stinks."

Beast scrapes a hand over his face. "It's a tough world we live in, Princess. Tougher for you."

"Because I'm a woman?" I ask.

"Yes, because you're a woman, but also because you're Carter's kid—"

"Daughter. I'm his *daughter*. I'm not a kid."

"Daughter," Beast corrects, his gaze dropping to my bare legs then quickly lifting back up again. "You have to be ten times tougher and twenty times smarter to survive. There ain't no getting away from that fact. This business we're in is full of men who will either want to fuck you or end you."

"And where do you fall, Beast? Do you want to *end* me or *fuck* me?" I ask.

His eyes flare with, what? Anger? Lust? I'm honestly not certain.

"Neither. I'm here to protect you. Guide you. Keep you safe from making stupid decisions," he answers and I swallow down the disappointment I feel at his lack of honesty. We both know he wants to fuck me.

"And yet you stopped me from shooting Saxon, from making a point that I'm not to be messed with. *That* was a stupid decision."

"I didn't stop you. You made a choice. The right one, by the way," he adds quickly.

"You and I both know that isn't true."

Guilt flashes across his features. "I was trying to protect you," he admits.

"I know that," I say with a heavy sigh.

"Princess, there's a time to take action, and a time when you need to take a step back. I've learnt that the hard way."

"So give me some tips on surviving this world, *oh wise one*," I say, trying and failing to bring a little levity to the moment.

"That's easy, you need to pay attention."

"Pay attention?" I shift on the sofa as he pours himself another drink, my gaze drifting to his thick forearms and the muscles that flex beneath his beautifully tattooed skin. "You want another?"

He catches me staring at him, but instead of pretending I'm not, I just nod. "Sure."

Our fingers brush as he hands me the glass, but I ignore the tingly feeling his touch gives me and wait for him to continue.

"Pay attention to what's going on around you, and trust your gut. Always."

"What else?"

"Surround yourself with people who are willing to kill for you, who are willing to die for you…"

His voice trails off as he swirls the bourbon in his glass, watching me intently.

"Can I count on you, Beast?"

"I'm Carter's second in command."

"What does that mean exactly?"

"He hired me to look out for you, so that's what I do."

"But being paid to look out for someone, and doing it because you care about them are two very different things. Which side do you fall on, Beast?"

"Does it matter? I've got your back either way," he replies.

"It matters to me," I say, taking Beast's glass from him and resting it on the coffee table alongside mine. "You said I need to pay attention. I already do. I see how you look at me."

"Princess, listen," Beast begins, but I take his hands in mine. He tenses, but he doesn't pull away.

"No, *you* listen. I pay attention. You were going to stab the King tonight because you were angry at the way he was eye-fucking me. You brought me here because you didn't want me to get blind drunk and spend the evening with Hudson. You *care*. Why?"

"It's my job to care."

"No, it's more than that and you know it."

"Princess, I've said this before and I'll say it again, *nothing* will happen between us. Understand?"

"No?" I ask, dropping his hands and reaching for the hem of his t-shirt, ripping it over my head. Cool air rushes over my skin and my nipples pucker under his attention as my hair falls over my shoulders, brushing against the tops of my breasts.

"Princess, what the fuck?!" he exclaims, his gaze lifting from my bare breasts as he glares at me. "Put the fucking t-shirt back on."

"Why?"

"Because I won't be that man."

"What man?"

"The one who takes advantage. Now put the t-shirt back on."

"No," I shake my head, my fingers curling into the material of his t-shirt that I'm still holding. "You want to touch me, just like I want to touch you. I'm eighteen in a few weeks. I'm an adult."

"The fact you even need to say that tells me you're not. Stop fucking around," he warns, licking his lips as he resolutely keeps his gaze fixed firmly on my face.

"Earlier you said I was the *perfect vision of beauty and badassery* which, by the way, was pretty fucking poetic."

"I was trying to make you feel better. Christ, what the fuck is this?"

"Touch me," I whisper, shifting closer, dropping the t-shirt and resting my hands on his knees.

When he doesn't shove me away, I decide to just go for it and clamber onto his lap. With my knees pressing either side of his hips, I grip his shoulders, looking down at him.

"Princess, this is what playing with fire feels like."

"I don't care. Make me burn."

His eyes flare and his chest heaves as he focuses on my face, refusing to look any lower, but despite his steadfastness, he doesn't stop what's happening. I settle onto his lap, my pussy pressing up against the hard ridge of his cock. Fuck, he's big.

"This isn't going to happen."

"You're hard for me," I whisper, grinding against him. He stays silent, still, and his hands remain stubbornly by his side. "Why won't you touch me? I know you want to. I feel how much you do."

"Princess... *Kate*, you need to stop this," he says through gritted teeth.

"I want you to fuck me, Beast," I whisper, running my palms over his shoulders, revelling in the way he feels beneath my hands and between my legs as I rock against him. He's so masculine, so strong, so *him*. My piercing rubs against his shaft and I see the way his eyes flare with hunger. His mouth drops open, words forming behind the lust and I know if I let him speak this will be over. "My dad called me a whore, but the truth is *you* were right. I am a virgin, but I'd be a whore for you if you'd let me."

"FUCK!" he roars, his hands on my waist as he lifts me roughly off his lap and stands, pushing me away. I look up at him, my own chest heaving as he glares at me, fuming. "I told you, no!"

"But—"

"The word no means the same damn thing for a man as it does a woman. I said no!"

Shame creeps up my spine, and I grab the discarded t-shirt,

covering my chest.

"Fuck you," I hiss, the rejection hitting me hard as I quickly pull on the t-shirt. "You're a coward."

"I ain't no coward. If I wanted you, I would've taken you by now. I would've ripped that dress from your tight little body and fucked you against the wall the second you stepped into this flat. Your pretty little pussy would've bled for me, and I would've lapped up your blood and your cum, then fucked you over and over again until I buried my cock so deep inside of you, you'd be choking on it!" he roars.

"And an egomaniac!" I shout back, grabbing the bottle of bourbon and swigging back a generous amount to calm my racing heart and throbbing pussy. He snatches the bottle from me and slams it back onto the coffee table so hard that I'm surprised the bottle doesn't shatter.

"There's one thing you need to understand about me, *Princess*," he snarls, breathing heavily. "I'm a man of my word. I promised Carter that I would watch over you as if you were my own flesh and blood, that I would protect you like you were my little sister. You're off the motherfucking menu, not just because I gave your father my word, but because I don't screw my family. Got it?"

"Loud and clear," I grind out, wishing the fucking ground would swallow me up whole, but refusing to let him know how much he's got to me.

"Good! You can sleep on the motherfucking sofa, I'm going to bed."

With that he grabs the bottle of bourbon and storms into his bedroom, slamming the door behind him leaving me feeling humiliated and more alone than ever.

CHAPTER FOURTEEN

Hands to Myself

"Morning Carter, Dom said you wanted a word," I say the following morning as I step into his office at Tales.

Carter stabs out his cigarette, blowing a plume of blue-grey smoke up into the air. "Where's Grim?"

"Dropped her back home. Why?"

Carter narrows his eyes at me. "Where did you take her last night?"

"To my place."

"You *what?!*" he snaps, eyes narrowing at me as he shifts forward in his seat.

"It was either that or let her get blind drunk at Macey's with that fucker Hudson Freed. She slept on the sofa."

"The sofa?"

"Better that than my bed, right?"

"Beast, you're pushing your fucking luck!" Carter exclaims running his hands through his salt and pepper hair.

"She's like my kid sister. You don't have to worry about me," I say, knowing full well that's a damn lie.

When I clapped eyes on her in that red dress last night, I wanted her. When the King fucking undressed her with his eyes, I wanted to fucking kill him for daring to look at what's mine, and when she'd pulled off my t-shirt flashing me her perfect tits... Fuck, I *needed* her.

Despite all of that I didn't touch her. So he really ain't got shit to worry about.

I'm a fucking *saint*.

Carter nods, his shoulders relaxing. "Good. Take a seat, I want to discuss a few things with you."

"This about the King?" I ask, folding myself into the chair on the opposite side of his desk.

"Partly."

"Okay, I'm all ears."

Carter pulls another cigarette from his packet and lights it up, taking a deep drag. "The King wants a slice of the pie."

"I figured as much."

"He thinks we can expand the business by drawing in fighters from across Europe. He's got contacts all over the world. His reach is far. He wants to help this club get a reputation as the number one fight club in Europe, and wants a cut of the profits for helping to drive business and talent our way."

"Not being funny, Boss, but we can do that ourselves without his help."

"Perhaps, but it would take a lot more time, and I'm not a

patient man. Tales has been open almost a year and we're not seeing the kind of traffic through our doors as I'd hoped, despite my best efforts. We need a wider variety of fighters. I want the best of the best fighting in my club. I want fucking bloodshed. Nothing gets punters going like the possibility of a death in the ring."

"And I'm not the best of the best?" I ask, fucking insulted.

"You're a good fighter, sure, but you've done the rounds. I need fresh meat, and so do our punters. There's only so many times they can watch you fight and win. Gets boring."

"So find me some fucker who's actually a challenge and maybe it wouldn't be."

"Which is why I've enlisted the King."

"What does Ransom think about this, given he was the one who bankrolled Tales in the first place?"

"I paid off his loan three months ago. He no longer has a say in what I do with *my* club."

"You know what the King's about, right? He might have plenty of contacts but he's not the kind of man I ever thought you'd go into business with."

"What he does in his private life is irrelevant to me," Carter replies tightly, drawing on his cigarette, the tip sizzling.

"Yeah, and how about the way he eye-fucked Grim last night? How about that? Are you willing to team up with that arsehole when he's got a hard-on for your daughter?" I ask, knowing I've overstepped but not giving a shit.

Carter stubs out his cigarette roughly, then points at me. "Don't fucking question my decisions. This is happening. End of."

"Yes, Boss." I grind out, suddenly needing to beat the shit out of something. If I don't leave this office soon, it could end up being Carter's face. I move to stand, but Carter holds his hand up.

"I need you to do something for me."

"Yeah, what's that?"

"Keep a close eye on Grim."

"I already do."

"A closer eye then. If she sneaks off to meet anyone, I want to know about it. If she so much as looks at a man, I want you to rip their fucking dick off. She's to remain untouched. *Pure.* Got it?"

"Untouched. Yeah, I got it, loud and clear," I reply, pushing back the chair probably a little too roughly. Mostly because who the fuck does he think he is cock blocking her? But also because I'm just as much of a prick as he is as I'm more than happy to oblige. No fucker on this planet gets to touch my girl.

No one.

Not even me.

"And Beast..." Carter calls just as I reach the door.

"Yeah, Boss?"

"I'm throwing a party here at the club in a couple weeks for Grim's eighteenth birthday."

"She wants that?" I ask, knowing that the kind of party he's talking about won't be with Kate in mind.

He shrugs. "It'll be good for business. Besides, I'm bringing the refit on the club forward. Figured we'd squeeze in a knees up before then."

"Got it." I bite my tongue, holding back from telling him what I truly think about his *party* for Kate.

"Problem?" he questions, sensing my dislike.

"Nope. Is it going to be open or closed?" I ask, meaning will the club be open for business as usual on the night of the party or invite only.

"Closed. I'll put together a list of people I want invited. Can't have any old Tom, Dick or Harry attending Grim's birthday party now, can we?"

"Definitely not," I agree, already smarting because she'll be the centre of attention of a shit load of criminals, all of whom will be sniffing around her like she's fair game.

"I've also arranged for you and Dom to fight next weekend. I've invited the King, figured he needs to see how we run things here. Are you willing to take the headline fight on the night?"

"Are you sure I'm good enough?"

He smirks. "You're too good, that's the fucking problem. Maybe let your opponent get a few licks in before knocking him the fuck out."

"Sure, why not. I can play cat and mouse for a while. Who am I fighting?"

"You'll be fighting Clayton and Dom will be up against Ramone."

I raise a brow, impressed he's managed to lock down Clayton. The guy's known for putting up a good fight and is as prolific as I am when it comes to winning fights. "A challenge at last," I remark.

"Think you can handle it?"

"Without a doubt," I reply, pulling the door open, ready to go train in the gym for a few hours.

"Good... Oh, and one last thing," Carter says, just as his phone starts ringing. He looks at the screen, and punches the answer button asking the caller to hold for a minute. "I've booked Grim an appointment with Miranda at House of Imperials on Rathbone Street in a couple of hours so she can find something appropriate to wear for the party. I need you to go with her and make sure she doesn't end up choosing another whorish dress like she wore last night. Make sure Miranda knows to pick her out something sophisticated, know what I'm saying?"

"Yeah, loud and clear," I respond with a scowl, stepping out of Carter's office before I do something stupid and get myself shot in the head for rearranging his face.

He might be my boss, but he's still a fucking prick.

"WHY ARE WE HERE AGAIN?" Kate asks dryly, as we pull up outside House of Imperials, an upmarket clothing store for wives, daughters and mistresses of London's most notorious gangsters.

"Carter wants you to pick out an outfit for the party he's organising for you at Tales for your birthday."

"Party?"

"Yep. Must be his way of apologising."

"I don't need a party or clothes for that matter, but a sorry would've been nice," she replies guardedly.

"You and I both know that's never gonna happen. Carter never apologises," I say, putting the car in park and killing the engine.

"Did he mention to you anything about the King?"

"Yeah. He's got contacts around Europe apparently, and has access to a bigger range of fighters. Together they want to make Tales the best fight club in Europe, or so he said."

"We can bring in fighters ourselves, we don't need the King's help."

"My argument exactly."

"Carter didn't listen to you, I take it?" she asks, sighing.

I shake my head. "No. He's an impatient man and the King has offered him a way to get the club where he wants it to be quickly."

"For what price?"

"A cut of the takings, of course," I say.

"Of course." She frowns, chewing on the inside of her cheek.

"What?"

"I don't trust him."

She lets that statement hang in the air and I don't try to counter her view because I don't trust the prick either, and right now I'm having trouble trusting Carter as well. "Come on, let's get this over with," I say instead.

"Do I have to?" she groans. "I'd rather stick my nose in Dom's armpit after he's been training for two hours."

"The fuck?" I snap. Hell to the fuck no.

"What's the matter, Beast? Are you jealous?" she asks, the seriousness of our conversation making way for amusement.

"Just get inside the damn shop," I order, her laughter ringing in my ears as she climbs out of the car and strides towards the shop, my gaze following her jean-clad arse all the way inside.

The moment I enter House of Imperials, Miranda greets me with a flirty smile. "Good afternoon, Beast. So nice to see you again," she says, flipping her long blonde hair over her shoulder.

"You too, Miranda," I reply distractedly, casting my gaze around the store. It's empty apart from Kate searching through a rack of clothing at the back of the shop. "Not busy today?"

Miranda laughs, the sultry tone irritating rather than attractive as she presses her fingers against my arm, drawing my attention back to her. "We're a *by appointment only* store, remember? Kate will get our undivided attention for the next hour... As will you," she adds under her breath.

"Yeah?" I say, looking over at Kate who's watching us both with barely veiled jealousy. I really shouldn't get a kick out of that, but fuck, do I.

"Collette will be with Miss Davidson in just a moment. Can I interest you in a drink in our lounge whilst you wait?"

"As tempting as that sounds, I'm under strict instructions from the boss to ensure Kate picks the perfect outfit, but I'll take that drink," I reply, knowing full well that an invite into the lounge is just a euphemism for a blow job or, if the ladies are feeling extra generous, sex. It's why the majority of the gangsters bring their ladies here because of the extra services provided. Their wives and mistresses get a whole new wardrobe and turn a blind eye to what happens in the lounge. Fucked-up if you ask me.

"After work then?" Miranda asks, stepping closer as she bites on her bottom lip.

"Sorry, I'm washing my hair," I reply, which draws laughter from Kate's lips as I stride towards her.

"What's wrong, Beast? It's not like you to pass up an offer like that," Kate says, searching through a rack of dresses as she side-eyes me.

"I don't sleep with everyone that offers themselves up to me. As you well know, Princess," I say, dropping onto the armchair just outside the fitting room. I meant it as a joke, a lighthearted way to let her know there are no hard feelings but it comes out condescending and I mentally berate myself for being such a fucking dick.

Kate's fingers still on the rack, her shoulders stiffening before she grabs a bland-looking dress and twists on her feet to face me. "And I don't offer myself up to just anyone, as *you* well know."

"Princess—"

"Screw you," she snaps, striding past me as she enters the changing room and roughly draws the curtain closed behind her.

"See, that's the whole fucking problem, Princess..." I mutter, scraping a hand over my face as I try to figure out how to deal with this situation.

"Has Miss Davidson found something to her liking?"

I snap my eyes open to find a pretty redhead, short in stature but not in curves, staring down at me. Her eyes alight with interest, and if I wasn't having issues with my fucking tormentor cursing my name behind the pulled curtain, I'd definitely be interested. As it is, my cock has other ideas, because no matter how hard I try to stop it my dick only springs to life for Kate.

"Yeah, she found something," I reply, jerking my thumb over my shoulder. "She's trying it on now."

"Perfect," the pretty redhead replies. "I'm Collette by the way."

"Yeah, Miranda said." I give her a once over, still my dick remains comatose.

"Nice to meet you, Mr...?"

"Just call me Beast."

She smiles, her cheeks flushing a deep pink. "Beast," she murmurs, then turning her back to me, searching through the rack and picking several dresses, hanging them on another rack on wheels.

My eyes fall to her shapely butt encased in a short, form-fitting black dress, and I cock my head trying to imagine bending her over and fucking her from behind, which until recently would've been exactly what would've happened. Not anymore. I ain't interested which, again, is a fucking problem.

"I don't like it," Kate says half a minute later, her bare arm poking out from behind the curtain, dress in hand. "I feel like a bloody housewife in it."

"Okay, so the Gucci dress isn't to your liking," Colette says, taking the dress from Kate and hanging it back up. "I've taken the liberty of choosing some dresses that fit the brief. Any one of these should be suitable."

"Wait, what brief?" Kate asks, yanking open the curtain, hand on her hip.

She's only in her fucking underwear, which I know shouldn't come as a surprise given she's standing in the changing room of an upmarket clothing boutique, but still, I do not need a fucking reminder of all the things I cannot have. Especially when her tight body is encased in black lace.

"Your father rang ahead, he was quite specific in his requirements."

"He did *what?*" she snaps.

"He called ahead..." Collette repeats, her voice trailing off as she looks between us. It doesn't take a genius to work out that Kate is about to blow a gasket.

"What exactly were his requirements?" she asks through gritted teeth.

"No skirts above the knee. No bare shoulders. No thigh high splits. No low cut front or back. No corsets."

"So what you're basically fucking saying is he wants me to wear a shapeless sack!" Kate shouts, pointing at the row of dresses Collette has picked out which, to be fair, look pretty fucking boring and shapeless.

"Well, I wouldn't describe these dresses as sacks. I have an Armani dress here that would work perfectly."

Kate snorts. "If Carter thinks I'm going to wear any of those fucking monstrosities, he's got another thing coming," Kate growls, and I have to hold in a laugh at the look on Collette's face when she strides out of the changing room and grabs a dress that is the total opposite of what her dad had described.

"I'm not sure that's appropriate—" Collette begins.

"And I'm sure I don't give a fuck!"

Kate storms back into the changing room drawing the curtain closed all the while cursing Carter out with language that colours the air blue.

"I'm just doing my job," Collette mutters, more than a little shaken from Kate's outburst. "Mr Davidson was very adamant. I really don't want to lose my job over this."

Blowing out a breath, I get to my feet. "Don't worry, Collette, I'll sort this out."

"You will?"

I nod. "Just go grab me that drink Miranda promised and bring a glass of champagne for Princess too."

"Of course," Collette says, giving me a small smile before turning on her heel and getting the hell out of dodge. I don't blame her, Kate's a firecracker at the best of times, but when she's mad, she's nothing short of volcanic.

Casting my eye over the rack of clothes, I grab a black lace, floor length dress that meets Carter's requirements, but is also sexy as fuck in an understated way. I'm pretty sure Kate would look hot as fuck in it, but Carter wouldn't be able to say a damn thing given not an inch of flesh will be shown. I'm no expert in high fashion, but I know the female form, and this dress will hug it in all the right places. Correction, this dress will hug *Kate's* body in all the right places. Not every woman could pull this dress off.

"Princess, Collette's gone to grab us both a drink, but I've got this dress that I think you'll love *and* will appease Carter."

"I don't want to fucking appease him. I want to wear what the fuck I want, when the fuck I want to. How dare he dictate to me what I should and shouldn't wear. In fact, how dare he dictate what I do at all?!"

"I get it, I do—"

"I didn't ask for a fucking party anyway!" she adds, her voice thick with emotion.

That fucking crack in her voice does stupid things to me, and not thinking my actions through, I shove aside the curtain and step inside the changing room with her, closing it behind me.

Her head snaps up. "What are you doing?"

"I thought this would look really good on you," I say, ignoring the way her chest flushes pink as I hold out the dress to her. Really, what the fuck am I doing in such a confined space with her? All I know right now is that I've got a motherfucking death wish and I'm about to be the first person to die of *blue-ballitis*.

Her gaze flicks to the lacy material as she looks it over. "It's just as shapeless as the rest."

"Put it on and I promise it will hug your figure like a second skin."

"Like a second skin?" she questions, discarding the dress she grabbed in her anger and fingering the material of the one I'm offering.

"Yep, like a second skin." I swallow hard, my gaze hyper focused on the centre of her forehead so that it doesn't slip to dangerous places.

"I'm pretty sure Carter didn't have this in mind when he was reeling off his list of rules for Collette," she gripes, taking it from me.

"Well, maybe your dad needs to be a little more specific? Besides, you're not showing an ounce of flesh, which meets his requirements and, in my opinion, is just as fucking sexy as a low cut, arse-skimming number.

"Is that so?" She smiles, taking the dress from me and twisting on her feet so she can hang it on the hook by the mirror and undo the zipper.

Despite trying really hard not to stare like a fucking creep, my gaze drops to the dip of her waist and curve of her hips as she takes the dress off the hanger and steps into it, pulling it up her body. The material glides like water over her skin as she slides her arms into the long sleeves, leaving a gap at the back where the zipper is still undone. My gaze is transfixed on the two little dimples in her lower back that are just begging to be licked, or better still filled with droplets of my cum... *Fuck!*

"I'll wait outside," I say, forcing my feet to move.

"Can you help me with the zipper first?" she asks, meeting my gaze in the mirror.

I should really say no. But fuck me, I don't.

Stepping forward I reach for the zipper, pinching it between my thumb and finger. My knuckle grazes her spine as I slowly pull it upwards. When the zipper reaches her mid back, I sweep Kate's hair over her shoulder, moving it out of the way.

She shivers. My cock leaps.

Our gazes lock in the mirror.

And for just a moment the world stops fucking spinning.

It's just me and Kate, standing inches apart in this tiny changing room with nothing but my resolve standing in the way of me fucking her against the cool glass of the mirror whilst Collette and Miranda listen on the other side of the curtain. My fingers slide beneath the material ever so slightly and I can't help but let out a rumble of appreciation at the silky smoothness of her skin.

I swear to fuck electricity sparks between us, I can feel it zapping over fingers and heading straight to my cock.

"Beast?" she whispers, her eyelids drooping slightly as the pad of my thumb traces up her spine.

I stare at the strip of flesh wanting so badly to chase my touch with my tongue, to lick up her back and across her shoulders to her neck so that I can suck and lick and bite her in that erogenous zone that most men are too fucking stupid to realise turns a woman into liquid fucking pleasure. It ain't just about the tits and pussy, there are many places on a woman's body that touching, licking and sucking in the right way will turn her on just as much.

Like the spot behind a woman's knee for example, or her inner thigh, the curve of her ankle, the soft underside of her wrist, the mound of her pussy, the underside of her rib cage, the palm of her hand...

I could go on.

The pulse in my cock throbs, and every part of me is strung tight with wanting her.

Fuck. I really need to keep my goddamn hands to myself.

"Beast?" Kate questions, louder this time.

I swallow hard, forcing myself to zip the dress up the rest of the way, and removing my hands. "Sorry, the zipper got caught on the material," I lie.

Our eyes meet and she nods. "Thank you."

"S'alright," I reply gruffly, staring at her reflection in the mirror. I was right, this dress does fit her like a glove. She looks like an absolute knockout in it. "You look beautiful."

The words are out before I can stop them from falling out of my mouth.

Kate's cheeks flush pink but she maintains eye contact with me. My fucking balls ache at the look she gives me, and my dick can't understand why I'm not currently buried to the hilt inside her sweet, sweet pussy.

"You were right, this dress *is* perfect," she says, smoothing her hands over the material.

"It's not the dress that's perfect, Princess, and don't you ever let any arsehole tell you otherwise. You're a motherfucking goddess," I say before twisting on my feet and stepping out of the changing room and as far away from fucking temptation as possible.

CHAPTER FIFTEEN

Woman

"One, two, three, four!" Matty calls, counting the beat before the music kicks in.

My stiletto heels drag across the floor as I grab the pole and kick out, hooking my right leg around the pole in a move called an inside hook, followed by an extended fireman. I spin around, loving how sexy I feel when I dance the pole. It's invigorating, and it's been helping to rid myself of this excess energy I've been feeling of late.

And by energy I mean sexual tension.

I'm wired. Hot and horny. It's torture.

"Go girl!" Nancy says, clapping encouragingly from the side of the stage where she's been sitting for the last hour, giving me tips, and correcting me as I dance.

She grins at me, and I smile back, grateful for her support. Fuck knows it's dangerous being here at Nine Lives. Not just for me, but for Matty and Nancy too. If Carter finds out I've gone against his wishes and am continuing to learn pole dancing, he's gonna go fucking apeshit.

"Thank you!" I reply, breathing heavily, sweat sliding down my spine.

When I first started I had no idea how exhausting dancing the pole would be. It's a whole body workout, and there isn't a muscle in my body that isn't used every time I dance. Fortunately for me, I'm fitter and more flexible than most due to all the sparring with Beast and yoga that I do to keep myself supple.

"You want to take a break?" Matty asks, pushing off from the bar and striding towards me with a bottle of water. I step down from the stage, taking it from her and uncap the lid, glugging back half the bottle. She laughs. "Thirsty work, eh?"

"You could say that again," I agree as Nancy takes my place on the pole and starts doing a series of intricate moves that has me gaping in awe. She spins around the pole, transferring from one move to another effortlessly and making it look far easier than it actually is.

"Dancing pole is an art form really, isn't it?" I muse, watching her in wonder.

Matty rests her butt against the edge of the table next to me, her long lean legs stretching out in front of her. She's a beautiful woman. Older than most of the girls who work here by at least fifteen years, but you'd never know she's in her early forties given her smooth, wrinkle-free skin and perfect hourglass figure. She attributes her youthful appearance to her dark skin tone and respect for her body. Matty doesn't drink, has never taken drugs and works out at least four times a week. According to her, her only vice is sex.

"It is exactly that. The men who come here do so for the tits and arse. That's all they see. But like you, I see so much more than that. These women are dancers, not just strippers."

"Absolutely," I agree, watching in awe as Nancy flips her body upside down, wraps her legs and feet around the pole then arches her back and uses her core muscles to lift the top part of her body horizontal to the floor. "Nancy's an incredible dancer."

"She is, but she's also not afraid to embrace her sexual prowess."

"Sexual prowess?" I ask, interested to see where she's going with this conversation.

"There's a power in female sexuality that many men are afraid of, intimidated by actually. For a long, long time women weren't allowed to seek pleasure or embrace their sexual self. They were vessels for bearing children and that was it. God forbid they ever expressed their wants and desires or actually enjoyed sex."

"That's bullshit," I remark, agreeing with her. She's basically describing Carter.

"There are few men who appreciate a woman who embraces her sexual self. That's one of the reasons why I'm a lesbian, that and the fact we actually know where to find the clit."

I laugh at that and she nudges me with her shoulder. "Nancy is popular here because she embraces her sexual self and uses it to her advantage. She's also got a banging body too."

I glance over at her. "Are you and her...?"

"Once upon a time. She's got a new love interest now. She's quite enamoured with the brute. Loved-up, actually."

My heart skips a beat, but I try to maintain my cool. "Yeah, who's the lucky guy?"

"One of Carter's men. You know him well."

I take another glug of water, willing myself to calm down. I'm not sure what I'll do if she says Beast. I like Nancy, but I don't want to have to rip her eyes out. "Which one?"

Matty grins. "Dom, of course. He's been chasing Nancy's tail for some time now. I can't blame him, she's a good fuck. One of the best."

"Ah Dom," I say, trying to hide my relief behind a beaming smile. "He's a great fighter."

"Not the greatest though," Matty replies with a knowing smile. "How's Beast anyway? It's been a while since he's popped into the club. We're all wondering if he's got a woman."

"Not that I know of," I reply with a shrug, focusing on Nancy so that I don't give away anything on my face. "He's been busy with Carter lately with one thing or another."

"Well, that'll cheer the girls up, they've missed his attention," Matty says with a smirk.

"I bet," I say with a tight smile.

"I can see the attraction," Matty continues. "He's built, hard as stone, respectful of women and a legend in bed, or so I've heard."

"Yeah?" I reply, trying to remain completely nonchalant.

"Not that I've had any experience like the other girls, given I prefer the female form, but I heard that he made Nancy come so hard she squirted. Not normally something a man has the ability to do. He's a catch."

I choke on my water, coughing and spluttering as Matty cracks up laughing at my expense. She pats me on the back as I take in deep lungfuls of air.

"You alright?"

"Peachy. Thanks for that visual," I reply wryly, trying to cover up the fact that I'm intensely jealous of all the women he's slept with and beyond intrigued about his expertise in bed.

"Hung like a horse too, *and* pierced."

"Beast has a pierced dick?" I try to keep the surprise out of my voice and fail.

"Yep, he's got a couple apparently, and both of them are positioned to give the most pleasure to whoever he's fucking. He's got a barbell through his glans and a top ladder."

"A top ladder?" I ask, screwing the lid back onto my bottle, if only to give me something to do with my hands and hide the fact that talking about Beast's dick is both bizarre and a turn on.

"Barbell piercings across the top of his dick."

"Right." Now *that* visual has me squeezing my thighs together, and my cheeks flushing. Thank God they're already flushed from the exertion, otherwise I'll be giving the game away.

She nudges me with her shoulder, smiling softly. "Is that interest I see in your eyes?"

"Interest in Beast?" I point to my chest. "Not in the slightest."

"Hey, you've got no judgement from me. As I've already indicated, Beast is legendary around here."

"Exactly," I mutter, then catch the look in her eye, and say quickly, "I mean no disrespect to the women here. They can fuck whomever they want."

"Except Beast, yeah?" she asks me knowingly.

I don't answer, but I don't need to. Matty is a woman of the world and I respect her greatly. She rubs shoulders with many of the same criminals as my father does, taking it all in her stride. She's well-respected, not just for ability to defuse any dangerous situation at the strip club that might pop up, but for her discretion.

"Is that why you're here? To learn some tricks to impress Beast?"

"I'm being rebellious," I reply, which is partly the truth anyway.

"Your dad isn't keen on you learning the pole?"

"Not in the slightest." I wince, realising that by being here I'm putting Matty and Nancy in a difficult position.

"Hey, your secret's safe with us."

I give her a grateful smile. "Thanks."

"Both of them," she adds knowingly, giving my knee a gentle pat.

"Matty, I—" My words are halted as the backdoor to the club opens and a familiar figure walks through the door looking less than impressed.

"Speak of the devil." Matty sniggers, then motions to Nancy. "I need you in my office for a minute."

Nancy flips her legs to the floor, and gives Beast a wave, before stepping down from the stage. When she reaches me she grins. "Good job today, maybe you can practice what you learnt on Beast, I'm sure he'd appreciate it."

"I don't think that's a good idea," I mumble, as she sashays across the room and follows Matty out into the hallway beyond, leaving me alone with Beast. He stops before me, his gaze taking in my gym outfit, and more pointedly my shoes.

"Princess—"

"What are you doing here?" I cut in.

"What do you think I'm doing here? Saving your arse, of course."

"Let me rephrase that. How did you know I was here?"

He waves his mobile phone at me. "Tracker app."

"You've got me on a fucking tracker app?!" I exclaim, appalled.

"Don't look so surprised. It's my job to know where you are at all times."

"Your job?"

"Yes, my fucking job."

"This is bullshit!" I'm pissed off now. Not just because he keeps referring to me as his job, but because I feel hemmed in, *caged*.

"You need to wrap this up. Carter wants you home."

"I don't give a fuck what Carter wants," I reply, turning on my heel. Beast grabs my hand pulling me back around. "What?"

"He'll go apeshit if he finds out you disobeyed him."

"He's not going to find out though, is he?" I counter, yanking my hand free and folding my arms across my chest defiantly. "Unless you're going to be the one to grass me up?"

"I'm no grass, Princess, but I am your friend, and as a friend I'm warning you this isn't a good idea."

"I don't see the problem. It's just like a workout. I'm not stripping for anyone. I'm just dancing. There's no one here apart from Matty and Nancy. I don't see Carter losing his shit over me working out in a gym full of pumped-up, chest-beating men who, by the way, are constantly checking me out."

"Who?" he grinds out, pulling me closer so that I have to crane my head backwards to look up at him.

"Who what?"

He lowers his face towards mine, his eyes glinting with anger as he spits the words out through gritted teeth. "Who's been checking you out?"

I shake my head and laugh. "Every single man with a dick and two fucking bollocks. That's who."

"Even Dom? Mark?"

"They're men, aren't they?"

"The fuck?" he seethes.

"What are you going to do, Beast? Knock them all out?"

"I'll kill every last one of them!" He shouts back.

"Why? Because they want me, or they want something you *think* you own. You're just like Carter," I accuse, snatching my arm back.

"I'm nothing like him!"

"I'm sick of Carter thinking he can tell me what I can and can't do," I continue, pacing back and forth in front of Beast. "I'm sick of his attitude towards me. I'm sick of his bullshit. I'm my own person, and I will do what the fuck I want."

"Listen, I know you're frustrated—" Beast begins.

"*Frustrated?* I'm angry. I'm pissed off and I'm horny as fuck!" I shout, my voice rising with every word. "And most of that is your damn fault!"

Beast folds his arms across his chest, keeping his thoughts to himself, which is probably just as well because I'm at the end of my tether.

Whatever.

He doesn't want to argue and I'm done talking.

Spinning on my heels, I head towards the stage as *Woman* by Doja Cat starts playing through the speakers. I grin. Given our very recent conversation I'm betting Matty's behind this.

"Princess, what are you doing?" Beast asks me as I climb up onto the stage and exaggerate the sway of my hips as I walk towards the pole. This is the song I've been practising my routine to and it's so perfect for how I'm feeling right now.

"What does it look like I'm doing?" I respond sarcastically, refusing to be embarrassed by my outburst. I don't care that he knows I'm in a constant state of arousal. I don't care that he knows I'm attracted to him, and angry at him, and grateful for him for being here and trying to have my back even though the whole issue of my dad trying to curb my actions pisses me off.

"It looks like you're about to put on a show," he says.

"You know where the door is, you're welcome to leave at any time."

He reaches for a chair flipping it around, then straddles it, leaning his arms over the back rest. "You know what? I think I'll stay," he says, locking eyes with me.

"Suit yourself," I reply, then step in front of the pole, press my arse against the cold metal and slut drop to the floor, spreading my thighs open wide and flashing Beast my lycra covered pussy.

He keeps his expression neutral, his hands hanging loosely over the back of the seat as he watches me. If he thinks he can intimidate me into stopping, he doesn't know me very well.

Pushing back upwards, I reach up and grasp the cool metal in my hands then go through the routine I've been working on.

With every spin of the pole, I gain confidence, funnelling the lyrics and my inner sexual tiger. Pretty soon I forget that Beast is even sitting there, too consumed by the way dancing the pole makes me feel.

I'm powerful. I'm sexual. I'm sensual. I'm a *woman*.

Finishing off with a back hook spin, I drop my feet to the floor, panting and covered in a sheen of sweat. My eyes meet Beast's, and this time his fingers are grasping the back of the chair, his knuckles white from the tightness of his grip.

Slowly I saunter across the stage, pick up my gym bag and swing it over my shoulder before descending the stairs. When I reach Beast, I stop in front of him. A bead of sweat travels slowly down his temple and cheek. I capture it with my finger and smile down at him.

"You're sweating."

"It's hot in here," he replies, a muscle in his jaw jumping as he presses his lips in a firm line.

"It is, isn't it?" I agree, then place my finger in my mouth and taste his lust right there on my tongue before twisting on my heels and striding over to the back door. I shove it open, and as I leave I can hear Matty and Nancy whistling and cheering after me. A huge smile spreads across my face as I walk towards Beast's car, feeling every inch the powerful, sexual, not to be fucked with *woman* that my father doesn't want me to be.

It's liberating.

CHAPTER SIXTEEN

Oceans

I wake up in a cold sweat, not from a nightmare but from a fucking wet dream.

My dick is still as hard as rock. It punches against my joggers, and even though I can feel the familiar stickiness of my cum against my lower belly, I can also feel the familiar ache in my balls telling me that I still need release, that I'm not done yet.

"Fuck!" I exclaim, pulling back the covers and climbing out of bed, my dick bobbing as I move, the tip pushing against the waistband of my joggers, eager for the woman of my dreams.

Fucking desperate for her.

I head straight for the shower, pushing open the door to my ensuite and flicking on the light switch. Instead of seeing my reflection, I see images of Kate dancing around the pole, her hair flying out behind her as she swings around and around and around.

Fuck, she made me dizzy.

Dizzy from lust.

Dizzy from my need to stride up onto the stage and fuck her against the hardwood floor.

Dizzy from holding so tightly onto the back of the chair that I almost broke my own fucking fingers to stop myself from doing exactly that.

Dizzy from willing myself to stay fucking put.

It wasn't that she was as good a dancer as Nancy, or that her tight body was encased in lycra leggings and a crop top that made me want her so fucking much it was almost impossible to breathe. It wasn't the stiletto heels or even the way she commanded the stage.

It was her ballsy attitude. Her inner strength. Her great big fat fuck you to her father, to me, to any person who dare try to control, contain, or own her.

That's what made my balls draw tight against my body and dick grow thick and hard.

Kate oozed power, *confidence*.

And it was fucking breathtaking to watch.

On the stage she showed me a glimpse of the queen I know she'll become and I was hooked, captured, ensnared like a motherfucking bear in a trap. I've always assumed that I'd be a lone wolf, never truly needing or wanting anyone. Fucking when I wanted too, and walking away because I could.

Now all I want is her.

Princess, Kate, Grim.

I want every facet of her. I want the girl who longs for

someone to protect her from a world filled with danger. I want the woman who is kind, thoughtful and sassy as fuck. I want the warrior who'll stand in a ring and fight a man like me without fear, who will stare in the face of her father and call him out for his shit.

I want all of her.

Everything she has to offer, all the good and all the bad parts. I want her vulnerability. I want her insecurities. I want her sharp tongue and wit. I want her anger and her passion. I want her sexiness and her sensuality. I want her spite and her fight.

I want her virginity.

I want it all.

Pressing my palms against the vanity unit, my head dropping between my shoulders, I suck in several deep breaths trying to calm my racing heart and the desperate need to go to her, right the fuck now and damn the consequences.

I'm so close to getting in my car and racing to her. My need for her is like a burning in my very blood, a thirst I know that I'll never be able to quench, a desire that fucking yearns for her touch, her kiss, her pussy, her everything.

But I can't go.

Blowing out a long breath, I stumble towards the shower turning it on. Ice cold water flows from the showerhead and I rip off my joggers, shoving them across the floor with my feet, then step into the water. Sucking in a sharp breath through my teeth, I press my palm against the shower wall, dropping my head under the spray. The cold water is supposed to wake me up so that I stop seeing Kate in front of my closed eyes, and to shrivel up my bastard cock that's intent on fucking killing me.

It does neither.

I can't wash away this feeling.

I'm not even sure that I want to anymore.

Grabbing my dick, I press my forehead against the tiles and suck in a sharp breath as I slide my fist up and down my cock. I pump it hard, tugging on it aggressively as I try my damndest to purge my fucking self of these feelings.

I can't have her.

I can't fucking have her.

But that doesn't mean I don't want her.

Because, fuck, I do.

I do.

"I motherfucking do!" I shout, pumping my dick, fucking my fist, relishing in the feel of my balls tingling and the pleasure building in the base of my spine. All of it for her, because of her.

She's my sweet, sweet temptation.

I rock my hips, my fist curling as I press my forearm against the tiled wall. Water runs in rivulets over my skin, cold and sharp but the heat within me builds as I pick up speed, recalling the way Kate lost herself to the power she conjured up on that stage. When she stopped dancing for me, and started dancing for herself, every single atom in my motherfucking body was set alight. She transformed before my eyes and I was gone, lost.

A man cast adrift pulled and tousled within the eddies of her seduction. I was gasping for breath watching her twist and turn her body around the pole, just like I'm gasping for breath thinking about her now. I've never wanted to be a piece of metal more than at that moment. I wanted her legs wrapped around me, her hands on me, her arse and pussy pressed up against me.

If my heart wasn't hers before then, it certainly became it in that moment.

And that's what fucking kills me.

Because I made a goddamn promise.

To her father.

To myself.

And it kills me knowing that I can't have her.

"God-fucking-damn-it!" I yell, bashing my fist against the wall as I squeeze my dick, holding back the orgasm building, feeling fucking guilt and shame for wanting Kate so fucking badly. Punishing myself for something I shouldn't want, can't have, but need. Fuck I need.

In another fucking universe, she'd be mine already, but a man's word is his bond and I'm bound to Carter, to a promise I made him, and by extension a promise I made Kate.

I'm her bodyguard.

I protect her from everyone, *including* me.

Knowing that doesn't soften my dick though. It doesn't stop me from seeing Kate in my mind's eye. It doesn't stop me from remembering the way she'd sauntered over to me covered in a sheen of sweat, dripping with new-found confidence. It doesn't stop me from recalling how it felt to look up at Kate and know that I will never want anyone like I want her.

It's a truth I can't run from, that I will have to face every fucking day in her presence and then even when I'm not. I'm going to have to pretend.

I'm going to have to keep a tight lid on my emotions. I'm going to have to cut myself off from her emotionally. But right here and now...

Right here and now, I let go of the pretence, the barrier I've built between us, and for one fucking moment I allow myself to believe I can have her, that there isn't a fucking ocean between us filled with sharks all wanting to rip us apart. I allow myself to believe that she's my queen, and I'm whatever she wants me to be. That we'll be together for the rest of our motherfucking lives.

I allow myself this moment to see a future together, where I can touch her when I want, kiss her when I need to, and fuck her until we're both drowning in pleasure.

I let myself imagine what it's like to cup her breasts, to lick and tease her nipples, to leave my teeth indents on the mound of her arse, to bring her pussy to my face demanding she sit so I can suffocate in her scent and her arousal. I let myself imagine what it's like to slide my cock into her pussy all the while staring deeply into her soulful eyes. I let myself imagine how I will move slowly, drawing out her pleasure in a long, spine-tingly, toe-curling orgasm, until her eyes roll back in her head and she calls my name. I let myself imagine how I'd let her come down from that orgasm then fuck her hard and fast so she knows just how feral she makes me, how brutal, how animalistic.

Right now I let myself fuck her, I let myself rut into her as I pull on my dick roughly, and jerk my hips into the ghost of her image in my mind. My imagination runs riot and my dick engorges, the piercings making everything feel so much more intense. I imagine fucking her against the wall in my apartment in that sexy as fuck red dress she wore hitched up over her hips, the material bunched in my fist as I ram into her. She claws at me, her teeth sinking into my shoulder as she opens herself up to me.

"That's it Princess, take me deep," I say, the words slipping from my lips and muffled by the spray of the shower and the slippery wet sound of my fingers fisting my dick.

I allow myself to envisage that moment when her inner walls tighten around me and she milks my dick, when she tattoos her pleasure all over my cock, marking me forever just like I mark her insides with my cum.

"KATE!" I shout, coming with that thought burning in my chest, fast and furious like a star imploding. It blinds me, and I stumble against the tiled wall, weakened by lust, floored by need, consumed by her as my cum spurts in thick, white ropes over my fist, washed away seconds later by the spray.

I stand there with my back against the tiles, my chest heaving, my dick slowly softening as my heart returns to a steadier pace. As my orgasm fades, I push myself upright on unsteady legs, wash myself robotically and step out of the shower to dry myself off. With every passing minute I lock all my emotions down, forcing those thoughts into a box inside my mind, never to be opened again.

CHAPTER SEVENTEEN

Wicked Game

"Are you meeting me at Tales, or picking me up?" I ask Hudson a couple days after I danced for Beast at Nine Lives.

My phone is gripped between my shoulder and ear as I paint my nails a deep purple to match the tight leather trousers I plan on wearing to Tales tonight. Dom is up against Ramone, a well-known fighter in the underground fight scene. He has a regular spot at Dixie's Fight Club in Manchester and he's travelling down to face off with Dom. It's gonna be a close fight, both are certifiably insane and rabid in the cage. Then Beast is headlining. He's going up against Clayton, a South African guy just as big and as dangerous as Beast, but I know Beast will win. He hasn't lost a fight yet.

"Who are you talking to?" Beast asks as he enters my bedroom, making me jump. I drop the phone and manage to get purple nail polish all over my big toe.

"Ever heard of knocking?" I snipe, swiping up the phone and apologising to Hudson as I balance the phone between my ear and shoulder and soak a cotton wool pad in nail polish remover, dabbing at my toe.

"Princess, who's on the damn phone?" Beast glares at me.

I give him *the* look, the one I know pisses him off. He's been a grumpy shit ever since I danced for him. He didn't speak one word to me as he drove me home like he had a rocket up his arse.

More like a boner in his pants.

I let out a snort of laughter at my wayward thoughts which only seems to incite him further.

"Princess," he growls.

Pressing the loudspeaker button, I place the phone on my dressing table. "It's Hud if you must know. Are you always this fucking cranky before a fight?"

"I'm this fucking cranky when you won't answer my damn questions!"

"Alright, Beast? I'm looking forward to watching you fight tonight," Hudson says through the loudspeaker. I can hear the amusement in his voice, and I grin. I've told him all about how Beast's been acting lately and Hudson's advice was to fuck someone else to piss him off. When I asked if he was offering, he nearly had a stroke. Not that I'd go there. Hud and I are just friends. Nothing more.

"It's invite only, prick!"

"*I've* invited Hudson."

"Well, I'm uninviting them," Beast retorts, snatching up my phone.

"Oi! Give it back, you fucking brute!" I snarl, getting to my feet. "You're so fucking rude!"

"Don't care." He grins at me, holding my phone above his head. Even if I jumped, I wouldn't be able to bloody reach it, the gigantic bastard.

"Hey! Are you alright, Kate?" Hudson asks, his voice sounding panicked.

"You keep asking that question and I'm going to lose my shit. *Of course,* she's alright, dicksplash, she's with *me!*"

"That's a matter of opinion!" I screech, shoving him as hard as I can in the stomach. He lets out a grunt, but it's not enough to make him drop the phone. "Apologise now!"

"Not a fucking chance," Beast says, taking the phone off loudspeaker and pressing it against his ear whilst simultaneously deflecting my attempts at knocking him the fuck out.

"Beast, give me the damn phone!"

"Nope."

He thinks he's won. He hasn't. Sometimes you have to pick your battles. "Fine, knock yourself out," I huff, striding over to my wardrobe. "I'm over it."

"See here's the thing, Hudson," Beast continues, speaking into the mouthpiece, "You're not welcome at Tales tonight, or any night for that matter."

I spin on my feet. "YES YOU ARE! IGNORE THE FUCK!"

"So if you know what's good for you, I suggest you spend some quality time with your bros and forget about the invite, yeah?"

Hudson must be saying something interesting in response as

Beast's expression changes from one of annoyance to downright rage. "The *fuck* you say?!" he snarls.

"Oh, for fuck's sake!" I exclaim. "I'm getting tired of all this chest-beating bullshit, and sick to death of the men in my life— NOT YOU HUD— thinking they can treat me like I've got no say in any-damn-thing!"

Beast scowls at me and then holds up his hand, the universal sign language for *shut the fuck up*.

The *fuck* he didn't!

Anger courses through my veins at his bullshit attitude. I've had enough of men thinking they can silence me with a look or a comment or a motherfucking hand. Deciding that all of my fucks have flown out the window I decide to play dirty and get naked, because fuck him and fuck blowing hot and cold. This is my damn bedroom and if he insists on barging in uninvited he can deal with me getting changed. Pulling off my clothes until I'm down to my underwear, I grab my outfit from the wardrobe and lay it across my bed.

"What the hell do you think you're doing?" Beast snaps, finally noticing that I'm no longer fully clothed.

I grin at him. "What does it look like? I'm getting ready."

"No, not you, dipshit!" Beast shouts into the phone. "I'm talking to Princess."

When I reach up to undo my bra, his eyes practically pop out of his head. Inside I chuckle. Good. Deal with me naked, *arsehole*. It's not as if he hasn't seen my tits before, so he can suck it the fuck up.

"You could look the other way," I say, fluttering my eyelashes at him and dropping my bra to the floor. The cooler air and the way his gaze laser-focuses on my tits make my nipples pucker. When my fingers reach for my knickers, he shakes his head.

"Don't!" he warns.

"Give me the damn phone back then!" I reply, my fingers sliding under the waistband.

His eyes narrow at me as he continues to listen to whatever it is that Hudson is saying, but he makes no move to hand my phone back. He's trying to call my bluff. Well, he might be a man of his word, but he'll soon learn that I'm a woman who won't back down. "Fine!"

Slipping my fingers under the elastic of my knickers I slowly peel them down my thighs daring him to stop me.

He doesn't.

Instead the bastard leans against the wall and licks his lips before saying, "Alright, you win. Meet us at Tales at eight," before promptly hanging up.

Placing my phone onto the dresser he remains impassive. His gaze fixed firmly on my face. Heat creeps up my chest as my knickers fall to the floor revealing my pussy. I know for a fact that the landing strip of hair barely hides anything, so right now Beast is getting a full view of my well-tended lady garden, and it's as un-beaver-like as you can get.

"That wasn't so hard, was it?" I ask, referring to the fact he conceded and has allowed Hudson to meet us at Tales and ignoring the fact that I'm actually completely fucking naked in front of him.

"You're wrong, Princess. I can promise you it's *hard*."

Slowly his gaze drops, lowering over my tits, stomach and finally resting on my pussy. Heat trails his gaze and centres at my core, lighting me up from the inside out.

"It shouldn't be though, right?" I ask, and he knows full well that I'm no longer talking about Hudson but the very sizeable boner in his jeans.

"No. It fucking shouldn't," he states, gritting his teeth. "But just because my body is reacting the way it is, doesn't mean I'm going to change my damn mind and act on it."

"So leave then," I exclaim, exasperated, turned on, confused, frustrated and wishing with all my heart that he would just give in. He rocks on his feet, glancing at the door and back again, at war with himself.

"Just get fucking dressed! We need to be at Tales within the hour."

Snatching his gaze away he strides towards the door, and a sudden bolt of panic rips through me. "Don't go!" I say and it comes out far more needy than I'd intended.

He reaches the door, tensing, but he doesn't turn around. Instead, he grabs hold of the door frame with one hand, and the edge of the door with the other, his knuckles turning white from the tightness of his grip. "What the fuck now?" he asks, his back still to me.

Right? What the fuck now?

This is where I need to channel my inner badass bitch just like I did on the stage at Nine Lives. No more fucking about. I need him to understand that I'm a woman with needs, with wants and desires, and that he's the only man I want to fulfil them. Climbing onto my bed, I settle back against the cushions and rest my hand on my lower belly as I stare at the side of his face. He's trying so damn hard to fight this connection, and I know I shouldn't push it, but I want him and I want him to want me too. So fucking much.

"Even though I'm a virgin, I'm not innocent, Beast," I say, my fingers edging between my parted legs.

"It doesn't matter to me whether you're a virgin or experienced. I told you this ain't happening!"

My heart thunders inside my chest at what I'm about to do but I push on, willing him to turn around, willing him to let go of his restraint. "I'll be eighteen in just over a week. You're only five years older than me. My dad *likes* you. I know you want me. I've made it clear that I want you. Why torture yourself, why torture me?"

"It doesn't fucking matter what I want. I will not go back on my word. Your father trusts me and I won't fucking break that trust," he replies, still stubbornly facing the other way.

"Even if you want me?"

"*Especially* when I want you."

"Then I'll just have to give you something to think about."

"What the shit are you talking about now?" he asks, as I lower my hand to my clit and start pleasuring myself. I gently finger my piercing, my toes curling at the instant sensation it elicits.

I'm already so wet.

Jesus, just thinking about Beast turns me on. The sheer fact that I'm naked, that he's in this room with a boner for me, makes me crave him even more. It's potent, the attraction between us, undeniable. The air crackles with it. I can practically feel it fizzing over my skin. Letting out a moan, I work my finger over my clit finding the perfect rhythm as I finger fuck myself.

"Fuck!" I hear him mutter. "Fuck, fuck, *fuck!* I need to go."

"Stay." It comes out halfway between a plea and a demand as he grips the door frame like he's about to rip it from the wall.

"You won't change my mind," he bites out, but the need in his voice tells me he's on the brink of breaking every promise he made to my father and probably a few he's made to himself.

"Do you know how many times I've fantasised about you?" I ask, and when he doesn't respond, I continue on. "So many times, Beast. I've touched myself like this hundreds of times imagining it was your thick fingers working me, your tongue tasting me, your cock—"

"Enough!" he roars, pushing off from the door frame and slamming my bedroom door shut, his chest heaving as he turns around to face me. Anger billows off of him, but so does lust. It's as thick and as heady as my arousal. With my gaze fixed on him, my finger rubs in expert circles over my clit as I grasp my aching breast with my free hand, imagining it's his hands touching me.

"I'm wet for you, Beast," I say, dipping two fingers inside myself whilst pressing the heel of my palm against my clit, knowing that the barrier protecting both my metaphorical and physical innocence has long since disappeared. I'm not a kid. I'm a woman who's comfortable with her body, with her desires and I'm not afraid to show that.

With my heels pressed into the soft bedding and my knees bent and legs spread, I show Beast what he refuses to claim for himself. If this doesn't work, then absolutely nothing will.

All I know is that this is the last time I'll throw myself at him.

The very last time.

"Beast, I want you. I want *you* to make me come," I say, meeting his turbulent gaze with my own. "But if you choose not to, then you better believe I'll find a man who's willing to do what you won't."

Anger blazes in his gaze and I can't work out if it's because I've given him an ultimatum or the fact that I said that I will find another man to do what he refuses to.

Either way, he says nothing, does *nothing*.

Instead, he stands like a sentinel, locking himself down. I literally see every single muscle in his body stiffen, his fingers curling into fists, his jaw locking tight. He becomes a witness to my pleasure, but refuses to be a part of it. So with his chest heaving, his angry gaze blazing, Beast watches me finger-fuck myself refusing to go back on his word to my father, and whilst I find that an admirable trait, it pisses me the fuck off because he's denying himself something worth breaking his word for and I'm not just talking about sex. I'm talking about *us*.

So be it.

Stubbornly, and with a determination to get myself off, I use both hands to pleasure myself. With two fingers rubbing my clit, and two dipping inside of me, I draw out the pleasure coiling in my spine. Every part of my skin heats under Beast's gaze until all too soon an orgasm rushes out from my centre in a wave so powerful I'm screaming out his name.

Even to my own ears it sounds broken.

He'll never get to touch me now.

As my orgasm ebbs away, I slowly draw my legs together and open my eyes, focusing on the man before me. Beast's gaze cuts me like a knife, and I feel the sharp pain of it deep inside my chest.

"It's over. You have my word that I will never offer myself up to you again," I say, climbing off the bed and pulling out a fresh set of underwear from my chest-of-drawers. I get dressed slowly, something inside shutting down with every brush of material over my skin. By the time I've pulled on my boots and strode over to him, I've shored up my defences and tucked away my disappointment. "Shall we go?"

He lets out a long breath, pushing off from the door then says, "I will kill any man who dares touch you. *Understand?*" Then he turns on his feet, rips open the door and storms out of my bedroom leaving me whispering my reply in his wake.

"Perfectly."

CHAPTER EIGHTEEN

I Wanna Be Your Slave

I bounce on my feet, a sheen of sweat covering my bare chest as I glare at my opponent across the other side of the cage. I can smell a win. It's close.

Clayton has fought well and at one point caught me with an uppercut so powerful I'd almost, *almost* passed the fuck out. The crowd had gone ballistic as my head had snapped back and I'd fallen against the cage wall. They'd smelt blood.

Except the motherfuckers didn't count on me climbing back to my feet.

I didn't do it for them. I did it for her. For Kate.

Over the sounds of the crowd I'd heard her.

"Beast!" she'd screamed, and the pain in her voice, the fucking *anguish*, had ripped at my heart, squeezing tightly. Her fear had almost floored me and I knew in that fucking moment that I will only ever fall to my knees for *her*.

Only Kate.

So I shook my head and stood the fuck up, blood dripping from the gash across my brow, lip and cheek, and fought.

I'm still fighting.

Clayton is a worthy opponent and it's been ugly, fucking brutal.

There are no referees in this club, and you're only announced the winner when your opponent is knocked out cold or can't get back up again. I've put many men in the hospital. As reigning champion it's expected. Tonight, I'm being pushed to my limits, and if it weren't for Kate screaming at me to keep going I might've conceded already. As it is, I'm fighting with every last drop of energy I have left.

Clayton lands a left hook to my cheek that I only partially deflect with my arm. I feel the power of it like a sledgehammer and my strength is waning. Pretty sure I've broken more than a couple of ribs from the kicks he's managed to get in, as well as splits to my eyebrow, lip and cheek. I don't need to look in the mirror to know that I'm covered in bruises, and I'm pretty sure I've got a concussion, given I can see three of the fucker in front of me.

Still I fight.

Split and bloody knuckles meet sweaty, crimson skin. Two men equal in fitness, size and strength battle for supremacy. On and on and on we fight until the canvas is covered in our combined blood, but I can see that Clayton's weakening, and right now winning isn't down to who's the best fighter, it's down to who wants it more. Brute strength will only take you so far, but inner strength? That's what wins the fight. Hands down, every motherfucking time.

I *won't* lose.

Digging deep, I grit my teeth, and ignoring the searing pain in my ribs, launch myself at Clayton in a flurry of punches that he can barely defend, let alone respond to. I don't stop, not when he stumbles, not when several teeth fly out of his mouth, not when his nose breaks, not when he falls to his knees, and not when he holds his hands up in defeat.

I finish it with one last blow to the side of his head that knocks him out cold.

The crowd erupts and I tip my head back and roar.

When the punters rush the cage, slapping their palms against the wire and chanting my name, I find myself searching for the only person that matters to me.

Kate.

The girl I call Princess who's a temptation I'm finding harder and harder to deny.

Swiping at the blood and sweat getting into my eyes, I find her half a beat later. She's standing beside Hudson who's cheering like the rest of the crowd. There's pride in her eyes, relief too, but also a flickering of sorrow before she shuts it down and dips her head in acknowledgement. My fucking stomach roils and my throat squeezes as I'm reminded of what she'd said earlier.

"It's over. You have my word that I will never offer myself up to you again."

I hadn't believed her then. I do now.

I'm a man of my word, and she's a woman of hers.

I should be happy about that, I'm not.

Because I want her.

Not because she'd spread her legs and finger-fucked herself in front of me, not because she'd done so with courage, but because there's something deep within her that calls to me. Earlier I'd wanted so badly to take her in my arms and fucking love her the way she deserves to be loved, but loyalty to her father and my own self-imposed boundaries stopped me from taking that step. Though those same ties of loyalty hadn't been strong enough to force me to leave the room. Nothing could've done that. Instead, I'd watched, fucking transfixed on her glistening pussy, her fingers sliding between her parted folds all swollen and blush for me, and I'd drawn on every last drop of fucking willpower not to throw caution to the wind and take what I know is mine.

What will *always* be mine.

Except now Kate's closed the door. As she should.

Fuck.

Dragging my gaze away from her, I walk on heavy legs towards the cage door and pull it open, allowing Clayton's crew to enter before stepping out. The crowd of people nearest to me gather round, slapping me on the back as they congratulate me on my win. I grunt my appreciation, shake a few hands before they ease back and allow me to pass. Across the other side of the club, Carter's sitting at the bar, the King next to him. They both acknowledge me, Carter with a dip of the head and King with a raised glass. I consider giving the King the middle finger but decide he ain't worth the attention.

Heading towards the changing rooms, Joey steps out of the shadows with an ice pack and a bottle of whisky. "Let's get you fixed up, shall we?"

I nod, ready to follow him when my skin prickles. Kate's

familiar scent accosts me right before her fingers wrap around my bicep.

"Beast..."

I step into the shadowed archway that leads to the changing rooms and wait. Joey looks between us, gives Kate a dip of his head and says, "I'll be fixing up Dom whilst I wait for you to join us."

"Alright," I acknowledge.

"You're hurt," she blurts out, a frown creasing her brow.

"It ain't so bad," I lie.

"Yeah, and my name isn't Grim."

I almost say it isn't, that it's *Kate*, but I hold my tongue. "Where's Hudson?" I reply instead, searching the crowd.

"At the bar getting a drink. He thinks you're *fucking amazing*. His words, not mine." She gives me a small smile that quickly dies on her lips.

I press my palm against my chest, right over my heart. "Ouch, that hurt."

"You know what I mean."

Scanning the crowd, I nod. "Yeah, Princess, I do."

"He really is a good guy, Beast. If you got to know him, you'd see that."

"He's talking to Carter and the King," I point out.

She follows my gaze, shrugging. "And?"

"And that doesn't concern you?" I ask, stepping further into the shadows and pulling her with me as the King looks past Hudson and at us both talking.

"I trust Hudson."

"Should you?"

"I've no reason not to. He was a friend to me when no one else was."

"How did you meet exactly?" I ask, if only to prolong our conversation. I might hurt all over and need some painkillers and medical care, but I need to speak to Kate more.

"Two years back I got into a fight with a few of the kids at the care home his brothers still live at. It was pretty brutal. Hud intervened."

"Is that so?" I ask, not surprised that he would, but more so that she'd let him.

"He did. The fuckers tried to mug me, they didn't get very far. I knocked a couple of them out from sheer rage. Back then I didn't have all the right training. I fought with anger and not with skill."

"Still do sometimes." I grin, then wince as I feel the tear in my lip pull wider.

"Hudson has my back. Always will," she says and there's a fondness in her gaze which I rarely see, a softness that she hides from everyone. Knowing that Hudson has pulled it out of her stings a hell of a lot more than the cut to my lip.

"I'm glad he does," I reply, my gaze slipping past her and back to Hudson talking to Carter and the King.

"Yeah, me too."

Silence falls between us as her gaze flits over my face and drops to my chest. I must look a fucking mess, but it doesn't bother her. It's not like she hasn't seen me fight in the cage before.

"You lost focus today," she says eventually. "Clayton almost bested you."

"It was a momentary lapse of concentration. I had things on my mind."

"What things?" she asks softly, casting a tentative gaze over her shoulder to make sure no one close by is listening in on our conversation.

"You know full well what I'm talking about, Princess," I reply, my fingers twitching to touch her. I keep my hands at my side, knowing that if I did touch her, I might not be able to stop, blood, sweat and broken ribs be damned.

"He could've killed you," she whispers.

"No, Princess. I would never let that happen." I shake my head, chewing on my split lip, tasting blood.

Her gaze drops to my mouth and she frowns. "What?"

I breathe out slowly. "What you said earlier..."

She takes a step back, and I see her shutting down, closing herself off. "What about it?"

"Did you mean it?" I drill my gaze into hers, willing her to say what I want to hear. That, no, she didn't mean it. That she still wants me. That I'm the only man she'll ever want, that she'll ever let touch her.

She doesn't.

"Yes, I did mean it. I will *never* offer myself up to you again," she says firmly and without a shred of doubt in her gaze.

Biting back all the words on the tip of my tongue, I say the only thing I can. "Good."

"THAT WAS AN EPIC FIGHT!" Dom says, wincing a little from his own split lip and black eye from his fight with Ramone.

We're sitting in the fighters' rest room situated off the changing room getting fixed by Joey.

"Clayton nearly had you beat at one point," Joey says with a chuckle as he sews up the deep gash to my cheek. I barely register the pain, too fucking distracted by thoughts of Kate.

"Yeah, he did," I shrug, the dull ache in my ribs is nothing compared to how fucked-up in the head I am over Kate. I'd pushed her away, and whilst in the long run it's better for the both of us, it sure as fuck doesn't feel good. In fact, it fucking hurts in a way that messes me up far more than a few cuts and bruises do.

"First time ever you've been close to being bested, am I right?" Joey continues, tying off the thread.

"Guess so."

"What's up, Beast? You ain't gloating like you usually do after winning a fight," Dom says with a wink to let me know he means no disrespect.

"Absolutely nothing, mate," I say, taking a sip from the bottle of whisky Joey brought in place of any real painkillers. I grimace at the cheap as shit muck, but at least it's helping to take the edge off.

"You sure?" Dom pushes, rolling his shoulder and pressing against a bruise swelling on his bicep.

"Yep."

Joey catches my gaze, blotting at my face with a damp cloth. "You'll do," he finally says, giving me a terse nod as he gathers up the bloody cloth and used needle and chucks them into the bin.

"How's Ramone holding up?" I ask, if only to pull the attention away from me.

Dom grins, taking the bait just like I knew he would. "Broken arm, cheekbone and missing several teeth. But it's the bruised ego that's effed him up more." Chuckling, Dom smirks. "Thought he could get the better of me."

"We all knew you'd win. You're like a pit bull in the cage. I was surprised you didn't rip his ear off like you did Bonner's a couple of weeks back," Joey remarks with a wry grin.

Dom laughs. "If Ramone hadn't conceded, I might've."

"And Clayton?" I ask, rolling my head on my shoulders to try and ease the tension in my neck and back.

"You fucked him up good and proper, but he'll live," Joey says. "He got lucky this time. I've advised him not to fight for a while."

"Bet that went down like a lead balloon," Dom says with a smirk before taking a sip of his beer.

"Don't much care if it did. There's only so long you can avoid the grim reaper. Know what I'm saying?" Joey says, giving me a look that tells me he's no longer talking about fighting in the cage.

I flick my gaze to Dom, understanding Joey's got something to say but won't in front of him. "Can you give us a minute?"

Dom nods. "Sure thing. I've got to get back out there anyway. Carter wants me to meet the King now that he's officially going into business with him."

Joey's bushy eyebrows shoot up into his hairline, but other than that he keeps his thoughts to himself. He's a wise man. We both like Dom, but we don't have frank discussions about Carter in front of him, or any of the other men who work for the boss, for that matter.

"He told the rest of the crew already?" I ask.

"Yeah, earlier this evening before you arrived with Princess. I figured you already knew, given you're his right-hand man and all."

"Yeah, I did."

"Right then, best be off," Dom says, discarding his empty beer bottle in the bin. "The sooner we get this official shit over with, the sooner I can go get my dick wet. Tonight Nancy's invited me over to her place and I intend on blotting you from her memory." He grins, and I shake my head.

"Not possible, mate, but I respect you for trying."

"After a night of passion with me it'll be *Beast, who?*"

"Yeah, yeah."

"Why can't you just humour me? You're giving us mere mortals a bad fucking name," Dom retorts, before striding towards the door.

"Can't help it if I'm a god in bed, now can I?" I call after him, only to receive the middle finger in response. The door slams shut behind him and I take another sip of the whisky.

Joey smirks, packing up his medical bag. "I like Dom."

"Not enough to chat personal shit in front of him though."

"Nope, not yet anyways. He'll prove himself one day and then we'll both feel more comfortable. I've got a good feeling about him, same as that kid Hudson Freed. I've been around long enough to know who's a good egg, and who's rotten."

"That's why we're friends, right?"

He laughs. "Yeah, that's why we're friends."

"So what did you want to say?" I ask, waiting for the lecture that I know is coming.

"You're going to get yourself killed."

"How do you figure that?"

"I've got eyes. Something has happened between you and Grim, hasn't it?"

Scrubbing a hand over my head, I blow out a long breath and nod.

"I told you not to fuck her."

"I didn't."

"What then?" He takes the bottle of whisky from me and takes a generous sip, before swiping the back of his hand across his mouth.

"Let's just say she offered herself to me and I turned her down."

"She did?"

"Yep, she did."

"And you turned her down?" he repeats, narrowing his eyes.

"Yeah, I fucking did."

Joey squeezes my shoulder. "Wise move."

"Then why does it feel like it wasn't?"

"What're you saying?"

"My head's telling me I did the right thing even though it was the single hardest thing I've ever had to do, but..."

"But?"

"But my fucking heart ain't so sure," I admit, fucking surprising myself.

"You sure it's your heart and not your dick that's uncertain?" He folds his arms across his chest and leans back against the table, smirking.

"She was fucking naked, Joey, and I turned her down. I'm fucking certain."

Joey's eyes widen and he whistles. "Well, fuck. Quite the predicament you've got yourself in, Beast."

"Tell me about it."

"So what're you gonna do?"

"Nothing. She made it clear to me that she won't be offering herself up to me again."

"Is that so? Do you believe her?"

"Yeah." I sigh, knocking back another glug of whisky, then stand.

"And you're alright with that?"

"I thought you said I should steer clear?"

Joey swipes a hand over his beard, tugging on the end as he thinks. "I did, that's true. But fucking Grim and caring for her are two different things."

"I'm not sure Carter would agree."

"Perhaps not, but that's neither here nor there. You choose who you're loyal to, not him. Besides, we both know that girl has the power and the balls to run Tales. It won't be long before Carter will be stepping aside to make way for her."

"You'd think, but I ain't so sure now."

"What makes you say that?"

"Just a hunch," I say, meeting his gaze. When he opens his mouth to ask me about it, I shake my head. "I ain't voicing anything until I know for sure."

"Understood," Joey replies. "And this thing he's got going with the King, has that got anything to do with your concerns?"

"You could say that."

"I heard he's bringing new fighters to Tales from Europe, that he's taking a cut of the takings for the trouble."

"You'd heard right, but there's more to this partnership than Carter's letting on. I just haven't figured out what that is yet."

"You've got good instincts, Beast, trust them."

"I intend to."

"But I am gonna give you another piece of advice," Joey says.

I smirk, pulling on a clean shirt, buttoning it. "I'd worry if you didn't."

"Loving someone trumps everything else, even your own rules, *and* any loyalty pledged to another man."

"Who said I love her?"

Joey barks out a laugh. "A man who doesn't fuck a woman as beautiful as Grim when it's offered on a platter is a man in love. Besides, you've never spoken about your heart and a woman in the same sentence before. If that ain't love, then I don't know what the fuck is."

"Okay," I reply, not admitting to anything because I haven't even admitted that to myself. "What're you saying?"

"If you truly care about Grim, *love her*, then you look after her in *any way* you can."

"This ain't no fairy tale, Joey. We won't get a happily ever after. You know that."

"Maybe. Maybe not," he shrugs. "Either way, you gotta protect what belongs to your heart, no matter the cost."

I nod. "Yeah. No matter the cost."

CHAPTER NINETEEN

Take Another Little Piece Of My Heart

My feet pound against the belt of the running machine as I hit the button to increase the speed. Sweat trickles down my back and stomach, pooling at the top of my leggings. Around me the gym is filled with Carter's soldiers and a few of the regulars who fight at Tales. As always I'm the only woman.

Beast is nowhere to be seen.

In fact, he's ignored this past week since he won against Clayton and whilst I've seen him around, other than a polite greeting and checking in to see what my plans are so that he can keep an eye on me from a distance, he's barely spoken to me. Humiliation creeps up my spine at his rejection, but overriding that is this deep sense of loneliness.

I *miss* him. I miss our banter and the friendship I thought we shared.

Gritting my teeth and ignoring the stitch in my side as I run,

I turn up the music bluetoothed into my headphones and transform all the disappointment into anger, using that to fuel me. I'm not sure how long I run for, but eventually my body tells me enough is enough, and I slow down the speed gradually to a walk. What I need now is to shower and change, then head over to Hudson's place. He's got his brothers Max and Bryce over, as well as Cal. It'd be good to be in the company of friends instead of around Carter who can barely look at me and Beast who's doing everything in his power to cut me out of his life as much as he can given he's still my bodyguard.

Stepping off the treadmill, I snatch up the hand towel hanging over the handrail fixed to the wall and swipe it over my face and neck to soak up the sweat, then head towards the female changing room, which is basically my private changing room.

"Off to spar, Princess?" Dom asks me as I pass him by. He's spotting Mark on the weights and they're both bare chested and sweating as much as I am.

"No sparring today, or for a while actually. Beast has been busy with Carter."

Busy avoiding me more like it.

"You know any one of us will be happy to step in. I'd be happy to spar with you now if you want?" he replies as Mark lowers the weight and sits up.

"Aren't you forgetting something?" Mark asks, giving him a look.

"Forgetting what?"

"You've got someplace to be, right mate?"

"Shit, you're right," Dom says, checking his watch. He pulls a face. "Sorry, Princess."

"This place you need to be, is that the same place that Beast's been skulking off to all week?" I ask as casually as I can.

Dom smirks. "I fucking hope not. I know Nancy had a thing for him once but I'm hoping he isn't balls deep in her right now."

I raise my brows and nod. "Ah, well, have a *nice* time."

Dom laughs. "Princess, I plan on having a *really* fucking nice time." He turns his attention to Mark, squeezing his shoulder. "See you at The Crib Club later?"

"*The* Crib Club? Isn't that where all the posh people go to play cards?" I ask.

"Games are certainly played there, but it ain't just cards." Mark says.

"So what then?" I ask, looking between the two men who are now smirking at each other. Then I get it. "Oh, it's a *sex* club. Gotcha."

Mark grins, but Dom has the decency to look a bit sheepish. "Nancy and I ain't exclusive."

"She knows that, does she?" I ask, amused at the way his cheeks flush. I'm pretty sure Nancy's a big girl and doesn't need me nosing around her business, but I can't waste the opportunity to wind Dom up a bit.

"Yep, she's happy to share my monster cock—" Dom's eyes widen, then he smirks, casting his gaze to someone over my shoulder. I don't need to see him to know it's Beast. I can *feel* his presence.

"The *fuck* you talking about with Princess?" he asks.

Mark bursts out laughing and Dom winks at me. "Alright, Beast? Wasn't expecting to see you here."

"Yeah, I figured that," he snaps, stepping up beside me.

I glance at him, and he purposely avoids my gaze. Arsehole.

"Nice to see you too," I mutter, the heat from his body and his familiar scent makes a deep ache open up inside of me. I don't enjoy feeling like this and decide the best thing to do in the moment is to get the hell away from him. He's been avoiding me, so now he can have a taste of his own medicine. I move to walk away but Mark's question has me pulling up sharp.

"Weren't you going to meet us there?"

"You're going too?" I ask snapping my head around to glare at Beast.

"Carter needed me to pick up Princess and drop her off at her friend's house first. I'll go home and change then meet you there later," he replies completely fucking ignoring my question and me entirely. Even Dom and Mark appear to notice his rudeness and are looking between us with questions in their eyes.

I see. So this is how it's going to be.

"Well, have a good time tonight, lads, and remember to play it safe. I wouldn't want your dicks falling off from some *well-used* pussy. Oh, wait," I say, staring daggers at Beast and aiming the next part of my retort at him, "Looks like you might have some trouble with that, given your bollocks have already shrivelled up from overuse."

Twisting on my feet, I head towards the changing room to the sound of Dom and Mark cracking up. The fact that Beast doesn't join in takes the edge off the pain I'm feeling. Fuck him and his bullshit anyways. I'm not going to let him treat me like shit. Flirting with me one minute, bringing me the hearts of my enemies the next, not to mention turning down my advances. And then to top it all off by fucking ignoring me completely.

I'm over it.

As I cross the gym, I pass a few familiar faces and some not so familiar ones. Half of the men are undressing me with their eyes and the other half are avoiding eye contact completely. No one that knows who I am, and more importantly, who my father is, would dream of looking at me so openly like I'm an actual, desirable woman. It won't take long for the newbies to be filled in and then I'll go back to being fucking invisible again. But I'll know. I'll feel their eyes on me.

Just like I feel Beast's eyes on me.

With anger bubbling in my blood, I shove open the changing room door and head straight towards the shower cubicle, then strip and step inside, turning the shower on. I dip my head under the warm spray and close my eyes, allowing the water to beat down on my head and body.

How fucking dare he treat me like this?

I'd thought better of him.

If I was like any other woman I might allow the tears brimming behind my eyes to fall, but I'm not like any other woman. I'm Grim and I *refuse* to cry. He doesn't deserve my tears, or my affection.

Fuck him.

Forcing myself to move, I grab the shower gel and clean up, taking my sweet time. Once I'm thoroughly clean and pink all over from the hot water, I switch the shower off and grab the towel hanging from the back of the cubicle door, wrapping it around my body. The instant I step into the changing area, I know I'm not alone.

Beast is sitting on the bench on the opposite side of the room, legs spread wide, the back of his head pressed against the wall as he stares at me. He's beautiful. So beautiful that he makes my heart ache and my traitorous pussy clench.

"What the hell are you doing in here?" I ask, ignoring the flicker of indecision in his eyes as I tighten the towel around my body, and reach for the smaller hand towel hanging over a locker to dry my hair.

"Honestly, I don't fucking know. But if your father finds out I walked in here when you were taking a shower he'd probably kill me."

"Probably?" I laugh bitterly. "We both know that he would."

Beast gives me a look that tells me that Carter could try but he wouldn't succeed. He's right. One to one, Carter wouldn't stand a chance. Then again, my dad is as powerful as he is because he's not stupid enough to rely on one man to protect him or to dole out punishment. Beast could take on my dad, but could he take on all of his soldiers? Unlikely.

"Then it's just as well that I asked every fucker out there to leave and locked up before I took liberties and stepped in here."

"You did what? We don't close for another hour yet."

"And?"

"And you can't do that," I protest, hating the fact that the skin on my chest and neck heats at the thought of me being naked and alone with Beast with no one around to interrupt should something happen, which it won't because he's made that perfectly fucking clear.

Dragging a hand over his face, he leans forward, elbows on his jean clad knees, his hands hanging loosely between his spread thighs,. I try so hard not to stare at the way the veins on his forearms and hands ripple beneath his skin.

"And you're staring," he replies, doing exactly what he accuses me of as his eyes rake over every inch of me.

I stand my ground, refusing to feel intimidated. There are so many things I want to say to him. Sharp words sit on my tongue like angry little knives just waiting to be thrown into his chest, but underneath the anger and disappointment is longing. It's not just sexual either, but an emotional longing, the need to connect with the man who I care about as a friend as much as anything. I've missed being around him, and as weak as it might seem, I don't have to dig too deep beneath the anger to know that I want him still.

"Beast, what do you want from me?" I ask heavily, lifting the towel to my hair as I rough dry it, if only to make me appear more at ease than I am.

For long heated seconds he stares at me, that same indecision I saw in his eyes a moment ago bubbling to the surface. "You want the truth?"

My hand grasping the towel drops to my side. "I'm not sure that I do," I admit. "Your truths tend to hurt, Beast."

"I've not handled this situation very well," he says, pushing up off the bench and walking towards me.

"So now I'm a *situation*?"

"See, this fucking mouth of mine. What I meant was—"

"Don't," I say, holding my hand up to stop him from getting any closer. I'm still holding the fucking hand towel and we both look at it dangling from my fist.

He reaches for it, taking it from me. "Let me," he says softly, and before I can refuse, he's stepped behind me and is slowly dragging the towel over my wet hair.

"I ain't good at this, Princess," he admits, gently massaging my scalp as he dries my hair.

"You seem pretty good at it to me," I murmur, my eyes rolling in my head as he drops the towel to the floor and runs his hands through my hair, his large fingers gently massaging my scalp.

"That's not what I meant," he replies, a soft chuckle in his voice.

"Then what do you mean, Beast, because I don't understand what this is?"

He continues to massage my head, the heat of his chest seeping into my back as he steps closer. My eyes close and despite everything, I relax against him as his fingers work downwards and his thumbs gently massage the base of my skull. I can't seem to find the energy to step out of his hold. Instead, I allow this moment of human contact to happen, because Christ knows I've not had much of it in my life. My dad isn't exactly affectionate.

"Ask me again, Princess," he says, his lips pressing against my ear, the soft rumble of his voice connecting with that part of my body that weeps for him as his fingers wrap gently around my neck, then trail over my clavicle. My clit throbs, desperate to be touched by him as heat courses through my body, and I stifle a moan, feeling his erection pressing against my lower back, thick and hard for me.

"Ask you what?" I mumble, knowing exactly what he means, but not ready to face the truth of what can't change. No matter what, I will *never* offer myself to him again. I will never ask him to fuck me. My pride and my heart won't be able to take another hit. If he *truly* wants me, then he's going to have to do better than this. He's going to have to fight for me.

"Everything I am, every fucking part of me knows that what I want, that what I'm doing now is wrong but I can't..."

"You can't, *what?*" I whisper as his palm smooths up the front of my neck and gently cups my jaw, twisting my head to the side. I tip my head back as he stares down at me, his free hand wrapping around my waist as his palm presses against my belly, warming me there.

"I can't get you out of my head. Fuck knows I've tried, but I fucking can't," he concedes, his palm smoothing up my cheek, his thumb brushing over my lips.

"You're fucking with my emotions, Beast."

"It's complicated..."

"Only because you've let it be," I reply, twisting in his arms. He sighs heavily and I pull away, needing to put space between us. He allows me to shift back but he doesn't let me go.

"You're a temptation that I'm trying so fucking hard not to indulge in."

"Then don't," I say softly, shocked by my own words more than anything.

"What are you saying?" he asks, looking at me intently.

"I need to protect my heart, Beast."

"Your heart?" he cocks his head to the side, gripping me tightly back against him.

I press my hands against his chest, allowing myself some breathing space. "Yes, my heart. You have a habit of carving them out of people's chests," I say with a wry grin.

"Not yours. Never yours," he says, swiping the pad of his thumb against my bottom lip. He flicks his gaze from my eyes to my lips and back again as he leans closer, pressing a soft kiss against my mouth. It takes monumental effort not to melt against him, to let him take my first proper kiss, my first everything, but a sense of self-preservation kicks into gear and I shake my head, our noses bumping as I do.

"No, Beast. I meant what I said," I say, pushing harder against him. "You don't really want this."

"You've no idea what I want," he grinds out, holding me tighter, pressing me closer to his erection.

My fingers curl into his top. "I know that you're loyal to Carter, that you don't want to betray him. I know that you don't want to go against your own morals. I know that you'll keep blowing hot and cold with me until you get your head straight. I know that I won't *ever* allow a man to touch me who isn't a thousand percent sure that nothing else but *me* matters to him. I know that no matter how much I want you to fuck me right now, I *won't* let you."

"Princess..." he mutters, his fingers twining in my hair as he pulls my head back and forces me to look at him. I meet his fiery gaze with my own.

"It's *Grim*," I say firmly, locking down my emotions, forcing my feelings back inside the heart he bruised with his rejection and avoidance.

"You will always be Princess to me," he says.

"And that's why this will never work, Beast, because I was *always* destined to be queen," I reply, then step out of his arms and stride away from him.

He doesn't follow, just like I knew he wouldn't.

CHAPTER TWENTY

Honesty

"This isn't the way to Hudson's flat," Kate points out as we're driving along the motorway ten minutes later.

"Nope, it isn't."

"Beast…"

"Princess…" I counter, trying not to smirk as her irritation grows. Why does that get my dick so hard? I've never felt more attracted to anyone in my life, but it isn't just her body I'm drawn to, it's her. I'm drawn to her feistiness, her sharp tongue and her wit, her strength and her courage. I want to provoke her because her anger turns me on. She's no wilting flower and I fucking adore that about her.

"You can't keep doing this."

"Doing what?" I reply, pressing on the accelerator as we speed along.

"This!" she yells, the anger I sensed earlier rearing its head.

"You've ignored me for days. Barely spoke to me, *looked* at me even. Then tonight you walk into Tales like a bear with a sore head, chucking everyone out so you can make a pass at me without anyone around to witness it. Is that what I am to you, a dirty little secret?"

Gripping the gear shift, I punch it into sixth gear as the speedometer pushes ninety. "Would you have preferred it if I made a pass at you in front of everyone?" I retort, weaving through the flow of traffic.

"At least it would've shown me you meant it," she spits, reaching for her handbag and pulling out her phone. Pretty sure she's messaging Hudson, which gets my goat no end.

"You think I'm fucking with you?" I snap back, more angry that she's texting the one guy who makes me feel inadequate, not because of his looks or anything, but because he has Kate's affection. It pisses me off.

"I think you don't like it when a woman takes control."

"That's bullshit!" That's the last thing I dislike. I love a strong woman. Always have.

"I initiated everything and you turned me down, leaving me *humiliated*," she says, clamping a hand over my mouth when I try to respond.

Rather than drag it away, I let her keep it pressed over my lips, sneaking my tongue out to lick her fingers. Out of the corner of my eye I see her shudder, but she keeps her hand in place, refusing to let me know I've affected her.

"Then when I do the same to you," she continues. "You act like the meathead you are and do what the fuck you want rather than taking me to my best friend's house so I can be with someone who actually gives a shit about me!"

Dropping her hand, she shifts in her seat, staring out of the window, and the guilt creeps in. I did humiliate her, but I hadn't intended to. At that point I was in a state of fucking panic, knowing I was feeling things and not knowing what the fuck to do. I want to tell her that, but instead I make shit worse.

"I warned you over and over, Princess."

"And yet you *kept* flirting with me."

"It was banter," I bite back rather than telling her the truth. Which is the whole fucking point of tonight. Fuck, what is wrong with me? I keep digging my grave here. Her murderous gaze tells me I'm a hairsbreadth away from ruining shit between us forever.

She laughs bitterly and I feel her disappointment like a punch to the gut. "You were the one who held my fucking hands steady when Carter wanted me to shoot Saxon. You were the one who acted like a jealous boyfriend when I was dancing with John—"

"You mean Orlando," I interrupt.

"Who-the-fuck-ever!" she shouts, continuing her tirade, which I fucking deserve by the way. "You were the one who wanted to stab the King at the dinner table when he looked at me the way he did. You were the one who said I looked beautiful when Carter just thought I looked like a whore. You were the one who hurt me because you weren't brave enough to act, and now you expect me to just drop my knickers because you suddenly decide the time is right? Fuck you and fuck that!" she fumes, her whole body trembling now.

Fuck. This wasn't how it was supposed to go.

Blowing out a long breath, I ease my foot off the accelerator and slow the car down to a more road legal speed as we take the exit off the motorway and towards Camden Town. Chewing on my lip, I try to figure out what to say next. Because she's fucking right. Everything she said is right.

"Where are we going?" she asks eventually, breaking the silence between us.

"To my tattoo shop."

"*Your* tattoo shop? You don't own a tattoo shop," she says.

"I do. I just don't talk about it. I figured as I spend so much money covering my skin, I may as well buy a place and make use of the artists who run it for me," I reply, side-eying her.

She shakes her head in disbelief, dropping her anger for the moment. "You're full of fucking surprises tonight, aren't you?"

"Is it really that strange that I run a business that's not connected to your dad, or the other shit I do on his behalf?"

"Well, yes, actually it is."

"Then take this as a compliment. I'm sharing stuff about me with you. I don't do that with just anyone."

"But don't you have someplace to be?" she questions, sarcasm dripping through her words.

"Not until later. First of all we are doing this."

"You know, as curious as I am, the second you stop this car I'm calling a cab to take me to Hudson's, right?"

"Wrong," I snap.

"Are you trying to piss me off?!" she shouts, beyond frustrated now. I don't fucking blame her. I'm not handling this well at all.

"Look, I promise to take you to Hudson's, but I want to talk to you first," I say, and when she doesn't respond I add, "Please?"

"We could've talked at the club."

"No, we couldn't have."

"Or your place."

"Definitely not there either. Look, I'm trying here."

"Trying to do what?" she asks. "Act like a caveman, then slope off to a *sex* club with your mates so you can bang some pussy that meets your requirements."

"No. I'm trying to apologise for the way I've been behaving, and I'm not sloping off to a sex club with my mates. Carter needs us there. It's *business*."

"Yeah, sure."

"Princess, I'm not lying to you. I'm trying to make amends and you're making it really fucking difficult."

"You're trying to make amends by throwing everyone out of Tales so that you can make a pass at me and when I'm the one to put a stop to it, drag me off to fuck knows where—"

"Not fuck knows where, my tattoo shop," I interrupt.

"—Only to drive like a fucking maniac along the motorway?" she shouts. "How about just saying you're sorry for being a first class dick?"

"When you put it like that..." My voice trails off and I chuckle.

"It's not even remotely funny."

My smile drops. "You're right, it's not, but will you just humour me?"

"Fine. Let's get this over and done with."

Twenty minutes later I'm ushering Kate inside my tattoo shop and introducing her to my two employees. "This is Trent and Casper," I say, pointing between the two good looking bastards. Trent is black with hazel eyes and a shock of dyed red afro hair, trimmed short against his scalp. He towers a good few inches over Casper who's as pale as his name suggests, and has deep blue eyes. They're both covered in tattoos and various piercings and are as devoted to each other as they are to their girlfriend, Rachel, who I've never met but heard is a real catch.

"It's good to meet you both," Kate says, giving them a tight smile.

I wince internally, knowing that I've pushed her way too far tonight. If I hadn't played this all fucking wrong and made a pass at her at Tales, instead of fucking apologising, this introduction might've gone a little better.

"The pleasure is ours," Casper says, responding with sign language as he speaks. "Anyone who's a friend of Beast's is a friend of ours."

Kate gives him a confused look but Trent grins, pointing to his chest, then his ears. "I'm deaf. It's a force of habit for Cas. He forgets I can lip read. It's nice to meet you..."

"Grim," I say, using her dad's nickname to introduce her rather than Kate or Princess.

"Have you come for a tattoo?" Trent asks her.

"No, I have," I reply.

"You have?" Kate asks, staring at me.

"Yeah. Thought I could do with another."

"I'm not being funny, but have you seen you? Aside from your face there's no free space left," she points out.

I grin, thinking about my dick that I'm saving just for her pussy to tattoo its first orgasm all over its length. "Believe me, there's room for another tattoo."

Casper laughs, his eyes flicking to my crotch, the fucking flirtatious bastard.

"Who do you want to do the honours?" Trent asks, grinning.

"I'm going to do it myself. You two get off home to your woman, yeah?"

"So now you're a tattoo artist?" Kate asks, pulling a face.

"He happens to be one of the best. Did a few of my pieces," Casper explains, pointing to a beautiful depiction of a wolf howling against a mountainous backdrop that's wrapped around his forearm.

Kate's mouth drops open in shock. "Wait. *You* did that?"

"Don't look so surprised," I reply, shrugging off my coat and hanging it over the back of a chair. "I'm full of hidden talents."

"Yeah, I'm just realising that," she mumbles, causing my lips to quirk up in a smile as I remember how she melted against me whilst I massaged her head and shoulders back at Tales.

"Well, we'll head off then," Trent says, interrupting my thoughts.

"I'll shut up shop," I say, fist-bumping them both before they give Kate a warm smile and head out. Striding over to the door, I lock it and turn the sign to closed. "Shall we?" I say, pointing to a door on the left side of the shop where our clients are tattooed in the privacy of a windowless room.

"Sure, why not?"

"Make yourself comfortable," I say, shutting the door behind me.

Kate sits down on a chair in the corner of the room as I pick up a tattoo gun, some ink, and a fresh needle, laying them out on a metal table beside the recliner.

"You're not fucking about, are you?" she asks, watching me as I move about the room, setting everything up.

"Nope. In my former life I was trained as a tattoo artist. My mum always said to have a backup profession just in case what I really wanted to do didn't work out. I followed her advice."

"So your backup profession to being an enforcer was this?"

"No, my backup profession to being a *professional boxer* was this," I reply, fixing the needle into the tattoo gun. "I kinda fell into enforcement."

"You wanted to be a professional boxer?"

"Yeah. Things didn't work out as planned." I give her a sheepish smile that I shut down when she frowns. "Come here, Princess."

"Why?"

"Because I need your hand."

"My hand? You aren't suggesting that I tattoo you, right?"

I laugh "No, I don't have a death wish."

"So what then?"

"Will you just come over here?" I ask, sitting down and swinging my legs over either side of the recliner, tapping the space between my legs. "Hop on up?" I frame it as a question rather than a demand, needing her to be okay with this. I know I've pushed her to her limits and fucked things up, but I won't force her to do anything she's uncomfortable with.

She stares at me for a while, clearly debating whether she should do as I ask. Eventually she nods her head and climbs up on the recliner so that she's kneeling between my legs.

"It would be more comfortable for you if you scoot your bum closer and drop your legs over my thighs. I don't want you getting dead legs from kneeling."

"Are you suggesting I wank you off, Beast?" she blurts out, her cheeks heating as she drops her gaze from my face to my crotch.

I burst out laughing, and she shifts to move off the recliner. "No, shit. Of course not!" I exclaim, grabbing her hips to prevent her from leaving. "I just want you to be comfortable as it's gonna take a while for me to do this."

"What are we doing exactly?" she asks, allowing me to help her shift positions so that she's facing me with her legs dangling over my thighs, our crotches inches apart. She has to grip my knees to steady herself whilst I pull off my t-shirt and grab the tattoo gun, dipping it into some black ink. My pulse does something funny to my heart and I have to swallow hard at the way it rams against my rib cage, just like my dick is pressing against the seam of my jeans.

Fuck, I'm in so much trouble here.

"Put your hand on my chest. Right over my heart, Princess," I say, ignoring the way her neck and cheeks pink up. She's as attracted to me as I am to her, there's never been any doubt about that. My chest swells with possession and it takes a great deal of concentration not to act on that right here and now.

"What?"

"You heard me. Just do it," I say gruffly to cover up my fucking nerves. Right now I feel every inch a man out of his depth. I'm not usually like this with women. I take the lead, I'm confident, sure of myself. But Kate makes me nervous. She frowns, but does what I ask. I'm pretty sure she can feel the steady thrum of my heart beating beneath her palm, given how much I can feel it pound in my chest from her touch.

"Like this?" she asks, staring at her hand pressing against my chest. My dick springs to life, painfully so.

"Spread your fingers," I instruct, switching on the gun as I try to keep my hand fucking steady. "I'm going to tattoo around them, so hold still, okay?"

"Why?"

Pressing the needle into my skin just beside the point where the bottom of her thumb meets her wrist, I say, "Because I don't want to tattoo your fingers by mistake."

"No, I mean why do you want a tattoo of my hand over your heart?"

"Isn't that obvious?" I ask, hissing a little as the needle makes its first mark. I welcome it, the slight sting helps to distract me from the growing ache in my balls.

"I'm going to need you to spell this out to me because you've got a really bad habit of switching up on me," she retorts, as I slowly trace the outline of her thumb. It's not exactly easy to do given our positions, but then again nothing about the pair of us is easy, so it's kind of perfect. "Beast?" she prompts.

I can feel the heat of her gaze, but I don't look up mainly because I don't want to make a mistake, but also because I'm shitting a brick right now. "This isn't easy for me..."

"You're *nervous*—?"

"I am." I stop what I'm doing and nod, meeting her warm gaze. Her eyes are like two pools of dark chocolate and the way she's looking at me right now makes my dick try and make the great escape out of my jeans.

"It's just me," she whispers, the softness of her voice sending all kinds of electrical currents to my balls, making me weep precum.

"Fuck, Kate," I say, unable to control the need in my voice. When she's like this, soft and true, I'm a goner. Don't get me wrong, I adore her sass and whip-sharp tongue, but this, the rarity of her softer side does things to me that I can't describe. I simultaneously want to protect her from the world and stand by her side whilst she rules it.

"Beast?" She tips her head to the side, shifting slightly. Her thighs pressing down on mine, her scent filling my senses. I'm fucking punch-drunk on her right now as my nostrils flare and I breathe her in.

"You're not *just* anyone," I say, finding it hard to explain how I feel. At a loss for words, I place the needle back against my skin and trace the side of her thumb.

"Yeah, I know, I'm your boss's daughter." The regret in her voice pulls me up sharp.

"No! You're so much more than that, Princess. *Kate...*" I add, wanting her to know that I see her for who she is, not the persona her father has encouraged her to be, or the box I put her into to suit my needs.

She falls silent and instead of being a man and growing some big arse balls I fall silent too. For the next half an hour I trace the outline of her hand with the tattoo gun, loving the feel of her warmth seeping into my chest and her soft breaths across my skin. This is what wet dreams are made of.

Eventually I finish, and drop the tattoo gun on the metal table beside us. Kate shifts backwards slightly, lifting her hand, but I'm not ready for her to go just yet, so I grab her wrist, holding her palm in place.

"No. Let me say this with your hand pressed against my chest so you can feel my heart beating beneath it and understand that I'm not fucking with you."

She chews on the inside of her cheek, staring at the point

where our skin meets. "I think you've ruined that beautiful tattoo on your chest. Why would you do that?"

"Because I need you to understand a few things..." My voice trails off as I try to gather the words to express how I'm feeling, which is no mean feat given I *never* express my feelings. Ever.

"Can we just pull the plaster off please, because I'm not sure I can take much more of this," Kate says.

I nod, blowing out a quick breath before locking eyes with her. "You were right about it all. Everything you accused me of was true. I *was* flirting with you," I confess, holding her gaze. "I look for you in every room, and the second I find you I can't fucking tear my eyes away."

"You do?"

"Yeah, I do. You're too bright, too dazzling and I want nothing more than to stand in your orbit and bask in your glow."

Her cheeks pink and a small laugh escapes her lips. "There you go being all poetic again. Are you sure you haven't read your mum's romance novels?"

I laugh with her, shaking my head. "Not sure where that came from, but it's all true. I swear, Kate. I'm not fucking with you."

She nods, but it seems like I've still got a ways to go to persuade her that I mean every word. So I continue. "When I saw you dancing with that Orlando prick, I wanted to gut him so badly for touching what is *mine*."

"Yours?" she asks, tipping her head to the side as she looks at me. I'm pretty fucking sure she can feel the way my heart frantically beats against my rib cage confirming that it wants her just as much as every other part of my fucking anatomy does.

"Yes, *mine*... When the King was eye-fucking you, I was

ready to start a fucking war, and don't get me started on what I wanted to do to Carter for speaking to you the way he does."

"But I'm not yours though. You turned me down, remember?"

"I did, but I didn't want to," I admit.

"You humiliated me." Her gaze drops to my chest, and I see the way her shoulders slump just a fraction under the weight of that hurt. I feel like a ten-ton prick.

"And for that I'm truly sorry." Placing my finger beneath her chin, I tip her head back up. "Did you honestly believe I didn't want what you were offering?" I ask, searching her face. "Did you really think that I didn't want to touch every inch of your skin, taste you with my tongue, replace your fingers with my own? Did you think I didn't want to fuck you, or bury my face in your sweet pussy and taste your arousal? That is *all* I wanted to do. I want that and so much more."

"But why—?"

"Why didn't I?" I interrupt.

"Yes."

"For the same reasons I've mentioned before, because you're young. Because your father is my boss. Because I care enough about you not to take something precious from you without being a hundred percent certain that I won't fuck this up."

"So nothing's changed then?" She tries to pull back, but I just grip her tighter, refusing to let her go.

"Everything's changed," I insist, willing her to believe me.

"How?" she asks. There's a sadness in her eyes, a distrust, and it guts me to know I put that there.

"I don't do relationships with women. I fuck them, then I walk away. Every woman I've slept with knows this about me. I don't make promises I can't keep, and I refuse to be the same man my father was. I won't hurt you."

"So what are you saying? That you don't want me because I'm too young, but because I'm Carter's daughter?"

"Right now I *can't* have you, no matter how much I want that to be different."

She shakes her head in frustration, trying to get away from me. "Then whatever this is between us is over before it's even begun."

"You're not listening, Kate," I say, refusing to let her go as I slide my hand to the back of her head and grasp a handful of her hair, tugging on it gently, forcing her to pay attention. "I said this can't happen *right now.*"

She stops struggling to get away, and I can see the indecision crossing her features. I know her well enough to know that I've triggered her anger. I don't blame her for it.

"You expect me to wait? Until when, Beast? Until I'm old enough for you? Until you've fucked a million other women whilst you wait for me to become one. In case it has skipped your notice, I *am* a woman. Right here and now."

"It hasn't skipped my notice," I say, trying to control my own growing frustration, not at her but at the situation we're in, that I've had a hand at putting us in. "But it doesn't change the fact that I won't fuck you until I think you're ready."

She laughs bitterly. "You've no right to decide when you think *I'll* be ready. How dare you make that decision for me!"

"Let me rephrase that. I won't sleep with you until I know *I* can be the man you deserve. The man who has nothing standing in his way. If we're going to do this, I need to make sure I do it right."

"But even if I agreed to wait so that your morals can be satisfied, Carter will always be my father, and your loyalty to him will *always* get in the way."

"That's the part I'm struggling with right now. Just give me time to figure it out. That's all I ask of you."

"Whilst you fuck other women. I don't think so."

"Who said anything about fucking other women? I don't want to fuck anyone else, Kate."

"I don't believe you."

"I'm a man of my word."

"So you keep saying."

I grind my teeth, gripping her tighter, pulling her closer. "I'm a man of my word," I repeat slowly, dragging each word out to make sure that she hears me. "The next woman I bury my dick inside of will be you, and in the meantime I'll deal with my aching cock thinking of you naked, with your legs spread, your pussy glistening and wet for me as I pump my dick, night after night after night remembering how you made yourself come."

"And what do I get, Beast? Am I supposed to just wait, to save all my firsts for you, a man who may *never* act on what he truly wants? What am I supposed to do in the meantime? Tell me why I should wait for you?"

Despite her anger, her cheeks are flushed, her pupils blown wide. She wants me to do all those things to her as much as I want to do them.

"Because you feel the same way about me as I do about you. Because you're loyal. Fuck! Because my motherfucking heart is yours, Kate. Why do you think I just tattooed your hand on my chest, huh? This heart is yours. The only hand that gets to hold it, *is yours.*"

"Your heart is mine?"

"Yes, god-fucking-damn-it!" I say in frustration, making my words sound harsher than I'd intended. Releasing her wrist, I wrap my arm around her back, pulling her fully onto my lap as I bring her head closer. "It's yours."

"Mine?" she asks, her body relenting, relaxing in my hold. She shifts her hips, rubbing herself against my aching cock, intentionally or not it doesn't matter, the outcome is the same. I bite back a moan, needing her to understand that this is more than just physical attraction for me.

"Yours," I repeat, relief flooding my body as she gives me a tiny hint of a smile. I rub the tip of my nose against the bridge of hers before lowering my mouth, hovering over her lips. Fuck, I want to kiss her so badly. But I don't know if I'll be able to stop if I close the gap between us.

"I need to believe it," she whispers against my lips, her voice a long, drawn out caress around my aching cock.

"Will you wait for me?"

"Will you give me something to hold onto, *anything*, so I know this is real?" she counters.

I stare at her for a long, long time, but she doesn't close the gap between us and I realise she needs me to be the one to come to her. She has to know that I want this as much as she does, after giving her mixed signals for so long. Kissing her now is going to be both agony and ecstasy.

But I'm more than willing to prove to her I mean every damn word I've just said.

"I'll give you your first kiss," I say, brushing my mouth lightly against hers, "So long as you understand that I will kill any man who dares take all the other firsts that belong to me."

"I do," she says, cupping my cheek, the warmth of her palm sinking into my skin.

"So you promise to wait?" I repeat.

"I promise," she agrees, but just as I'm about to really kiss her, she presses her thumb against my lips before saying, "As long as you understand that if you betray me, or go back on your word, not only will I fuck who I want, when I want, I'll have no issue putting a bullet in your chest for breaking my heart."

"That's my girl," I reply with a smile, nipping her thumb before nudging it out of the way.

Her lips part the second mine touch hers, and she grants me access as I plunge my tongue into her mouth and pour every last ounce of lust and love into this kiss.

She wanted something to hold onto, and that's what I give her.

A kiss to remember.

A kiss that brands us both. That binds us together. That mocks every other kiss I've experienced before. This kiss is like an explosion, it demolishes every other memory of every other kiss I've shared with every other woman before and it forms a new memory, an everlasting one.

Kissing Kate is like the sun coming out after an eclipse, brightening everything, warming my skin, shining a light on the connection we share, the one I've been a fool to deny, and it feels good.

Fuck, it feels better than good.

It feels *perfect*.

She's fucking perfect.

There's no doubt in my mind that she's mine, that I'm hers.

That we fucking belong together. I don't give a shit about how that might make me sound.

I'm in love.

I'm. In. Love.

My heart doubles in size with that truth, competing with my cock that she mindlessly grinds against, her hips rolling as she grasps my face, pressing her tits against my chest.

No one has ever made me feel so fucking out of control. No one.

I'm consumed by her. I'm fucking lost. I'm lost in her taste, in her scent, in the way she feels and in the sounds she makes as she whimpers and moans.

But I know, I *have* to stop.

I must.

And it's the hardest fucking thing I've ever had to do as I grasp her shoulders and ease her backward away from me.

"Enough. No more," I say, and it isn't a command, I'm pleading with her to stop, wanting nothing more than to continue.

Her cheeks are flush, her lips are bruised, her pupils are blown wide as she heaves out a breath, nodding. "I don't want to stop," she admits. "I want you to kiss me until I can't breathe. Then I want you to fuck me until I can't stand," she says brazenly as she presses her hand back over my chest, her thumb rubbing gently backwards and forwards.

"Fuck, Kate, I don't want to stop either. I want to kiss you until all the fucking oxygen has left my lungs and I want to fuck you until there is no you and me, only us, but I *have* to stop. We have to."

"Just one more kiss," she says, leaning close, her lips brushing against mine softly, her eyes pleading.

"Fuck, I would give you the world if you asked me."

"I don't want the world. I just want one more kiss."

"It has to be our last... *for now*. But know this, the last kiss I ever give you will be on my motherfucking deathbed because only death has the power to keep me away from you."

"You promise?"

"I promise," I mutter against her mouth, pressing my lips against hers in a kiss that I hope tattoos that promise right across her heart.

A heart that I go ahead and break just a few days later.

CHAPTER TWENTY-ONE

Family

"You look happy," Hudson remarks as I step into his flat. I can hear chatter coming from inside the living room and recognise the deep rumble of Bryce's laughter.

"Yeah?" I reply, not giving up the reason why. I don't want to share what happened between Beast and me just yet, and especially not in front of the others. They'll only take the piss. Max loves to joke about everything and Cal is always trying to find ways to wind me up.

"Beast finally let you out of his clutches then?" Hudson asks with a knowing smile.

I shrug. "He had stuff to do."

Hudson trails behind me as I walk towards the living room. "With your dad?"

"Yep. Him and a few of the others are going to The Crib Club tonight. Carter's doing business there."

"Business at The Crib Club? Sounds like my kind of business," Bryce says from his position on the sofa as I step into the living room. He grins at me, winking in that flirtatious way of his. Next to him Max snorts with laughter.

"Yeah, you wish. The women in that club are way out of your league, bro!"

Cal smirks. "Mate, Bryce could pull Jennifer Lopez if he wanted. Have you seen the size of his dick?"

"Wait, you've seen Bryce's dick?" Hudson pulls a face that makes us all laugh.

"Are you kidding me? Nearly every time he's over here he's walking around the flat fucking naked. It's hard to miss."

"Ever heard of averting your eyes?" Hudson says, looking affronted.

"I never thought you were a prude," I say, poking him in the rib and grinning mercilessly. "You should see the fighters at Tales, they're always talking about their dicks or comparing sizes."

"And that's why you're the only female member. You're a cock hoarder," Max says, and the three of them burst out laughing.

"Yep. Love a cock or twelve," I reply, grinning. "Unlike Hud here, who's clearly affronted by a nice big dick."

"Shut the hell up! I just don't want to look at my brother's dick, or hear about how well hung he is either. He's barely a fucking adult."

"Mate, have you seen the hair covering my body? I'm more adult than you are," Bryce says, lifting his t-shirt to show us the rug covering his chest. Fuck, he *is* hairy.

We all crack up laughing and before long I'm squished on

the sofa between Bryce and Hudson, whilst Max and Cal sit on the two-seater opposite us. For the next hour or so we all eat pizza, down a couple of bottles of beer and watch some mindless trash tv. I've always felt comfortable in the presence of Hudson and his brothers, Max and Bryce. They kind of come as a package deal. If you're friends with one, you're friends with the other two. They may not be brothers by blood, but the bond they have from growing up in the same care home is much stronger than many I've seen. Cal is their very good friend, but he doesn't fit in their tight-knit threesome in quite the same way. Not that it makes them care for him any less, just differently.

When it's pushing eleven o'clock, Cal jumps up. "I gotta head off. Are you coming?" he asks Max and Bryce who're both fighting over the last slice of now cold pizza.

"Yeah, you should get back to the children's home before they send someone over to drag your arses back there," Hudson says, gathering up the empty boxes and nudging Bryce's leg to give him room to pass.

"We've literally got a few weeks left until we're eighteen and can leave. Why do they care whether we stay out past our curfew?" Max asks, running a hand through his blonde hair. He's cute to look at, all four of the boys are, but none hold a candle to Beast. I bite down on a smile, remembering the conversation we had earlier.

Hudson notices, narrowing his eyes at me and giving me a look that says he'll find out what's making me smile just as soon as everyone leaves. "Because, Max, I don't need to give those nosy arseholes in social services any more of a reason to give me a hard time, not when we're so close to being together at long last."

"Ah, you make it sound so romantic," Cal jokes, grinning.

"Are you jealous?" Bryce retorts, standing.

He's so tall that he looks way older than his almost eighteen years, that and the fact he is covered in more hair than the three of them put together. If I wasn't so hung up on another man, he'd be tempting. There's nothing more attractive than a manly man, in my opinion. I guess that's why I'm so drawn to Beast, because he's most definitely an alpha male, that's for damn sure.

"Jealous of you three fuckwits? Nah. I'm good," Cal replies, but this time his smile doesn't quite reach his eyes. Hudson frowns.

"Hey, Cal, you know our home is your home, right? We've said all along you can be a Freed just like us," he says, gripping his arm and making him wait.

"Yeah, I know," Cal nods, placing his hand over Hudson's and gripping it briefly. "But I've got a family still and whilst they might not be the best it wouldn't feel right taking on another name. You understand where I'm coming from, yeah?"

Hudson nods. "Of course."

I don't know the details of Cal's past, but I do know he ended up in the care home with the others for a couple of years whilst his mum got her shit together. He's back with her now, but the friendship the boys made is still as strong as ever. I don't think that will ever change.

"Don't worry, Cal, you'll always be our number one sidepiece," Max jokes, earning him a punch on the arm.

"Fuck you, arsewipe," Cal grins.

"Ow, fuck. You know I'm only joking, that honour belongs to Grim. Right, Grim?" Max asks, winking at me.

"Ha ha! You should know by now that I'm no man's sidepiece," I reply, raising a brow and giving him my best death glare, but my lip twitches and I end up smiling because there isn't one person on this planet that can stay mad at Max for long. He's a lovable fool and completely harmless. Though I'm pretty sure his wit is a defensive mechanism. We've all got one, his just happens to be humour.

"Tell that to that big bastard that calls himself Beast. Pretty sure he wants all your pieces," Max replies, wiggling his brows.

"Funny!" I shout, picking up a cushion off the sofa and throwing it at him as he runs from the room.

A few minutes later, the flat is a lot quieter and it's just me and Hud sitting on his sofa sharing his last beer. "Those two eat me out of house and home. The sooner they leave the children's home the sooner I can set them to work."

"What's the plan?" I ask, curious to know what scheme he's come up with to get them all out of the gutter. His words, not mine.

"For the last three years since I left the children's home I've been working my arse off."

"I know you have. You're the hardest working person I know," I say with a smile.

"Wow, Grim, is that a compliment?"

"Don't get used to it. I need my best friend to remain un-bigheaded."

"Not possible," he grins, pointedly looking at his dick.

"Eww, fucking gross! I did not need that visual in my life." We both laugh and then I nudge him with my shoulder. "So you were saying?"

"I've managed to secure a loan from the bank and have added that to my savings," he continues. "And I'm going to put a deposit down on a tiny studio flat on the other side of town."

"What's wrong with this place?" I ask. His flat isn't huge by any means, but it does have two bedrooms and it is low rent given it's owned by the local authority.

"Absolutely nothing. We're not going to live at the studio flat. The deposit is for a mortgage."

"You've managed to get a mortgage from an actual bank? How in the hell did you pull that off?"

Hudson grins. "I have my ways. Anyway, we're gonna do the flat up and flip it for a profit. The plan is to keep doing that until we've got enough equity to buy our own place outright."

"Wow, that's... ambitious," I reply, impressed.

"You don't think I can do it?" he asks, trying not to look affronted even though I can tell that he is.

"Of course I do! I just... Well, I'm impressed. You're not just a pretty face, are you?" I joke. Hudson is smart, one of the smartest people I know.

"Talking of pretty faces, how are things with you and Beast?" he asks, changing the subject smoothly.

"Same as usual," I lie, avoiding his gaze and taking a sip of beer.

"That's not what your loved-up face said earlier. "

"A face can't get loved-up, you moron."

"You're not denying it then?" he asks, taking the bottle from me and finishing it off in one long gulp as I try to figure out what to say. I trust Hudson one thousand percent, but I don't know how to talk about my relationship with Beast because at the moment we don't officially have one. Just a promise.

Maybe I should start with that?

"I kind of made a promise. No, *we* made a promise to each other," I begin, chewing on the inside of my cheek, feeling my cheeks flush at the memory.

"A promise?" He swipes a hand through his dark hair, tousling it up. If he wasn't my very best friend and I didn't have completely platonic feelings towards him, I'd absolutely be attracted to him. As it is, I appreciate his good looks, but that's it.

"Yes. He has an issue with getting together with anyone under the age of twenty—"

"Okay," Hudson says slowly. "I mean, I get that he's cautious. You're not eighteen yet and he is older. People could frown on it."

I pull a face. "Don't you start. I'll be eighteen in few days."

"And then there's the pretty fucking major issue of your dad being his boss. Beast hooking up with you crosses several boundaries and then some. Not to mention Carter is a certifiable nutcase when he wants to be. You being his daughter makes being together tricky, don't you think?"

"I thought you said I should bang someone else to make him jealous, that would imply all the things you've just said aren't actually all that important," I grumble, blowing out a breath.

"That was before I knew how serious this was. I just figured you had a crush." Hudson shrugs, and I punch him on the arm. "Ow, what was that for?"

"For assuming I had a *crush*. Crushes are for kids. Seriously, Hud, when have I ever *really* liked someone?" I ask.

"You liked me once upon a time," he points out, much to my dismay.

"I did not!"

He raises his brows and pulls a face. "I'm pretty sure you threw yourself at me."

"I was pushed into you! I did not throw myself at you!"

"Technicalities," he smirks, teasing me.

"Those shits shouldn't have started on me."

"They totally didn't realise who they were up against. Though to be fair, you were a shit fighter back then. Beast's trained you well."

"I was *not* a shit fighter. Pretty sure I knocked out two of the five boys who thought they could try and mug me."

I grin when he bursts out laughing. "Touchy, touchy tonight, aren't we? Is it all that pent-up sexual frustration?"

"Ha-bloody-ha."

"Seriously though, I'm glad you came into my life, our lives. If it weren't for those pricks I would never have met you—"

"You know *you're* my favourite right?" I ask, interrupting him. I really like Max, Bryce and Cal, but Hud and I have a special bond.

"Of course," he jokes, then gets serious again. "I love you, Grim, you mean as much to me as Bryce, Max and Cal do."

"Did you just say the L word in my presence?" I joke, feeling my heart warm at the words even though I'm trying my hardest not to let him know how much hearing that means to me. I don't think my dad has ever said he loved me. Never.

Now I've had two men say they love me in the space of a few hours. Maybe the words didn't actually leave Beast's mouth, but I know that's what he meant. Hudson gives me his serious look and I wait for whatever it is he's going to say.

"Grim, you're like a sister to me. You're my best friend and a really fucking scary badass bitch all wrapped up in one. I'm glad those shits from the children's home started on you, otherwise we wouldn't be mates now."

"Yeah, me too," I say.

He nods, putting an arm around my shoulder. "So this thing with Beast is serious then?"

I relax into his arms. "Yeah, it's serious."

"But you have this weird love-hate relationship with him. I never thought you'd fall for him."

"I haven't fallen for him," I mumble.

Hudson chuckles softly, dropping a kiss to the top of my head. "You know you can tell me how you really feel. I swear to you, Grim, I won't breathe a word."

"Not even to Bryce and Max... To Cal?"

"Not even them. Whatever you say in this room remains between us, okay?"

"Yeah, okay," I reply.

"So?" he gently prompts.

"I'm in love with him," I admit.

"Fuuuuck," he replies.

"I know, right?"

"Are you certain?"

I pull back and give him an *are-you-shitting-me* look, because he knows I don't love easily. I can't even tell my best friend that I love him, even though he knows I do, that I'd do anything for our friendship, for him. "Yeah, I'm certain."

"And Beast, how does he feel about you?"

"I think he feels the same way."

Hudson raises his brows. "You think?"

"Tonight he tattooed the outline of my hand on his chest, right over his heart," I explain, smiling a little at the memory.

"That's why I'm late. He took me with him to get it done because he needed my hand."

Hudson grins. "I'd say that's a pretty good sign."

"It barely showed up against his other tattoos on his chest…"

"I don't think that was the point, do you? He wants *you* to know it's there."

"I guess."

"You don't believe he likes you?"

I frown, thinking for a moment. "I do. It's just…"

"It's just easier to expect the worst from someone than it is to trust they'll look after your heart, right?" he asks knowingly.

"Right," I reply.

"Listen, Grim, I know trusting people isn't easy for you, but for what it's worth, I believe him. I see the way he is with you."

"You do?"

"Yep, I do. In all honesty, I thought he was going to kill me that day I got concussed by Slimy who, by the way, has gone radio fucking silent. I think we scared him off?"

I keep my expression as neutral as possible. There's no need to make Hudson an accomplice by telling him what actually happened to Dougie and his cronies. "Yep, we totally scared him off," I agree.

"Not only that, Beast is a man of his word. If he's made a promise to you then he won't break it."

"If he does, I'll kill him," I reply, only half joking.

"Fuck, Grim. Remind me not to get on your bad side. You're more like your dad than you let on."

"Lately I feel like I'm more of a disappointment for Carter than anything."

"Why? The way he was talking about you to the guy at

Tales that night Beast mullered Clayton said otherwise. He dotes on you."

"You mean the King?"

"Wait, that was *the* King... I didn't realise *he* was the guy who came on to you."

"The one and only."

"No wonder Beast was giving us all daggers. I thought he was still pissed at me for getting you involved with my shit. Sorry, Grim, if I'd have known, I wouldn't have been so chill with him."

"Don't worry about it. So what was Carter saying about me that night, exactly?" I ask, my curiosity piqued.

"You know, how proud he is of you, that kind of thing."

"Proud of me?" A laugh bursts out of my mouth. "Come on, Hud, what did he *really* say? You don't need to soften the edges. I can take it. I've lived with Carter my whole life, remember?"

Hudson grimaces, and I know for sure Carter wasn't complimenting me at all. "He mentioned you were still helping with the refit."

"And?" I question, knowing there's way more to this than that.

"And he said you'd make someone a fine wife one day..."

"Did he now," I scoff, "And you agreed with him, I suppose?"

"Of course, I did," Hudson replies, earning him a punch on the arm, which he takes without complaint.

"I'm not *wife* material. There's more to me than that!"

"Of course, there is! But it's not as if I could disagree with your dad. I do actually want to live to see my next birthday."

"Fair enough," I concede, because he has got a point. "And what did the King say?"

Hudson frowns and I roll my eyes.

"Shock, horror, he agreed with Carter too, right? I'm the perfect wifey material. Urgh, he's such a prick. I feel for whoever ends up with that arsehole."

"Actually, no. He kind of said the opposite, in fact."

"What?" I ask, curious.

"He said that most women are born to fall in line, but there are some women who are born to break all the rules."

"And the rules he's referring to are made by men for men, right?" I scoff, shaking my head.

"Yeah, but then he said that the ones who were born to break the rules were the most fun because who wants a boring housewife anyway."

"What was my dad thinking, going into business with him? Once I take over the company I'll be cutting ties with that prick the second I get the chance."

"I couldn't agree more," Hudson replies. "The sooner you're free of that man, the better."

"The sooner the better," I echo, a sudden chill scattering down my spine.

My gut tells me the King is bad news, and my gut is never wrong.

Hudson puts his arm around my shoulder, squeezing me against his side. "Don't worry about all of that shit now. First things first is your birthday party. Soon you'll be the centre of attention. Are you looking forward to it?"

I pull a face. "Not really, but Carter is keen to throw me one, so I'm just going with the flow."

"What can I get you for your birthday?" Hudson asks me. It's sweet, but we both know money's tight.

"I don't want anything," I reply, meaning it.

"I can't come empty-handed. Come on, give me *some* ideas."

"You being there is enough. I need someone who's got my back just in case things go pear-shaped."

"Are you expecting trouble?"

I laugh. "I *know* there'll be trouble. So you'd better buckle up, buttercup, because every party Carter throws ends in blood and violence."

"Fuuucckkk," Hudson drawls.

"Yep. It's not a good party unless someone winds up dead," I joke.

We both laugh, neither of us aware that's exactly what's going to happen.

CHAPTER TWENTY-TWO

Cross Me

Driving to The Crib Club after reluctantly dropping Kate off at Hudson's place, I relive our kiss over and over again.

I'm still hard.

Painfully so.

I'd wanted to give Kate a kiss that proved how deeply I feel for her, but instead of being sensual it had ended up being passionate, raw and ball-crushingly painful. Fuck, I ache for her. My balls feel like a vice is tightening around them, and don't get me started on my dick.

It hates me right now.

I hate myself right now.

That kiss took me to the brink of madness, and I'm fucking drowning in the aftermath.

Even my goddamn thoughts are poetic, but that's nothing

compared to the way it felt to finally kiss her. I'd gone in soft and ended up in a motherfucking duel for dominance.

Our teeth had clashed and our tongues fought. She was mad at me, I felt that in the way she kissed me, how she'd climbed into my lap and rubbed her hot, jean covered cunt over my raging hard-on. She'd wanted me to break, and in all fucking honesty, a huge part of me wanted to break too. I wanted to rip off her jeans and knickers, ram my dick inside her tight heat and smash through the thin barrier of her virginity, finally claiming her as mine.

But I hadn't.

Instead we kissed for long, long minutes and it was breathless and sloppy and fucking perfect. Fuck knows I wanted to throw caution to the wind, but I kept my word, forcibly removing myself from her even though it felt like I was cutting off all of my limbs. Even now I feel as though part of me is missing, my balls certainly think it's my dick.

I've never craved someone as much as I have Kate.

Never.

Pulling into the car park beneath The Crib Club, I pull the handbrake up and give myself a moment to calm the fuck down. My goddamn heart has been racing ever since Kate climbed up on the recliner and pressed her palm against my chest so that I could tattoo her handprint forever on my body. Over the coming weeks I intend to fill it in so that everyone sees it and knows my motherfucking heart has been claimed. I run my fingers over the tattoo now hidden beneath my shirt and grin, the slight sting and the lingering pleasure a reminder of the girl I love…

Love.

"Yeah, *love*," I say, shaking my head in disbelief.

Fuck. I need to get a hold of myself. I made a promise to Kate and I intend on sticking to it. First and foremost, there's the not so small fact she's not yet at the age I would even consider fuckable. I have an issue sleeping with anyone who has the word 'teen' at the end of their age, even if they hit eighteen and are classed as an adult. As much as I know Kate's a woman, and is as far removed from a child as a person can get, given how she's grown up in the environment she has, I can't and won't sleep with her until she hits twenty.

Call it whatever the fuck you want.

I won't do it.

Secondly, I still haven't figured out how to deal with Carter. I'm not afraid of him in any shape or form, but I do still have enough respect for him not to carry on with his daughter without speaking to him about it first. I owe him that much. Luckily I've got time to figure that out.

Two fucking years to be precise.

I'll be lucky not to die of *blueballitis* by then.

Tonight I just need to get my head back in the game, and be the man Carter hired me to be. Honestly, I'm not sure why he wants to conduct business at The Crib Club, but then again why do I care? If he and the King want to whack off to a couple of hot sex workers in a legit club to close their business deal then who the fuck am I to question it? I don't like the King, but so long as he gets his rocks off with anyone other than Kate, I'm fucking good.

Not that I've forgotten how he'd looked at her, because I haven't.

If he so much as looks at her the wrong way, I will remove his eyes from his face and damn the consequences. With that thought in mind, I rearrange my rapidly deflating cock, grab my gun, holstering it at my waist, then head inside the club.

"GOT THINGS SORTED WITH PRINCESS?" Dom asks me as we head over to the private room Carter has rented for the evening. The Crib Club is filled to the brim with high class hookers and patrons that are into all manner of kinky shit. There's a main stage area with strippers and pole dancers, and a dozen or more private rooms around the edge of the club that have a lockable door and a glass screen that allows you to view whatever sexual fantasy you've paid to watch. For those wanting a more personal experience, the whole first floor of the club is filled with bedrooms that you can rent for the night. There is even a part of the club designated for gambling. If card games are your thing, with a little sex on the side, then this place is for you.

"What's up, Beast, trouble in paradise?" Dom persists when I don't respond straight away.

"None of your fucking business," I retort, not in the mood to share. Not that I would, even if I was. What happens between me and Kate stays between us.

"Is that boyfriend of hers, Hudson, causing shit again?" Dom asks.

"He's not her fucking boyfriend!" I snap, shoving open the door to Carter's private booth.

His head snaps around. "Do you fucking mind?"

"Apologies, boss," Dom replies, side-eying me when I don't say a word.

"Is he here yet?" Carter asks, turning his attention back to the curvaceous blonde who's currently lying on a round bed covered in pristine white sheets getting railed by a redhead wearing a strap-on.

"I thought he'd be here already," I reply, taking a seat on one side of the door as Dom takes the other, completely distracted by the show.

"Fuck me," Dom mutters, his eyes glued to the women. "Those two ain't mucking about!"

Not that the women are paying us any fucking attention, and why would they? We might be able to see them, but they can't see us. Privacy of the patrons attending The Crib Club is paramount and we're watching behind two-way glass.

"He was supposed to be here half an hour ago. As were you," Carter says, twisting in his swivel chair to face me. "Was Grim giving you trouble?"

"Not in the slightest. There was traffic. Accident on the motorway."

He nods, narrowing his eyes at me as though he reads the lie written in neon across my face. "She's not been getting up to any shit, has she? You know what I said, she needs to remain—"

"Yeah. All good in that department," I quickly cut in.

Out of the corner of my eye I can see Dom frown. He's no idea we're talking about Kate's virginity and the fact her dad's weirdly obsessed with it as of late. Not sure what's up with that, but it's a big fucking red flag if you ask me.

"Good," Carter replies with a terse nod before turning back to watch the women fuck. "Because if I were to find out that my daughter was whoring herself out, there'd be hell to fucking pay, but not before I chopped off the dick of the motherfucker fooling around with her and fed it to him."

I meet Dom's gaze and the way he looks at me is a cross between incredulity and concern. Despite all the ribbing, I'm pretty sure he knows how I really feel about Kate, even though I deny it on a regular basis. The sheer fact he's not given me away tells me a lot about him. Joey was right, he is one of the good ones.

Giving him a minute shake of my head, I stare at the back of Carter's head and say, "Don't worry boss, I'd have the prick hung, drawn and quartered before you even had a chance to chop off his dick."

Dom smirks knowingly.

"Glad to hear it," Carter replies, grabbing his drink from the side table beside him and taking a sip.

After another half an hour of watching Carter eyeball the two women fucking, I become a little restless. Sitting in a locked room whilst my boss rubs his cock over his trousers isn't my idea of a fun night out, no matter how much I'm getting paid.

"You want me to go see if the King's arrived yet?" I ask, ready to fucking bolt.

"Yeah, and bring me another Jack and Coke whilst you're at it," he replies with a distracted wave of his hand.

Dom swallows a smile, knowing full well I ain't happy about being the fucking waitress, but I take it on the chin and step outside the booth into the club that's ten times as busy as it was when I first arrived.

Heading to the bar, I scoot around the edge of the dance floor, glancing around the space for any obvious cause for concern. No matter what I'm doing, or where I am, I've got my radar whirring. I can sense trouble a mile off, and can normally pinpoint someone out of place within a few seconds. It's a force of habit, and whilst I told Kate that I always wanted to be a professional boxer, I always knew that I had a gift for sniffing out trouble. It's that gift that has me bypassing the bar and heading towards a dark corner of the club where two familiar figures are standing in an alcove, deep in conversation.

It ain't easy to hide a physique as big as mine. I stand out like a sore thumb for the most part, but I use the dim lighting and throng of people to my advantage and get close enough to make out the King and Rodriguez deep in conversation.

With my back pressed against the wall, I listen.

"Are you certain everything's in place?" the King asks.

"We're good to go. No problems on that front," Rodriquez replies.

"Good. Won't be long now until I get my hands on *everything* that I want."

They fall silent, and when a flirtatious female voice starts talking I take that as my cue to leave. I knew that motherfucker was up to something, and I'm going to take great pleasure in ending the bastard, but the cherry on the cake is Rodriguez signing his death warrant.

Torturing them both is going to be so much fun.

So. Much. Fun.

After making my way back to the bar and ordering Carter his drink, I make a show of looking for the King, coming across him, minus Rodriguez, chatting to a pretty blonde who's a double for Pamela Anderson in her heyday.

"Carter's been waiting for you," I say, not bothering with

fucking niceties. I didn't like him before, and I sure as fuck don't like him now.

"Ah yes, just got distracted sampling the goods," he replies, his fingers trailing across the woman's arse, before he gives her a slap. She laughs and he presses his lips to her ear, whispering something to her.

"See you later then," she says breathily.

I make a mental note to make sure that never happens. The King ain't one for treating women well and I'm betting he's not the type to let them know he's a sadistic bastard up front either. Besides, I'm hoping by the end of the night he'll be in my special room at Tales getting his toenails pulled out with pliers and buried in his eye sockets, so she should be good.

"Shall we?" the King asks, watching me carefully.

"After you," I reply, stepping aside so he can go ahead, not because I'm feeling polite but because I don't trust the cunt not to stick a knife into my back.

When we reach the private room, I grip the door handle before he can. "Allow me," I say, my gaze purposefully trailing to the gun holstered to my waist. Just like I knew he would, he follows my gaze.

"Is that for me?" he asks.

"That depends."

"On what?"

"On how well you behave."

"You're very distrustful, aren't you, Beast?" he says, a smirk pulling up his lips.

"It comes with the territory."

"Do you trust anyone?"

"Very few."

"That's wise," he agrees, broadening his smirk into a million-watt smile that's even more insincere than this stupid fucking conversation we're having now. I move to open the door, but he rests his hand on my arm. "I do have a piece of advice for you though."

"Yeah, what's that?" I ask, half a second away from snapping his fingers off my arm.

"Some men were born to rule, and some men were born to be ruled. There's only room for one King, so if I were you I'd back the winning side."

"What the fuck is that supposed to mean?"

"It means *I* have the power to give you what you want most of all."

"And what's that?"

His eyes drop to my chest, and even though I'm wearing a shirt that covers my fresh tattoo, it feels as though he's seeing me fucking naked and staring right at Kate's handprint etched into my skin.

"*Her.*"

I straighten up, my fingers slowly uncurling from the door handle as I ready myself to take action. "You've got thirty seconds to expand on that statement before I load a fucking bullet in your head," I reply, wrapping my fingers around the handle of my gun that's strapped to my waist.

The King smiles, a slow stretch of lips across his face. "Then let's talk."

CHAPTER TWENTY-THREE

Him & I

I'm wearing the dress Beast picked out for me. It hugs my body in all the right places and makes me feel beautiful *and* deadly. I feel like one of those knockout nineteen fifties actresses like Ava Gardner or Grace Kelly, ready to take on the world. Who knew that an item of clothing could make you feel so powerful?

    I smile at the memory of Beast sliding up the zipper of my dress, recalling the hunger in his eyes and the way his fingers lingered on my skin as he stared at my reflection in the mirror just like I'm doing now. Thinking about him makes me wonder if it's possible to miss someone who is still a part of your life?

    Because I do. I miss the man who could relax enough to kiss me. Who could cup my cheeks in his huge palms, fuck my mouth with his tongue and make me wonder what having sex with him would be like.

    Since we kissed, he's gone back to being less handsy and

more gruff. Over the past couple days that we've been in each other's orbit, it's been tense, to say the least. I'm not sure if it's all that pent-up sexual tension or the fact that Carter has asked Beast to fight again tonight, this time with a man called Derby, brought in by the King no less. I've never heard of him before, not on the fight scene and not as a name to be familiar with in the criminal underworld.

Still, that doesn't mean anything.

Just because I've never heard of him doesn't mean he isn't a threat. It's more likely that he is one tonight because Beast will be going in cold to the cage with nothing to go on. Not that I'm afraid for him. On the contrary, Beast is the best fighter out there. Hands down.

He'll win. He always does.

He won me, didn't he?

I grin at that, my bright cherry-red lips complimenting my smoky grey eyes. I've purposefully gone for the glam but sexy look. Instead of wearing my hair down like I usually do, with the help of Nadia, I've got it pinned up in a low bun that sits at the nape of my neck with tendrils of hair hanging loose at my temples, adding a softness to my features. In all honesty, I feel like a knockout, and I'm more than ready to floor Beast.

Satisfied with my reflection, I slide my feet into my favourite Louboutin heels, the same ones I wore that night I met the King. Who, despite my reservations, is attending tonight. Just like all of Carter's business associates and acquaintances are. It stings a little that this night isn't about me, or my eighteenth birthday, but about my dad and his business...

Our business?

I'm still not certain whether he wants me as his partner

anymore. He's barely spoken to me these past few weeks, and has certainly avoided even being in a room with me since the night I didn't shoot Saxon.

Which is why I have to prove myself tonight.

I will be the perfect Davidson. Strong, beautiful, and not to be fucked with. Whatever goes down tonight I will take it all in my stride, because like I said to Hudson, it's not a Davidson party without a little—*a lot*—of bloodshed.

"WHO THE FUCK IS THAT?" Hudson asks as a man not dissimilar in size to Beast steps into the cage.

Around us the chat quietens as everyone focuses on the new guy who is as bulky as Beast but maybe a couple inches shorter. He's so pale, he's almost translucent, except for his face where he has a skull tattooed into his skin. If he's going for the intimidation look, it looks good on him.

Beast isn't easily scared. I've never seen him look even remotely concerned in the cage, but there's an edge of apprehension in the way he carries himself, and that in and of itself is cause for concern.

"Is that who I think it is?" Tony, a small-time gangster who I've been talking to for the past ten minutes, mutters under his breath. He's actually one of the few men I recognise here tonight. There are a lot of new faces, most of them brought in by the King according to my father, including Beast's opponent.

"His name's Derby, right?" I ask, repeating the only thing I know about the new fighter and hoping Tony can fill in more details.

"Yeah, it is. He's to the King what Beast is to Carter," Tony explains, the excitement in his eyes sparking concern in mine.

"He's an enforcer?"

"Yeah, he worked for the King once upon a time. Rumour has it Derby banged his ex-missus and that's why they're getting a divorce."

"And he's still alive?" I ask. The King doesn't strike me as a man who'd let anyone get away with sleeping with his wife.

"Looks that way. All I know is that this fella is fucking hardcore. I heard he once ripped a man's throat out with his bare hands."

"Fucking hell," Hudson mutters.

A nervous laugh bubbles out of my throat and I make a kind of choking noise trying to cover it up. "He ripped out someone's throat, with his *hands*?" I repeat, hoping my voice doesn't give away the panic expanding in my chest.

"Put it this way, Beast might be undefeated in this cage, but Derby..." Tony smirks, "He's the Grim fucking Reaper. Know what I'm saying?"

Hudson shifts on his feet. "Fuuuuuck!"

"I'm not worried. Beast's got this," I say firmly.

"You might want to tell that to him," Tony adds, pointing to the cage as Beast steps into the spotlight.

"He does look worried," Hudson comments, earning him an elbow-dig to his rib.

"It's his game face, he's *not* worried," I retort, even though the look on his face tells me that he very much is.

Shit.

Circling each other, Beast and Derby face off. Where Beast is tense, Derby is relaxed in a way that doesn't speak of arrogance, but confidence. He thinks he's going to win. Beast might have the edge in height and build, but there's no denying the fact that he doesn't seem to intimidate this guy in the slightest.

"Do *they* know each other?" Hudson whispers. "There's a lot of eyeballing going on."

"Appears that way," I reply, and when Derby drops his chin and gives Beast the briefest of smiles, revealing a set of gold teeth, a thread of anxiety bubbles up in my stomach.

Everything feels off.

"Ladies and gentlemen," Carter says, interrupting my thoughts and drawing my attention to him as he steps into the cage. "Or should I say *Grim* and gentleman..." He laughs at his own joke as a spotlight appears over my head, highlighting me to the room and the fact I'm the only female within it.

"Oh shit, he's not going to sing you happy birthday, is he?" Hudson mutters, raising a laugh from Tony and some of the other arseholes nearby.

"Fuck," I mutter, keeping my lips in a tight smile.

"Come on up, Grim," Carter says, motioning me over.

I want to say no, but this is Carter and no really isn't a word he takes kindly to. Instead, with the smile plastered on my face, I head towards the cage. All eyes are on me, and as I stride across the room, I can see the King and Rodriguez step out of Carter's office. Rodriguez is smirking and King is watching me closely. My gut flips over.

The moment I step inside the cage Carter jerks his chin, fishing in his pocket for something. A moment later he pulls out a coin and gives me a beaming smile that's so fake, I almost wish I'd worn shades.

"Carter?" I question softly, turning my gaze to Beast who

briefly meets my eyes with an empty gaze. There's not even a flicker of acknowledgement. My gut twists. I know he has to keep up pretences but fuck, that hurt.

"Tonight you're all here to help celebrate my daughter's birthday," Carter continues, addressing the crowd and doing nothing to temper my growing unease. "Tomorrow, Grim will be turning eighteen, and as such I've arranged for Beast and Derby to go head-to-head, all for your viewing pleasure." The room erupts into cheers and whistles, only quieting when Carter raises his hands. "But for tonight only we're going to change the rules of the cage."

I glance at Beast with a question on my face, because we all know the only rules that apply in the cage are that there *are no rules*. The last man standing is the winner, that's it.

"What?" I ask, but my question is lost amongst more cheers and whistles from the crowd. Why do I get the feeling they already know what Carter is talking about?

Pinching the coin between his finger and thumb, Carter says. "In a moment I'm going to ask Grim to toss this coin."

"Carter?" I repeat, quieter this time.

He throws the coin to me and I catch it, frowning at the weight and the warmth. It's one of those old sovereign coins that are no longer in circulation but are often mounted in jewellery as a nod to the *old days*. I wonder where he got it from.

"Tonight Beast is up against Derby, a worthy opponent," Carter continues, dragging my attention back to him as he strides around the edge of the cage. He looks pumped. No, he looks *wired*. There's a jittery kind of energy pouring off him. It's not fear, but excitement, and I'm not a hundred percent sure it's the natural kind. His pupils are blown wide and he's sweating.

"As usual anything goes. The only difference is that tonight we allow *weapons*."

"What?" I exclaim, my eyes widening. Again I find myself looking at Beast and this time he shakes his head minutely, warning me not to protest. Swallowing hard, I bite back my concern and say nothing. Carter raises his brows, looking between us both as he notices the silent exchange.

"Grim will throw the coin. If it lands on tails, Beast will get to choose his weapon of choice first. If it falls on heads, Derby will." He motions over his shoulder to someone in the crowd. "Bring me the weapons."

Rodriguez steps into the cage, wearing his usual shit-eating grin. I grit my teeth, hating the way he smirks at me like he's in on the joke and I'm the fucking punchline.

Maybe I am.

Standing between Beast and Derby, Rodriguez waits for further instruction. On the large silver tray are several weapons. Notably, a twelve inch butcher's knife with a slightly curved blade, a pair of knuckle dusters with clawed tips, nunchucks, a crowbar and finally, a baseball bat.

Jesus Christ.

This is madness.

I stride over to my dad, pressing my hand against his arm. "Carter, what are you doing?" I hiss.

"Why? What's it matter to you?" he replies, eyebrows arched.

"Toss the coin, *Grim*," Beast orders, cutting in.

The sheer fact he calls me Grim and not Princess or Kate has me feeling all kinds of ways, and the look he gives me makes my stomach flip and my spine tingle with fear. Rodriguez, the prick, laughs, adding to the already building tension. What the fuck does he find so damn funny?

"Yes, toss the coin, Grim," Carter adds smoothly, turning his back on us all and moving to stand at the edge of the cage as he addresses the crowd. "Tonight the winner is the last man standing. This is a fight to the *death*."

"No!" I shout, unable to stop the word spilling from my lips, but it's just background noise, lost as the crowd goes wild. Like a pack of baying wolves they're out for blood.

This is a fight to the death.

To. The. Death.

"NO!" I repeat, striding over to Carter, anger firing in my blood and my heart beating out of control. I grab his arm, unconcerned now at how this looks to the crowd, to him. "What the hell are you doing?!"

Whilst the crowd goes fucking crazy, Carter grips my elbow and forcibly pulls me towards the centre of the ring where Rodriguez stands with the weapons and Beast and Derby eyeing each other up. "I'm doing this for you!" he hisses.

"What do you mean, for me?" I reply, glancing at Beast who shakes his head subtly.

Carter ignores me and Beast looks away, leaving me in total confusion as Carter once again raises his hands to quieten the crowd. "Grim is about to toss the coin. Let's see who gets to choose first."

"Do it," Beast insists, softer this time as he meets my gaze. A thousand words and a whole host of emotions pass across his features. "It's *okay*. I've got this."

This time Derby laughs. He steps close to me and I freeze, not because I'm afraid that he might touch me, but because if he does Beast will lose his shit and show everyone how he truly feels and he'll wind up dead anyway.

"Toss the coin, sweetheart, let the fun begin."

I toss the coin.

The crowd falls silent as the gold sovereign flips in the air. I watch it in slow motion as gravity pulls it down, my stomach dropping out at the same pace until eventually I catch it, covering the coin up with my hand.

"Call it," Carter demands as my racing pulse fills my ears with white noise.

Slowly I lift my hand, my eyes dropping to the coin nestled in my palm. "Tails!" I announce loudly, a rush of relief that's quickly overridden by a powerful dose of fear, because it doesn't really matter if Beast gets to choose his weapon first, he could die anyway.

"Tales you win, heads you lose," Beast shouts as he steps towards the tray of weapons, picking up the butcher's knife and gripping the handle tightly. He taps the tray twice with the blade, pointing it at Derby. "And the fighters of Tales *never* lose!"

Then he turns to me and places his left hand over his chest, right where my handprint is tattooed into his skin. My stomach flips with apprehension and dread, but also *love*.

I love him so much it hurts.

"Beast—" I begin but around us the crowd go apeshit, and my words are drowned out by their hollering. "I know," he mouths. "I know."

And whilst the crowd might not be aware of the unspoken words between us, my father certainly notices. The look he gives is deadly.

He knows.

When the crowd settles, Carter steps forward and withdraws his gun from the holster at his hip, placing it on the tray. "Let's up the motherfucking anti, shall we?" he rasps out on a laugh that has all the blood draining from my face.

"Dad?" I question, shaking my head in disbelief. "That's not fair."

"My club, my rules!" he snaps, jerking his chin at Derby. "Choose."

Derby smirks, or at least I think he does because I can't really tell beneath his skull tattoo. He glances at the gun and I wait for him to grab it. Only he doesn't. He picks up the crowbar instead.

Rodriguez looks as shocked as Carter, but the crowd doesn't care, they want a fight not an execution, and that's what they're going to get. With a tight jaw and even tighter voice, Carter addresses the crowd one last time.

"May the best man win!" he yells, then grabs my arm and pulls me from the cage and marches me towards his office, shoving me inside before I can even blink, let alone watch the fight unfold.

The moment the door slams shut behind us and Rodriguez —who has followed us both into the office like a bad fucking smell—the crowd goes insane.

"What the fuck, Carter?!" I round on him, trying and failing to disguise my fear as my gaze flicks to the window in his office and the fight unfolding in the cage. Derby wastes no time and lunges for Beast, who ducks, the crowbar missing the top of his head by mere inches.

Fuck!

"What's the problem, Grim, afraid of a little bloodshed?"

"What's my problem? Are you insane?! Beast could die!" I shout, snapping my head back around.

"You don't think he'll win?" My father questions, canting a look at Rodriguez who places the tray on the desk and smirks in that infuriating way of his.

"What the fuck do you find so amusing?" I snarl, ready to punch his fucking lights out.

He holds his hands up. "Absolutely nothing. No disrespect meant," he replies, completely insincere, the smarmy bastard.

"Get the fuck out!" I snap, reaching for my father's gun and pointing it at him. The feel of the cool metal in my hand is comforting.

"Don't be hasty," he stutters, his fucking smile dropping as he looks to Carter.

"You heard Grim. Get the fuck out."

Rodriguez spins on his heels, not needing to be told twice. When he opens the door, I catch a glimpse of Beast receiving a blow to his upper arm, the tip of the crowbar scraping across his bicep. Blood bursts from the wound and I swear I can hear Beast's grunt of pain over the roar of the crowd.

"Beast!" I yell, my desperate call lost behind the door slamming shut.

"It's true then?" Carter questions.

"What's true?"

"That you and Beast have been fucking."

"What? No!" I exclaim, my fingers curling around the handle of the gun even as my arm hangs loosely at my side. "He's a *friend*."

"Like Hudson is?" Carter asks, looking over my shoulder. I

turn to figure out what he's looking at and see that Hudson's on the other side of the window, being prevented entrance by Rodriguez who's apparently guarding the fucking door now.

I whip my head around and glare at Carter. "What is this?" I question. "Hudson is a friend. Beast is a friend. That's it, that's all."

Carter shakes his head, stepping towards me. "You're a liar!"

"We haven't been fucking, Carter!" I counter, my voice rising in distress.

It's not a lie, we haven't, but not from lack of trying on my part.

He laughs, and it comes out cold and distant. "Hudson is your friend. I *believe* that. It's one of the reasons why he's not fucking dead already."

"What?" I whisper, dread creeping over my skin as his gaze darkens with malice.

"You're *my* daughter, Grim. You forget that I know you."

"Carter... *Dad*," I plead. "You've got to believe me, we're not together. Put an end to this madness. Now!"

Gripping my arm, he twists me on my feet and pushes me towards the window, pulling up the blind so that I can see the fight more clearly. Hudson sees the movement and shouts at me through the glass.

"You alright?"

I nod, warning him with my eyes to back off before he gets himself hurt, but it's Rodriguez who forcibly manhandles him out of the way. Hudson puts up a fight, throwing a punch that hits Rodriguez on the chin and forces him back against the door with a loud crash.

"Maybe Hudson has more than just smarts," Carter says, a

note of respect in his voice as Rodriguez retaliates and the pair get into a brawl. "Wonder whether he'd be up to fight in the cage?"

"Absolutely not!" I exclaim, moving towards the door so I can break up the fight then put a stop to the one in the cage.

Carter laughs, snatching my arm and yanking me back against his chest. "Yeah you're right, I can't have that pretty head of his losing any brain cells. I think he'll come in handy down the line."

"Useful how? What are you—?"

My question is cut short when Mark appears from the crowd and strides over to the pair, forcibly pulling Hudson off Rodriguez. Hudson's face is pitted with rage and he spits out a glob of blood before casting his gaze to me. I shake my head, warning him not to continue, but it's only when Mark drops his mouth to Hudson's ear that he finally backs off. That and the fact Mark has a gun pressed against his side. With one last look at me, Hudson grits his jaw and follows Mark to the other side of the room, disappearing from view.

"Carter! What the hell is Mark doing?" I ask, panic crawling beneath my skin.

"Don't worry, Mark won't shoot him. Like I said, he's going to come in useful in the future. Mark will escort him home. Make sure he gets back safe and sound," Carter says, but that doesn't reassure me in the slightest. It only concerns me more. Hudson's a good guy. He's working hard to get himself and his brothers out from beneath the stigma of being a child in care. Crime is the road he never wants to walk down.

Another roar from the crowd has my gaze snatching back to the cage. Beast has just slashed his knife right across Derby's chest, spilling blood that sprays across the canvas as they continue to fight.

"Dad, you've got to believe me. End this."

"See, here's the thing, Grim. I don't fucking believe you. I know Beast touched what's mine!" he replies sharply, grabbing the back of my neck and forcing me to watch the fight.

"Dad..." I plead, hating the way my voice gives me away. This is all my fault. Every part of it. "There's nothing going on!" But even to my own ears it sounds false.

"DON'T BULLSHIT ME!" he roars, squeezing my neck tighter, his fingers digging painfully into my skin. "Now watch the fight!"

"Don't do this," I argue. *Beg*, actually.

"This is for your own good, but if you fight me on this then I will go out there right the fuck now and shoot him in the motherfucking head," he hisses into my ear. "Do you understand me?"

"Yes," I whisper, giving Beast the only chance I can because Carter is many things, but a liar isn't one of them. Beast has to win this fight so that together we can convince Carter he's wrong.

It's the only chance he has. The only chance *we* have.

As my gaze lands on Beast, I silently mouth the words he'd uttered just minutes ago inside the cage, sending a silent prayer to the man I love.

"*Tales you win, heads you lose, and the fighters of Tales never lose.*"

He has to win.

He has to.

CHAPTER TWENTY-FOUR

Danger

Death is pretty fucking painless when all is said and done.

I don't feel a goddamn thing, not the broken ribs, not the gashes to my arms, chest, back and thighs from the crowbar Derby is wielding so expertly. I don't feel my broken nose or cracked eye-socket. I don't feel the bruises or the deep gash to my head that sent me free-falling into the arms of darkness.

I don't feel anything.

But I do hear something.

A scream.

A fucking cry of pain so loud, so deafening, that even in the throes of death it drives a hook into my soul and drags me back from the motherfucking light at the end of the tunnel.

A light that shouldn't welcome the likes of me, but *does*.

It comes again, and again and again. Her screams punctuated with my name.

Beast. Beast. Beast. BEAST!

It's familiar, her voice, and the pain within it is like a fist wrapping around my heart and forcing it to pump faster, harder, until death crawls away and the light fades, leaving me with nothing but excruciating pain and a banging fucking headache.

Right now, I can do nothing other than feel.

Feel the pain.

Feel the bloody canvas beneath my cheek.

Feel fingers pinch my skin as someone tries to roll me over.

Feel a heart breaking open with every second I don't respond.

"Beast, please wake up!"

Princess.

Kate.

But try as I might, I can't fucking move.

I can barely fucking breathe.

I'm incapable of anything other than holding on to her voice, using it to ground me, to lure me back to consciousness, one painful breath at a time. More noise filters into my brain that's rapidly trying to make sense of the situation. Memories piece together as the sound of a man yelling at everyone to get the fuck out rings in the air.

Dom.

Deeper voices merge with the cacophony of sound, Kate's sobs a burden as she lies across my back, pawing at me now. Yet I remain still, weighted down by her grief. Fuck knows I want to reassure her, I want to tell her that I'm alive, that I've survived the single hardest fight of my life, but that would be a lie.

The biggest fight is yet to come.

So I lay here instead, on the blood-splattered canvas, and

wait for my other senses to return one by one, drawing on every last drop of strength left in my body and gathering it together so I can do what I must and protect the woman I love.

After sound and touch, scent returns. The smell of blood, metallic and meaty. I'm surrounded by the stench of it. Fucking choking on it.

Next it's sight. Spots of colour invade my vision as I slowly crack open my eyes a sliver. The world reappears in shades of red first. There's blood everywhere, a huge fucking pool of it that I'm lying in. But as I focus, trying to ignore the metallic stench of butchered flesh, my gaze falls to a wide-eyed Derby, his sightless eyes unseeing, the knife I impaled him with sticking out of his gut, the serrated edge making mincemeat of his bowels. Didn't stop him from bringing down the crowbar on my head though. The last thing I remember is blood spurting from his lips before the world went black.

He's dead.

I'm the victor.

Except I'm not.

Not yet.

Because our fight was just a show, a fucking good one at that, given death had me in its grasp only moments ago and Derby has stepped into the afterlife. The King wanted Derby dead for fucking his wife and Carter wanted me dead for loving his daughter. They both needed revenge. Looks like I fucking delivered, at least partly.

"Remove the bodies. Get this shit cleaned up," I hear Carter order, his voice a cold, unyielding hammer to my painful head.

"Yes, boss," Dom replies, the heaviness of his voice as

painful to hear as Kate's distress is. If I didn't know any better, I'd think he was gutted by my apparent death.

"Get the fuck away from him!" Kate yells, her weight pushing off of me as she stands. I watch through slitted lids as she strides towards Carter, gun in hand, oblivious to the fact I'm not actually dead.

Not fucking yet, anyway.

She's holding a gun, and that makes me feel so much better because fuck knows I've been worrying about her from the moment she stepped out of the cage with Carter. I'd lost sight of her almost immediately, too busy trying not to fucking die and knowing that I had to win this fight in order to keep her safe from him.

Except she isn't safe.

She never will be whilst *he* remains alive.

"Lower the gun, Grim!" Carter demands. "There's no need for dramatics. Everyone's fucking gone."

"Fuck you, Carter!" she replies, refusing to do as he demands.

Good girl.

Rodriguez, the King and Dom are standing just outside of the cage, right in my line of vision. Both the King and Rodriguez are watching this all unfold, neither paying me any attention. Clearly they think I'm dead, just like Kate and Carter do. Dom's gaze however falls to me, his eyes widening a fraction as I blink at him a couple of times, willing him not to rat me out. I'm praying I've read him right and he's going to keep his mouth shut. I've got one chance at this, and one chance only. He gives me the tiniest nod, then looks away. I make a mental note to buy him a fucking drink when this shit is over.

"You're a fucking monster!" Kate yells.

I've never seen her so enraged, so fucking broken, so radiantly beautiful in her anger. I want nothing more than to stand by her side, to back her whilst she takes on her father and any other motherfucker who dares try to control her. Instead, I use these few precious moments to gather my wits and concentrate on mentally checking my body. I hurt, there's no denying that, but that's a good thing. Hurting means I'm alive, and that's all I need to be to end this.

"Grim, lower the gun and *behave*."

"Behave?! Screw you!" Grim continues, screaming at her father now, her rage undeniable. "You killed him!"

Carter shakes his head. "No, he did that all by himself by fucking you and fucking *me* over. He knew the rules. He broke them. There was only ever going to be one motherfucking outcome. Betray me and die. End of."

"We've never fucked!" she screams, lifting the gun and aiming it at Carter's chest. "Beast is loyal, so fucking loyal that he *refused* to sleep with me even when *I* offered myself up to him!"

For a moment Carter appears taken aback, then a smile glides across his face. "You think I'm fucking stupid? No man would ever deny themselves a hot piece of ass, so your lies are worthless to me. Beast made *me* a promise, Grim, and he broke it when he went after you. He betrayed me."

"He didn't!" Grim exclaims, her broken voice taking on a hard edge as they circle one another. I watch transfixed, enraptured by the woman who's snared my heart so thoroughly. She's a lioness, prowling, baring her teeth at her dad, a man who was willing to sell her to pay off his debts.

Yeah, he's *that* man.

Looks like The Crib Club has been a home away from home for Carter over the last six months, and all of Tales' profits have been sunk into card games and pussy. Turns out the bastard was willing to sell his daughter to the King to clear the debts racked up by his gambling habits and addiction to pleasure.

A debt that *I* will clear the moment I kill the cunt.

Carter might be acting holier than thou right now, but he's the fucking villain, not me, and because of that he won't live to see another day.

The moment he has his back to me, I launch myself upright. Adrenaline and the need to protect the woman I love propelling my feet forward the few paces to rip the knife from Derby's body and then drive it into Carter's back, straight through his heart.

He dies instantly.

He didn't see it coming and neither did Kate.

Her face is a mixture of astonishment and relief as she stares at me, oblivious in the moment that her dad is dead in my arms. Her eyes brim with tears, tears that never fall as relief is quickly replaced with shock, then bewilderment as blood gurgles up Carter's throat, spilling from his lips.

I watch in slow motion, breathing heavily from the exertion and pain as she tries to make sense of what's happened. Her eyes widen and her body stiffens as realisation dawns.

Drawing the knife free with one hard yank, I let Carter's body fall to the canvas with a loud thud. He falls onto his back, blood pumping from the wound and mingling with the viscous pool beneath my feet.

"Kate," I murmur, my arms falling to my side as I drop to my knees with exhaustion right beside Carter. His sightless eyes stare up at me, and even though I know he's dead, I need to make sure. Ripping at his shirt, I pull it open, revealing his bare flesh. Blood oozes from the wound on his chest, streaking down his skin in rivulets. Despite the leaking blood, his chest is still.

"Carter?" she whispers, her voice trembling with emotion as her gaze drops to him.

"It's over," I reply, looking up at her.

She's pale, ghostly, her mouth hanging open as she blinks with confusion. "Beast?"

"It's over," I repeat.

Only that dark part of me, the part that is more beast than man, still needs to prove to her that I'm willing to cut the heart out of *any* man who dares hurt her, that I'm willing to do whatever the fuck it takes to protect her. So, with a bloodcurdling roar, I stab the knife through Carter's sternum, using the serrated edge to saw through his bone. She deserves nothing less than his bloody heart, and I'm going to deliver it to her right the fuck now.

"Stop!" she shouts, her demand stilling my hand.

My head lifts, the rage I feel at the man who so easily wanted to sell his daughter making way for another emotion, *empathy*.

She looks broken.

Defeated in a way that guts me.

I drop my hands from the knife handle, falling back on my arse as I watch the woman I love drop to her knees. "Kate, listen," I reach for her, but she shakes my hand away, flinching from my touch.

"Don't!"

"*Kate...*" But the look she gives me quietens me faster than any weapon ever could.

"Dad?" she questions, resting the gun on the floor beside her then cupping Carter's face. "Dad?"

Her voice is no more than a whisper as she twists his head to the side, ducking closer to him and ignoring the twelve inch knife sticking out of his brutalised chest.

"He's dead."

My head snaps up as I watch the King step into the cage, followed by Rodriguez and Dom. I'd almost forgotten about them. Rodriguez is uncharacteristically quiet, and Dom gives me a small nod. He's a smart man, he knows that I would never do something like this if I didn't have a good fucking reason for it. There will be time for an explanation, but that time isn't now.

"You!" she hisses, grabbing the gun and getting to her feet, aiming it at the King. "This was you!"

"No, Kate," I interrupt as I force myself to my feet, readying myself to act if the King decides to go back on his word. Fuck only knows it gets my goat backing the cunt, but this is all part of the deal I made to keep Kate safe.

"Shut the hell up, Beast!"

I want to tell Kate everything, and I will when I can ensure her safety, but right now I just need to get her through this night without starting a fucking war. Keeping Kate in the dark for a short time will protect her in the long run. It has to.

"You'd be wise to listen to your boyfriend, Grim," the King says, unperturbed by the fact she is pointing her gun at his head.

"Trust me, Kate," I urge, willing her to see past the carnage. To think and not act this time.

At The Crib Club I made my own deal with the King after he revealed Carter's plans. The King had said that he'd never intended on taking Kate for his own, and whilst I didn't believe a word of it, I was willing to suspend disbelief to get what I wanted for Kate.

Her security, her safety, and her father's debt paid in full.

All I had to do was kill Derby and Carter.

The King would remain a silent business partner, and continue to provide fighters, taking a cut of the profits. In turn he would keep her in business under his protection, and whilst the whole part about him giving her his protection is a bitter pill to swallow, I'm man enough to know that I'm only one man, and one man does not an army make.

At least not until Kate and I can build one ourselves.

And we will.

The caveat to this agreement was that I take full responsibility for killing her dad, hiding the fact that a contract was drawn up between the two men. To be honest, after the King showed me their contract, killing Carter was the easiest fucking decision to make.

Not killing the King for agreeing to it, the motherfucking *hardest*.

I don't like the man. Don't fucking trust him, and I certainly don't believe he will keep to his side of the deal, but for the time being I'm willing to let him live so that Kate and I can make a plan, and build a fucking army. There will come a day when we'll both have our revenge, but in the meantime we use him, then take him out when the time is right.

"This is on you," she snarls, her rage fucking beautiful to behold.

She may be at her most vulnerable right now, but she is *fierce*, and one day soon she'll be unstoppable.

"This has nothing to do with me," the King says without even flinching. I'll give him that, the guy has balls of fucking steel and the best poker face I've ever seen.

"You're a *liar*," she accuses, her finger tightening over the trigger.

"Kate, this is on me," I say, stepping over Carter's body and standing between her and the King, stumbling a little as my head pounds like a motherfucker. I fucking hate that I'm in this position, protecting the King, but it's only temporary. His time will come.

"Bullshit. What do you have on Beast?" Kate presses, stepping to the side, trying to get a clear shot at the King. I move in front of her again and she bares her teeth at me.

"Not a thing," the King replies. "I'm as shocked as you are about how this all panned out."

"Bullshit!" she shouts, fury leaking from her now.

"Kate, listen," I say, holding my hands up and trying my fucking best not to pass the fuck out. "This is on me. *I'm responsible*."

"What?" she asks, snapping her gaze back to me.

"I went to Carter this morning about us. I explained everything to him. I tried to make him listen. He wouldn't."

"And he didn't kill you the second you told him?"

I shake my head. "No. He said if I won the fight tonight then he'd allow us to be together. I took him for his word, Kate," I lie, because I didn't say a damn thing about us. As far as I was concerned he knew nothing. I only realised that wasn't the case when he asked Rodriguez to bring the weapons into the cage.

Right now I'm not a hundred percent certain which fuck told him, but given the look on Rodriguez's face, I'm guessing it's him. "He wanted me dead. That's why he allowed weapons into the ring. He also wanted a bloodbath, and he fucking got one."

"Yet you survived," she whispers, sadness brimming in her eyes as she aims the gun at me now.

"Kate, what are you doing?"

"You killed my dad, Beast."

"I *had* to do it. He would never have allowed us to be together, Kate," I say, covering up the fact that I did it to protect her. That *he* was the fucking monster ready to sell her off to the King to save his own arse.

"And I have to do this," she replies, her sadness replaced now with a hardness that is so much like her dad it makes my blood run cold.

"We can work this out," I say, watching as she shuts down her emotions one by one.

"I will never be respected in this business if I let you walk after what you did."

"Kate, I was protecting you!"

"Don't you see, it doesn't fucking matter. We could've found a way around this *together*, but you chose to murder Carter instead. How can I let that go? Tell me how?" she pleads.

"Princess, think about this..." Dom says, his voice trailing off when she snatches her head around to look at him.

"It's *Grim*," she snarls.

"Grim, listen, you're in shock," he says quickly, and the room around me fucking spins as darkness claws at my brain. "Understandably so, but even I can see that Beast did what he had to do."

"And where does that leave me?" she shouts, her voice cracking. "Carter is dead and Tales is mine." Her gaze flicks back to me now and the anguish in her eyes almost floors me. "It's too late for me to choose. They'll walk all over me if I *don't* do this. You know that."

"No one would dare fuck with you, not with *my* backing, Grim," the King interjects. "I have a reputation enough for the both of us."

"And what makes you think I want your backing, huh? This is *my* club now," she snaps.

"Well, see, that's where things get a little complicated," the King says, and my fucking stomach bottoms out because I know why that is. Carter well and truly fucked the gravy train on this one.

"What do you mean?" she asks, the gun moving from my chest back to the King's.

"In order to get my backing, your father signed over a percentage of Tales to me. I now own a forty-eight percent share in the club, and that will remain in place for as long as it is profitable for the both of us or you're able to raise two million pounds to buy me out."

"Two million pounds? You've got to be fucking kidding me!"

"Those were the terms of our deal, Grim," the King says, conveniently leaving out the most important part, that Carter was going to sell her to him to clear his debts and secure the deal.

I glance at the King, not liking the way he's fucking smirking like he assumes she'll never be able to raise that kind of money. He's a fool to underestimate her.

"Or I could just shoot you dead and rip up the contract now," she replies, bringing a smile to my lips. "I'm feeling particularly trigger happy."

"You could, but we both know that wouldn't be wise. I have men who know where I am and what time I'm expected back. If I don't turn up they'll rain hellfire down on you. You stand alone, Grim, with one man barely alive."

"She has me too," Dom says.

"Three against two hundred loyal men. You do the math," the King retorts.

I can see the defeat written across her face as she tries hard to figure out what to do. We both know that acting out of passion and anger now will be a mistake. She's smart enough to know that what she needs is time to figure everything out, to make a plan.

That's what I've given her, *us*. Time. "You're right, it wouldn't be wise to kill you."

"That's a good girl," he replies, the fucking patronising prick.

"But don't for one second think you can walk all over me. I'm not a bleeding heart. I'm a Davidson... No, I'm *Grim* and no one fucks with me. Let this be your warning."

"Understood," the King retorts evenly.

She shifts her attention back to me. "I warned you not to break my heart."

"I was protecting you!" I protest.

"No, killing Carter wasn't about you protecting me, it was about you protecting *yourself* and believing that I'm incapable of finding a solution to a problem that affects the both of us."

"That wasn't what—" I begin, but she cuts me off.

"Once again you failed to consider that I had a say in all of this. *Me*. I don't need a man to make decisions for me, I need a man who's willing to stand *beside* me whilst we find a solution together. You're just like all the rest."

"Kate, you don't understand…"

"Don't. Not another word, Beast."

"I did this for us, for you. I fucking *love* you," I say, willing her to believe me. Needing her to know, if nothing else, *that's* the truth.

"Love?" she laughs bitterly. "People like you and me don't get to love."

Then she points her gun at me and pulls the motherfucking trigger.

TO BE CONTINUED in **Heads You Lose**, book two of Grim & Beast's Duet…

AUTHOR NOTE

Phewf!

If you haven't got the female version of blueballitis then I've not done my job properly!

I hope you've loved Beast & Grim's story so far. As you already know, their standalone has turned into a duet. I couldn't shove all of their love into one book, it just wasn't possible.

So, I hope you'll stick around to find out what happens next!

Most of my readers already know that the pair get their fairy tale ending because you've met both characters in the Academy of Stardom series (set after this duet) where they are happily together, BUT if you know me, the path to true love never runs smoothly.

I mean, come on, this is Beast and Grim we're talking about.

Expect lots of grovelling, more fireworks, more banter, violence and of course copious amounts of steam!

Rest assured, the build up in book one will lead to all the

angst and tension and steamy, knicker-drenching sex scenes we've all been waiting for, including me.

Like I've said before, my characters do what the hell they want, and I'm just a human vessel for them to use to write their story. All I know is that Beast will make good on his promise of fucking well and Grim has a few tricks up her sleeve too!

You have been warned.

For those of you who are new to my books, and that gorgeous cover brought you to me and this is the first book of mine you've read, firstly welcome! This duet was written for my readers who needed Beast and Grim's love story. It's been promised for some time, and now I've finally gotten around to writing it! Secondly, if you're interested, all of my contemporary books so far are set in the same world and this is the recommended reading order:

Brothers Freed trilogy (featuring a future Hudson, Max and Bryce)
    Academy of Misfits
    Beyond the Horizon
    Finding Their Muse
    Academy of Stardom
    Their Obsession Duet
    Beast and Grim Duet

As always, thank you for continuing on this journey with me and my characters. Most days I'm still awed that people actually want to read what I write. So, to you, dear reader, I am indebted.

To be certain that you keep up to date with all my new

releases and author news, please do come and join my Facebook group, *Queen Bea's Hive*, where I'm most active.

Once again, thanks for sticking with me. Here's to plenty more stories to come.

Love, Bea xox

ABOUT THE AUTHOR

Bea Paige lives a very secretive life in London... She likes red wine and Haribo sweets (preferably together) and occasionally swings around poles when the mood takes her.

Bea loves to write about love and all the different facets of such a powerful emotion. When she's not writing about love and passion, you'll find her reading about it and ugly crying.

Bea is always writing, and new ideas seem to appear at the most unlikely time, like in the shower or when driving her car.

She has lots more books planned, so be sure to subscribe to her newsletter:

beapaige.co.uk/newsletter-sign-up

ALSO BY BEA PAIGE

The Deana-dhe Duet (dark reverse harem)

#1 Debts & Diamonds

#2 Curses & Cures

Grim & Beast's Duet (M/F second-chance, bodyguard romance)

#1 Tales You Win

#2 Heads You Lose

Their Obsession Duet (dark reverse harem)

#1 The Dancer and The Masks

#2 The Masks and The Dancer

Academy of Stardom (friends-to-enemies-lovers reverse harem)

#1 Freestyle

#2 Lyrical

#3 Breakers

#4 Finale

Academy of Misfits

(bully/academy reverse harem)

#1 Delinquent

#2 Reject

#3 Family

Finding Their Muse

(dark contemporary reverse harem)

#1 Steps

#2 Strokes

#3 Strings

#4 Symphony

#5 Finding Their Muse box set

The Brothers Freed Series

(contemporary reverse harem)

#1 Avalanche of Desire

#2 Storm of Seduction

#3 Dawn of Love

#4 Brothers Freed Boxset

Contemporary Standalone

Beyond the Horizon

For all up to date book releases please visit

www.beapaige.co.uk

Printed in Great Britain
by Amazon